ASCENDANT

ASCENDANT

BOOK 1

EmergencyComplaints

Podium

Cover design by Iromonik

ISBN: 978-1-0394-4527-7

Published in 2023 by Podium Publishing
www.podiumaudio.com

ASCENDANT

Prologue

Exarch Niramyn reclined on a cushion of air, basking in the bright light of the rising sun that bathed his home isle of Vislarg. Clouds drifted through the sky below the floating island, which gave his alabaster palace a brilliant glow from the unobstructed sunlight. The glow was a deliberate choice, one made to set his palace sparkling like a beacon when it absorbed the power of light and charged the hundreds of arcana batteries embedded in the walls. They would have been more efficient without the glow, but he wanted everyone to know that they were approaching the palace of an exarch.

He enjoyed the warmth of the sun on his skin, though of course the temperature was regulated by his magic. It would be exactly as warm or cold as he desired, all with barely an effort from him. He'd long ago infused the essence of his will into his home, and it was no more work than to think it for it to become warm or cold, bright or dark. Today, he wanted warmth and light.

A decanter hovered in the air next to him, full of a sparkling blue liquid. Niramyn wasn't sure what it was exactly, other than it was tribute from a lesser-ranked ascendant who owed fealty to him, and that it tasted divine. Arcana had been infused into the drink itself, an uncommon practice due to the layer of complexity it added to actually consuming the beverage. It was all too easy to poison oneself with arcana, but Niramyn wasn't an exarch for nothing, and the task was childishly easy for him.

The decanter was about halfway empty when Niramyn felt the stirring of arcana he'd been waiting for. A visage appeared in the air in front of him, hazy and mirage-like. His fellow exarch and rival, Myzalik, stood before him in projection, fresh from his latest defeat. This was the only room in the palace that would allow projections without being keyed to his warding, and so the only place someone like Myzalik could project into. Considering Niramyn's latest victory had taken place last night, the other exarch has no doubt been checking regularly for his chance to confront his rival. Niramyn smirked at the visage and opened his mouth to gloat, only to pause and cock his head to one side.

He'd been sparring with the other immortal for over a thousand years. They'd met on every battlefield imaginable, from literal duels to political maneuverings to economic clashes. Niramyn had consistently come out the victor, and he knew his opponent's reactions well. Right now, Myzalik wasn't wearing the expression he should have had for someone who'd just been beaten. Suddenly, the all-too-easy victory seemed suspiciously like a trap.

Perhaps it was the arcana-infused wine. Maybe Niramyn had just grown careless, secure in his supremacy. Whatever the cause, he had only a split second to register the sneer on his fellow exarch's face as a mask of contempt, not the cold anger he'd come to know when Niramyn had secured yet another victory. Then Myzalik's magic washed over him.

At first, he was confused. The rival exarch appeared to have cast the immortality spell that kept all ascendants' mortal avatars young and hale, which was an utterly ridiculous course of action. There was a twist in the spell though, and Niramyn sobered up instantly as he realized it. Somehow, Myzalik had modified its spellform, defied all known rules of magic, and spun it around to anchor on Niramyn instead of himself.

The spell took hold, and Niramyn felt the familiar twinge in his muscles as it refreshed his vitality and started to reverse his aging. Normally, that would have been fine, except that without any control over the source of the magic, he couldn't stop it! His reversion was wild and uncontrolled, the many, many precise adaptions he'd made to his physiology over millennia coming unraveled. He appeared as a man in his early thirties, then late twenties. Then the unthinkable: he was pushed past the boundaries of immortality and back into the reaches of mere humans.

Whatever Myzalik had done, there was no time to break it, so Niramyn did the only thing he could think of. He reached into the arcana, already sitting in his soul well from the wine. It was a calculated maneuver. Even with an exarch's knowledge, it could take a full second that he didn't have to penetrate the Bulwark and pull greater arcana from the Echoing Vastness. His options were limited by his response time and the weak arcana of the Astral Sea, mere third-layer power. Rather than try something more complicated, he launched himself into flight. The wind whipped around him and shredded his clothes as he burst out into open air.

In the blink of an eye, he crossed miles of open sky. Still the immortality magic clung to him, and his shredded clothes would have hung loosely off his now-teenage frame if they'd still been whole. Another second passed, and Niramyn was thirty miles away from his home. The magic started to loosen with distance, and the exarch grinned in wild triumph. A spell localized to affect only the caster couldn't support a long-range connection, despite the impossible modifications.

By the fifth second of Myzalik's attack, his would-be victim had reached full speed. He was a few hundred miles from home over open water and wearing the body of a preteen boy. His physical body couldn't support what mere moments before had been a trivial amount of arcana anymore. It buckled under the strain, and Niramyn desperately diverted what resources he could to protecting himself as he hurtled into the ocean.

An explosion of water shot a hundred feet straight up, and Niramyn plunged deep under the surface. The shock of the cold penetrated the kinetic barrier he'd put up, causing him to gasp and swallow a mouthful of seawater. Hacking and coughing, Niramyn breached the surface and skimmed forward. He felt the tether binding him to the reverse-aging magic finally snap at that moment. It didn't matter. He was too weak to fight back, and Myzalik's hunters would be coming for him.

His speed greatly reduced, it took another thirty seconds for him to reach the shore. In that time, he analyzed what he needed to do to hide himself away and spent what little arcana he'd held on to to act on that fact. Then, exhausted beyond words, he collapsed onto the sandy beach. His once-splendid clothes, woven from solid strands of arcana, were little more than rags where they hadn't been ripped away from his body completely. It was only thanks to their superior quality that his skin was still more or less intact.

From the moment the visage appeared to Niramyn's crash landing into the sand, the entire battle had taken forty-two seconds. In less than a minute, countless millennia of uncompromising superiority had been undone. For the hundreds of victories he'd won over his rival, it had only taken one loss to utterly undo him. At least there was the small consolation that Myzalik had needed to craft an impossible magic to claim victory.

In those forty-two seconds, Niramyn had cast twenty-six spells. Despite everything, he was still an exarch, the uncrowned king of magical knowledge, technique, and raw power. He'd reached into the twelfth layer and claimed its reality-warping powers as his own. Myzalik had won an overwhelming victory today, but Niramyn had already set into motion everything he'd needed to complete his rise back to power.

His mind unraveled, and he fell unconscious. Still the magic worked on him. It broke down who he was and stored it away, somewhere safe from both the prying eyes and searching hunters and from himself until he'd regained enough of his power to reclaim it. In that way, Niramyn gave up who he was to deny his pursuers the chance to find him, a necessary sacrifice, but one he vowed to repay his rival back for a hundredfold.

The magic finished its grim business, and the exarch, now trapped in the body of a child, battered and weary, fell to true sleep. There was an odd sort of paradoxical peace to his slumber. Without his memories, his personality, his sense of his true self, many of his worries and stresses fell away. In that way, Niramyn passed his first night as a child of a new world.

Myzalik's rage knew no bounds when he was in his own palace. "This close!" he screamed, unleashing a bolt of star-spawned lightning to rake the surface of the scrying pool. Jagged-sharp plasma burst across the liquid obsidian and hurled it into the air, dispelling the image and hardening into a storm of razor-edged needles that peppered the room. None struck the exarch, of course. It was barely even the work of a thought to deflect their trajectories away from him.

"I had him! Another two seconds and he would have been reduced to a child too young to properly hold the smallest sliver of arcana! Even as quickly as he reacted, he shouldn't have been able to do half of what he did to escape! There was no time for him to pull in arcana. Explain to me how this happened," he demanded of his servant, who had not been quite so quick to defend himself and had been pierced by several of the shards.

The ascendant did his best not to cringe beneath the exarch's glare. He telekinetically plucked the obsidian back out and returned it to the pool while sealing the wounds. It would not do to let a drop of blood reach the carpets and stain them, never mind that they were made of astral silk and a simple current of arcana would return them to pristine condition.

"We believe this is the cause of the miscalculation," the servant said, plucking an image from the stream of time and forming it into an illusion in the middle of the room. It showed Exarch Niramyn lounging in the air, drinking from a decanter that radiated magic. "It appears to be some sort of arcana-infused beverage. Our theory is that he burned what he already had in his body to boost his resources and outdistance the spell's range before it could complete the transformation."

Of course that self-indulgent prick was drinking wine laced with pure, unfiltered, deadly arcana. Niramyn's arrogance knew no bounds. "Are you saying," Myzalik began slowly as he struggled to master a sudden tick in his left eye, "that the plans I have spent close to a century laying, the research and fortunes spent on modifying the immortality spell to weaponize it, all of it was beaten because on the day we chose to strike, he wanted to show off that he could get drunk while giving himself and surviving arcana poisoning?"

"I . . . Exarch Niramyn was still affected by the spell. He will be weaker than a human mage right now. It's only a matter of time until we capture him, exarch."

Myzalik turned to fully face the servant. "You had better hope so, for all your sakes. I want him back here under my control, or I want his body. I'll drag his soul back to this reality myself if he's already dead. We will not let all the work that went into this be wasted."

He dismissed the servant and silently fumed. Unlike his servants, he wasn't so confident in his rival's defeat. Myzalik needed to take steps to ensure this was a total victory for him and not merely a setback for Niramyn. This couldn't be a repeat of the incident at the Castle of Storms.

With a snarl, he reached through Transcendence and into the Crushing Void to wrest arcana from it. He filled his soul well and cast a spell to split his conscious into fourteen separate beings. They teleported away to attend to a variety of tasks, several moving to present the appearance of a normal day, but the majority taking personal command of the units of hunters being sent out to scour the surface of the world below the clouds.

Five minutes had passed from Myzalik's attack, a bare three hundred seconds. And yet, Niramyn had slipped away completely and utterly. None of the Myzaliks could find a trace of him, nor could any of the ascendants they led.

He'd done the impossible in creating a spell to defeat Niramyn, and somehow the infuriating man had managed to out-impossible him in mere seconds by escaping. After weeks and weeks of searching, he was forced to concede the hunt. His rival had escaped, and there was nothing Myalik could do except consolidate his position and prepare for the inevitable counterstrike.

CHAPTER 1

His whole body ached, a dull but insistent pain. His eyes were crusted shut, and it was almost too much of an effort to pry them open. Even then, the world was a blur of blue-and-white sky. That was strange, but he couldn't say why, like looking at something familiar from an unusual angle. His mind struggled to catch up, but it took several more seconds for him to register what had woken him.

"Wake up!" a woman's voice yelled. "You'll get dragged into the cove with the tide!"

Her voice pierced the fog over his mind, and he struggled to sit up. For something so simple, it felt like a monumental task, and he couldn't manage anything better than rolling over and climbing to his hands and knees. Then a wave struck him and bowled him over.

He tried to crawl farther up the beach, but his limbs were too weak to drag him. The next wave flattened him again and pulled him away from safety. He kept trying, but it was a losing battle. By the time the woman reached him, the water was up to his chest and he'd been dunked underwater several times. She grabbed his arm and started dragging him back up the beach.

He didn't remember much after that. The woman helped him to his feet and held him upright. Without her, he would have toppled over, unable to support his own weight. With her assistance, they trudged up the beach and navigated a narrow trail up the bluffs. He blacked out somewhere near the top, and after that, he had only hazy memories of scrub bushes and dusty fields.

The next time he opened his eyes, it was evening. Pale light illuminated a ramshackle room, filtered through cracks in the wall and holes in the ceiling. He was in a bed with a threadbare blanket draped over him, which did little to ward off the chill of the coming night.

He could hear two people in the other room talking, though their voices were soft enough that he only caught bits and pieces of the conversation. He over-heard a man mutter about arcana poisoning and a death sentence, and the other voice, the woman who'd saved him, insisting on something. They kept arguing, the volume gradually increasing until finally the man said, "I've given you my diagnosis. Do whatever you want with it."

There was the sound of a door slamming after that, so hard that the walls shook and he felt it through the rickety legs of the bed. He struggled to sit up, but he was so weak that even the weight of the blanket was too much. After a brief surge of effort, he sagged back down onto the bed and closed his eyes again.

When he woke, daylight was coming in through the cracks in the walls. He tried to sit up again, and this time managed to prop himself up on his elbows before a wave of vertigo hit him. He rolled to the side and hurled his guts out onto the dirt floor, then collapsed back into the bed. The noise was enough to summon his rescuer, who entered the room with an earthenware cup that had a crack running down half of its length.

"You're awake?" she asked, nodding to herself when she saw his eyes open. "Good. You should be past the worst of it now, if Magister Tormin was right. He said you had arcana poisoning somehow and that you were as good as dead. You're looking pretty alive to me though, so what does he know?"

He could barely follow the woman's voice. Mostly, his eyes just followed the cup in her hand as she talked, and she fell silent when she realized what was distracting him. "Ah, sorry. You must be thirsty. Here, let me help you up and you can drink this."

The woman sat next to him on the bed and helped him into a sitting posi-tion. The world spun again, but he managed to keep himself from spewing all over her, or at least from dry heaving in her general direction. There wasn't much of anything left, and he was pretty sure he'd hacked up all the seawater in his belly a minute ago.

The water in that cup was warm and gritty, like drinking from a mud puddle that someone has sprinkled a fresh layer of dust on top of. To his parched throat, it was delicious. He tried to drain it in one swallow, but the woman kept a hand on the cup and only let him sip at it. Still, she remained patiently at his side until it was gone.

"Better?" she asked.

"Yes," he croaked. "Thank you."

"You're welcome. You know, you've got to be about the luckiest kid in the world. You look like you survived a shipwreck and somehow washed ashore in Bloodfin Cove in one piece. There are more sharks in the waters off the coast here than there are people in Palmara, and you were right at the thickest of it."

He didn't feel very lucky. Mostly, he just felt sore and sick. His head was killing him, and his stomach was still threatening rebellion. It was sheer will-power and grit that kept the few ounces of water he'd been given inside of him.

The woman kept talking, but he'd stopped listening. It wasn't until she'd repeated herself for the third time that he realized she'd asked him a question. "Sorry," he told her. "Tired still. What did you say?"

"I said my name is Ciana and asked what yours is," she told him, not a hint of impatience in her tone.

"My . . . name?" He thought about it for a second and felt his mind drifting. It was harder to focus, hard to remember anything.

He mumbled something and sunk back down onto the bed. His eyelids were too heavy to keep open, his limbs too weak to move. Whatever Ciana said next, he was already too far gone to hear.

What finally woke him hours later was the smell of cooking food. It took him a few attempts to sit up and swing his feet around to the edge of the bed, and then there were a few more false starts before he finally got upright and was able to wrap the ratty old blanket around his shoulders. He hobbled across the room to the door.

Ciana was tending a metal pot hung over top a firepit in the center of the room. There was no chimney that he could see, but given the nature of the shack he was in, one was hardly needed. None of the boards that formed the walls had been sealed in any way, and even if they'd been square when they were constructed, time and the elements had conspired to warp and pull them. The roof wasn't in much better shape, and the smoke that rose from the fire simply passed through the many, many holes instead of lingering.

"Finally awake again?" Ciana said, looking up at him. "I knew the smell of a hot meal would get you out of bed. Come on over and have a seat. It's almost done."

He walked across the room, each step deliberate and wobbly, and all but collapsed on a driftwood log that had been carved into something like a bench and set up near the firepit. He watched in silence as the woman ladled out two scoops of whatever was gurgling in the pot into wooden bowls and passed him one, along with a spoon.

"Here you go, Nym."

"Nym?" he asked.

Ciana frowned. "Sorry, did I get it wrong? I thought that's what you said your name was."

He blinked and considered. He remembered her asking, and he'd said something as he was passing back out. "I don't know what my name is," he told her. No matter how hard he considered it, he couldn't really remember much of anything specific to his identity, not his family or where he was from or even how old he was.

"That's awful," she said. "Maybe the magister can help you get your memories back. For tonight, we'll call you Nym, okay? When you're feeling better, I'll show you the way to town and we can ask."

"Okay," Nym agreed quietly. He ate the stew in front of him slowly, lost in thought. The oldest thing he could remember was waking up on the beach and getting pounded with waves. Ciana had been yelling at him from the trail at the top of the bluffs and had somehow made it down to the shore in time to drag him back out of the water.

Whoever he was, whatever he'd been doing prior to that, he had no idea. He didn't remember being on a ship, or what had happened to it. She didn't know who he was, so he guessed he wasn't a local. Really, there were no clues at all, and it was a struggle to even string those thoughts together.

Ciana didn't say anything while they ate, a small mercy Nym was thankful for. She gave him the time he needed to start to put himself together. The two sat in silence, interrupted only by the crackle of the small cooking fire. Nym took a moment to study the woman who'd saved his life.

She was in her early twenties, plain faced and lanky. She had tanned skin with a splattering of freckles across her nose and cheeks, and brown-red hair that hung down past her shoulders in a braid. Her clothes were in better condition than the blanket he had wrapped around him, but still showed plenty of signs of wear. Her hands and feet were heavily calloused, and scars showed on her bare arms.

"Why are you helping me?" he asked.

She seemed surprised by the question. "Why wouldn't I help you?"

He gave her a wry smile and looked around. "Can you afford to? You don't look like you have much? Not that I'm not grateful, but . . ."

Ciana shrugged. "I'm not going to let a kid get turned into chum, and I'm not going to let one die if I can do anything about it. Sure, I don't have a lot, but I can spare a bed for a day and a meal."

Nym wasn't sure that was true. There was a hollowness in her cheeks that told him times had been tough for her, and that maybe she was giving away more than she could afford. He looked down at the empty bowl in his hands and felt guilt squirm through his guts.

"Thank you," he told her.

She smiled. "Don't even worry about it. I'll survive. I always do. And you're going to survive too, right? We'll see about healing your mind tomorrow and then figure out how to get you home."

"That . . . sounds good," Nym said.

"But first, we need to find you some pants!" she told him. "That blanket is more holes than not anymore."

He looked down and realized exactly how much of himself could be seen through it. His face flushed, and he shrugged it off his shoulders to bunch up extra material around his waist.

Ciana laughed. "Not your fault, Nym. And nothing I haven't seen before. No need to be embarrassed."

But there was need. Oh yes, yes there was.

"I am going to lay back down again. Thank you for saving me."

She waved him off. "Anyone would have done it. Sleep well. Big day tomorrow."

He laid back down and watched the sun set through the wall slats while he pondered her words. Somehow, he doubted anyone else would have saved him, let alone offered him shelter while he recovered his strength.

He owed Ciana big time. He'd have to find some way to repay her. Paying back debts seemed like the kind of thing that was important to him. Sleep took him while he turned that idea around in his head.

CHAPTER 2

The sound of arguing woke Nym up. Ciana and another man were talking, and the conversation was getting heated.

"I'm not bringing you food to waste on some shipwrecked orphan who's going to die by next week!" the man shouted. Nym could see him throw his hands up through the wall slats.

"No one asked you to bring me anything! I'll take care of myself and him too!" she yelled back. Though the man was a foot taller than her, she had no problem getting right up in his face. "I appreciate all the help you've given me since my father died, but I don't need your permission to live my life however I want. If you don't want to help now, then get out and stop trying to tell me what to do."

"Ciana," the man said in a quieter voice, trying to regain control of the situation. "You will starve. Food is already tight. You can't afford to feed this kid. You're too nice. You did him a good turn, and no one can fault you for saving him, but he's through the worst of it, and you need to cut him loose."

"Get out," she said coldly. "You're a worse person than I thought if you'd leave him out to die. The boy doesn't even remember his own name."

"That's very sad," he said, stomping to the door. "But all you're doing is dooming yourself along with him."

The door creaked open on rusted hinges, then slammed closed. Ciana sat down on the driftwood log heavily and let out a huff. "The nerve, trying to run my life for me," she muttered.

"Who was he?" Nym asked, once again wrapped in the ragged blanket and standing in the doorway to the bedroom.

Ciana shot the front door a sour look and said, "His name is Senman. He's been sniffing after me for about two years now trying to get . . . Well, never you mind what exactly he's trying to get from me. Point is he's not getting it, no matter how many times he shows up with a coney. And he's got no ground to tell me what I can and can't do."

Nym thought about it for a minute. "But was he right? Am I too much of a burden?"

Ciana crossed the room and folded him into a hug. "Don't you ever think that," she said into his hair. "I'll figure something out. For now though, let's get you into a pair of pants and a shirt."

The clothes weren't even close to his size, but they were better than wearing a blanket around his body. He held the pants up with a length of twine Ciana gave him after rolling the legs up several times so they were snug against his calf. The shirt was sleeveless and about a foot too long, stopping just a bit above his knees. Nym was tall, but so was Ciana, and she was more than twice his age.

There were no shoes for either of them, and he lacked the calluses she had, so it was a slow trip into Palmara. The town was only three miles away, but it took about two hours to get there, and Nym's feet were thoroughly blistered and bruised by the time they made it. Once he saw it, he thought that *town* might have been a bit of an exaggeration.

It was barely more than twenty or thirty shacks that might have been a bit better quality than Ciana's all huddled together around a dirt road that snaked its way through the center. She led him into it and straight to one particular shack that was maybe in a bit better shape than average. Unlike hers near the cove, the ones in town had some sort of earth packed into the slats to give them some weatherproofing, and the one they stopped in front of had some carvings running up and down the door frame. There was a plaque mounted next to it.

"What does this mean?" Nym asked as he studied it. A symbol was carved into it, a solid circle in the center with a pair of rings going around it. A single line was drawn from the center circle to bisect both rings.

"This is Magister Tormin's home. He's the one who looked you over when I first found you and said you had arcana poisoning."

"The one who said I was going to die from it?" Nym asked.

Ciana nodded. "Good thing he was wrong, huh? I guess you're tougher than you look."

The door opened to reveal a middle-aged man with a receding hairline, a bushy beard, and a potbelly. He was wearing the same style of clothing as Ciana, but with a brown robe loosely belted over his waist and a pair of shoes.

"What's this then?" he asked, staring down his nose at the pair of them. "Standing at my door gossiping about me? How rude."

"No, magister," Ciana said, soothing his ruffled pride. "Nym here was just curious about what the symbol on your sign means, and I was telling him it's a magister's symbol."

"Yes, quite," the magister said. "Second circle, you know. My talents are utterly wasted here, but that's life for you. I see your stray managed to survive his arcana poisoning."

"Uh, yes, magister. Thing is, he can't seem to remember anything. We're not even sure Nym is his real name. I was hoping you might be able to help him."

Magister Tormin cocked an eyebrow at her before turning his gaze to Nym. "And how exactly do you propose I do that?"

"Well, uh . . ." Ciana gestured helplessly to the sign next to his door. "Second circle?"

The magister let out a heavy sigh. "Come in then," he told them, moving to the side and gesturing them through his door.

Unlike Ciana's shack, the magister's home had two doors off the main room. Even the main room itself had a large bookshelf and a table with two chairs. The firepit was set in the back corner, which had some metal sheathing to keep the heat of the flames off the wall.

The magister fished a book off the shelf and started flipping through it. After a minute or two, he stopped and started reading a passage. "Very well," he told them. "Hold still and stay quiet. It will not look like I am doing anything, but trust me, I am. And it's not easy."

Magister Tormin closed his eyes and steadied his breathing. Nym waited as seconds turned into a minute, then two. Finally, he saw a faint movement around the magister, like a shadow crossing over his face and stretching out into the distance. It slowly strengthened and grew until it enveloped his entire body in a misty blue light.

The mist rolled across the magister as it sunk into his skin, disappearing and being replaced by more and more, slowly building in brightness until he was almost glowing. Finally, almost five minutes after he'd started, the magister's eyes snapped open, and he laid his palm on Nym's hair.

The mist spread out from the magister's hand to encompass Nym's head, but didn't seem to do anything else that he could tell. Then again, it wasn't like he could see into his own head. If the magister saw anything though, he didn't say a word. Sweat started to bead on his forehead, which was steadily turning red despite the veil of blue covering it. A single vein stood up near one of the magister's eyes and started pulsing rapidly.

Another minute of awkward silence passed with Nym shooting Ciana a look and her rolling her eyes behind the magister's back. "Stop fidgeting," Magister Tormin said when Nym shuffled in place.

"Sorry, sir," Nym said.

Finally, the magister let go of him and let out a soft wheeze. He wiped his face on his sleeve and plopped down heavily in the chair. Ciana opened her mouth to say something, but paused when he held up a finger. "Give me a minute," he said.

It was more like five minutes, but Magister Tormin did eventually catch his breath. "Alright," he said, addressing Ciana. "I've used the most powerful, targeted body diagnostic spell there is in the second circle. There are definitely remnants of arcana poisoning like I already told you. There are a lot less than there were a day ago, which would be a mystery to take to the healers at the Academy if you could afford it. He shouldn't have survived, and he shouldn't be in as good a shape as he is right now. I don't know how he did it.

"As far as this supposed memory loss goes, there is no physical basis for it that I can find. Nor is there any magical malady here, though who would bother to curse a little kid with something powerful enough to completely obliviate his memories is beyond me."

The magister turned to glare at Nym. "Now, come clean with me. I've wasted a good deal of energy on this farce. Who are you really, and why are you playing this game? There's nothing wrong with your head."

"I'm not lying!" Nym protested.

"Either you are a liar or this is related to your mysterious case of arcana poisoning. I am not a medical expert when it comes to magical maladies, but any second-circle magister knows that some snot-nosed kid can't even pull that much arcana into his soul well, let alone survive the backlash. You haven't even pierced the first circle. Whoever you are, and whatever you're playing at, I advise you to come clean before you make it worse."

"I'm telling you the truth," Nym said hotly. "I don't know what you want from me."

The magister sniffed. "I wash my hands of this. Don't bring this child back to me unless it's to offer an apology for his behavior," he told Ciana. "There is nothing wrong with him, and he's making a fool of you. I won't waste precious time and energy I could be using to solve actual problems on him."

That said, Magister Tormin promptly threw them both out onto the street. He refused to listen to either of their protests and slammed the door in their faces so hard that his plaque rattled against the wall.

"You believe me, right?" Nym said.

Ciana gave a long sigh and told him, "I do. But I don't know what to do to help you now. I guess let's just go back home and figure it out later. Maybe your memories will come back in a few days when you start feeling better."

He didn't have a better idea. "What can I do to help?" he said. "I don't want to put you in a bad spot because you gave me too much."

Ciana gave him a small smile. "Sure, Nym. You can help. Not tonight though. You're still not recovered. Maybe in a day or two."

"I can help now!" he told her. "Just tell me what you need me to do."

"We'll see. For starters, we've got to walk back. How do your feet feel?"

They hurt. Every step was a small agony on each of the blisters he'd acquired, and they'd get worse on the walk back. That wasn't something she needed to worry about. There was nothing she could do. She didn't even have shoes for herself, let alone a spare pair to offer a stranger. He'd suffer through aching feet, and soon they'd be calloused over.

"They're fine," he lied. "Let's go home and I'll help you get lunch together."

It was a slow walk back, even slower than the first trip, but Nym did his best not to hobble along, and if Ciana noticed, she didn't say anything.

That was a small mercy. He had his pride too, after all.

CHAPTER 3

Ciana wouldn't let Nym help that day. She just kept insisting that he needed to recover his strength and telling him to rest. If he was being honest with himself, she wasn't wrong. He could barely walk on his own, and he was still feeling weak from the arcana poisoning he'd somehow given himself prior to forgetting every detail about his life.

"What even is arcana poisoning?" he asked while she diced some vegetables pulled up from a scraggly garden right next to the shack.

"I don't know much about it, just what Magister Tormin told me when he came to check on you the first night. I guess it comes from trying to pull too much arcana into your body—um, he called it a soul well, I think—at once. It escapes from where it's supposed to be and gets into the rest of you, which makes you sick until it dissolves. The more you take in, the sicker you get, and it can kill you if you have too much at once."

"How would you pull arcana into your soul well?" Nym asked. "I must have done it somehow."

He thought about what the magister had done, that pale-blue mist that had come from somewhere and been sucked into his body, and tried to remember if he'd ever done anything like that. If he had, it wasn't coming to him. He didn't even know how he'd start. He should have asked the magister for a hint when he had the chance.

He did have arcana poisoning, so that meant he could draw arcana into his body despite what the magister had said. Or maybe there were other ways to get arcana poisoning that he didn't know about. But he had plenty of time to sit there and think about it, since Ciana had him back on bed rest. She wasn't impressed with his fortitude or, as she termed it, mule-headed stupidity.

It wasn't like he was expecting her to give him a piggyback ride home. There was nothing to be done about his feet, so there was no use complaining.

He'd cleaned the blisters out as best he could, though the salt water stung enough to bring tears to his eyes, and now it was just a matter of time until they healed.

Ciana didn't have much to offer him in the way of mystical arcane knowledge, for which he could hardly fault her. It wasn't like he had much of that kind of knowledge either, or any other knowledge for that matter. He was wearing borrowed pants, so his life was pretty much defined by accepting acts of charity at this point.

He would pay that debt back someday, hopefully soon.

It was sometime in the middle of the night when his eyes snapped open. The last bits of arcana in his body had finished dissolving, and it felt like something in his chest broke open. A channel he hadn't even known existed was suddenly unclogged. There was an empty space inside him that he could fill. He just needed to reach out and . . .

And he didn't know what came next, but it gave him a starting point. Working mostly on instinct and still half-asleep, his consciousness reached out and pierced the boundary of physical reality. The conduit was forged, and his soul well slowly began filling. Nym willed the blanket off of him to float in the air above him.

It drifted up like it was caught on a strong breeze and flapped in place in the air. Nym gave it a sleepy smile and reached out to grab it, then pulled it back down into place. Tomorrow would be a new day, and he'd be able to start repaying Ciana for her generosity.

He was up with the dawn, well before Ciana. Nym practiced creating the conduit that let arcana into his soul well over and over, expelling the magic in acts of minor telekinesis. He discovered that even though the magic was doing the lifting, it still tired him out as if he'd done it physically. It wasn't possible for him to lift anything too big either. The limiting factor seemed to be his own body. Anything that was too heavy for him to lift couldn't be budged by the magic either.

Where it really shined though was in time management. Sure, it was just as hard to move something with magic as it was physically in terms of sheer weight, but he could move lots of small things at once, and with remarkable finesse once he'd gotten a bit of practice in. Nym wasn't even sure he had as much dexterity in his fingers as he did with magic.

Ciana came into the main room and stopped, her jaw hanging open and her eyes popping out when she saw five wooden spoons and two bowls swooping through the air in a large circle in front of Nym. He saw her and turned with a big grin on his face. "I figured it out!" he said. "It was the arcana poisoning that was blocking me. Once it cleared up, I could touch the magic and pull it in. I was careful not to pull too much though."

"That's amazing," she told him. "Does that mean your memories came back too?"

The spoons clattered as they fell all at once. Nym picked them up again with his magic and put them away. "No," he said softly. "Nothing came back to me. Even all of this is just what I figured out in the last few hours. It seems really easy to do though, way easier than what Magister Tormin made it look like. Maybe I already knew this before."

"Maybe," Ciana agreed. She came over and sat down next to him. "Good job either way. How are you feeling today?"

"I feel fantastic!"

"And how are your feet?"

"Uh . . ." Nym looked down at them and wiggled his toes. "They're alright I guess."

"Good to hear. Tell you what. You stay here and keep practicing and I'm going to go check my snare lines to see if we caught anything for breakfast."

He nodded eagerly. "I can do that."

Once she'd left, Nym dove back into the magic. He wanted to see if he could fly, but it turned out he couldn't pick himself up. Nym didn't know if that was because he couldn't lift his own weight, or if that was just a rule that telekinesis didn't work that way. It inspired him to try levitating a broken branch and hanging off it, but all that happened was as soon as he tried to put his weight on the branch, it fell down.

That wasn't really conclusive evidence either way. He needed to find another kid about the same size and see if he could lift them up with his magic. There had been a few out and about that he'd seen when they'd taken their trip to Palmara; he was sure he could find one that fit the bill. That was an experiment that would have to wait though, since he didn't think Ciana would be taking him back there until he was able to walk long distances.

He felt like he should probably get up and at least attempt to walk around, but he was getting tired from the magic. When Ciana did get back, she found him on his back on the ground, chest heaving as he watched the clouds go by.

"Are you alright?" she said.

"Might have overdone it," he told her. "Just catching my breath. I'm fine."

"Well, look. Nothing on the snare lines, but one of the traps in the cove caught a crab. We'll have a nice meal after all."

Nym groaned as he rolled over and forced himself upright. "What can I do to help?" he asked.

"Just come in when you're ready."

It didn't take long for the smell coming out of the shack to set his stomach rumbling. Deciding he'd rested enough, Nym scrambled to his feet and went inside to float out the bowls and spoons for Ciana to fill.

The next day, his feet had healed enough to run around. The calluses weren't thick yet, but they were there. Ciana was deeply suspicious of the speed at which he'd developed them, but she just shrugged and told him that since nothing else about him had been normal, there was no reason for this to be any different.

She showed him the route she took from trap to trap she'd set around the shack, both on land and underwater. The land traps rarely caught much as there weren't a ton of small game animals living so close to the sea where the soil was sandy and plant life was scarce. There were forests farther inland with better hunting, but her father had made his living as a fisherman, so her home was right on the coast.

Most of the food she caught came from the underwater crab traps. The problem was that Bloodfin Cove was not safe to swim in, and there had even been occasions of the local sharks tipping over rowboats. The shallows were only marginally safer as the young sharks could get around in as little as a few feet of water and would happily take a bite out of a person's leg.

Ciana had a wide boat that looked more like a box she floated around in, hauling up the traps one at a time to check the contents before sinking them back down to the seafloor. Usually they were empty. Unfortunately, there was very little in the way of fish in the cove, and attempts at line fishing usually resulted in losing the hook to whatever shark took it.

It was dangerous work, but Nym thought he could it do relatively safely if he stood on the beach and used his magic to pull the traps up instead. It even worked, for about two traps. The weight was too much for him after that, and he had to take a break to recover. It would be the work of the entire day to check every trap, so that idea was dead unless he came up with some clever way to determine which traps were full and only pull those up.

He did figure out that distance was a factor. The ones that were closer were somewhat easier to pull up, although hauling anything through the water was a chore. If he went out in the boat, he could do more, but that defeated the point.

Instead, Ciana took him out in the boat, and they alternated hauling up the traps to check them. They were almost all empty. The next day was the same story. By the third day though, they'd noticed something strange.

"Nym," Ciana said slowly as she pointed out into the water. "Why is this shark following you?"

"What?" he said, following her finger to see a shark circling around them. "They all look the same. How can you tell?"

"It's got that scar near its fin, see? Every time you come out on the boat with me, this one shark shows up. I never see it otherwise."

"Uh . . . maybe it thinks I'm good-looking?"

Ciana gave him a flat stare. "I am sure that is not the reason."

"Well I don't know. Is it a problem? There's always sharks out there."

"No, I guess not." She watched it swim another circle. "As long as it doesn't try to tip the boat. I just don't like that it seems obsessed with you."

She shook her head and handed him the hook she used to fish the trap line off the buoy it was tied to. "Here, your turn to pull one up."

He scooped the rope up, eyeing the shark the whole time. Once the rope was in the boat, he started hauling up hand over hand until the empty trap broke the surface. With a sigh, he let it sink back down and grabbed the oars to head over to the next buoy.

The shark followed them like a puppy as they did their circuit around the cove. It didn't disappear until they beached the boat and dragged it up above the tide line.

CHAPTER 4

Days turned into weeks as Nym and Ciana settled into a new routine. He went into town a few times and subsequently learned that there was a whole section they hadn't visited during their original trip. That was farther up the road, and while there were only three homes there, all of them were for rich people and could easily house four or five families.

They stayed far away from that part of town at Ciana's insistence. There was no reason to go that way, and nothing good could come from it, according to her. Those people were always willing to use others to further their own agendas and just as willing to discard people once they'd squeezed them for all they were worth. Nym didn't miss a note of bitterness in her voice when she lectured him on staying away from the rich side of town.

Nym didn't see the harm, but it was what Ciana wanted, so when he went into town to run errands for her, he stuck to his business and didn't go exploring. That did not stop trouble from finding him, as he found out soon after his first month living near the village of Palmara.

He walked out of the general store, carefully holding on to a large bag of onions he'd traded the owner three crabs for. The bag was Ciana's and had a hole near the bottom where a seam had split on the side, so he was using both hands to both hold it upright and keep the seam pinched closed. Consequently, he wasn't paying as much attention as he could have been to his surroundings and practically bowled over a boy a year or two older than him who was about to enter the store.

"Oh! I'm sorry," Nym said, struggling to keep the onions in the bag. Two of them had already escaped and were rolling away down the road.

"Watch where you're going, you idiot!" the other boy yelled as one of his friends reached down to help him to his feet.

"I said I was sorry," Nym said, not looking at him as he hopped around trying to stop the rogue onions with his foot. He had a moment's warning of magic stirring near him before something struck his back and sent him sprawling. Onions rolled everywhere where they weren't pinned between his chest and the dirt.

"It's a good look for you. A peasant rolling around in the dirt with some moldy vegetables. How appropriate."

Nym rose back to his feet and spun to see the boy for the first time. He was dressed in nice clothes, clothes with no patches or holes, clothes that had buttons and buckles. He wore shoes, had a finely tooled leather belt circling his waist, and the glint of a pair of rings was visible on his finger. His friend, whom Nym mentally downgraded to lackey, was dusting him off while he smirked at Nym.

More importantly, he had the same misty glow of magic around him that Nym had seen around the magister when he'd first washed ashore. Nym narrowed his eyes as he examined it. The power output was low, but given the speed with which the boy had generated the effect, that seemed about right. It looked something like his own telekinetic experiments, except instead of the magic molding around the object to hold it, it was just a flat square of force used to shove something.

"Ooooh, is that the new magic you learned?" the lackey said.

"A good debut for it, don't you think?" the boy said back. "Putting a rude peasant back in his place."

"Oh yeah, real fancy," Nym said. "But I'm really interested in the magic you're using to see where you're going."

"What would a peasant like you know about the noble art? And why would you think I need magic just to see?"

"No magic to see? I'm sorry, I just assumed. If it's not magic, how do you see with your head so far up your own ass?"

The boy's sneer transformed into red-faced rage in an instant, and the glow of magic surrounded him again as he pulled in more power. This time Nym was ready for him though, and when the force shove came at him, he used his own magic to deflect it off to the side. The boy's eye twitched as he stared at Nym.

"What's wrong, Amos?" the lackey asked. "You're not doing anything."

"I'm doing magic, moron," the boy snapped at him. "I just . . . It's a new spell."

Magic flared up around him, again and another force shove flew from him to Nym. Nym knocked it aside again, this time at a downward angle so it tore up some dirt from the road. "Stop doing that."

"What . . . How are you . . ." Amos trailed off, his brow furrowed. He eyed Nym, focusing on the tears in his clothes and giving a pointed look at his bare feet covered in dust. "There is no way you're a mage."

Nym shrugged. He'd already forged his conduit and filled his soul well with magic, so he reached out and telekinetically picked up eight of the onions. They floated through the air back into the holey sack. As they fell in, new ones rose up until he'd recovered everything that had fallen out when he'd been shoved.

"Not sure about being a mage. Just a thing I can do." Nym was confused though. He could easily see the flow of magic around the other boy. He'd seen it on the magister too, on several occasions when he'd bumped into the pretentious man while running errands for Ciana. It sounded like Amos couldn't see the magic, maybe not even feel it. That meant he was at a severe disadvantage in a magical shoving match, since he wouldn't be able to see what Nym was doing to counter it.

The smart thing to do was walk away and not antagonize Amos any further. Ciana had warned him specifically about not getting entangled with the rich folk from the far side of Palmara. He should just leave. But the other boy was a smarmy, stuck-up jackass. So Nym made his own little force shove and used it to sweep Amos's legs out from under him.

The rich kid went down onto his butt with a startled cry. Nym snickered and said, "Well, it was fun to meet you, but I've got stuff to do. Later, rich boy."

"Don't you dare walk away from me, you filthy peasant!" Amos screamed at him, scrambling back to his feet. Magic surged again, and Amos flung out a powerful blast of telekinesis big enough to literally scoop Nym off his feet and hurl him forward. The boy was red-faced and panting from the effort, but he succeeded in knocking Nym over and spilling the onions again.

"Okay, look, this was a misunderstanding. I said I was sorry. We knocked each other down. I have to pick up my food again. Can we say we're even now?" Nym said.

The sneer was back. "I don't want to be even."

The glow was getting stronger now, showing the same misty qualities that Magister Tormin had when he'd used his diagnostic spell on Nym. Whatever Amos was up to this time, it was going to be a lot stronger than a shoving spell. Of course, there were no adults around to stop him, which meant Nym had to fend for himself.

He had no idea what the other boy was planning, so it seemed like the best defense was a good offense. He reached into his own soul well, still filling rapidly from the conduit he'd forged, and let out a telekinetic wave of energy that arced out to strike Amos's entire body. It didn't make it halfway before the rich kid struck.

A sudden spike of pain shot through Nym's chest, and he lost control of the telekinesis. He let out a strangled, hoarse cry that seemed to alarm the lackey and made Amos smirk with satisfaction. "What . . . what did you do?" Nym gasped out.

"What, you don't know?" Amos asked in mock surprise. "Good. Magic isn't for people like you. Go back to grubbing in your dirt, peasant."

Nym's vision started going dark, and he felt a foot press against his shoulder. It kicked him backward, and the laughter of the other two boys rang out as they walked over him. The last thing he saw was the lackey scooping up one of his onions to throw, then it struck him in the face and everything went black.

"Wow, you walked right into that, huh?" a girl's voice said.

Nym groaned and rolled onto his back. There was a blurry person-shaped outline standing over him looking down. He blinked a few times, and it resolved itself into a teenage girl dressed in the same style of simple clothing he was, although hers was hole free and didn't even have any patches.

"Here, let me help you up."

She held out a hand and pulled him to his feet when he grabbed it. "Oof, heavier than you look. How are you feeling?"

"Like I got kicked by a horse," Nym told her.

"I bet. You just stood there and let Amos hit you with an arcana injection. You'll be fine tomorrow, I'm sure. But today is going to suck for you."

"What's an arcana injection?"

The girl just sighed. "Come on, pick up your onions and come with me. I'll tell you all about how the world works, new kid."

The girl led him between two huts and into a grassy field with a few trees scattered through it. "Here, have a seat," she said, patting the ground next to her once she'd sat down.

Nym wasn't sure what was going on, but his whole body hurt, and his chest was worse. If for no other reason than he needed a bit to catch his breath before he started the walk home, he decided to stay.

"Good boy," the girl said. "Let's start with introductions. You're the kid who washed up in Bloodfin Cove somehow right? The one who can't remember anything?"

"That's me," Nym said slowly. He supposed it was a small village, and they hadn't made a secret out of it, so it made sense that people knew about him. At least, some people did. Amos didn't seem to have any idea who he was, but then again, Nym doubted he cared about anything that didn't involve him personally.

"Thought so. My name is Lathia, what's yours?"

"Nym."

"Nice to meet you. So like I was saying, you're new here, and it looks like you can do some first-circle magic. Most people can't, but it's not super uncommon or anything. What I'm saying is that there are other things that are way weirder about you, you know?"

"Uh . . . yeah. I guess?"

"Right, so what Amos did was prepared a needle of second-layer arcana, and when you opened your soul well to let the magic out, he jabbed it into you. Basically, he gave you a mild case of arcana poisoning by flooding your soul well with arcana you aren't strong enough to handle," Lathia explained.

"How did he know when to do that? It didn't seem like he could tell when I was using my magic."

"Well, obviously he cast an aura-reading spell first. How else would you know when to use a disruption spell if you couldn't see when your enemy's soul well was vulnerable?"

Nym frowned and turned that thought over. If he was understanding Lathia right, that meant that most people couldn't just see magic. They had to do something special, which gave them feedback that may or may not have been the same as what he saw. That meant he had an advantage next time.

It also raised a new question. If people couldn't see magic without casting special spells to help them, why could he? And more importantly, was it a good idea to tell anybody, or should he keep it to himself?

CHAPTER 5

How do you know all of this? Can you use magic too?" Nym asked.

"Er, I live next to the magister. Amos goes there for lessons twice a week, and I overhear a lot. He was on his way back from his lesson today when you bumped into him."

Nym noticed she hadn't exactly answered his second question, but he decided to gloss over it. If she didn't want to talk about it, he wasn't going to force her. Besides, she'd been nice and helpful so far. It would be rude to pry into her personal life if she decided not to share.

"What's wrong with him anyway? I've never met anyone so arrogant. Is he nobility or something?"

Lathia let out a laugh. "He wishes. His father is a wealthy merchant. If they could buy a noble title, I'm sure they would. Failing that, the whole family makes sure we all know that they have money and we don't. Thus, we are all inferior human beings in their eyes."

"If that's how they feel, why do they even live here?"

Lathia shrugged. "Money reasons, I assume. The Nestar family has never deigned to speak to me, and I am very happy to keep it that way."

He started to laugh, only to wince and grab at his chest again. "Owww," he groaned. "So this will go away on its own?"

"There is a thing I overheard Magister Tormin tell Amos once. He said it was a meditation technique used to purge the body of arcana and speed up recovery from arcana poisoning in case Amos actually overdrew himself and flooded his soul well."

"That sounds like it would help."

"Yeah," Lathia agreed. "The thing is, I don't know how to teach it to you. I only know what I overheard them talking about. So it might not help unless you can get Magister Tormin to explain all the parts I can't tell you about."

"That's fine. Anything would be better than nothing."

"Okay, I'll do my best to explain it the way I heard it. First, you have to be able to feel the arcana in your body. That's what the meditation part is for. It's to help you figure out where the arcana spread to. Once you know that, you have to figure out how to manipulate it. Magister Tormin said the key was to take it in small chunks and break it down in your soul well, then make a reverse conduit to drain it back to whatever layer it came from.

"That was very important too. I remember him stressing that a lot to Amos, to not try to release the first layer into the second layer or the other way around. That was a bad idea. If he didn't think he could hold his conduit stable in the second layer to discharge extra arcana, he was better off waiting for it to break down naturally."

Nym was silent until he was sure Lathia was done. "I have . . . follow-up questions," he said. "What is a layer? What's the difference between a first and second circle? How are you supposed to siphon the arcana out of your body into your soul well?"

She just gave him a helpless shrug. "I'm just telling you what I heard the magister say. I don't know how to do the technique itself. Why would I?"

Lathia was protesting a little too hard for it to be honest, in Nym's opinion. Whatever she was keeping secret though wasn't his business. Nobody had forced her to help him, and he was learning a lot from their conversation. "But the circle thing? And the layers?"

"Right, those. That I can tell you a little bit about. The way magic works is there are what they call layers of reality, and the act of magic is bringing in some of the essence of one of those layers to ours. The further you get from the real world, the harder it is to bring in the magic, but the more powerful the spell. According to Magister Tormin, almost everybody who can use magic of any kind is only able to draw on the first layer, which lets them use first-circle magic.

"Some people who are super talented or lucky or whatever can pull from the second layer, like the magister and Amos. There's supposed to be a third layer past that, but you've got to be a real prodigy to reach that one. Third-circle mages are really rare, and their magic is so powerful that they're all rich and important."

"So . . . by that logic, I can't meditate away this arcana poisoning because it's from the second layer, and I can only reach the first."

"Oh, hrmm." Lathia frowned. "Yeah, I guess you're right. Sorry, I didn't think of that."

There went all Nym's hopes. It was going to be a long, unpleasant slog home. Every muscle in his body ached like he'd been beaten with a stick, and in some cases that was basically true. He just knew he'd have a bruise across his back from Amos's shoving telekinesis attack, and that foot plant on his shoulder had been pretty hard too.

"I guess I should start the trip home then. Probably going to need a lot of breaks to rest," Nym said. He stood up with a groan and used his own magic to fetch the sack of onions. It hurt, and the magic came sluggishly, but not as much as it would have to bend over and pick the onions up. Plus it was easier to keep them all in place until he managed to pinch the split seam closed.

Lathia watched him with a frown. "How did you do that?" she said. "You shouldn't be able to do any magic right now."

"Why wouldn't I be able to?" Nym asked.

"Because . . . the disruption?"

"Wait, that's supposed to completely stop me from using any magic? It just feels like things are sore."

Lathia stood up and dusted her pants off. She held out a hand for Nym to shake, but he had both of his full with his onions. "Sorry," he said, presenting an elbow to touch her fingers instead. He wiggled it up and down in an approximation of a handshake.

"You're a weird kid, but I like you. You keep doing things that you shouldn't be able to do. Swimming with sharks. Using magic while suffering from arcana poisoning. Plus I saw how many things you picked up at once."

"I suppose if the only alternative is Amos, I can see why you'd prefer a weirdo like me."

"Exactly! That one's my house right there, next to Magister Tormin's like I said. Come visit sometime. It's nice to have someone to talk to about all this magic stuff."

They parted ways there, with her going back across the field to the village and him starting the long slog back west to the coast. It took him twice as long as normal, which was still an hour faster than his first trip ever.

He got back and set the bag of onions down near the front door, then went to lay down. Ciana was nowhere to be found, to his surprise. Her chore was to check the snare lines while he went to town, and she should have beaten him back by a wide margin considering the extra time it took to walk home. Hopefully the delay was due to an abundance of wild game and they'd eat good for the next few days.

With nothing better to do than reflect on what he'd learned, Nym stared up at the ceiling from the pallet they'd made for him so Ciana could reclaim her bed. It was strange that Lathia wanted to hide her own abilities. She obviously had more than a passing interest in magic if she was listening in on all the lectures the magister was giving to the rich twat. Maybe she didn't want to admit that she was basically stealing classes from him. If she couldn't do magic, it was just stuff she overheard, but if it was useful information, someone would probably want her to pay for it.

Or maybe he was overthinking it. Maybe she really couldn't do magic herself but wished she could and was deeply fascinated by it. That would be awful for her to be so close to the topic without actually being able to participate. Nym hoped that wasn't the case, and that she could do magic but didn't want people to know.

The meditation technique she'd described sounded interesting, but learning about the layers of magic was more immediately relevant to him. He couldn't use the technique to clear out arcana poisoning even if he did know exactly how to do it. But reinforcing his conduit so that he could pierce through the first layer to reach the second was something he could practice.

That's what he did for the next half an hour, until the pain became too much and he needed a break. Trying to make a magical breakthrough while suffering from an enemy attack on his soul well wasn't the best idea he'd ever had. He was too stubborn to give up completely, and once the pain had subsided, he started working on it again.

Nym had to admit that he didn't really know what he was doing, and experimentation was both tedious and, for now, painful. After the third round of trying to figure out how to tap into the second layer, he was forced to concede defeat. It was something to practice later, and he was starting to get distracted by the fact that Ciana still hadn't returned yet.

The sun was sinking into the ocean and he'd started preparing vegetables for the stew pot when she finally stalked through the door, empty-handed. "Checking the lines didn't go well?" he asked.

She stomped over to the log they shared when they were eating and snarled, "That damn Senman. I just found out that that son of a bitch has been stealing from my snares. Every time he came by to give me some extra food he caught, it was something he took off my traps!"

Nym peered at her. It was hard to tell in the fading light and with flickering shadows from the fire dancing across her face, but he was pretty sure. "Is that a black eye?" he asked.

Ciana turned her head away. "I may have had some strong words with him when I caught him looting one of my snares. Things . . . may have escalated."

"I guess you didn't win?"

"What makes you say that? You should see what he looks like now!"

"Well," Nym said slowly, dragging the word out. "I guess I just thought that if you'd caught him in the act and had a fight with him about it, you would have come back with some food if you'd won."

Ciana scowled at him. "You're too damn smart for your own good."

"What are you going to do?"

"Talk to the captain of the guard. Can't prove anything, but hopefully it'll at least get some eyes on him, and they might catch him up to no good. But enough about me!" Ciana turned to glare at him. "I heard all about your escapades today. Tell me, what in God's name possessed you to pick a fight with the son of the richest man in town?"

"Oh, uh, you know about that, huh?"

She snorted. "Yeah, brawling in front of Apari's store. She's such a gossip. Everyone knows about it. By the way, everyone also knows you can do magic now. But don't try to sidetrack me! What were you thinking?"

Nym wanted to protest that he wasn't the one who was dragging the conversation around, but he was smart enough to read her mood and knew better than to argue. He was already in trouble as it was.

"It wasn't my fault. I bumped into him on accident, and he was unreasonable about it."

"Of course he was. He's rich! Rich people don't have to be reasonable about anything they don't want to. Worse still, Magister Tormin's been polishing his ego for going on two years now when they found out he could do magic. They think he's good enough to head up to the Academy in Abilanth for serious training."

"Well it's not like I knew that! I didn't even know who he was. I was just trying to keep the onions from falling out of that hole in the bag when I was leaving the store and there he was."

Ciana sighed. "Tell me everything that happened. I want it straight from your mouth, and then we can work on damage control. Trust me, a little shit-head like him being humiliated by you, this isn't over. You'll be seeing him again."

That was just great. Nym had his very own rich bully who could probably get away with anything. He was hurting and hungry and it'd be nothing but vegetables in the stew. Tonight couldn't get much worse. Almost on cue, the fire popped, and some cinders fell on his foot. Nym yelped in pain and scooted back.

There it was. It was worse. Perfect.

CHAPTER 6

Nym worked on it for the next week but failed to make a breakthrough into the second layer. It wasn't really a surprise, but it was frustrating. What he did figure out though was that he could use magic to do more than lift things with his mind. It started with him trying to expand the garden and realizing they didn't really have good tools for it. Ciana had borrowed them from a friend of her father's years ago and had been making do with what she could do by hand.

That got him wondering if he could use his magic to form a tool. When that worked, it progressed to wondering if he could also wield the tool via telekinesis, which was difficult but possible. The better he got at it, the bigger he went. By the end of the week, he was mentally dual wielding a hoe and a spade at the same time as he expanded the garden. Ciana picked up the seeds from Apari's general store after telling him that she couldn't trust him to go into town on his own without picking a fight anymore.

Nym rolled his eyes and gave her a light mental shove, then went back to work. Once she'd returned with the goods, they'd started working on planting. It was a bit late in the season to expand, but it never really got too cold this far south, and if the vegetables grew a bit stunted, it was still better than growing nothing at all.

She also taught him how to make the crab traps that she had placed all over Bloodfin Cove. They'd gathered the materials and made dozens of them to replace some of the older ones and set new ones and were moving around the cove placing them when Ciana said, "Your shark is back."

"Why does he have to be my shark?" Nym groused, watching the scar-marked shark circle around the boat.

"Never behaved like that before I met you. I don't see him when it's just me out here. Maybe you were right about him having a crush on you."

Nym rolled his eyes and used his magic to help push them through the water while Ciana rowed. It tired his legs and arms out like he was actually swimming behind the boat and pushing it, except he was significantly less likely to get eaten. They got to the next drop spot and sank the crab trap, leaving just two more to go before they were finished.

"I don't know how I'm going to check all of these without you," Ciana said.

"Why? Am I going somewhere?"

"Look, Nym, I'm not kicking you out or anything, but, like . . . don't you want to get your memories back? Maybe if you saw some other places, some stuff would come back to you."

"You think so?" Nym asked, distracted as he forced the boat to turn toward their next destination. They'd already seeded the buoys to tie the trap lines to and, using his magic, even recovered a few traps whose lines had been snipped by curious sharks. As they approached, Ciana fished the buoy out of the water.

"I don't know. I ran out of ideas for you after that jackass magister called you a liar and kicked us out. You're welcome to stay here. I kind of like having a little brother, but don't feel like you have to. Big Sis will survive if you want to go on a trip in a few years when you're older."

"Big Sis, huh? I guess you are though."

"Yeah, yeah. Don't get all sappy on me. Here, hand me that next trap box."

Nym leaned down to grab it for her, and she started weaving the rope through it before she dropped it into the water. It was almost out of sight when a shark cruised in and took the whole thing in one bite.

"Damn it, I hate when they do that. Wait, is that your shark? Tell him to behave, Nym!"

"He's not my shark. I don't have any control over him." Nym glared down at the retreating form in the water. "You think maybe he can smell magic or something? Maybe I'm the tastiest thing he's ever smelled."

"He eats another one of my traps and we'll be having shark-fin soup tonight," Ciana threatened.

"I've never had that," Nym said.

"That's because these sharks are terrible eating. It's not even close to worth the effort; plus it's dangerous to harpoon them. Best case you'll probably lose the harpoon, worst case they'll capsize the boat if you've tied a line to it."

Nym shuddered. The odds were not good in getting back out of the water alive if he had to swim to shore. Even with his magic helping him, he didn't like his chances. It wasn't like there was always a shark in sight, but they regularly came close enough to the surface to see a silhouette or a fin cutting through the water.

"Why are there so many sharks here, anyway?" he asked. "Shouldn't they be spread out more so they get enough to eat?"

"It's because of the currents in the open water. The sharks go out to hunt in the shoals, but it's nice and calm here. So they come back in to rest between hunts. They're all the way up and down the coast here. The bigger trade ships can ignore them, but the fishermen in the smaller boats are taking their lives in their hands every time they go out on open water. That's why I stick to the cove, where the water's calm."

"Makes sense. Still annoying though. Especially you, my finny little stalker!" Nym shook a fist at the scarred shark still circling their boat.

The shark swerved in and bumped the boat with its snout, rocking it and throwing Nym against one side. "Hey, watch it!" he yelled at the shark.

"Nym! Sit down and brace yourself!" Ciana snapped out. A second thump rocked the boat. If not for her warning, he might very well have been thrown out. The shark circled around and came up directly from below, lifting the boat and setting it to spinning in place.

"What's wrong with this thing?" Nym said, eyes wide.

"I guess you got its attention," she told him grimly. She set the oars and stopped their spin, then started rowing back toward the beach. "We'll do this last trap some other time. It's not worth it to—ahh!"

One of the oars was ripped out of her hand as the shark caught it in his mouth. "You've got to be kidding me," Ciana said, dumbfounded. She immediately pulled the other oar out of the lock and started alternating sides as she paddled.

Nym fell into his magic and cast the boat-speeding spell again. Sweat started to pop out across his skin, and they picked up speed, but not nearly fast enough to outpace the persistent shark. It snapped at the remaining oar several times, but Ciana jerked it out of the water whenever the fin approached.

That worked until a second shark joined in. The two of them circled the boat relentlessly, each lap they took bumping up against its hull. Despite Nym's efforts, the boat slowed to a stop and started spinning in place. "Are they doing this on purpose?" he asked, a hint of panic in his voice.

"They're sharks! How could they be coordinating this?" Her eyes darted back and forth, tracking their circuits. A third shark joined, then a fourth. "What is going on here?" she whispered.

It was impossible to get the oar back in the water without one of the sharks taking it, and they were bumping up against the boat enough that if Nym or Ciana stood up, there was a decent chance they'd be thrown in the water.

"I got this," Nym said, his voice clearly strained. Slowly, the boat started moving toward the shore again. Each time a shark bumped up against it and diverted the course, he worked to correct it. Inch by inch, they crawled closer to shallow water and safety.

That was the plan, at least. Nym felt his stamina giving out on him halfway, and Ciana didn't have any real way to help. The boat slowed down and drifted to a stop again. "Sorry," Nym panted. "Can't . . . keep . . . going."

"Nym, if we get out of this, you are never allowed on a boat with me again."

"Ha . . . funny."

Just because the boat stopped didn't mean the sharks were done. If anything, there were more of them. It was harder to keep track with them occasionally dipping under the boat and pushing on it, but Nym figured they were up to six or seven now.

A loud crunch caught his attention, followed by a blistering string of curses from Ciana. She'd tried to use the oar again, and a shark had quickly taken it from her. "Okay, Nym, this one is all on you. Take your time here. Breathe in. Get your strength back. Let me know when you're ready. I'm going to use the harpoon to try to keep them away from the prow so we can keep a straight heading."

"Thanks . . . for the . . . pep talk," Nym gasped out.

Another bump nearly tipped them into the water. "No pressure here, but how long do you need before we can start moving again?"

"Working on it," Nym said.

He took a series of deep breaths and forged a conduit to the first layer again. His vision doubled, then blurred, and he found himself on his knees in the bottom of the boat, trying not to heave his guts out. With great effort, he started forcing arcana into his soul well and shaped it into a set of paddles. They were invisible to Ciana, but he could see them as two misty shapes.

Since she no longer had oars, it was easier for him to give his legs a rest and use his arms. In fact, once he thought of it, he wondered if Ciana would be able to use the oars he'd shaped. "Give me your hands," he said.

"What?"

"Just do it!"

He took her hands and placed them on the oars. "Can you feel them? I made oars with magic."

"I don't feel anything," she told him.

"Your hands are wrapped around them. Do a rowing motion, see if it helps."

"How about that?" she whispered to herself as she pulled on the invisible oars. "It does feel like I'm rowing."

The boat shot forward a few more feet. "Again," Nym said. "Just keep going. I'll try to hold them in place as long as I can."

It was maybe less effort than it would have been to row himself, but there was still a strain on both his mind and his muscles. Ciana made the rowing motions as fast as she could, unaware that each motion cost Nym a little bit. It wasn't just time that was a factor, but usage.

Still, it looked like they were going to make it. They lost one of the oars when a shark bumped into the paddle and the whole construct fell apart, but Nym spun a new one out of the ether, and they kept going. Nym was barely still upright, weakly clinging to his seat as sweat rolled down skin that had turned bright red. It was taking everything he had not to hurl and hold the magic in place.

Suddenly the boat was sideways, and he slid off his seat into the water. It crashed back into place still upright next to him, and he heard Ciana's panicked screaming. She reached out to grab hold of his arm as he fought weakly to stay above water, but it was too late. He slipped under the surface and saw his stalker shark coming straight at him, mouth open wide.

CHAPTER 7

Nym could barely see grim death coming his way through the murky water, but he knew what being out of the boat meant. The other sharks were still circling, but his shark, the one with the scar near the fin, was coming straight at him. He appeared in the dark water, barely feet from Nym, jaws open as his powerful tail propelled him forward.

Then his arm was in the shark's mouth and teeth punctured his skin around his biceps. Skin broke, blood wafted into the water, and pain blocked out any rational thoughts Nym might have had left. Time slowed down to a stop as the teeth bit down. And in that frozen fragment, everything was washed away, and he found himself somewhere else.

A woman floated in front of him, supported on cushions of air. She smiled down at him and said, "One more time. You've almost got it. The conduit is strong enough to hold, you just need to stretch it farther. Just copy what I'm doing."

She was surrounded by a brilliant corona of colors, magic pouring into her soul well from at least four different layers. He could make out multiple conduits, each one connected to a different layer, but that was still too advanced for him. While she wouldn't or couldn't drop her connections to the higher layers, she'd forged the conduit to the second layer specifically for him.

"Can you make it again?" he asked.

"Of course."

And she did, slowly so that he could follow along. Laboriously, he forged the conduit one strand of willpower at a time. Instead of a needle like he'd used to reach the first layer, he wove his will together into something stronger and sliced through the metaphysical layer they called Phase Shift to connect to the second layer, what they called the Edge of the Horizon. He barely had the strength to breach Phase Shift, but he did have it. What he lacked was the technique to mold his willpower and force the magic to obey him.

The mental construct fully realized, he forged the conduit and quested out of reality with it. The first layer was as easy to find as it had always been, and he drove his will into it like a splinter under its skin. The farther he pushed, the harder it got, but he refused to let the arcana of the first layer into the conduit. It could reach farther, he knew. It would reach farther.

There was something at the edge of his awareness. That was his goal, to stretch his conduit to touch it and to punch through. Seconds passed, and he was just about to admit defeat again when he broke through. It was by a fingernail's width, but it was enough. The conduit was at the Edge of the Horizon, and he opened it greedily, letting the wash of second-layer arcana flood his soul well.

"I did it!"

"Good, now let me show you how to use the magic . . ."

They worked for hours as he learned how to weave it in different patterns, internal and external, to a variety of basic elemental effects. He was sitting on top of his own cushion of air, legs crossed and a globe of water orbiting his body, when a door opened to reveal a tall, thin man dressed in opulent robes with long hair tied back behind his head in an intricate pattern.

"How is he doing?"

"See for yourself," the woman said, indicating the boy with the wave of a hand. "He's working on multicasting from a single conduit right now."

"How long did it take him to learn to reforge his conduit?"

"Two hours."

The man's eyes glittered as he regarded the boy. "Excellent. I'll have Omarin come in tomorrow to start working on combat casting. He'll need to learn to defend himself while working his magic."

"So soon?" the woman protested. "He's only three."

"So what? Do you think his enemies are going to care? As soon as it becomes known how quickly he's advancing, he will be a target. It's better for him to learn to defend himself now."

The boy's concentration faltered as he listened to them, and he sprawled out of the floor. Tears came to his eyes as he picked himself back up, but rather than comfort him, the man said, "There, see? This is exactly what I mean. Just paying attention to a conversation is too much for him. What is he going to do when someone hits him with an arcana injection?"

The man squatted down in front of the child and looked him in his tear-rimmed eyes. "Understand this, son. All the world is against you, and the only thing you can truly rely on is your own strength. You will grow strong, stronger than anyone else, or you will break one day when it turns out you are too weak."

The woman gave the man a frosty look but didn't contradict him. "If that is all, you may go," she told him.

The man stood up and told her, "Omarin will be here at dawn to commence his combat training." Then he disappeared, leaving the boy alone with a scraped knee and a woman who made no effort to comfort him.

Time resumed, and Nym wove his conduit with a speed he hadn't known he possessed. It pierced the second layer easily, struck something outside his awareness, and started to unravel, but nonetheless flooded his battered soul well with arcana. The water around his arm hardened, forcing the shark's jaw open and letting him slip his arm back out.

The puncture marks were barely skin-deep, not enough to cripple the muscle. Nym forced the water around him straight up and burst into open air. His flight wasn't supported though, and as the water settled back down, he started falling. He landed half in the boat with his legs in the water, and Ciana grabbed hold of his shirt to haul him the rest of the way to safety.

"What was that?" she demanded.

"Second layer," Nym said, coughing and trying to stop his head from spinning. "Hydrokinesis. Much more efficient than . . ."

He trailed off and looked toward the center of the cove. There was . . . something . . . there. He couldn't see it, but he knew it was there. It was down at the bottom buried in the sand and silt. Now that he thought about it, they'd been getting close to that when his stalker shark had gotten aggressive.

It could be a coincidence. That shark was weird anyway. It followed him all over the cove, but usually it just circled around, making its presence known without doing much to interfere. It could be that they'd just spent too long on the water or it was just hungry enough to try something today.

"Focus," Ciana said, shaking him by his shoulders. "We're still on the water with no way to move. Can you get us back to the shore?"

Nym forged a new conduit using the weaving technique he'd remembered, but he was still weak from his explosive burst of arcana, and the best he could manage was a first-circle spell to push them to the shore. Ciana took up the harpoon and menaced any sharks that got too close to the prow, and they slowly made it into the shallows.

She dug the harpoon into the sand and used it to drag the boat forward until the water was barely a foot deep. Then she hopped out and dragged it up onto the sand. "Out," she ordered. "This thing is heavy enough already."

Nym dragged himself onto the beach and promptly collapsed face down. "My everything hurts," he said. "Think I gave myself arcana poisoning again."

"I'll take care of getting the boat above the tide line. Think you can make it home without help?"

"Just going to lie here for a bit," he said. "Too tired to walk now."

And that was what he did, for the next six hours. He only moved once, when water started lapping at his feet, and then only to crawl a few feet higher up the beach. Ciana came down to check on him a few times, but he just waved her off and told her he was fine.

He lay there and thought about what he'd remembered, his first returned memory. He had no idea what it meant, but he was pretty sure he'd seen his parents. The faces were unfamiliar to him, and the conversation seemed extreme. He had to wonder if they were really his memories. It was too outlandish to be real.

There was no denying the technique worked though. He'd been trying to reach the second layer with no results, and it honestly felt like cheating to just get handed the solution like that. He hadn't earned it that way. On the other hand, not losing his arm to a shark was pretty nice too. He liked having two arms. In light of that, he was willing to take the dirty victory.

Nym wondered what other skills he could uncover hidden in his lost memories, but not at the expense of literally swimming with sharks to gain them. Once he was recovered, he had plenty to parse anyway. Reaching the second layer was just the first step. The arcana was richer, rife with impossibilities that were truly magical. The woman, his maybe mother, had been floating in the air. He could do it too.

Nym looked at the bluffs and the narrow trail leading up them. His first goal was to float himself to the top. Second goal, he amended. His first goal was to stand up without anything hurting or getting dizzy. Once he'd recovered enough to have coherent thoughts and give himself a mental once-over, he considered the meditation techniques Lathia had told him about.

It wasn't exactly the same situation, but now that he had reached the second layer, maybe he could find something useful there. He rolled onto his back and closed his eyes, trying to feel the arcana that had leaked out of his soul well into his muscles and bones. To his surprise, he found it was easy to locate. The problem was that there wasn't actually all that much there.

It seemed that his aches and pains were plain old muscle fatigue. The first-circle magic he'd been using was hard on his body in the same way physically performing the actions would have been. He'd put himself through the wringer and was extremely sore, and there just wasn't a lot that he could rush fixing. Time was all he really needed.

He did work on extracting some of that excess arcana, but it turned out finding it and moving it were two very different skill sets. The arcana was dissolving on its own faster than he could remove it, a process that still took hours. Eventually though, as the sun was setting on him and Ciana had just come down to check on him for the fifth time, he felt well enough to make an attempt.

Staggering to his feet, Nym crossed the sand and stepped onto the scrub grass that bordered the base of the bluffs. With one hand on the stone wall, he forged a new conduit and sent it out to the second layer. It took about thirty seconds to fill his soul well, a mildly uncomfortable act still, like poking already-bruised flesh, and then he set about weaving the arcana into thick cushion of air.

Pressure pushed against his legs and hugged his chest. It lifted upward, and his feet rose off the ground by a few inches. Nym's confidence grew with each second, and he flew higher. The bluffs were maybe thirty feet tall, and even though he wasn't really ascending any faster than if he'd just walked, he was still flying.

With a broad grin, he manipulated the cushion to push him forward once he crested the ridge. Both feet touched down on the prickly grass, and he let out a deep sigh of contentment. "Honestly," he said aloud, "it was kind of worth the shark. The arm barely even hurts anymore."

CHAPTER 8

With the loss of the oars and Ciana's general refusal to let Nym go out by himself, they no longer had the ability to check the crab traps. Unfortunately, that combined with Senman's interference with the snare lines, left them with nothing but vegetables to eat and not much to trade or sell in Palmara.

The two of them stood next to a line that had been very obviously cut with a knife. "This is too far," Ciana muttered. "Senman's messed with my traps for the last time."

"What do you want to do?" Nym asked.

"Go talk to the guard captain again. I've got evidence of tampering this time. If he won't listen . . ." She trailed off as she reached down to pick up the remains of the trap.

"If he won't listen, what?" Nym prompted.

"Senman's not the only one with a knife," she muttered darkly. "I've had enough of him messing with me."

"That seems like a bad idea," Nym said.

"Trying to starve me because I won't let him between my legs is a bad idea. He's about to find that out. You head back home. I'm going to Palmara."

Nym gave her a look of surprise. "You don't want me to come with you?"

Ciana shook her head. "This is going to be messy. You're still a kid. I'll handle it."

"Okay. I will . . . uh . . . weed the garden?"

She gave him a playful shove. "Why don't you work on that fancy magic? Maybe you can get another memory back. It sounds like you were part of a rich, important family. Someone is going to come looking for you eventually, and the more you remember, the better prepared you're going to be."

That was true. He'd explained what he'd remembered the night before, and together they'd gone over every detail he could recall. They had a lot of theories but nothing concrete, though the fact that the techniques he'd remembered learning all seemed to work was strong evidence that it was a true memory. Ciana had started calling him Prodigy to tease him. It beat being called Shark Bait, which was her other nickname for him now.

Truth to be told though, if he used Amos as a measuring stick, it was kind of impressive. He'd apparently been significantly younger than the other boy, who was being groomed to attend a prestigious magical school by Magister Tormin, when he'd achieved his breakthrough into the second layer.

Even now, barely a month after washing ashore with no memory, he had reconstructed enough of what he'd learned to start catching up. Nym wasn't sure he'd win in a serious fight with Amos, but he suspected he'd give a better showing if it came down to it.

What he really wanted to do was talk to Lathia again. Now that he had a stronger foundation, he had all sorts of other questions. He wondered if she'd let him sit in on some of the lectures she eavesdropped on. Maybe he could trade her some of the things he'd remembered for access. That presumed she could actually do magic, which he hadn't confirmed and wasn't going to push her on. If she wanted to keep that to herself, he wouldn't try to pry the secret out of her.

That was a plan for another day though. For now, he finished checking the rest of the snare lines with Ciana, where they found another three lines cut and nothing caught in any of them. Then they parted ways, with him going back home and her going to town by herself with the sabotaged traps. He occupied himself on the walk back by flying instead of walking.

It took a fair bit of concentration, but it was only half a mile, and he could actually fly faster than he could walk once he'd gotten a chance to practice at it. It wasn't much faster, not even twice as fast as walking, but the novelty of floating above the trail made for a nice change of pace. At least, it did until he accidentally smacked his head on a tree branch when he wasn't paying attention.

"Ow! Damn it!" he cursed, his concentration broken and his butt in the dirt. Now he had a headache and his tailbone hurt. Nym decided to just walk the rest of the way. Soon enough, he'd reached the two-room shack he shared with Ciana and found a nasty surprise.

Senman lounged in the main room, sprawled on the carved driftwood log they used for seating and idly carving out chunks of it with a hunting knife. He glanced up when Nym opened the door and snorted.

Nym froze, trying to process what he was seeing. "What are you doing here?" he asked, his face darkening in anger.

"None of your business. Where's Ciana?"

"Went to town to talk to someone about someone messing with the traps," Nym told him. "Sure hope you weren't involved. You could get in trouble."

Senman didn't play along though. He went still for a second, and his eyes got an evil gleam in them. "So if what I'm hearing is right, you're saying that she won't be back for an hour or two. It's just you and me."

That didn't sound good. All of a sudden that knife in Senman's hands seemed a lot more sinister, and Nym recalled how the older man had argued to get rid of Nym when he was still sick and recovering. It was very clear to him that Senman was possessive of Ciana in a way she wouldn't tolerate and refused to accept any decisions she made that didn't line up with what he wanted her to do.

In a flash, Senman was on his feet and lunging across the room to grab Nym. Nym danced back out of the doorframe and spun around to run, but he didn't make it three steps before Senman grabbed hold of him. "Guess I didn't waste my time coming out here after all," he said.

"Let go of me!" Nym fought, but he was no match for the older man's strength. Senman got an arm around his chest and lifted him off the ground, then carried him the hundred feet or so to the bluffs overlooking the cove.

Nym kicked at him, but the angle was all wrong. He felt his heels connect against Senman's legs, just not in a way that did anything. One kick that landed a bit higher up caused the man to curse and punch Nym in the head, at which point the boy fell limp and stopped struggling.

"Sure is a shame that the sharks got you after all. But honestly, who could expect to get lucky twice swimming in that cove? No one will ever know for sure where you went. Don't worry though, I'll console Ciana and convince her it was for the best that you moved on. You got what you wanted, you little vagrant, and hit the road to find your next mark."

Nym didn't bother answering. He wasn't going to outrun or outmuscle the man, so he needed to rely on the one advantage he had over Senman: magic. The problem was that he was finding it difficult to concentrate, and he didn't have much time to pull everything together.

If Senman had been content to chuck him off the bluffs right in front of the shack, Nym never would have made it. The hunter-turned-murderer had a different plan in mind though. The closest spots all had beach below them, but farther down they led directly to the water, and it looked like Senman wasn't planning on taking any chances on Nym surviving the drop.

This meant he had to go almost three times farther though, and that was where he made his mistake. Nym doubted he would have been able to pull together any magic while he was lying in the sand with a few broken limbs or a concussion. Senman could have easily tossed him over the edge, then taken the trail down and finished dragging him into the water.

Instead, he gave Nym the time he needed, and the boy was determined not to waste it. He controlled his breathing and reached out into the layers of adjacent reality. The first one couldn't give him the strength he needed, but the second layer was far enough removed to allow for the impossible. Conduit forged, he began drawing in arcana and forming it with his will.

They were ten steps from the edge. Eight. Five. Two. Nym struck. Magic roared through him, and the ground under Senman's foot erupted. They were both flung into the air, and Nym used the opportunity to shove away from the older man. Senman was so surprised that he let Nym go without a fight, and then they were tumbling end over and end toward the cold water below.

He landed on a cushion of air and skidded sideways across it, almost sliding off completely. Desperate, Nym curved the edge up to catch him and slide him back into the middle. Below him, Senman let out a hoarse, panic-ridden cry as he splashed into the water. He immediately resurfaced and clawed at the slick stone walls of the bluffs, trying to gain purchase and haul himself back up to safety.

Nym stared down at him, no mercy in his eyes. There below him was a man who had casually planned to murder a child in a bid to manipulate a young woman into a vulnerable state so he could take control of her. If Nym hadn't been able to defend himself, it would have been him flailing desperately at the rocks below, trying to haul himself to safety while being tugged around by the currents running up against the bluffs.

It was within Nym's power to save him still. There was even a chance the man would make it on his own. Nym didn't think he'd make the climb, but he might make it to the beach. It was only a few hundred feet of water. If Senman was lucky and a strong swimmer, he could make it.

It was also within Nym's power to finish the job, to make a barrier of solid air to force Senman's head underwater, or make the water itself drag him down. He considered his next course of action, his gaze cold and calculating.

Senman was a problem, plain and simple. Ciana probably didn't want to kill him though, however mad she was at the moment. Nym doubted she'd lose much sleep though if he just . . . disappeared. He doubted there would be any repercussions at all, unless someone knew Senman was here. If questioned, it would be easy enough to say he'd never seen the man.

Decision made, he cast a spell to form a tendril out of the water and snake it around Senman's leg. "What was it you said?" Nym called down to him. "No one will ever know for sure where you went."

He willed the tendril to pull down, and Senman had just enough time to take one last desperate lungful of air before he was pulled under. The tendril dragged him away from the bluffs and out toward the middle of the cove, where Nym held it in place for a few minutes, long after Senman stopped fighting.

Nym floated gently back to solid ground. Except for the ruptured patch of dirt, there was no trace that anything had happened. The blown-out rocks rolled back toward the hole he'd made and piled in, then covered themselves with a blanket of dirt that inched along like some sort of fat slug. It wasn't perfect with the grass patches missing, but he doubted anyone would notice.

Nym walked slowly back to the shack and sat down. His father had been right after all.

Understand this, son. All the world is against you, and the only thing you can truly rely on is your own strength. You will grow strong, stronger than anyone else, or you will break one day when it turns out you are too weak.

CHAPTER 9

W hat happened here?" Ciana asked as she examined the driftwood log. Nym shrugged. "It was like that when I got here."

"It looks like someone started carving it up with a knife."

"Sure does."

"You don't own a knife though."

"Nope."

"So who did this?"

"That is a good question."

Ciana squinted at Nym. He looked back at her, expression blank. "You know something," she said. "And you're acting weird."

"How was your trip into town?" he asked, changing the subject.

"Worthless waste of time," she growled. "Watch captain's still telling me I've got no proof of who it is, could be anyone. I'll have to deal with Senman myself next time I see him." She paused thoughtfully and looked at the log. "Senman, huh. Okay, spill. What happened here?"

"How should I know?" Nym protested, but there was no real resistance in his tone. Ciana wasn't stupid, and there wasn't much he could do to hide the evidence that someone had been there. Of course she'd figure it was Senman. He was the only one who ever visited. "I told you it was like that when I got here."

That was technically true. The log had already been hacked at with a knife prior to him getting back. She didn't need to know that Senman had still been there when he'd arrived, or anything else. No good would come from that.

"Sure, but you know more than you're telling me," she pressed.

"I figure it was Senman who did it. He's been screwing with you for weeks. Probably got bored of waiting for you to come back."

Ciana studied him some more. "Fine," she said finally. "You're still hiding something though. Everything okay?"

"I'm fine," Nym said. "Hit my head on a tree branch practicing flying earlier. I have survived worse."

And that was the end of the matter, at least for that day. Dinner was a collection of foraged nuts and berries and a pair of potatoes from the garden. It was sparse, but it was what they had. As they ate, Ciana sighed and said, "We should get a loaf of bread. It's been forever since I had that."

Nym didn't have anything to say to that. He was feeling particularly out of touch with reality and wondered what precisely the cause of it was. He'd channeled more arcana than ever before in such a short time, even more than their escape from the sharks. Ciana had been right: he wasn't exactly acting normal, and he was starting to wonder if drawing so much arcana at once was the cause of it.

Or maybe it was the man who'd tried to kill him, or the subsequent killing of that man. Or maybe it was the memory he'd recovered. All of those were viable options. He wasn't particularly bothered by how numb he was to everything though. It was just a thing he noted, examined, and put behind him.

He thawed out over the next few days and returned to the boy he'd been for the first month after he'd washed up on the beach. It was a strange feeling, like he'd been a passive observer in the events that had happened with Senman. He remembered them. He was there for them. But it was like some other person was moving his body. He wasn't sure he liked that. It wasn't so much that he felt regret for defending himself from Senman's murderous intentions, but he'd taken steps to ensure the man drowned in a place where his remains would never be discovered. And he hadn't told Ciana the truth.

About a week after the encounter with Senman, they received a visitor. He was an older man in his fifties with salt-and-pepper hair and a lean build. They saw him approach while they were working in the garden, where he stopped at the edge and said, "Hey there, Ciana. Do you have a few minutes?"

"Who's that?" Nym asked.

"Guard Captain Mordat. The one I've been talking to about Senman screwing with my snare lines." She straightened up and cracked her neck. "Can you finish this up while I go see what he wants?"

"Sure," he agreed. The pair went into the shack, which was right next to where he was working anyway, so it was easy to overhear the whole conversation.

"What do you need?" Ciana asked.

"It's about Senman," the captain said. "When was the last time you saw him?"

"Hmm . . . A few weeks ago when I got into that fight with him after I caught him stealing out of one of my traps. Before that it was when he showed up to fight with me about keeping Nym here. I never did find out who told him about that. Somebody was running their mouth though because he was right out immediately."

"And you've had no other interactions with him since then?"

"No. Why?"

Mordat ignored the question. "What about what you told me before? You said you caught him cutting the lines on some of your other traps."

"No, but I know it was him. Believe me, if I had caught him, I'd have torn into him. I've been looking for him to give him a piece of my mind for a week now."

"That's the thing, Ciana. We don't know where he is. He's been missing for a few days now, and according to his friends, he was planning on coming out to visit you. Nobody's seen him since he left."

The shack was silent.

"Ciana?" Mordat prompted.

"I haven't seen him. If I do, you'll know because I'm going to give him a black eye. Maybe two black eyes."

"That's your official stance? You know this makes you look bad, right?"

"I've been to your office twice about him harassing me. It's not like it's a secret that I'm not friendly with him. He's always showing up sniffing around me, trying to tell me how to live and what I can and can't do. I don't know where he went when he was done causing trouble with his friends, but I haven't seen him."

"Alright then. Thanks for your help."

"You see him, you let him know I'm still pissed about him messing with my traps."

"I'll do that. Have a good day."

The door opened, and Nym squatted down and started working on pulling weeds. The watch captain spared him a glance before he turned to the path and started walking back to Palmara. Ciana appeared in the doorframe and watched him go.

"Nym," she said without moving her head, still watching.

"Yeah?"

"Come inside for a minute, will you?"

"Sure thing."

He followed her in and stood in front of their driftwood log bench. With one hand, she gestured toward all the notches and nicks in it. "Tell me the truth, now."

The game was up. One part of Nym was panicking. Another part of him descended into that calm, emotionless state he'd found. That part won. "I went home when you went to Palmara. Senman was sitting right in front of where you're standing, whittling away at the wood with his knife. He was waiting for you, but when I told him you'd gone to town, he decided he'd stumbled onto an opportunity.

"He grabbed me and carried me out to the bluffs. He was going to throw me straight into the water to get rid of me. We both went over the edge, but I could make myself fly and Senman couldn't. Last I saw him, he was underwater in the cove."

Ciana didn't say anything for a while. Finally, she asked, "He's dead then?"

"Yes."

"Why didn't you tell me?"

"Would it have made a difference? By the time you got home, it was already over."

"You should have told me. I asked you what happened. You lied to me, Nym!"

He nodded. "I suppose I did. I don't regret it. Nothing good would come from dragging you into what happened."

"I don't know. It would be nice to know that I was involved in his disappearance. You ever think of that? Did you think I'd be mad at you? He tried to kill you, and you fought back."

Nym thought about that for a second. "I didn't know if you'd believe me. And like I said, it was too late to change what happened. It was easier to just not talk about it."

He stared straight ahead, not really seeing anything as he confessed to covering up murder. He'd have to leave now. She could tell them what he'd done when they came around to question her again. If he left immediately, he could get a decent lead. The ground here was relatively flat, but he was sure he could find somewhere where being able to fly would give him a terrain advantage.

When Ciana put her arms around him and pulled him into a hug, it shocked him out of that numb state. "What . . . what are you doing?" he asked, his voice cracking.

"Nym, you should have told me. I know better than anyone what kind of person Senman was. I'm surprised he would go that far, but he's been going down that road for months now. He was obsessed with me in a scary way. It wasn't healthy. This was just the point of no return for him."

"I—"

"Hush." Ciana squeezed him tighter. "We still need to tell Mordat what happened to him."

"That's an awful idea."

"It's the right thing to do."

Nym sighed. "One last way for him to screw with you, huh?"

"We'll survive."

That was easy for her to say. She wasn't the one who'd killed him. An image of Senman's wild-eyed stare as he struggled to stay above water while Nym's magic ripped him off the rocks and drowned him came to mind. Ciana didn't really understand what had happened. That wasn't her fault. She wanted to believe the best of him, that Nym hadn't had a choice. That he'd defended himself the only way he could.

That wasn't the truth. Nym could have restrained Senman on the bluffs. He didn't have to throw him into the cove. He didn't have to take extra steps to ensure the man died. He'd done it because he'd decided not to leave an enemy alive. Senman had been willing to kill him. Nym had been willing to return the favor.

The numbness settled back into his thoughts.

If he confessed and they arrested Nym or tried to execute him, he couldn't see himself meekly complying. He wanted to live, even if that meant killing someone else to make it happen. He had his magic, but he wasn't nearly strong enough to think he was invincible. Something told him that he would be an utter fool to ever believe that no one could hurt him.

"Nym?"

"Hmm?" he came back to himself with a start, belatedly realizing that she'd been talking to him while he stared at nothing.

"Let's have lunch. We'll go into town after and talk to Mordat after."

"Okay," he said.

He wasn't doing that. Ciana had been good to him, better than anyone had a right to ask. But it was time to leave. He needed to work on his magic, and the resources in Palmara were practically nonexistent. The magister was a weak source at best, and Nym suspected he was already reaching the point of surpassing the old man. Never mind the fact that the magister wasn't a resource he personally could tap into.

"I'm going to go take a walk," he said.

He found himself standing at the bluffs, looking out over the cove. With a thought, he stepped into thin air and floated down to the sandy beach below. Somewhere in the water was whatever the sharks had left of Senman's remains. He doubted it was very much.

A familiar fin broke the water, cruising parallel to the shore. Nym could see the scar at the base. He shook his head. "What is your problem with me anyway?" he asked the shark. Of course, it didn't answer.

Farther out, past that, was that thing in the water. He could still sense it. It dug at his thoughts. He couldn't get to it though, or could he? His magic wrapped around him again, and he drifted through the air to the center of the cove. The shark followed him the whole way and circled around him, occasionally rolling on its side and staring at him with its dead black eyes.

Whatever was down there called to Nym. He tried to grab it with his magic, but he couldn't find anything to hold on to. Shaking his head, he flew back to the shore. It was invisible, intangible, but there was something there. He knew it.

One day, he'd come back to claim it.

CHAPTER 10

Nym returned from his walk and ate mechanically, not really tasting the food. He didn't really have a plan beyond not turning himself in to the guards. He was painfully aware of a lack of resources and that adults wouldn't take him seriously. Whatever he decided to do, it was going to be a rough road.

"I'm going to Palmara now," he said.

Ciana blew out a long sigh. "Right. Let's get this taken care of. I'm sorry, Nym. This isn't going to be a fun conversation."

"You don't have to come with me."

"No, I should. Senman tried to kill you because you were in the way of him getting at me. I'm so sorry that happened to you. I'll come with you."

"Really, it's fine," Nym said.

There was no arguing with her though, and soon enough the pair of them were on the road. They walked in silence, Ciana no doubt planning to talk to the guard captain, but Nym just thinking about what he was going to do next. He really didn't have any good ideas beyond continuing down the road. He could hold his flight for ten minutes easily and stretch it to half an hour if he didn't mind being completely wiped out. While flying, he could move at about a jogging speed without pushing himself.

His biggest problem was going to be getting a clean break away from Palmara. There was every chance that Mordat would just run him down, but he thought if he could get far enough east to reach the forest Ciana had told him about, he could hide there. That was the plan then, to fly straight to the forest at top speed. He'd have to gamble that he'd make it to cover before he ran out of stamina.

They stopped outside of Palmara. The road stretched out before them, leading into the poor part of town. Past that, around a bend, was where the richer citizens lived. Of course, the guardhouse was in the rich part of town. That's where they wanted the guards. Nym had never gotten a chance to really see that side of Palmara as Ciana had warned him away from it after his run-in with Amos.

It was a shame. He wasn't planning on actually entering the town. When he stopped at the outskirts, Ciana stopped and looked back at him. "You don't need to be nervous. I'm going to be right there with you."

"Ciana," Nym began. "I . . . Thank you. You saved me, even though everyone told you to kick me back out. You gave me food and a place to sleep."

"It was the right thing to do," she said. "I don't know if I ever told you, but I'm adopted. My parents were killed at sea when I was a bit younger than you are now. It's hard living here, and in some ways it's harder to be a girl. The man who became my father took me into his home and kept me from starving to death or worse."

"Why did he do it though?" Nym asked. "Everyone is struggling here. Well, not everyone. Was he rich?"

Ciana laughed softly. "No, he was a fisherman, just like my parents. It took a lot of years for me to really understand the sacrifices he made. I was a lot older than you before I realized how much it cost him, and when I asked him why he'd done it, he said the same thing I told you. He did it because it was right."

She led him off the road and sat down in a dusty patch of grass. "I know you're scared. But you do know I'm not going to abandon you, right?"

"I know that. Big Sis is looking out for me. But what does it cost you?"

"You're too young to worry about that kind of stuff. We'll survive, you and me."

Nym let out a deep sigh and looked over at the town. "You say that, but . . . I killed someone. They're not just going to shrug and let me go because he had it coming."

"I'm not going to let them hurt you, Nym."

He wanted to believe it, that they could just let the guard captain know so they didn't waste time looking for Senman and everything would go back to normal. He wasn't that naive. Cold rationality dictated that if nothing else, Senman's friends would want some sort of payback. Ciana hadn't even been able to convince the guards to do anything about him messing with her snare lines.

They were barely surviving as it was. The garden was coming along, but they'd lost all the meat from the crab traps. Ciana would have an easier time on her own, especially without Senman interfering. The boat was still sound; she could get new oars for it. That shark would probably disappear if he wasn't with her.

He stood up and dusted off his pants. "I don't think this is a good idea. We shouldn't tell them."

"I'm not going to be a hypocrite," Ciana said. "I know it's scary, but I will keep you safe."

Nym shook his head. "How? How do you stop them when they say, 'We need to run this kid out of town,' or 'Lock him up,' or even 'Hang that boy'?"

"No one's going to hang you, Nym!"

"But they could! And you can't stop them if they decide that's what they want to do. We shouldn't even give them the chance."

Nym stopped himself from saying more. The conversation was going in circles. Ciana insisted everything would be fine but really had no way to prove that. Nym was afraid the worst would happen. It was time to go.

"I'm leaving," he said. "Thank you for saving me. I'll pay you back some day."

"What? Where will you go?"

Nym forged the conduit into the second layer and lifted himself into the air. "I don't know. Someday I'll come back, when I know that I'm strong enough to protect myself, and you too."

"Wait, Nym! Don't leave!"

But it was too late. He'd made up his mind, and he started flying east, skirting the edge of town and heading toward the forest. Hopefully he'd given himself enough of a lead that no one could catch him.

He flew when he could, walked when he had to, and didn't stop for a break until he'd reached the trees. No one followed him, as far as he could tell. He was free. Free . . . and alone.

Exarch Myzalik was not happy. He should have been celebrating his greatest and final victory over Niramyn, but they could not find the body. He'd spent a month, objectively, but more like three when he included all the time his copies had invested into the search. Over twenty ascendant hunters had been tasked with fetching the weakened exarch or finding his corpse.

All of them had failed. It was impossible. Even if the corpse had been devoured by wild animals, there would still have been an arcana imprint. Niramyn had pierced the twelfth layer! It was not possible for him to just vanish like he'd never existed at all. No, it was proof that the rival exarch was still alive. It had to be active obscurement, a veil so powerful that Myzalik himself couldn't see past it.

Myzalik didn't understand why Niramyn would do that, and it was making him unreasonably angry. He'd always had a volatile temper, but lately the servant golems had started collaborating to track his movements and ensure they stayed out of his way. It would have been amusing to teleport around just to screw with them if he wasn't in such a foul mood.

If Niramyn was alive, which he had to be since they couldn't find him, why hadn't he come back? If he still somehow had the power to reach into the Edge of Reality and beyond to the Hungering Chasms to wrest back the purest arcana anyone had ever found, if he was *still* an exarch, where was he?

His team of ascendant hunters had done everything they could think of to track him down. They'd performed powerful temporal scrying to try to track Niramyn's progress as he fled using a simple supersonic-flight spell, of all things. He hadn't even reached full speed. It didn't matter though because the scrying had been rebuffed by the enchantments woven into the exarch's robes. Even as tattered as they were, the magic held strong. They'd tried conventional scrying using projected destinations. There was nothing anywhere along that trail.

They'd divided the globe up into quadrants, and each ascendant had meticulously combed through for some trace of a powerful arcana imprint. They'd found plenty of humans that had reached the third layer. Surprisingly, there had been not one but five humans who had managed to break into the fifth layer.

But none of them were Niramyn in disguise! Myzalik had personally checked each of the supposed archmages to ensure it. They were barely more powerful than an ascendant child, if maybe more skilled in a wider array of subjects. If all five of them got together and attacked an ascendant who hadn't managed to get past the seventh layer, it would be an amusing battle.

He'd briefly considered recruiting humans to help search, but dismissed the idea. If a team of a dozen ascendant hunters couldn't find Niramyn with magic, no human had even the smallest chance of succeeding. Myzalik himself was an exarch, and he couldn't do it. Some might argue that it was hypocritical of him to punish his minions for failing to do what he couldn't achieve either.

Some might receive a lightning bolt to the face if they pointed it out.

He fumed as he paced back and forth in front of an acceleration pod. There was a copy in there, working under a temporal dilation to comb through the arcana imprints on the timeline from a month ago. It was tedious work, and it had already been a full day of waiting. Considering the massive dilation ratio in there, his copy had been at work for months already. He'd expected results after a few hours and wasn't happy about the delay, not to mention the cost.

Powering the acceleration pod for so long was stressful, magically speaking, and it would push up his next rejuvenation cycle by at least a decade. He avoided looking at the mirror and seeing the physical evidence of the advanced aging. Yes, he was immortal, but that didn't mean he wanted to look old. He couldn't afford to be stuck in stasis for days while he regained his youth right now, maybe not anytime in the next few years.

Despite the fact that they couldn't find Niramyn or his remains, they were proceeding as if it had been a complete victory. The facade had to be maintained, after all. He'd steadily taken over his rival's businesses and assets, converted his staff, personally ensured the loyalty of the high-ranking ascendants, and pillaged Niramyn's vaults.

With a hiss of released air, the pod opened, and his copy stepped out. He looked even worse than Myzalik himself, appearing frail and stooped, a man of at least eighty years. "Results?" Myzalik demanded from the copy.

He shook his head. "Nothing."

With a scream of rage, he raked the room with lightning. "How is he doing it? It's impossible. There is no way he's hidden himself this well!"

He absorbed the copy back into his consciousness so that he could review the full results of his own work later. Immediately he sagged, the excess years settling onto his shoulders. At the rate he was burning through his time, he'd be in stasis inside a week.

He needed to come at this from a different approach. If he couldn't find Niramyn through magic, perhaps revisiting the idea of recruiting humans to help had merit after all. A network of thousands of humans under compulsion scattered over the world would never know they were secret eyes and ears but would report back if they ever spotted Niramyn. It would be hundreds of hours of work for each ascendant assigned to the task to plant the compulsions, but that's what minions were for.

He scowled in distaste. It was a brute-force solution completely lacking any sort of elegance. Niramyn was probably laughing at him right now. With a deep scowl, he waved a hand and reset the room back to when he'd placed a temporal lock on it. The air blurred and furniture reformed, exactly as it had been when he'd set the lock a few weeks ago.

Myzalik took a moment to compose himself, then reached out to his commanders to issue their new orders. Niramyn hadn't beaten him, not yet. Not by a long shot.

CHAPTER 11

The forest was cold, and surprisingly wet. The only climate Nym knew was that of the coastal village, which wasn't even that far away. There had been a lot of sand and bare ground and few trees over there though, and apparently that made a difference.

It wasn't so bad during the day, but as night fell, the temperature plummeted, and he became keenly aware of the holes in his pants and the lack of sleeves on his shirt. His first instinct was to turn to magic to fix the problem, but he'd spent most of his time working on elemental air manipulation with a splash of water. Earth was barely a footnote, and he'd never done anything with fire.

Not keen on the idea of accidentally cooking himself from the inside out, he decided to forego any experimentation with magical heating for now. Instead, he found a semisheltered spot where a trio of trees had grown close together and were tangled overhead, scooped himself out a circle of pine needles and dirt to make a firepit, and started breaking branches to throw in it.

That was when he learned the difference between green wood fresh off the tree and deadwood that had been left out to dry for weeks. After trying and failing to ignite the green wood for an hour, he gave up and scavenged some fallen branches instead. Then, with a deep breath, he forged a new conduit to the second layer and tried to condense heat into a single point to spark the wood.

"Air was so much easier than this," he grumbled as he failed to ignite the wood again. He was doing something wrong, but he had no clue what it was.

The memory he'd recovered and shown him how to reach into the second layer, what his maybe mother had called the Edge of the Horizon, and funnel arcana into his soul well. Creating a basic elemental effect involved altering the arcana from pure potential reality into a physical state to form a connection with earth, air, or water. Creating fire was a bit different, and apparently that meant he didn't have a clue what he was doing.

Forget about cooking himself from the inside out: he was liable to freeze to death if he couldn't manage to even magic up a single spark. He probably wouldn't freeze tonight, but it was only going to get colder as summer turned to fall, and even now it was too cold to not have a fire.

It was amazing how a bare thirty or so miles of travel and a canopy of branches overhead had drastically reduced the temperature. The sea wasn't even that warm, so why was it so much warmer by the coast? Nym tried to channel some of that warm breeze to use as inspiration for his own fire, but just wanting it wasn't enough to make the magic work.

It was fully dark before he finally figured out the trick of it. He'd been trying to light the branches directly, and it wasn't until he started experimenting with other material that he got the concept of tinder. As soon as that clicked, he felt incredibly stupid. He'd watched Ciana start a dozen fires to cook, and he'd never really stopped to think about the process.

Things got a bit easier after that, though the green wood he'd piled into the hole never really caught. It blackened a bit and looked singed, but the next morning, it was still there, and he woke up shivering since the fire had gone out in the middle of the night.

"I am not very good at this," he said, looking at the blackened sticks in his makeshift firepit.

With a heavy sigh and a shake of his head, he dumped all the dirt he'd scooped out last night back into the hole, burying the ash and some of the smaller sticks. Then, because he had no idea where he was, he flew straight up over the treetops.

One advantage of flying was that it became a lot harder to get lost. If he flew up high enough, he could still see Palmara off in the distance. It wasn't much more than a collection of brown dots on the lighter-brown canvas that was the coast, but it was there. He could head straight to it if he wanted.

More importantly, he could see the road going northeast, skirting the forest and heading to the town of Zoskan. That was Nym's destination. A single night in the woods had convinced him he was meant for civilization, even if he didn't know how he was going to survive when he got there. He had magic; he'd think of something. Lathia had said that third-circle mages were rich. He was only one step away from that.

Zoskan was not in sight, unlike Palmara. Nym figured if he followed the road, he'd find it eventually, but he didn't want to risk running into anyone who would try to capture him there, so he decided to fly over the forest and walk through it when he had to rest.

"I hate the forest," he said to no one halfway through his third walking segment. He'd gotten tangled up in a bush he'd been trying to squeeze past. There were thorn scratches on his arms, and he was bleeding in three different spots from where they'd dug deeper. "You are lucky I can't just turn you to ash, you stupid bush. Because I would. Oh, yes, I would."

Day turned into night, and this time Nym was smart enough to gather dead wood. He broke some down into tinder and ignited it, then sat down and felt sorry for himself. He was hungry, and there had been very little in the way of foraging available to him. He'd found one berry bush that he'd gorged himself on and then promptly felt sick. Water at least was plentiful.

The next day wasn't any better, and it seemed like the deeper into the woods he got, the colder it got. Everything was older, wilder, scarier. The darkness was deeper, the trails more overgrown when they existed at all. He stopped seeing small game or birds halfway through the day. Everything was silent, unnervingly so.

Nym stopped walking completely. He flew over the treetops when he could and rested high up in the branches. His original plan of cutting straight through the woods no longer sounded like a good idea, and he resolved to turn north and find the road again. Even if it was just close enough to keep it in sight, he'd feel better.

Darkness caught up to him before he made it, and Nym was left with the difficult decision of descending into the woods to start a fire or shivering in the treetops, trying to sleep and hoping he didn't fall out and break his neck. It was incredibly tempting to stay up high, just because being at ground level was really starting to creep him out.

He tried to convince himself that he was just being paranoid. He'd been in the forest for two days, and the worst thing that had happened was he'd lost a fight with a bush. Still, he couldn't shake the fear, and found himself sitting on a branch with his back leaned up against the trunk as the last rays of the sun disappeared into the ocean.

Nym fell asleep, tired and shivering and uncomfortable. He missed that pallet Ciana had helped him make. He missed Ciana too. Everything would have been just fine if Senman would have left them alone.

Something was tugging at his arm. Nym groaned and tried to pull away, only to be brought up short. "Huh?" he said groggily, peering down at his sleeve to figure out what it was caught on.

Except it wasn't a sleeve. His shirt didn't have sleeves. There was something sticky on his arm, thick, gray cables of it that he was being tangled up in. He blinked a few times and followed the cable to its source.

It was anchored to a branch above him, and strong enough that when he pulled, the branch flexed and snapped before the cable broke away. "What is this?" he said out loud.

A nearby clacking caught his attention, which was when he realized his leg was also tangled up in the same stuff, but anchored to a much thicker branch. Seated on the cable was a spider the size of Nym's chest, covered in dark-green chitinous plates and staring at him with eight eyes. He jerked back from it, only to find that he couldn't really move.

Nym scooped up the branch that was stuck to his arm and swung it at the spider, which nimbly hopped back. It clacked at him again, the sound of its armored body plates rubbing against one another, and advanced. The next swing caught it solidly, and while it might not have actually hurt it, spiders didn't weigh that much, and the force was enough to send it flying away into the darkness.

More clacking came to him. With a sinking feeling in his chest, he realized that he was in the middle of a whole colony. He could see dozens of shapes scurrying around in the darkness. "Nope. No. No way. Not doing this," he said.

He quickly pulled arcana into his soul well and sent a pulse of hardened air to strike the thicker branch anchoring his leg. It took four shots before it snapped, and only then in conjunction with Nym working it back and forth, and he went straight up as soon as he was free, dragging the broken limb behind him.

"Screw this, I am done with this forest," he said. Immediately, he started flying straight north with no plans on stopping until he found the road.

That plan lasted about half an hour before he ran out of energy and had to take a break. It was still very dark, and he made sure to thoroughly poke around the tree he picked as his perch before finally landing. He spent most of his rest time trying to remove the sticky webbing from himself, with minimal success. He was at least able to tear off the branches that had been flapping along behind him, but by the time he was ready to move again, he still had a web sleeve on his arm and leg. The stuff seemed to cling even worse to his pants than it did to bare skin.

Dawn broke a few hours later, and it didn't take Nym much longer to spot the road. He followed it east, staying over the trees when he was flying and walking on the road itself when he couldn't, despite the potential danger. He couldn't bring himself to walk through the forest again, not after the spider incident.

The downside of his new travel arrangement was that there was no foraging at all. Noon came and went, and his belly rumbled, but he had nothing to put in it. Ciana had told him it was about a four-day walk to Zoskan, but Nym had hoped to make it much quicker by a combination of flying being faster and able to move in a straight line. In the end, the slowdown of walking half the time probably balanced it out.

Or maybe not. A few hours after that, the town finally came into sight. It was only visible when he was flying, but he could at least see his goal. He altered his direction to head straight to it and, two hours later, walked up to the gates.

There were three guards there, lounging in the shadow of the wall. They wore leather armor, and each had a spear leaning up against the wall next to them. When he walked up, they casually scooped the weapons up and placed themselves dead center in the road.

"Hey now, what troubles you been getting into?" the center guard called out.

"No troubles if I can help it," Nym said back.

"That so? What's that all over your arm then?"

Nym glanced down at the spider cable still stuck to him. He'd broken most of it free, but it had frayed into smaller bundles rather than come off in one chunk, and the stuff he had pulled off had taken skin with it.

"Long story," Nym said.

"Best get to talking, boyo. You're not getting into town looking all suspicious like that."

CHAPTER 12

I t was sorely tempting to just fly right over the walls. He doubted the guards could stop him, but it would just draw more attention to him, and he'd come here to blend in and hide. He'd try to talk his way in first. If they refused to let him, he'd just go around and over the wall somewhere else once it got dark.

"I tried to take a shortcut through the woods," he told them. "There were some spiders. I hit one with a stick. It was not fun."

"And . . . who are you?"

"My name is Nym. I'm just trying to find a place to get some food, and I guess a bath. Wait, this is Zoskan, right?"

One of the guards nodded slowly. "That's right. How long you been on the road, boy?"

"I'm not sure. Three days?"

"Aww, let him in Lagram. Poor kid's had a rough week," one of the guards said.

"Shut yer mouth. People don't get in just because they're pitiful."

Of all the possibilities Nym had tried to plan for, the gate guards refusing to let him in was not one of them. "Uh . . . sorry, but why can't I go in?" he asked.

"Well, 'cause we don't know if you're a criminal or not. You could be a bandit for all—"

"He's not a bandit," one of the guards said. "Could he even shoot a crossbow without it knocking him flat on his ass?"

"Okay, that's true. He's probably not a bandit. But a thief! Master pickpocket right there. We don't know."

"Are you serious, Lagram?" another guard said. "The kid is wearing rags and is half-covered in spider webbing."

The stubborn guard jutted out his chin and said, "Well fine, but he hasn't told us his business. Why'd he come to Zoskan in the first place?"

Because he was a criminal, Nym thought. He wasn't about to admit to that though. Instead, he said, "Got no family left. Some rich guy's jerk kid started giving me a hard time back home, making my life miserable. Seemed easier to just go somewhere else. It's not like I was leaving much behind."

There was some bitterness in his voice, which Nym made no effort to hide. If anything, he felt it helped sell the story. Lagram opened his mouth again, but before he could say anything, one of the guards on his side said, "Stop grilling the poor boy. Just let him in. What harm's he going to do?"

"Bah. Fine. You can go in. Make sure you stay out of trouble!"

"Thanks, sirs," Nym said. He moved to walk past, but the guard who'd spoken up for him stopped him.

"There's an alchemist on Spinder Street who could probably help get that webbing off you. It'd be a bit easier on your skin than scrubbing at it at least. You go talk to him, his name's Cern. You tell him Toren at the west gate sent you. I know him, he'll help if he can."

"I'll do that. Thanks!"

The guard gave him a pat and moved back to his post. They waved him through the gate, and Nym got his first good look as Zoskan.

It was probably a hundred times bigger than Palmara. The streets were made of cobblestone, and the houses were properly fitted wood with shingled roofs. It wasn't necessarily clean everywhere, but it was cleaner than Nym. He got a few looks as he trudged through town, reading the signs and looking for Spinder Street. The damn spider webbing was so much worse in town, where it stuck to the stone streets with every step and took a bit of effort to peel back up.

After half an hour of wandering, Nym was forced to admit he was lost. "Excuse me," he said to a nearby man who was walking into a tavern. "Can you tell me where Spinder Street is?"

"Spinder Street?" the man said thoughtfully. "Not really sure. Maybe that way?"

Nym looked toward the direction the man had waved him in. He'd already checked that way. "Thanks," he said, suppressing a sigh and trudging off.

Once he reached the next intersection, he turned and asked a different person for directions. That one just told him to piss off and aimed a kick Nym's way when he didn't move fast enough. Finally, after much wandering and no real help from the locals, Nym found Spinder Street. Unfortunately, he had no idea which way the alchemist's shop was.

A few more questions that got him a variety of unhelpful answers, and he stumbled across it. It was a squat building, only a single story tall and almost twice as wide as the ones next to it. The storefront was a glass window showing off various vials, jars, and bottles full of different colored liquids, pastes, and ointments. Signs touted the wonders of the concoctions, claiming to do everything from relieving muscle pain to curing impotency.

Nym pulled open the door and limped in. "Hello?" he called out, not seeing anyone around.

"Hello there," said a voice from right next to him.

Nym jumped a foot in the air and spun in place. There, standing in a spot that had clearly been empty moments earlier, was a thin, middle-aged man with a thick beard and even thicker eyebrows. He wore a smock that was liberally stained and thick, heavy shoes. His clothes were rough, but solid and thick.

"Sorry about that," the man laughed. "I was trying out an elixir I crafted that makes the imbiber light as air. Seems to be working."

Once Nym's heart rate slowed back down to something approaching normal speed, he realized there was an open door nearby that the man had probably come out of. Still, the man didn't really look sorry. He looked gleeful, like a kid playing a prank.

"That was not very nice!" Nym told him. "Are you Cern?"

"That's me," the man confirmed. "Nice to meet you."

"Uh, likewise. The guy at the gate, Toren, said I should come talk to you, that you could probably help with my . . . um . . . problem." Nym waved around an arm that still had strands of spider webbing stuck to it.

"Oh, interesting. From the giant spiders in the forest, right? How did you get so much of it stuck to you?"

"Fell asleep in the wrong tree."

"And you're still alive? That sounds like an interesting story."

"I woke up before they could . . ." Nym trailed off and shuddered. He finished lamely, "Finish whatever they were doing."

"Probably for the best," Cern agreed. "But how did you escape them?"

"Oh, that part was easy." Nym filled his soul well with some arcana and lifted himself up off the ground.

"Ah, very good, young mageling! That is solid control over a basic air elemental construct, practically unheard of in someone so young. But how long can you keep it up?"

"Depends how fast I want to go," Nym told him. "Long enough to get away from some spiders at least."

The alchemist laughed. "Fair enough. So Toren sent you to me to see about removing those stubborn webs. Bless his heart. Not only would I be happy to remove them for you, but I'll pay you a bronze wedge to keep them."

"Deal," Nym said instantly. Ciana got three wedges for each crab she brought into town to sell, enough for a cheap meal at least. He had come to Cern's shop just hoping to get away with a few hours of chores in exchange for the man's help. This was a deal beyond his wildest hopes.

"Very good then. Come with me and we'll get you cleaned right up."

Cern led him into the side room and started rooting around in one of his baskets. "Ah, here it is," he said, holding up a bottle with a brush cap stuck into it. He gave it a good shake to mix the contents up, which turned them a pale, pasty green, before removing the cap and using the brush applicator on Nym's arm.

"Don't mind the smell," he said. "It'll fade in an hour or so. There we go, just let that soak in for a few minutes."

While he was working on Nym's leg, with Nym hovering in the air to make it easier for him, Nym asked, "That elixir you mentioned, that makes a person light as air, did you mean that literally?"

Cern got a gleam in his eye. "Ha! I did. Well, not actually as light as air, but it would in fact make it easier for you to fly farther as it will reduce your weight by roughly thirty percent. That's what you were thinking, right?"

"It was," Nym admitted.

"I'd be happy to sell you a bottle, but—and not to be rude—I think most of my goods might be out of your price range," Cern told him. "Although, you're highly mobile, willing to venture into the forest, nerves of steel it seems. I can always use more ingredients. Are you interested in a bit of work?"

Finally, some good luck came Nym's way. "I sure am!" he said. "Wait, it's not getting more spider webbing, is it?"

"Oh, goodness no. Not at all. This stuff is only situationally useful and doesn't last very long even when properly preserved. I wouldn't want it at all except I have a client who's looking for a potion that this is the main ingredient in. He's been bugging me for two months, but I never have any of the webbing in stock, so it was a bit of good luck you came in with it. I can finally get him off my back!"

The two shared a laugh, and then Cern started peeling off the spiderweb. "There we go. Just let the rest of the solution dry on your skin for another ten minutes and then it'll turn to powder and you can brush it off," the alchemist instructed.

Nym nodded happily. He hadn't realized how irritating it was having his limbs gummed up with that webbing until it was gone. He wiggled his toes with a smile and flexed one hand. "That is so much better."

"I imagine so. Now, young man, let's discuss what other things I need that a brave and enterprising soul such as yourself might be able to provide. You seem to be in dire need of funds, and I am in casual need of some materials to experiment with, so I think we should be able to work something out."

Cern pulled out a sheet of paper and started jotting down things he wanted from the forest along with descriptions of where to find them and a sketched map of the local woodland. He focused on plants that grew high up off the ground, fully planning to take advantage of Nym's ability to fly.

He also added a second sheet of paper listing some of the dangers Nym was likely to find, including the green armor-plated spiders he'd run into. There were also giant owls, living-vine snakes, and if he went deep into the interior of the forest, something that Cern called frost wraiths. Nym was advised to run far away very quickly if he encountered one of the monsters.

"And I think that should about do it. You, er . . . you do have a pack of some kind, right?" Cern eyed him up, looking at Nym's bare feet and patched and holey clothes.

"I don't," Nym admitted. "I'll have to make the first run using my shirt to hold stuff until I can afford one."

Cern sighed and shook his head. "Here," he said, "one bronze wedge for the spider webbing, and an extra two as an advance on the first load of supplies. Now I want skywort blooms from the waterfall cliffs first. You take a right out the door here, go down two blocks, and buy yourself a pack, then bring me back those plants and we'll call it even."

Nym nodded along with the directions. "I'll be back before it gets dark," he promised.

CHAPTER 13

Skywort bloom, as it turned out, grew in significantly denser patches just under the waterfall where everything was wet and loud and extra difficult to get to. Nym resorted to a combination of flight and hydrokinesis just to get a look at the stuff, which looked like lichen studded with little flowers glistening with waterdrops.

Actually harvesting the blooms was a bit more complicated for two reasons. First, he didn't have anywhere near the strength needed to divert the waterfall enough to get into the good, thick patches near the top of the cliff. Second, a flock of some sort of bird that Cern had not seen fit to mention nested on the cliffs, and they were not happy about Nym's intrusion.

The birds were small and not really life-threatening, but it was still hard to concentrate on two different spells at once when they were dive-bombing him. Another layer of complication was that the best way to quickly harvest the skywort bloom was to dust off his old first-circle telekinesis spell. There were other patches closer to the ground, but they were well-known by herbalists out hunting for the same thing, and nothing compared to the harvest Nym could take off the top of the cliffs, if he could manage three spells at the same time while fending off an angry flock of small birds.

That was easier said than done. Nym retreated from the waterfall to practice near the stream. There wasn't anywhere to land, but holding his flight while he worked the other two spells was part of the training anyway. He floated in the air above the water and forged a second conduit to the first layer. That was something the returned memory had shown him how to do, but his three-year-old self made it seem a lot easier than it actually was.

There were two main problems. First, it was much harder to hold open two conduits at once than it was to widen one conduit. Second, the arcana from the first layer didn't like mixing with the arcana from the second layer. He initially thought he could just fill his soul well up halfway with one type, then switch to a shallower conduit and fill it up the rest of the way.

That made him violently ill. Some poor, unlucky fish got to swim through a cloud of his vomit as it drifted away in the water below him. Nym dry heaved for a solid half an hour until he managed to drain his soul well again. That of course cost him his flight spell, and he ended up soaking wet when he plunged into the stream.

He knew it was possible, but he couldn't remember how he'd managed to both hold open two conduits and keep them from mixing arcana inside his soul well. If he wanted that big payday waiting for him at the top of the waterfall, he needed to figure it out. The air cushions he used to fly were not delicate enough to harvest the skywort blooms, and even if he found a place to perch, he still needed to use a second-circle hydrokinesis spell and the first-circle telekinesis at the same time.

The hydrokinesis was the bulk of the drain on his arcana anyway. Flight was just to give him an angle to see what he was doing, and it was a lot easier to lift his own weight than to divert thousands of pounds of rushing water. When he'd first tried, he couldn't move it at all. It was too heavy and too fast for him to alter. What he'd ended up doing was speeding up the water before it got to the fall so that it flew out farther than it normally would.

That was still a strain, but it was manageable for at least a few minutes. That and the flight spell together were pushing the limits. Nym wasn't sure how he was going to mix in a telekinesis spell from the first layer. He wondered if it would be easier to figure out a new telekinesis spell that used second-layer arcana. Surely there had to be a second-circle version of it.

Nym hadn't focused too hard on learning to do new things for a few reasons. First, he had no one to train him and no books to study from, so he was inventing everything from scratch. Second, he was still picking the low-hanging fruit of air and water manipulation. Third, there was a limit to his stamina that he was steadily expanding, but too slowly.

He was determined to crack this problem though. He could see the skywort blooms, and even if they weren't the most valuable things on Cern's list, there were a lot of them right in front of him. They represented food, new clothes, shoes, and maybe, just maybe, some magical instruction. That was at the top of his list once basic necessities were met. All he had to do was manage to find a way to get up there and harvest them.

Eventually, Nym was forced to give up. It was getting dark, and he needed to come back with something to cover the advance Cern had given him. Instead of the mother lode of skywort blooms, he scoured some of the easy-to-reach ones that were near the waterfall, but high enough up that people who couldn't fly didn't want to bother climbing. He spotted a few other things that looked right, but Cern would have to be the one to determine that, and called it a day.

The flight back to Zoskan was short. He took a break just outside the forest to catch his breath, and then skimmed over the ground for another twenty minutes until he was close to the walls. It might have been meaningless to hide his magic from the guards, but he was operating under the assumption that if someone from Palmara came looking for him, the local guards would be their first stop.

So he walked the last quarter of a mile and this time was let in without any fuss since he was able to show that he'd been picking herbs and reagents in the forest to sell in town. There were some mutterings about him being too young to be in the forest unattended, but nobody stopped him. Nym worried they might block him from going back out next time.

The door to Cern's shop was locked when he got there, but he could see the alchemist moving around inside the store cleaning. He knocked on the window and held up the backpack when Cern looked up at him and scowled. He strode over to the door and unlocked it.

"You're late," he said.

"Sorry."

"Ah, whatever. What'd you find for me?"

Nym handed over the pack, and Cern peered eagerly into it. "Hmm . . . let's see. Bluecaps, good. A garnet root, just one? Too bad, I need four or five to do anything useful. A few skywort blooms, in good condition. Good. What is this?"

Cern held up a slab of bark covered in moss. Nym internally winced. He hadn't been sure if he'd identified that right. "Shadar's slab?" he asked.

"Not even close. The moss is too light, and the texture needs to be smoother. It only grows on trees that have fed on arcana, which can be identified by the zigzag pattern in the bark. This is garbage. The rest is good." Cern considered for a few seconds. "Taking off the two bronze wedges you owe me, let's say three shims and eight wedges. Eh, let's call it four shims, and I'll just keep the pack. You can borrow it whenever you want to do another run."

Nym found himself with four circles of copper pressed into his hands and was shooed out of the shop. "I recommend you spend two of those on a room at the Trough and Saddle. No one there will give you a hard time about being a kid, and if they do, you tell the owner. His name is Babkin, and he'll sort out any trouble right away. They'll get you a hot meal, a bath, and a place to sleep. You need all three."

Nym felt his cheeks flush. It had been close to a week since his last bath, not counting his dunk in the river. "Thanks for the advice," he said.

As embarrassing as it was to be called out for smelling bad, Nym couldn't deny it. He got directions and went straight to the Trough and Saddle. It was a sleepy little place at the north end of town near the fields that catered primarily to farmers who had stopped for a drink. He went right up to the bar, where a reed-thin man with an equally thin mustache was filling a mug with beer.

"We don't serve kids," the man said before Nym could say anything.

"Cern the alchemist said I could get a room, a meal, and a bath for two shims," Nym told him, placing the shims on the bar. "He also said to ask for Babkin if there was any trouble with that."

The man huffed and shook his head. "I'll go get him. Let me finish up here first."

He poured two more beers and slid them over to the farmers sitting at the bar. Then he scooped up the shims, crossed the floor, and disappeared through a door he closed behind him. Nym looked down at the counter where his money had been, then back up to where the man had disappeared.

"Um," he said.

The guy on the seat next to him started laughing. "He's not gonna run off and cheat you, son."

A few minutes later, the man came back out and called Nym over. "Babkin wants to talk to you. He's got your money. Just follow this hall to the end and go in."

"Thank you," Nym said.

The man waved him off and went back to work, leaving Nym to find his own way. There were doors every ten feet or so, with one at the end of the hall that led into an office. There, seated in a padded chair, was a wide man with a thick beard, spiky hair, and a pipe hanging out of his mouth. Everything about him seemed squished to be extra thick, from his arms to his fingers to his belly.

"You are the kid Cern sent me?" he asked around the pipe.

"Yes, sir. I ran some errands for him, and he recommended I come here for a room and, uh . . . a bath." That last part was mumbled.

Babkin crinkled his nose and said, "Yes, I can tell. You are a paying customer now, so you are entitled to a bath, a meal, and a room for the night. We do not serve beer to children. Do not try to sneak any or I will evict you. If I catch you stealing, I will break your hands before I evict you. You eat in the common room tonight and a second meal for breakfast. You either clear your stuff from your room by noon or pay for another day."

"I don't have anything, sir," Nym said.

Babkin's expression softened a bit. "Of course you don't," he grumbled.

"Sorry, sir."

Smoke rolled off the pipe as Babkin thought for a moment. He absently reached behind him and pulled a key off a peg on the wall. With a glance down at it, he handed it over. "Room closest to the kitchen's yours. Stay out of the kitchen. Don't go in there begging for scraps."

"I understand."

"Good enough," Babkin said. "I will send someone to your room with the tub soon."

Nym left the office and found his room easy enough. Being that close to the kitchen let him smell everything being prepared, and it was maddening. He barely stayed in the room long enough to confirm the key opened the door and that there was a bed before he was back out in the common room and sitting at the bar before the reedy man.

"I thought I told you we don't serve kids," the man said.

"Can I get my meal?" Nym asked with a grin.

CHAPTER 14

ym didn't want to speak ill of Ciana. She'd literally saved his life after all. She'd been there for him every single day, and he missed her terribly. He would always be thankful for what she'd done for him.

But the Trough and Saddle's cook was so much better than her.

It wasn't really a fair comparison. Their meals had consisted of a lot of root vegetables and small game, with occasional seafood. The cooking method was pretty much always a stew or broth. She worked with what she had, and he hadn't missed too many meals when he stayed with her.

But . . . bread! Cheese! A real slab of meat! The cook had fried things; there was butter involved in the process. There were seasonings, including the best seasoning of all: almost a week of going hungry in the woods. Nym barely even registered some of the noises he made while he was eating.

"Enough, lad," said the farmer sitting next to him. "If I didn't know better, I'd think you were my wife back when we were first married."

Nym cocked his head to the side. "It's really good," he explained.

The whole bar started laughing. "Leave him alone, Shep. Poor kid's so scrawny, he probably hasn't had a real meal in years," a different farmer said. "Besides, that's a perfectly normal reaction to having Shary's cooking for the first time."

There was a chorus of agreements and the raising of a few mugs, but after that the farmers ignored him, and Nym lost track of their conversation. Before he knew it, the plate was empty, and a woman was sliding a second one in front of him.

"Here ya go, darling," she said.

Nym paused. Part of him wanted to tear into it, but he needed to save up his remaining money. He wanted clothes without holes, maybe a coat. Shoes seemed less important since he spent so much of his time flying now, but still, cold toes were uncomfortable. He was expecting a few more long days in the woods scrounging up materials for Cern just to afford a full set of clothes, and if he spent the money now, it'd just be that much more work.

"Thank you, but I can't afford it," he said quietly.

"Aw, don't you worry about that. Just this one time, it's on me," she told him.

"Are you sure?" he asked with a frown.

The empty plate disappeared from the bar, and the woman leaned forward. "Just because you appreciate the food so much, just this one time, you can have an extra plate," she said with a wink.

"Hey now, we appreciate your cooking, Shary!" one of the farmers called out.

"I know all about what you appreciate about me," she said back. "You can pay full price."

"Don't be like that!"

"Yer lucky I don't charge you extra."

Nym lost track of what was going on again as he devoured the second plate. It was in fact every single bit as good as the first one, but by the end he was starting to slow down. There just wasn't enough room in his stomach, and it was a bit of a struggle to finish. "Whew," he said at the end. "That was so good."

Stuffed to bursting, he waddled across the floor to find his room, where he found a big wooden washing tub. If he'd been an adult, it would have been cramped, but he had plenty of room. There was a brush on a handle and a block of soap left there for him too; both sat on top of a folded towel left on the bed.

Nym couldn't remember ever having a warm bath. His sole memory had been of him very young in a room where everything looked expensive, from the clothes to the decorations. He was sure he'd been accustomed to all sorts of luxuries in his early life, luxuries he couldn't even imagine now. Just a hot meal and a bath were novelties to him.

He scrubbed a week's worth of dirt and grime off, leaving behind water that was more brown than clear, and regarded his clothing dubiously. He didn't really have any plans to go anywhere but bed now, and though he was missing a washboard, he did his best to scrub the pants and shirt in the dirty tub water.

A quick application of hydrokinesis dried them back out. They were . . . marginally cleaner. He shrugged and put them back on. They felt less stiff at least. Maybe. It was hard to tell. But then he looked at the nice clean bed, a real bed too, not just a pallet on the floor, and then back at his own clothes. They came right back off before he jumped into bed.

It was sized to hold an adult, which meant he had plenty of room to roll around, and even if it wasn't all that much more comfortable than what he normally slept on, it was infinitely better than the piles of moss and pine needles he'd been using lately. Nym fell asleep before he even realized it, and barely even woke up when someone knocked on the door.

"Wha—?" he asked sleepily, the blanket wrapped around him.

"Sorry, but we need the tub back. Gonna be a few minutes getting the water drained so we can haul it out," the teenager at the door told him.

Without thinking, Nym used telekinesis to open the window and sent the water out in a long, undulating tendril. It splashed out into the yard while the teen stared at him, slack-jawed. The tub floated up a few inches and flew forward to bump against the teen. "Go 'way," Nym told him, closing the door on him and collapsing back into the bed.

The smell of breakfast woke him up before the sun rose. He staggered out of bed and dressed himself, then shuffled into the common room and climbed up onto one of the barstools. There was no one there yet, so he just leaned over the bar and laid his head back down.

"Go back to your room if you want to sleep," Babkin said from behind him.

Nym groaned and sat back up. "I am so sore," he complained. "I think I'm sick."

"You're too young to be sore," Babkin said. "I must speak with you. Please join me in my office."

That woke Nym up. "Am I in trouble?" he asked.

"Should you be? What did you do?"

"Nothing!" Nym protested. It was even true; he hadn't done anything wrong in Zoskan, but he supposed someone from Palmara might have followed him here. Nobody should know where he'd went when he left, and Ciana was the only one who'd seen which way he'd gone.

"We shall see. Come with me please."

Nym followed the huge innkeeper back to his office. The man took his seat behind his desk in an overwide chair and picked up his pipe. After a few moments of fiddling, he had it lit and was puffing away at it. He said, "No, you're not in trouble here. I just need to get some things cleared up. First, you're a mage."

"No, I'm not."

Babkin shook his head. "You scared my son when you emptied that tub out for him last night. By the way, if you stay here longer, don't dump water out of your window again. We have a place for it. But you showed that you can use magic, and not just basic first-circle spells. You're a mage."

Nym thought about that for a second. He could do second-circle magic, true, but there had to be more to it than just that. Also, he had no idea what Babkin was talking about. He only vaguely remembered someone knocking on his door and waking him up, something about the tub.

His eyes widened. He'd done a first-circle telekinesis spell and a second-circle hydrokinesis spell. He thought about it, trying to remember if he'd done them simultaneously. He barely even remembered doing them, let alone the mechanics of it. Had he forged two conduits at once and held first- and second-layer arcana in his soul well?

A simpler explanation would just be that he'd done them sequentially. That was much more likely. He decided that had to be it. There was no way he'd done by accident while half-asleep what he'd spent hours struggling and failing to achieve yesterday.

Back to the issue at hand. Was he a mage? "What makes someone a mage? Is it just that they can use second-circle spells? Don't they have to have a master or go to school or something?"

"Mage isn't a profession," Babkin told him. "It's just a description of who are you, like saying I'm dark-haired or my son is blond. You can use magic, therefore you are a mage. You will always be a mage, and the only way that changes is if you become even more of a mage and reach archmage status."

"Oh. I guess I am a mage then. I never really thought about it before," Nym said. He paused for a moment to consider that fact, then added, "Is that a bad thing?"

Babkin shrugged. "I do not care. Some people would. It's very unusual though. You're too young to have such strong control over your magic. Maybe if it was basic first-circle spell, but it's rare to see anyone with strong control over elemental magic younger than fifteen. Someone must have invested a lot of time and energy into teaching you, but you look like you're homeless. Is someone going to show up and blow the door off my inn looking to bring you back home to the family castle?"

"No . . . no one like that is looking for me." Maybe a guard from Palmara might make a scene, but Nym doubted anyone would show up who was capable of what Babkin was afraid of.

Babkin grunted and took another puff off his pipe. "Does Cern know you can do magic?" he asked.

"Yes, sir. That's how I got the money for the room. He sent me out to gather stuff for him in the forest."

"He did what?!" Babkin demanded, coming to his feet. "You're a little boy. Even with magic, you are far too young to be roaming around the forest on your own!"

"It's . . . it's fine. Really. I was out there for days on my trip here anyway. It's not so bad, except for the spiders." Nym shuddered at the memory of waking up partially encased in webbing.

"Unacceptable. I will find some work for you to do here to earn your keep. Do not go back into the woods. You're going to get yourself killed."

Nym shook his head. "I need the money."

"Boy, promise me you are not going to go back into the forest for Cern," Babkin insisted.

"Sorry. I can't do that."

The innkeeper let out a rumble. "Very well. Come with me. We're going to talk to Cern about this."

"I don't think—"

"Come along," Babkin said. He strode out of the office and walked through the kitchen to the back door. Nym followed along his in wake, and the two of them stepped outside.

It was only a few minutes to the alchemist's store, and Babkin didn't stop pounding until he answered the door. Cern was wearing a robe loosely tied at the stomach and not much else. "By all that's holy, what do you want? It's not even dawn yet."

"Cern," Babkin rumbled, his pipe billowing smoke. "Did you send a ten-year-old boy alone into the woods to find mushrooms and flowers for you?"

The alchemist's eyes widened to a comic degree, and he shot a glance over at Nym, who was standing behind and off to the side of the innkeeper. He groaned out loud. "You told him?" he asked, exasperated.

CHAPTER 15

The three of them were seated at a table in Cern's kitchen. It was fascinating to see what his home looked like, if only because it was a bizarre mix of work and personal life. Intricate glasswork filled random counters and tables. Jars and vials were filled with liquids of different colors and thicknesses. There were drying racks for herbs and leather bags full of powders.

All of this shared space with cutlery and flatware. There was old, hard brown bread on a plate on the table with a half-eaten wedge of cheese. Right next to it was a mortar and pestle full of sparkling green dust. A small wooden bowl of fruit shared counter space with a giant steel funnel that had dried gunk all over the inside.

"You need to hire someone to clean up after you," Babkin said. "It cannot be sanitary living like this."

"Bah. They'd just mix everything up and ruin my experiments." Cern waved a hand at a table over by a window that had been given over to an elaborate contraption that seemed designed to produce a gently fizzing liquid one slow drop at a time.

Babkin grunted and reached up to light his pipe. "No smoking in here!" Cern snapped. The innkeeper just scowled.

"Fine. Now, tell me why you thought it was a good idea to pay a little boy to run errands for you in the forest."

Cern shrugged. "He's a mageling. A bit young, but competent. If he gets into trouble, he can just fly away. Plus he already had experience in the forest."

"You can fly?" Babkin asked, turning in his seat to give Nym a surprised glance. Nym nodded, and he added, "How long? How fast?"

"Maybe twice as fast as I can walk, for about an hour. Or really fast for a few minutes."

"See, he's fine!" Cern said.

"Air and water," Babkin said thoughtfully. "Have you mastered earth and fire too?"

"Not really. I've only been practicing for a few months. Not quite two."

"Wait, what?"

Both men were staring at Nym now. Slowly, Babkin said, "You implied that you don't have a teacher or master. No formal training. You are self-taught?"

Nym nodded.

"And that you have only been using magic for almost two months. And you are how old?"

"Ten, I think."

"You don't know how old you are?" Cern asked.

"I don't remember anything before a few months ago," Nym said. "Someone found me washed up on a beach on the coast and took care of me for a bit."

Nym didn't want to say more than that. He'd probably already said too much. No one needed to know he came from Palmara, and they especially didn't need to know why he'd left. He liked Cern, who treated him like an adult, and Babkin was nice in his own way. Neither needed to know that Nym was a murderer fleeing his crime.

"The mystery gets deeper and deeper," Cern said.

"Indeed. But regardless of his talents, the boy is still too young to go into the forest unsupervised.

"You're not the boy's father, Babkin. He can do what he wants, and I can pay him a fair wage if he brings me in things I can use."

Babkin rose from the table to loom over Cern. "You are correct, of course," he said. "And if you ever want to taste Shary's cooking again, you will not buy any of the things Nym finds, and thus he will have no reason to go into the forest looking for them."

"That's playing dirty!" Cern cried out. He slammed a hand down on the table and shot to his feet to glare at Babkin, nose to nose.

The burly innkeeper was unmoved. "I am not playing with you."

The argument devolved from there, but Babkin was unmoving despite Cern's pleas, arguments, and threats. "Fine," Cern finally said, "How about if Nym only goes out with my regular group? That way he won't be out on his own, and he can still fly to get the harder-to-reach stuff for me."

"Which group?" Babkin asked. "Therm's or Risto's?"

"Therm's. Risto is completely irresponsible. I couldn't trust him to look after anybody."

"That . . . would be acceptable, I suppose." Babkin gave Nym an appraising look. "Therm will watch out for you and keep you safe. You will be able to harvest the things Cern needs to run his business. And you will be able to afford food and shelter, and have extra money to expand your wardrobe."

Cern just sighed. "Therm's group only goes out twice a month. He'll come by tomorrow afternoon to get a list of what I'm looking for. Come by then and I'll introduce you to him. This whole arrangement depends on him agreeing to it. Don't see why he wouldn't. He'll make more money with you along."

Nym had kept quiet throughout the whole conversation. He wasn't necessarily happy about the two adults deciding what he could and could not do, but he did want to keep staying at the inn and eating Shary's cooking, and the work Cern wanted him to do seemed easy enough for the pay. There was just one problem though.

"If they only go out twice a month, and I earned four shims for a trip on my own, how am I supposed to make enough to afford to stay at the Trough and Saddle?" he asked.

The alchemist opened his mouth, thought for a second and closed it again. He turned to look at Babkin and said, "He's got a good point. You're the one who's got a problem with this. How do you expect him to pay for room and board if you won't let him work?"

"I didn't say the boy couldn't work. I said it was too dangerous for him to be roaming the woods all day long every day. I can find the occasional odd job for him, and I'm sure a smart lad like him will find plenty of people who need an odd job done around town."

It seemed the matter was settled between the two men, all without Nym's input or his wishes considered. To say that he was not impressed with the whole thing would be a gross understatement.

Shary had a plate of food ready for Nym when they got back to the Trough and Saddle. Somehow, it didn't taste as good as last night's meal had. The more he thought about it, the more he was annoyed with Babkin. He hadn't asked for the man's help, and in fact the innkeeper had crippled his only source of income before he could even get started.

Worse, the man obviously thought he was doing Nym a favor. He'd spent the better part of a week living in that forest, and the worst of it was some cold weather and one run-in with some spiders. Of course, just because Babkin had decreed what Nym could and could not do didn't mean he had to listen to the old man. Cern would probably be willing to buy from him anyway, as long as Babkin never found out.

And if he wasn't, there were probably other alchemist shops in town. And if none of that worked, well, he could do magic. That was a unique enough talent that somebody would pay for it. He probably needed to practice some more, since he really only had a handful of spells he could do reliably, and more than that, he needed some resources to learn from. A teacher would be ideal, but he'd settle for a few good books if that was all he could get.

He was busy planning out his next steps when a shadow fell over him. Babkin stood over him, watching him eat. "When you're done, come back to my office. We had more to talk about before our detour."

Nym grunted sourly around a mouthful of ham. That seemed to satisfy the wide innkeeper, since he just grunted back and walked away. Somehow, that made the rest of the meal taste even worse. He finished it anyway and left the plate at the sink, where the teenage boy from yesterday was working, then went to go see what Babkin wanted.

He found the man comparing a ledger to some notes scribbled on a paper and shaking his head. Every few seconds he sighed and made another mark on the paper. When he was done, he put the book down. "I am trying to teach my son the numbers he needs to know to run a business," he explained. "He needs more practice."

Nym just stared at him, not feeling like talking. Babkin sighed and lit his pipe. "I'm sure you think I'm being unfair, and harsh, and interfering in your life. That's fine. You are correct to think that. I am interfering. The forest is dangerous, and the fact that you survived as long as you did is a testament to how lucky you got, not your skills. Cern should never have sent you back there. He knows better.

"But that's not what I want to talk to you about. I want to talk to you about your magic. The more I learn, the more impressed I am, but also the more concerned I am. You are entirely self-taught?"

"I am," Nym said.

Babkin nodded to himself. "That's right. I think you might even have said that already. I also think it is probably reasonable to assume then that you have very little knowledge of the dangers inherent to magic. Now, I am no mage myself, so understand that what I tell you is secondhand knowledge. To start, there is a thing called arcana poisoning."

"I know about arcana poisoning," Nym cut him off. "Gave it to myself twice, once fighting off a shark that was trying to eat me and once when another boy hit me with an arcana injection spell while I was casting."

The innkeeper's eyebrows shot up. "You have fought a mage duel at age ten?"

Nym regretted saying that immediately. He was giving away too many clues about where he was from. Now Babkin knew that wherever he'd been before, there had been another boy there who was talented enough to cast a second-circle spell. He didn't know how much that narrowed it down, but nothing good would come from giving anyone hints.

"Regardless," Babkin continued, "arcana poisoning is one possible danger, and it is comparatively benign. Conduit-degradation backlash is another big one novice mages are warned to be careful of. That's when you try to make a conduit with holes in it so that you can draw arcana from the first and second layer at the same time. It mixes in the conduit and can blow it out. That can permanently damage your soul well if it's bad enough."

For a man who claimed to be sharing secondhand knowledge, the innkeeper sure seemed to know quite a bit. He rambled on for a while, listing conditions like matrix destabilization, fused lung, temporal blindness, and something called phallic-engorgement discombobulation. He refused to elaborate on what exactly that was or tell Nym what any of the symptoms were.

"Now, do you have a license?" Babkin asked him.

"A license for what?"

"That's what I thought. The mage guild issues a license to any mages who want to perform magic inside the walls. They are expensive, and you have to pass rigorous exams to get them. I don't think you could pass them, given the obvious gaps in your knowledge, even if you could afford to take the exams. There are penalties for casting without a license, especially second-circle spells. Don't do any magic in town again."

Nym groaned. It was just problem after problem cropping up. He couldn't go to the forest. He couldn't do magic in town. How was he supposed to survive like this?

"We're not going to turn you in, of course. But for your own safety, be careful what you do. Even first-circle spells can get you slapped with a fine that I doubt you can afford to pay."

Nym sighed heavily. "Okay. Thanks for letting me know."

"Moving along," Babkin said. "Let me tell you about what kind of creatures you need to be aware of when you do go out with Therm's group."

Nym had to suppress another groan. In the last few months, he'd almost been eaten by a shark and a man had tried to kill him. Somehow, this was still the worst day of his life.

CHAPTER 16

The mage guildhall was the largest building Nym had ever seen. It was three stories tall and filled an entire block by itself, not even including the support buildings and fields taking up space next to it. It was actually the only place he'd found in Zoskan with open fields. Space was at a premium inside the walls, and the whole town felt crowded and squished together. Apparently being mages allowed them to claim an extra-large chunk of land.

He'd passed a church on the way there that was fancier looking, but the guildhall dwarfed it in terms of sheer size. It was also in a more expensive district. Nym saw a lot more guards patrolling than he'd seen by the Trough and Saddle, including some that were permanently stationed in front of certain stores that dealt in what he assumed was expensive merchandise. He got a lot of dirty looks from those guards.

Nym was nervous at first until he figured out what was going on. He was too poor to afford anything, and he was dressed in rough clothes that showed exactly how little money he had. There was no good reason for him to be there, so they all assumed he was looking for things to steal. He wasn't, but that was infinitely preferable to wondering if they were deciding whether he matched the description of the child murderer they'd gotten from Palmara.

He reached the guildhall without anyone stopping him and, with a deep breath, pushed open the door. His first view of the interior was a disappointment. There were some benches and chairs set up, and a long counter with two men conversing behind it. The rest of the room was empty. It was decorated with some notice boards and a few tables with pamphlets scattered across them.

It was a weirdly depressing room to be in. Nym couldn't quite put his finger on why, just something in the air. The two men ignored Nym until he walked up to the desk. "Hi," he said.

"Hi there," the man on the left side. "Need something?"

"I wanted to ask some questions about magic," Nym said.

"Oh yeah?" Both of them were leaning on the counter looking down at him.

"Um . . . yes. I heard that you have to have a license to use magic in town. Is that true?"

"Sure is. Too many amateurs who couldn't control their spells causing damage. And then they can't pay, and someone is looking at the guildhall like it's our responsibility just because someone else could use magic. So they decided that if it was going to be our problem, we were going to charge to take care of it."

"That makes sense," Nym allowed. "What do I need to do to get a license?"

Both men started laughing. "You're about five or six years too young to even be worried about it," the first one told him.

"But I can do magic," Nym said. "And I don't want to get in trouble for it."

"I'm sure you'll be safe. This is really only for big stuff. You're not going to destroy a street or knock down a building with your magic, are you?"

"I just don't want to get in trouble for flying. Can I do that without a license?"

The man whistled. "Flight's pretty complicated. I can see where you'd be concerned. Tell ya what, you do a lap around the ceiling for me, and I'll start getting the paperwork ready for you to apply."

Nym drifted up until he was eye level with the men, then higher. He skimmed the walls just below the ceiling, intentionally going faster than what he considered long-distance speed. Neither man was laughing when he came to a stop, still floating in front of them.

"Blight my eyes," one of them muttered. "Little shit really can fly."

The one who'd been doing the talking just stared at Nym for a second. Then he shook his head and reached into a drawer to start pulling out paperwork. "Deal's a deal. Here's the forms," he said. The man hesitated a second, then added, "It's five shields for the application. That covers all your exam fees too."

Nym fished out his two remaining copper shims. "This is all I have."

With a sigh and a shake of his head, the man told him, "That's not even the right kind of coin. You'd need fifty of those to equal five shields. I'm sorry, but you can't submit an application if you don't have the fee."

Nym wilted. "And I can't fly in town without the license? What if it was only flying and nothing else?"

"If you get caught, you'll be fined. But honestly, and no offense kid, I'm not sure you could pass the exams if all you can do is fly," the talkative one said.

The other one scratched his chin and eyed Nym up and down. "How good are you at flying? Can you change direction rapidly? Ascend and descend in response to attacks?"

"Maybe?" Nym told him. "I can dodge around trees a bit. I guess it would depend on how fast I'm going."

The first man caught on to whatever his friend was thinking. "Hey, that's a good idea. You think Brogan would take him on?"

"Maybe. Tell you what, why don't you come with me? We've got an aerial obstacle course, and the guy who runs it could make a special pass for you that's just for flight if you can impress him. I can't promise anything, but it doesn't hurt to ask, right?"

"I guess not," Nym agreed. "How do we do that?"

"You want to watch the front desk for a bit and I'll take him back?"

"Sure. Let me know how it goes. Good luck, kiddo."

The pair of them walked down a hallway. The mage said, "My name is Navarim. What's yours?"

"Nym."

"Nice to meet you. So here's what I'm hoping will happen. I'm going to go introduce you to the flight master, Brogan. Hopefully he'll be interested enough that you can fly so early and let you do the obstacle course. If you can impress him, he might give you a kind of pseudolicense that lets you fly *and nothing else* without you having to pay all the fees and do the other exams."

Navarim led him through a confusing maze of hallways and adjoining rooms, and soon Nym was hopelessly lost. Eventually they reached a room that had a dozen circular platforms embedded into the floor. Each one was carved with symbols and glyphs that had wisps of arcana coming off them. Some glowed brightly, others flickered, and a few in the back were completely dim.

"This is the guildhall teleportation room. It's for mages only, but it should be fine since you're with me and I'm on mage business. Step up onto this one and we'll go to the flight field."

Nym examined the runes he was standing on while Navarim activated them. His arcana mist was a washed-out green color, and as the mage worked, it flowed through him into the platform below them. Light spread across the lines, at first making a circuit around them that brightened and faded, but gradually filling until the whole platform shone in his sight.

Then the world became flat and constricted around him, like someone scrunching up a drawing. Everything went black for a moment, and when Nym could see again, they were in a small shed. The walls were unadorned with any sort of decoration, and a wide double door was thrown open to reveal a field full of the strangest equipment Nym had ever seen.

There were hundreds of poles of different heights seemingly scattered at random. Sometimes giant hoops were set into the sides of them, all painted in reds or blues or yellows. There were giant boxes the size of two-story houses made out of logs all spaced apart by a few feet. The interiors were filled with ropes stretched at various angles over and around one another, like a giant knot that had been blown open.

Mages of various ages zipped around and through the obstacles, sometimes diving gracefully through hoops, sometimes clipping them and spiraling out of control. Nym saw one particularly agile fellow rocket through a rope house at full speed, contorting spectacularly to avoid getting tangled.

"Wow, this looks like fun."

Navarim chuckled. "Maybe for you. Brogan's standards are difficult to achieve. This field was six months of hell for me when I was a student."

"Mage Navarim," a voice barked from behind them. "What do you think you're doing bringing a child onto my airfield?"

Navarim jumped in surprise and spun in place. "Flight Master Brogan," he said. "We have a bit of a situation that we were hoping you could help us resolve."

An old man, probably at least eighty or ninety and looking more like a wrinkled sack of skin with hair sprouting out of places hair had no business growing than he did like a person, stared at the two of them with a severe frown. He was wearing thick leather pants with a matching coat and a long scarf that seemed to alternate between white and pale blue as it drifted out behind him and held what looked like a willow switch in one hand.

"What kind of situation would possibly require my intervention to resolve?" he asked.

"Well, you see, sir, this boy here has already learned how to fly. And he wanted to get a license so he could fly in town without getting in trouble. Very responsible of him to seek us out, don't you think? The problem is he can't afford the licensing fees, but you know, that's really more for property damage stuff. All he wants to be able to do is fly."

Brogan shifted to look at Nym. "He can, huh? What are you, six? Seven?"

"Ten," Nym said.

The old mage grunted. "Still young. Good, can never start too early. But I fail to see what you expect me to do here, Mage Navarim."

"Well, I thought that maybe you could just do the flight exam and, if he passes, he could get a special permit to allow him to just fly, rather than go through the whole thing."

"Huh . . . a flight license. That's an interesting idea. Not much call for it, since everyone learns all the other stuff when they complete the curriculum. I'm afraid I cannot help you. The rules are the rules. You need to clear this space."

Navarim wilted in place. "You can't make an exception? He's really good. He demonstrated for us, did a lap around the entrance. He even skimmed the ceiling, tight corners, everything."

"There is no such thing as a flight license," Brogan told them. He waved them off and went back to watching the mage trainees loop through the air.

The words were a clear dismissal. Navarim let out a heavy sigh and said, "Sorry, kiddo. I thought maybe, but . . . Well, let's head on back."

"I want to try the obstacle course," Nym announced.

"What?"

Both mages turned to look at him in surprise.

"It looks fun," Nym explained. "And we're not in town now, right? We teleported somewhere else. So I can fly here and I won't get in trouble?"

"That is technically true," Brogan agreed. "It's really not a playground though. You could get hurt."

"I'll be okay. I'm good at flying."

The old mage gave him a noncommittal grunt. "Even if you get to the end, even if you broke my own personal record, I still won't give you this flight-license thing you want. It does not exist."

"That's fine. At least I'll get to practice here."

Brogan thought about it for a second, then nodded. "Fine, you show me that you have full control over your flight and you can try it. I'll even spot you myself to make sure you don't get hurt. Mage Navarim, you can power the enchantments."

Navarim blanched. "By myself, Flight Master Brogan?"

The old man gave him a wicked grin. "It was your idea to bring this boy here, was it not?"

CHAPTER 17

Navarim was sent off to a waist-high pedestal to be what Brogan called the arcana battery of the operation. He did not look happy about being assigned the task.

"Alright, what's your name?" Brogan asked.

"Nym."

"Just Nym? No great house or family?"

"Just Nym."

"Fair enough. Better in some ways. Nobles play too many politics. It gets in the way of the magic. Well, Nym, while Mage Navarim is powering up the obstacle course, I want to see you do some of the basics. Fly around in a circle for me, eight feet up, keep it level to the ground, nice and wide now."

Nym opened up his soul well to arcana and filled it completely. He suspected that by the time Brogan was satisfied with his performance, he would be running dry. Then he lifted up and spun himself around in a circle overhead before stopping on front of the flight master mage.

"Not bad. Hard air style, cushions are a bit big, but you've got solid control over the size, so that's just a matter of practice to narrow them down. Okay, head straight up as fast as you can for three seconds, then come back down as fast as you can and stop twenty feet off the ground."

Nym took a breath, poured arcana into the spell, and shot off into the air. He was high enough that by the time he reached the count of three, Brogan was a black dot on the ground. Nym let the flight spell break, and gravity pulled him back down. New cushions of air formed above him and pushed to help speed him up, then broke apart to be replaced by a full-body cushion that hugged him and slowed his descent until he was hovering in place above Brogan's head.

"Less good. Speed was alright, but the full-body brake is inefficient."

"You said to be as fast as possible, not as efficient as possible."

"Hah! So I did. So I did. Last test. Follow me."

The old mage drifted upward, his scarf billowing out behind him as he rose into the air. "Ready?" he asked. Then, without waiting for Nym to answer, he yelled, "Go!"

The mage zipped off at an astonishing speed, leaving Nym gaping at him for a second before he pushed his own arcana into acceleration and caught up. Brogan wasn't so easy to keep pace with though. He shot off at odd angles, changing direction with such tight turns that Nym couldn't match him. He was forced to make wider, ponderous turns every time Brogan went a different way, and each time he fell farther and farther behind.

That wasn't to say that Nym wasn't nimble in the air, just that an old master like Brogan changed direction without an inch of wasted space or losing any of his momentum. First he'd be going one way, then in a blink he'd shoot off in a completely different direction, as fast as if he'd always been going that way.

Nym narrowed his eyes against the wind and dashed tears out of them with his hand. He was flying as fast as he could, half-blinded by the sheer speed, and he still couldn't keep up with the old master mage. But each time Brogan altered his direction, Nym got a look at the arcana around him, and he was starting to figure out what was happening.

Experimentally, he loosened the constraint on the cushion of air supporting him. His flight became less stable, but when he rotated his body, the cushion moved with it, allowing him greater control over his trajectory. It worked great in theory, but in practice, the next time he tried to make a turn, he found himself rolling through the sky and had to reinforce the cushion to right himself.

The speed he'd bled off in those few uncontrolled seconds allowed Brogan to pull away from him again. The old man regarded him with a wolfish grin, easily visible from a hundred feet away. "Nice try! You're learning," he called back. "You got to know where to keep it tight and where to give it some freedom to breathe!"

With a howl of laughter, Brogan picked up speed and all but disappeared from Nym's sight. Nym put on his own burst of speed and caught sight of the man skimming the treetops at the edge of the airfield. Somehow, he'd tripled the gap between them in a second. That was when Nym realized the old man had been playing with him the whole time. Nym was going all out just to keep up with him, and the geezer was just screwing around.

Brogan shot straight up into the sky, and Nym curved his trajectory to meet him rather than follow the exact same path. That wasn't nearly enough to catch up, and the old man just flew over his head back to the beginning of the obstacle course where Navarim was still laboriously working over the arcana-battery pedestal.

Nym landed next to Brogan a few seconds later. His chest heaved up and down, and despite the breeze of high-speed flight, sweat covered his face. In contrast, Brogan merely straightened out his scarf and regarded the boy. "You're . . . really . . . good," Nym panted out.

Brogan snorted. "Been flying for over a century now. I've spent twenty years teaching every new mage that comes out of the Academy. I literally wrote the book used to teach new mages how to harness the wind. I would have to hang up my scarf if I lost to a little sprout like you."

On the ground, Brogan lost most of the wild cheer he'd displayed while they were flying and regained his more serious, almost military-like manner. "Mage Navarim!" he yelled. "Is the obstacle course charged and ready yet?"

"Almost," Navarim yelled back. "Thirty seconds to finish."

"Too slow. Looks like you need to revisit your basic exercises if you can't channel arcana faster than that."

Brogan led Nym over to the start of the course. "This one has three sections. The first is the logs. They'll change height and width randomly, so you need to be able to weave between the openings quickly before they disappear, and also react in time to avoid crashing into the logs when they pop up in your way.

"Second is the hoops. Once the magic gets flowing, they move up and down the length of the poles. Time your speed and predict where they'll be when you reach them. Of course, you want to fly through each one as fast as you can.

"Finally the rope course. Eheheh, this one is a personal favorite. The ropes you see, they are alive. This one is all about reflexes and defense. If the ropes touch you, you'll get shocked. The more you get shocked, the harder it will be to keep control and not bump into the next rope. Then you get shocked again. The solution is of course not to touch the first rope."

The first two were fine. Nym could do those. The last one sounded difficult. He thought of how Brogan had made instantaneous direction changes and tried to imagine the old man doing it inside a giant box full of taut ropes. It couldn't work. There had to be a different way to do it. Nym was half his size, and he wasn't sure he had enough control over his flight to worm his way through those ropes.

If he took it slowly, he could pick his way through, but that didn't seem to be the point of the obstacle course. It was all about how fast he got from start to finish. It just didn't make sense to have one obstacle at the end that slowed him to a crawl. But he didn't know what he was missing.

"Ready," Navarim said. He slumped back from the pedestal and wiped his face on his sleeve. "Were these batteries always this big?"

"Nope," Brogan told him. "We upgraded them two years ago. Should be enough arcana to run the whole course four or five times now."

"What! Why did I have to fill it all the way then?"

Brogan shrugged. "Because you were here."

Muttering darkly to himself, Navarim stomped off to the side and sat down on the grass. He shot Brogan a nasty look when he thought the old man wasn't looking, but based on the smirk Nym saw on his face, he guessed the flight master knew exactly what Navarim was thinking.

"Are you ready, or should I give you a few more minutes?" Brogan asked Nym.

He needed more than a few more minutes before he'd be back to full, but Nym straightened up anyway and said, "Ready!"

"Right. Good. Don't die up there." Brogan lifted his hand and announced, "Three, two, one, go!"

Nym shot up twenty feet and flew into the forest of pillars. He weaved through them at max speed, trying his best to fly through the empty spaces where the pillars couldn't appear. That trick didn't work long before two pillars would pop up on either side, then swell to three times their normal thickness. The first time it happened, Nym was so surprised that he couldn't stop in time. He rolled onto his side and flattened himself out as much as possible, barely managing to squeeze through the gap.

The next time, he used the trick he'd picked up from Brogan and swerved straight up. He overcompensated, and his feet flipped up, leaving him hanging upside down when he tried to start moving forward again, but Nym leaned into it and completed the rotation until they were behind him again, then pushed forward.

He completed his aerial acrobatics in what he felt was a respectable time. He might have done better if he was completely fresh, but the log-forest part of the course had been more about reacting to new situations, and he doubted he would have reached max speed in there anyway. The second part was where he knew his building exhaustion would hurt him.

Nym wasn't a quitter though. He looped up high and soared through the first ring, then dipped low for the second one. He almost misjudged the timing, but a quick bump down from a new air cushion placed over his back corrected his course.

The rings started moving up and down faster after the first few, but Nym managed to squeeze through the rest without any serious issues. His strength was fading at the end, but he was confident he could complete the last segment. It needed precision, not power. He could go slow and steady. With that thought in mind, he flew through the gap between two of the logs on the outside framework.

That was when he discovered he'd completely misinterpreted what the last segment of the obstacle course was. Brogan had even told him, but he was so distracted trying to figure out how to navigate it, he hadn't listened. The ropes were alive. They thrummed with power and hissed out sparks. From the outside, they looked taut, but nothing could be further from the truth.

The rope closest to him reared back like a serpent about to strike, then shot forward. Nym cried out in surprise and spun to dodge it. The rope shot past him, but its entire length undulated, and a coil smacked into Nym's arm. He cried out again, in pain this time. His arm started to go numb, and he tucked it tight against his chest to avoid being struck again.

More ropes were coming to life around him, and even the first one that he'd only semisuccessfully gotten past was curling around to attack from the back. There was no way Nym was going to make it through the rope course. He didn't know how anyone could complete such a sadistic obstacle.

Still hissing sparks, the ropes all lunged for him at once.

CHAPTER 18

Desperately, Nym conjured up a full-body cushion of air, one that was thick and solid, strong enough to stop a grown man's fist from hitting him. He could only hope it would be strong enough to protect him now. The ropes arced in from every different direction, and Nym curled into a ball, as tight as he could.

The air cushion held. At almost a foot thick all the way around his body, it deflected the ropes back as they lashed at him. Small burns appeared on Nym's exposed arms anyway as the discharged lightning coursed through the air to sting him, but it was nothing compared to direct contact with the ropes.

The arcana was draining out of his soul well faster than he could pull in more. Worse, the constant shocks were making it harder and harder to hold his conduit open. He had no choice but to retreat back out of the log framework before the magic unraveled completely. There was no way he could beat the last segment.

He shook his head in denial. There had to be a way. Brogan had chosen this course, and the old man must have thought he could do it. A more cynical part of his mind pointed out that maybe the flight master just liked watching people get shocked. Maybe nobody ever beat the rope course. Or maybe they did, but Brogan had overestimated him.

Nym retreated out of the range of most of the ropes and shifted the barrier he'd made out of air to only cover the front half of him. Whatever he decided to do, he needed to do it soon. The actual distance to the other end of the rope course was only thirty or forty feet. He could fly it in a second if the ropes weren't in the way. He hadn't considered it as an option initially because he'd misunderstood what the obstacle was.

But the ropes were really only tied on one end. They were an obstacle he could force his way through, as long as he didn't mind getting shocked. There was no way he could take that many direct hits. The ropes would cook him alive, and he'd probably pass out from the pain well before they got to that point.

On the other hand, they'd only really hurt him if he touched them. He formed a new cushion and used it to push away a rope that was snaking in to attack. It coiled around the cushion and resumed its descent, but it proved the theory at least. His magic could push the ropes away.

Strategy decided, he took a deep breath and flexed his conduit to open as wide as possible. Arcana poured into his soul well. Seconds passed by while he filled himself up and set up the spell he would need. Then, with a yell, he flung his hand forward and unleashed a blast of gale-force air. It whipped through the rope course and flung everything in its path away.

Immediately, Nym darted forward, using every last sliver of arcana for pure speed. He didn't try to dodge anything, just trusted his first spell to clear a path for him, and aimed for a gap between two logs on the far side of the house.

He wasn't nearly as fast as the supercharged blast of air, but he still made it three-quarters through before the first rope fell back into position on him. Nym forced the barrier to shift around, breaking it into free-floating pieces that slapped away incoming ropes. The first one bounced off, spitting sparks as the tip sped off in the wrong direction.

He blocked a second one coming from head-on, but then one of the ropes came at him from behind and lashed across his exposed back. Nym cried out in pain and clenched his eyes shut, but he held course. At the speed he was going, if he hit one of the framework logs instead of clearing the gap, he might not survive it.

It had not even been a second since he'd begun his desperate charge. He was practically clear when the first rope hit him. By the time the second rope struck him, he could hear the wind ripping around the log. A third one caught him on his way out, and the pain overwhelmed him. He was through the logs, but he lost control of his magic and tumbled into a high-speed free fall.

Barely conscious, he saw the world spin around him rapidly as he lost altitude. Instead of crashing straight into the earth, he gently eased down as he bled off speed until he finally landed on wobbly legs. The air current that had caught him disappeared, and he collapsed to his hands and knees.

"Nym! Are you alright?" Navarim came running up to him.

In response, Nym hurled his guts out onto the grass.

"That was the stupidest thing I've ever seen a new recruit do," Brogan told him. Then he sighed and added, "Well, no. It was pretty stupid, but you'd be amazed what some of these idiots come up with. It almost worked. I imagine if I hadn't taken so much from you with our little game of tag, you could have pulled it off."

Nym rolled over onto his back and groaned. "Think I gave myself arcana poisoning again."

"That'll make it much harder to heal you," Brogan said placidly. "Foolish child, so intent on showing off that you didn't take even a second to consider the risks. This will be a good learning experience for you. Maybe you'll think more next time you're considering something stupid for the sake of your pride."

Several mages landed nearby, having seen the spectacle from some of the other training courses. "Flight Master Brogan," one of them said, "is everything alright? Is there anything we can do to help?"

Brogan waved them off. "Get back to work. I have this under control."

"Yes, of course. My apologies, flight master."

They took off again, leaving Nym alone with the sadistic old man and the younger mage who'd gotten him into this mess. Nym looked over at Navarim and said, "I blame you."

"Me? How is this my fault?"

"You charged the course too good!"

The two older mages looked at each other and burst out laughing. "I think he'll be fine," Brogan told Navarim. "Still can't give you a flight license, but if the boy wants to come back and use the training field, he's got my permission. He's a bit reckless, but he's got enough talent to be an interesting project. With proper training, he could be almost as good as me."

Nym choked in outrage. "Almost as good? I'll show you, you sadistic old man! Just you wait until I catch my breath!"

Still laughing, Brogan flew up into the air. "Take good care of him, Mage Navarim."

Then he was gone, and Navarim was helping Nym to his feet. "Come on, let's get you back to the teleport platform. Tell you what, I'll buy you lunch, how's that sound?"

Nym gave Brogan's retreating form a glare. "Humph. I'll be back, old man."

"How'd it go?" the mage they'd left behind asked.

Navarim shrugged. "No special flying-only license like we were hoping, but he impressed Brogan, and you know that's no easy feat. Damn near killed himself doing it, but he did it. Probably would have broken his neck on the landing if Brogan hadn't caught him."

"That was him at the end?" Nym asked, remembering the air currents that had bled off his momentum and deposited him safely on the ground.

"Well of course. He said he'd spot you. He wasn't going to let you fall to your death when you ran yourself completely dry of arcana."

The two older mages got talking about the adventure on the airfield, and Nym excused himself to a nearby chair to sit down. He missed most of the conversation due to the amount of pain he was in, both from being shocked repeatedly and from the mild case of arcana poisoning he'd given himself. He must have dozed off, because when Navarim put a hand on his shoulder, he jerked in surprise.

"Easy there," the mage told him. "Come on, I'm off for the day, and I did say I'd buy you lunch to make up for putting you through Brogan's torture chamber."

Navarim led Nym to a nearby tavern that was significantly classier than the Trough and Saddle. He ordered food for the two of them and sat down at an empty table. "So you're a curious fellow. I'm sure you'll get sick of hearing this soon if you haven't already, but you're too young to be using second-circle magic. How'd that happen?"

Nym shrugged. "Started casting first-circle magic, and things kind of progressed from there. I'm still figuring it all out. I've been trying to hold two conduits at once so I can cast a first- and second-circle spell at the same time. No luck so far. Every time I try, I just end up feeling sick because I can't figure out how to keep the arcana separate in my soul well."

"Wait, you already figured out how to hold multiple conduits open?" Navarim asked. He gave a low whistle. "That is impressive. You're a monster, Nym."

Nym's cheeks flushed. "Thanks. I didn't do anything special though. It was just kind of the same as opening one conduit, but . . . doing it again."

"It takes a lot of willpower and concentration to maintain two of them though. You are going to kick all sorts of ass when you're old enough to go to the Academy. And I'll be able to say I met you way back when before you were famous."

Nym sighed. "Not any time soon, I think. Unless you know a way I can make a lot of money in a hurry?"

Navarim laughed. "Don't we all wish we did? I can't help you too much with that."

Nym thought about that harvest of skywort blooms hidden behind the waterfall, just waiting for him to come clean them up. He sighed. "I think I'm poor by anyone's standards. I was going to be supplying an alchemist on the north side of town, but the deal kind of fell through. Someone else interfered. Are there other alchemists who might need fresh ingredients?"

"Here? Not really. I didn't even know we had one to begin with. Zoskan is such a small town, there's not a lot here. If you were to go to Abilanth, there'd be a much better market. All sorts of magical research goes on there, and they produce tons of unique stuff thanks to all the magic going on. I'm sure you'd have an easier time there. Zoskan is a bland place by comparison."

"I don't even know where Abilanth is."

"Well, if you've got two crests, it's on the other end of the public teleport platform in the guildhall. Otherwise your best bet would be to attach yourself to a caravan traveling east. Keep doing that at each town you come to and you'll probably get there inside a year, unless things go horrifically wrong."

Nym's heart sank at the news. Even assuming he just flew, he was looking at months and months of travel. And as far as teleporting there went, he didn't even know what a crest was! There were too many types of money. Between wedges, shims, and now shields and crests, things were too confusing. Nobody in Palmara used anything but wedges.

They ate their food in silence, and Nym thanked him for the meal after. Navarim nodded and told him to come by any time in the mornings and he'd take Nym over to the airfields for an hour or two. Nym left the tavern, lost in his thoughts. He needed to find a good source of money. There were things he wanted to buy!

CHAPTER 19

Nym spent the rest of his money on a second night at the Trough and Saddle. In the morning, he walked over to Cern's shop to wait for the team he was supposed to go reagent hunting with to show up. The alchemist just shoved him in a corner and said he didn't have time to deal with Nym.

Nym might have been offended by the brush-off, except right at that moment, something in the back room let out a large boom that rattled the glasswork on display. Cern ran back off with a cry of dismay, and smoke started filling the shop.

"Cern, do you need help?"

"It's fine! Everything is fine! Oh damn it, no, don't do—where did I put, aha! Just . . . need . . . oh no!"

There was a second boom, even louder. Nym lunged toward a rack that had tipped over and caught it before it hit the floor, then formed six air cushions to catch additional things. He set them down gently and dismissed the magic, hoping no one saw it. It was probably fine. He'd only be fined if he got caught, and even then, he could probably get Cern to pay it since he'd just saved him probably a lot of money.

The smoke was coming out thicker now, and the alchemist retreated out of his back room with a soot-covered face and singed eyebrows. Flames licked at the bottom of his beard, which he was furiously patting to try to put them out. Nym looked around to make sure the smoke hadn't drawn anybody's attention, then pulled some water out of the skin he'd filled for his reagent-hunting trip and splashed it on Cern.

"Eh? Oh, erm, thanks." The alchemist stepped over to a mirror on the wall and studied his reflection. With a heavy sigh, he said, "Six months without an explosion. It was coming in so nicely too."

"What happened?" Nym asked.

"Complicated, but the short version is a bad thermal regulator wasn't holding the enchantment anymore, and I didn't realize soon enough. I thought I could compensate and save the batch." He gestured to his burnt beard. "Obviously I was mistaken."

"What in God's name happened in here?" a new voice asked from the front door.

A tall man stood there, hands on his hips. He was exceedingly handsome, with short blond hair and a muscular, athletic build. A sword was strapped across his back, long enough that the end came down to his knees and the tip of the hilt stuck up over the top of his head. He had a pack slung over one shoulder.

"Oh, hello, Therm. There was an incident. I, uh . . . I had today's list, but it's . . . gone."

Therm raised an eyebrow and shot a pointed look at the back room door, which still had smoke coming out from it. "Is everyone safe?"

"Of course we're safe! What kind of alchemist do you think I am?"

Therm gestured toward the door. Cern looked at it, then back to Therm. He scowled. "Nobody's perfect! Anyway, I'll have a new list for you in a few minutes. In the meantime, meet Nym. He's going to go with your group today."

"What? Did you take on an apprentice? He's a bit young, don't you think?

"No, no. Nym is a mage. He's going to help you gather materials."

Therm looked doubtful. He gave Nym a once-over and said in that patronizing tone adults sometimes used on him that he found infuriating, "I guess you'll be with me then. I'll show you what we're looking for and keep you safe."

Nym understood that he was a kid. He knew adults always thought they knew better, but he was getting really tired of being looked down on and underestimated just because he wasn't as old as them. "Cern, are you sure this is necessary? I could just go by myself, and we won't tell Babkin."

The alchemist shuddered and shook his head. "Not a chance am I crossing Babkin after I gave my word. It's Therm's group or nothing. If you don't go with them, I won't buy anything you bring back."

If anything, Therm looked more confused. "What is going on here?" he asked. "What's that old battle-axe got to do with this kid?"

"Nym needed a place to stay, so I sent him to that inn Babkin started when he 'retired,' and then the next thing I know, I've got them both banging on my door before the sun was even up, and he's chewing me out for letting Nym go into the woods on his own to harvest. So this was the compromise. I promise you, he's not going to slow you down. If anything, you're slowing him down."

"That so?" Therm was looking at Nym with new respect. He thought about it for a second and nodded. "Okay, if Babkin thinks you're good to harvest as long as it's with a group, that's good enough for me."

"Excellent. Give me just a minute to find a pen that hasn't been disintegrated and I'll get you a new list. I'm going to have to change up what I need a bit. How do you feel about doing a second run this week? I won't know how much stock I just lost until I get a chance to start cleaning up."

"I'll run it by the group. I think Aliat is leaving town tomorrow, but as far as I know, it should be fine for everyone else."

"Fantastic! I'll have a second list for you when you get back tonight."

Soon enough, Therm had a list in his hand and Nym was leaving with him. "Alright, so normally we just spread out and hit the spots where we know stuff is at. How familiar are you with these plants?" he asked.

Nym shook his head. "I know a few of them. I am a mage, I guess, so I was kind of cheating by flying around to collect things. But then Babkin said it was too dangerous for me to go alone, and here we are."

"You can fly?" Therm brightened. "Oh, this is going to be a very profitable day for everyone. We'll show you all the best places to find stuff, and you can get all the stuff that's not worth the effort to climb up and get normally. Come, let's go meet the rest of the group and we'll get started."

There were five of them, including Therm. Aliat and Rosunde were women in their early twenties, the same age as Therm. Both were dressed in a similar practical manner, though without the giant sword that Therm sported. The other two were men, one in his thirties and the last one at least fifty. Their names were Kalrow and Dumont.

Each had a specialty when it came to collecting, and they traveled together for safety while dividing the forest up. Aliat was an expert diver and was able to harvest along the river and underwater, for example, while Kalrow focused heavily on digging things up. Nym was paired with Dumont though, as the old man had the best eyes and was the group's spotter.

The group chatted easily with one another. There were gasps from some and laughter from others as Therm described the state of Cern's shop when he'd arrived, and the whole group clamored for a demonstration when they found out Nym could fly. They waited until they were past the walls, and then he flew a few laps around them to the applause of Rosunde and Kalrow.

"I always wanted to be a mage," Rosunde told him. "I'm terrible at it though. I can barely forge a conduit to the first layer, and the mage who examined me said my soul well is the smallest he'd ever seen. I can't extend my basic telekinesis spell more than a foot past my hand."

She winked and brandished a knife out of nowhere though. "Not to say that I don't have some handy tricks."

"Me too," Nym told her, and she floated up into the air.

Rosunde squeaked in surprise, then flapped her arms around a bit, which completely failed to move her since Nym just altered the air cushions around her movements. "Okay, that's pretty amazing. How high can I go?"

Nym shrugged. "High enough to reach the tops of the trees if we need to."

He'd realized yesterday that he'd only been supporting himself with the magically controlled air, but that was just him being narrow-minded. Brogan had wrapped him in air to save him at the end. It was obviously possible. He just hadn't thought to try. It turned out it was very easy to move another person with air, and they were considerably more durable than skywort bloom.

"Save some for the forest," Therm said. "Don't want you running out of magic halfway through the day."

Rosunde protested, but Nym brought her back to the ground. "Oh, fine," she said, sticking her tongue out at the back of Therm's head. "We'll go flying later, okay?"

"Sure! Flying is lots of fun."

They reached the woods and split up, though they never got more than a few hundred feet away from one another. Therm and Kalrow anchored the group, with one or the other always keeping an eye out for trouble.

Dumont pointed out various plants for Nym to get, and occasionally asked to be lifted up to harvest the more delicate specimens himself. They quickly filled a pack and dropped it off with Therm to grab a fresh one.

"It feels like we're cheating," the old man told Nym. "Easiest I've ever filled a bag. Cern's not going to have enough to pay us when we get back."

The boy grinned at him. "I hope so. I wanted to get a coat for flying. It gets kind of cold when you're moving really fast. Maybe some shoes too if I have extra money."

The old man's expression flickered for a second, but he hid it before Nym could ask what was wrong. "Yeah, that sounds good. I think I know a good shop that can make something in your size too. Remind me about it when we get back and I'll point it out to you."

"Thanks! I'll remember."

It was a thoroughly uneventful afternoon. The worst Nym saw was a tree snake that seemed just as surprised to see him as he was to run into it. He was gone before it could do anything. By the time late afternoon came around, they had nine full packs. Nym held the tenth one, and it was already half-full. He finished scraping a fuzzy blue moss out of a crevice about sixty feet off the ground and deposited it into the pack, then flew back to the group when he heard Therm calling his name.

"Alright team, this has been a fantastic run. I'm going to put this haul at two shields six for each of us, and that's a six-way split instead of our usual five. Nym, you are welcome to come back anytime. Don't forget, Cern wants a double order, so I'm going to be back out here in two days for another run."

The group let out a general cheer when Therm announced his estimated payout for their haul. They started back, two bags to a person. "What about me?" Nym asked. "Shouldn't I carry one?"

"Don't even worry about it. You've done more than enough today."

"It's not a problem, really. I need the practice anyway." Six bags floated up into the air around the group.

"Okay guys, it's official. I vote Nym replaces Therm as the new leader. He's too useful to let him go anywhere else," Rosunde announced.

"Hey now!"

The whole group trouped back home amid laughter, a trail of bags drifting through the air behind them. Nym smiled and joked and laughed with them. It was another good day for him. He could get used to that.

CHAPTER 20

I t took a day to get a coat in his size made, but Nym was happy with the results. He decided to hold off on the shoes until the group made their second run for supplies and used the rest of the money to pay ahead for his room at the Trough and Saddle. He debated heavily on it, but in the end, it wasn't much cheaper to buy meals without the room, and he liked having a bed to sleep in. He'd gotten used to a warm bath too.

He visited the guildhall in the morning, and Navarim took him to the airfield to practice. He didn't stick around since Brogan said he could send Nym back through the teleporter. The old man worked Nym until he was ready to pass out, sticking him with a group of kids five or six years older than him and using him as a prod to motivate them.

"Look at this! This boy is barely half your age and he's outflying every single one of you!"

Nym won the races against them. He beat their times in the obstacle course. He emerged victorious when they played a game where everyone stood on a pole and they all tried to knock one another off with concentrated gusts of wind. At first, it was a rush, but it didn't take long to notice the glares the mages were giving him.

Brogan was not helping matters. In fact, he was actively making it worse as he rubbed the class's collective noses in it each time they were beaten by Nym. The glares got less and less subtle every time Nym won. He considered throwing a few games on purpose, but he hadn't held back at all, and the gap in abilities was obvious. No one would believe if he all of a sudden cut his maximum speed by half, which was what he'd need to do to even give them a chance.

After an hour, Brogan sent the whole class to break and dragged Nym off to the side for a talk. "I'm going to be honest with you, I figured you'd win the first one or two and then be too tired," he confessed. "Things have gotten kind of ugly now, so I wanted to apologize. Nothing left to do but ride it to the end, but I'll keep a close eye on you. No one is going to take it out on you."

Nym wasn't sure what to say to that. In hindsight, of course Brogan had realized things were getting out of hand, but his decision to double down on it instead of putting an early end to it baffled Nym. "Why did you do it?" he asked.

"At first, to motivate them. This class is lazy. Nothing new there. Most all classes are lazy, and teenagers are easy to provoke into working harder. But then you just kept going, and going. You didn't have this kind of stamina a few days ago. I wanted to see how far you could push before you gave out. But you beat them all! The entire class is wiped, and you're good to do another lap."

"Probably because I didn't play tag with you again," Nym told him.

Brogan shrugged. "My miscalculation, either way. Son, I understand that you are . . . not financially stable. When you have the opportunity, you should have the mage guild perform an aptitude test. I say this in the best possible way; you are not normal. You're too advanced for your age by every metric I can casually measure. The only category you even approach standardization in is your knowledge base, and even then, you've figured out stuff in your narrow band of interest that's too advanced for your level of development."

There were a few words in Brogan's speech that Nym was guessing at the meaning of, but he thought he had the gist of it. He only had a single silver shield left after paying for his new coat and a week's stay at the Trough and Saddle. He needed to save it for shoes and maybe a second set of clothes, or if things got desperate, food. So really what it came down to was one simple thing. "How much will it cost me, and is it really necessary?"

"Ask Mage Navarim when you get back. I took that test a hundred thirty years ago, and I didn't know what it cost then either. As for necessary, it is if you want to go to the Academy. I think you should. You're obviously talented and smart. I know money is an issue for you, but I'm sure you'll find a way."

"Maybe if you're offering to pay for it," Nym said.

Brogan grunted. "Not on my salary," was all he said.

The conversation died off as they watched the class he was teaching recover their breath. Finally, Brogan said, "Let's get you back to town. Zoskan, wasn't it? Think about what I said. If you can find a way to make it work, I guarantee it'll be worth it. Abilanth has one of the best schools in the world."

Navarim was happy to answer questions, but once Nym found out it would cost him five shields, he lost interest. Every service the mage guild offered was so expensive. He briefly wondered how much it would have cost him to use the teleportation platforms to go to and from the airfield. He decided not to ask, lest Navarim mention repaying that expense.

The only thing to do was keep gathering things from the forest for Cern. The alchemist was his only real source of revenue, and Nym used the second outing to purchase a second set of clothes and shoes. He was left with four shield three, as they said, or four shields and three shims. It was almost enough to take that licensing exam so he could fly in town, and Nym considered pushing for it.

Navarim warned him off. There were many other subjects he listed off that Nym had never even heard of, and there was no way he could pass the entire exam. It wasn't designed for just one topic, but it was an all-or-nothing grade. Either he passed everything, or he got nothing except a wasted five shields.

He felt rich with the weight of the silver and copper in the pocket of his new pants, but Nym was afraid to spend it. The second trip into the forest had seen them hitting new spots, deeper in, trying to find places that they hadn't already cleaned out. There was a reason they normally only made one trip every other week, and while having Nym along expanded what they could reach, it didn't completely negate the fact that stuff needed time to grow back.

With that thought in mind, Nym allocated one shield to covering a second week's stay until the group's next trip. Since he still had some money left, he had Navarim point him to a bookstore that sold texts for apprentice mages, but the older mage's warnings about the prices proved all too true. Even the cheapest of beginner primers would completely drain all Nym's reserves. Regretfully, he left without a purchase. The shopkeeper and the guard both gave him suspicious looks the entire time he was in the store.

Stymied by a lack of funds and out of ideas, Nym simply left town to practice flying on his own. The forest wasn't as good an obstacle course as the airfield, but he didn't need anyone's help to get there, and no one was pushing him to compete against the other students. He took his own pack with him and just wove around, stopping occasionally to scoop up some of the things he recognized from Cern's list. Maybe he could slip them in with the next haul, or find someone else to buy them.

He flew back to the city when the sun started going down. By now, the gate guards on every shift knew him by sight, and nobody was giving him a hard time about getting in and out. He paused when he saw Toren was on duty today. "Hey, Toren, got a question for you."

"What's up, Nym?"

"I was just wondering, do you know if anyone besides Cern needs anything from the forest? I kind of have more than I can sell to just him."

"Wait, you're going into the forest?" Toren asked. "By yourself? I knew you went a few times with Therm's group, but that's incredibly dangerous to go in on your own."

Nym shrugged. "I haven't had any problems yet. So . . . bagful of mushrooms and flowers and moss used by an alchemist. Any ideas?"

Toren just shook his head. "Cern's the only alchemist in the city, as far as I know. Though some healers do also use herbs from the forest. I'm not sure they'd want anything you have today, but you could try a few of the clinics set up around town."

"Thanks, I'll do that," Nym told him. He went into town and headed straight for the closest clinic. Toren was right though, there wasn't a lot of overlap between the kinds of things Cern wanted and the kinds of things a healer wanted. Moreover, the healers all seemed to align with Babkin's way of thinking and refused to tell him anything they collected from the forest so that he would not have a reason to go there.

It was annoying. He'd spent three days living in it, had gone back in half a dozen times now for various reasons, and he was fine. Yes, there had been one close call with some spiders, but it wasn't even that close. He'd gotten away easily and hadn't been hurt. It wouldn't even have been an issue except he'd needed to sleep, and they'd gotten the drop on him. It wasn't like he slept there anymore.

Nym just knew if he was older, this wouldn't have been a problem. The struggle to get adults to take him seriously was never-ending. In some ways, being a child probably helped, as it seemed like a few adults were more inclined to give him some leeway or a good deal, but it wasn't worth the aggravation of them constantly thinking they knew best and trying to tell him what to do.

He walked into Cern's shop, only to find it half-dismantled. "What happened?" he asked the alchemist, who was working with two mages Nym had seen around the guildhall recently.

"That little mishap a few days ago reminded me that I forgot to renew the antishatter wards on the baseboards. It's such a huge pain to do that I kept putting it off. I was just lucky that nothing broke the other day, though quite a few things ended up on the floor." Cern gave Nym a shrewd look. "I guess I owe someone a thank-you for that. Must be the glassblower."

Cern nodded his head toward the two mages who were busy at work. Nym got the message. Cern knew he'd used magic to catch everything and was grateful for the help but wasn't going to announce in front of two mages from the guild that Nym was unlicensed and using magic in town. "Uh, right, yes. Anyway, why are you tearing the place apart?"

"Some of the potions and elixirs react badly to having wards cast near them. It's easier to just clear the whole space for them to work, then put it all back when the wards have settled."

"That sounds expensive," Nym remarked. "Is it really cheaper than just occasionally dropping something?"

Cern snorted. "If it were just me, you'd be right. That's one of the reasons I don't have them in my labs. But the . . . ugh . . . customers can paw at them here. Half of these vials are display only. Just colored water and if someone wants to buy one, I spin them a story about it being old but I have a fresh batch in the back. And still, just the cost of the glass and the few real brews out here, no, it's cheaper to keep the antishatter wards working on the floor."

He noticed the pack Nym was carrying and gave it a curious look. "What do you have there?"

Nym handed it over, and Cern flipped open the top to reveal the harvest. Slowly, he poked through it. "Nym, why do you have this?" he asked. He did not look pleased.

CHAPTER 21

was practicing and just picked up a few things here and there as I saw them."

"You were practicing. In the woods. By yourself?"

Nym shrugged. "I needed a place with things to dodge around."

"Are you trying to get Babkin to kill me?" Cern asked.

"You don't have to buy them. I just thought you might be interested."

Cern handed him the pack. "You know I can't. This was not the deal we had."

Nym took it back and tried to pretend he didn't care. "No problem. I'll just go dump these into the garbage then."

The alchemist's eye twitched. He looked at the bag with undisguised longing, but then shook his head. "Nice try. The answer is still no. And stop going into the forest by yourself!"

"Nope," Nym said. He shouldered the pack and let himself out. "See you later, Cern."

As the door swung closed behind him, he heard the sound of the two mages laughing over Cern's cussing.

Nym went by the guildhall next, but Navarim was already gone for the day. He left the contents with the mage on duty and explained it was a gift to them to be used for their alchemy classes, as he had no other use for the supplies and they wouldn't stay good forever. The mage was confused, but politely thanked Nym and cleared them away.

Nym returned to the Trough and Saddle for dinner and retreated to his room. By his figuring, he could scrape together enough for the license exam, but he didn't have a prayer of passing it. Getting the funds to afford a teleport to Abilanth was possibly doable, but only if he started sleeping outdoors and scrounging for food again. Too much of his annoyingly limited income was going to room and board.

He was getting a decent discount thanks to his willingness to help Shary in the kitchen, though that usually amounted to nothing more than washing dishes. It was probably more than the job was worth, but that didn't make Nym feel better. If he could have gone into the forest for supplies every day instead of once every other week, he could easily have afforded to buy books on magic and save up for tuition at the Academy. Babkin had killed that dream in its infancy.

He suddenly found he hated staying at the Trough and Saddle, but he'd already paid up through to the end of next week. Once that was done though, he was going to find somewhere else to sleep. In fact, opportunities in Zoskan seemed to be drying up completely. It was too close to Palmara too. Nym decided his best move was to scrape together two crests and get a teleport to Abilanth.

At the rate he was going, it'd be another two months at least. He'd encountered plenty of adults sympathetic to his struggles, but none willing to help him out by offering some work besides Cern. And Cern was too afraid of Babkin to do any more than he already had. Nym needed to figure out something else. He resolved to head back to the guildhall in the morning and ask Navarim if he had any ideas.

Nym didn't sleep well that night. He had too much on his mind and was impatient to get started on it. In the morning, he helped Shary with breakfast and wolfed down his plate, but before he could get out the door, Babkin's shadow fell over him. Nym didn't even have to turn around to confirm, he had such a unique breadth to his shoulders and was the only one who liked to sneak up on people without saying anything.

"What?" Nym asked, turning around from cleaning his plate.

"Please see me in my office," Babkin said. He turned and walked to the back of the inn.

It was uncanny how a man so big could move so silently. There was definitely more to him than being a simple innkeeper, and Nym had picked up enough hints to know that nobody wanted to cross the man. He just didn't know why. He'd already made up his mind to leave though, so that was a mystery that could remain unsolved.

For the next week or so, he still had to deal with Babkin. As satisfying as it would be to just walk back out of the inn and ignore the innkeeper's request, Nym dried his hands off and trudged over to the office. Babkin was waiting for him, pipe clamped between his teeth and hands clasped behind his back. He was staring out the window and didn't turn around as Nym opened the door.

Neither of them said anything. The only sound was the background noise of Shary working in the kitchen. Silence stretched out between them, Nym's face getting stormier with each passing second. Finally, Babkin asked, "Why are you in such a hurry to grow up?"

Nym wasn't really sure what he meant by that question. He opened his mouth to retort, thought better of it, and took a second to really think. Babkin must have taken his silence as an answer in and of itself because he continued. "Cern came to see me last night. You went back into the forest on your own. I thought I'd made it clear that you were not to venture into that place alone. It is too dangerous."

That did it. "You're not in charge of me," Nym said. "What I do is my business."

Babkin finally turned around to look at Nym. "I see. I have tried to help you as best I can, Nym. 'He is a child,' I say to myself. 'He does not know any better.' You have no idea what kind of threats you dance around in your ignorance, one misstep from disaster. I think to myself, 'If I can remove his reason for going into the forest, he will not go.' That was my mistake. I tried to use an adult's logic to direct a child's whims away from danger."

"No one asked you to do that. I don't want your help. If controlling what I can and can't do is the price to stay here, then give me back the shims I already paid in advance. I'll go find somewhere else to sleep."

Babkin fished the money out of a purse on his desk and set it out for Nym. When the boy reached out to scoop it up, he said, "Spend it wisely. Cern will no longer buy anything from you, and you are not welcome in Therm's harvesting group. This money will have to last you for a while, until you can find some safer way to support yourself. You are correct. I cannot stop you from taking your own life in your hands in that forest. I can only remove as many incentives as possible and hope it convinces you to stop behaving so foolishly."

Nym scooped the money up and dropped his room key in its place. "I hope I never have to deal with someone like you 'helping' me again."

The burly innkeeper sighed around his pipe and sank heavily into his chair. "Please leave the Trough and Saddle, as you are no longer a patron of this inn. If you wish to rent a room in the future, you will be welcomed back on the condition that you do not enter the forest again."

Nym was in a foul mood. A quick trip to Cern's confirmed that his only source of income had completely dried up. The alchemist was apologetic, but adamant that he would no longer do business with Nym. Nym stomped out, spitting out every foul word he'd ever heard in one long, unintelligible string of sounds.

Babkin had cut off all his options. It was time to move on. Either Navarim would have a way for him to make some money, or he'd follow the road on to the next town. He still had an hour or two to kill before the guildhall opened, but some of the stalls were open early enough that he could stock up on food. He was going to need that whether he stayed or went, so he filled his pack with some long-lasting staples.

After negotiating a nice cloak to be rolled up in his pack and used as a blanket, since he would now be sleeping outdoors again, Nym headed over to the guildhall. When he got there, there was already a crowd of people standing at the desk. He knew it wasn't that big of a deal to wait a few minutes, but it was just one more annoyance on top of an already awful day.

He sat down in an empty chair in the corner and resigned himself to a wait. At least they all seemed to be one group, so whatever they were doing, it would hopefully not force him to sit there for too long. The way the day was going, they'd likely be tying up the front desk for an hour, at least.

Nym didn't pay much attention to what was going on until he heard Navarim say, "It's five crests to send three people to Abilanth. With all this luggage, it's six."

That was semirelevant to Nym's interests, so he perked up and started studying the group. That was when he realized he knew almost everyone in it. There was the guard captain from Palmara who'd shown up at Ciana's house at the front, talking to Navarim. Next to him was Amos and that other boy who'd always been following him around. Two more of the local Palmara guard he knew by sight but not name were there too, as well as some people who had the same color hair and similar clothes. Presumably they were Amos's family.

They didn't even balk at the price tag. Amos, his friend, and one of the adults from his family separated from the rest of the group, and Navarim led them off to the teleport platform. Nym gritted his teeth in annoyance and jealously. That little shit who'd bullied him was going to the Academy to learn magic, and Nym was stuck in Zoskan, unable to even afford transport to Abilanth.

The injustice of it rankled, and he cursed Babkin yet again for his interference. If he had stayed out of it, Nym would have had more than enough to buy a teleport already. He was so focused on how unfair it all was, he stopped paying attention to anything else around him. That lasted until the guard captain was standing in front of him.

"Aren't you . . . Ciana's boy? The one she saved?" the man asked.

Internally, Nym panicked. But he did his best to put on a confused expression and said, "Sorry, I don't know what you're talking about."

Now that their attention was drawn to him though, the rest of the group was looking him over. "Yeah, I think that is him. You're right, captain," one of the guards said.

"Yup. She's been worried sick about him."

"You have me confused for someone else," Nym insisted. He stood up and walked to the door, acting confident enough that nobody moved to stop him.

"Why are you leaving?" one of Amos's family members asked. "Didn't you need assistance from the mage guild? Isn't that why you're here?"

"I just remembered I have an errand to run," Nym lied.

The captain grabbed hold of his arm. "Hold on there. I remember now. You're definitely Ciana's boy. What was your name again? Nam? Nin?"

Nym jerked away from him. "Don't touch me!"

He darted for the door, and the sudden movement startled all the guards. Rather than shy back though, the captain darted forward and got hold of Nym again. "Hold up there. We just want to ask you a few questions. You'll need to come with us."

"I said don't touch me!" Nym yelled. He pulled arcana from the second layer and flung out a blast of air that knocked the captain off his feet. Before anyone could do anything else, he was out the door and straight up past the roof of the guildhall.

CHAPTER 22

Nym touched down on the roof of the guildhall and crouched low. He peered over the edge and watched the guardsmen from Palmara pour out the door and spread out to look for him. None of them looked up, but he wasn't willing to wait around for them to think to. The real question was how he was going to get out of Zoskan. The fastest and most direct way would be to fly straight over the wall and not look back.

He already had supplies for the road and had gotten back the rest of his money from Babkin, so Nym was, through fortuitous coincidence, as prepared as he possibly could be to flee. The only problem was that he didn't know where to go. It wasn't safe to talk to Navarim now, and he didn't know if he'd be able to return to Zoskan once he left. The ultimate goal of getting to Abilanth seemed less and less likely.

Nym shook his head. He'd figure things out later. His immediate problem was getting away from the group from Palmara. He could do that. It was as simple as flying over the guildhall and landing on the street behind it. Then he just walked away and left town through the nearest gate. Though it was still early, the guards didn't stop him. Apparently, word hadn't spread, or if it had, the Zoskan guards weren't interested in helping detain him for questioning.

Once he was far enough away, he took to the sky and flew off into the woods. It was unlikely anyone knew where he was or was quick enough to follow him even if they did. He had time to consider his options, though there were distressingly few left to him.

The first and simplest was to just keep going. He could cut through the forest for a day or two, find the road again, follow it to the next town, and start over. That plan had a number of drawbacks, like the fact that he didn't even know where next town was, and he didn't like the idea of foraging for food and water again. He also wasn't keen to be sleeping in the forest, not after the incident with the spiders, but he'd already resigned himself to sleeping outside again even before he'd run into the guards.

The second idea he had was to lie low for a few days, maybe even a week or two. He'd run out of food eventually and have to start foraging or risk a trip back into Zoskan, but it gave him time to see if the Palmara guards would hang around looking for him or give up and go home. If they did, there was a possibility this was all just a minor distraction and he could resume living his life once they left. That would be ideal, as he still wanted access to the airfield and to eventually use the teleportation platform in the guildhall.

He had other—worse—ideas like going on the offensive, lifting men up with his magic and dropping them from great heights. That idea made him a bit queasy, and he immediately wrote it off. In the end, he decided to treat the whole thing as an extended camping trip. He'd stay out for as long as he could, and then use the gate guards to judge if it was safe to go back. If they tried to stop him or capture him, Nym would just fly away, come back at night, and fly over the wall so he could resupply before he hit the road for good.

Decision made, he flew deeper into the forest to find a good campsite. It would ideally be far enough away from the edge of the woods to avoid casual detection and be open to the sky so he couldn't be trapped. A source of nearby fresh water would be necessary too. That sounded simple enough to find.

Humming to himself, Nym started exploring. Everything was going to be just fine.

By the second day, he'd decided he missed hot meals more than anything else, although a comfortable bed was a close second. The cloak was a good purchase, and he silently congratulated himself for buying it. There had been no other incidents with things like giant spiders coming up on him in the middle of the night, which was his biggest concern.

He spent his days practicing his magic. Nym felt he'd gotten pretty good at air magic, but his skills with water magic had lagged behind, and his earth and fire abilities were practically nonexistent. If he ever wanted a solution to a problem that didn't involve running away, he needed to fix that. He didn't have much of a lesson plan beyond just figuring it out as he went.

Water wasn't too hard to practice. It was easier to find a stream to work at so he'd have an abundant source of it, but then it was just a matter of creating some drills to improve his coordination, finesse, and gross power. Water was heavy, and moving a little bit at a time was easy, but even using second-layer arcana, he had trouble controlling large volumes at once.

Still, Nym felt like he was making progress. He was able to sling water around to slap against trees with resounding cracks that shattered bark and branches, if not with as much accuracy as he would like. He could see himself getting visibly better the more he practiced. It was just a matter of time and effort to catch up to his abilities with air.

Earth, on the other hand, was frustrating. The problem was that unlike air and water, it wasn't flexible. He could rip a large chunk of dirt out of the ground and fling it around, but it felt like there should have been so much more he could do. Forcing it into a shape like he did with air and water was impossible. Even moving it around was exhausting.

Nym felt like he was doing something fundamentally wrong when it came to terrakinesis. What should probably have been his strongest defensive element barely functioned at all for him. He could see the shape of his magic reaching out to it, rearranging it and bending it to his will, but it was a fight. The earth didn't work with him like air did. Using a light touch resulted in nothing happening.

In the end, Nym decided to ignore it for now. He could see better gains working on literally anything else, and there was plenty of work to do on his hydrokinesis spell. That left only one other basic element: fire. The less said about that, the better. Nym could generate enough of a spark to light his campfire if he was careful about shredding his tinder as small as possible. If moving earth was like pushing against a wall, fire was like fighting a whole swarm of insects. It was impossible to keep it corralled and under control.

They went on his list of things to get help on, hopefully in the form of an instructor, but a few good books on the subject would be minimally acceptable. Once again, he cursed Babkin for cutting away his ability to generate money. There weren't a ton of resources to be had in Zoskan, but he hadn't been able to get even a single book from the bookstore. Brogan was as close as he'd gotten to hiring a tutor, and the old man didn't so much teach him as allow him to observe what others were doing and copy it, then build on it.

The best thing that had come from his time on the airfield was a throwaway comment he'd overheard one of the student mages make. Nym hadn't recognized its importance when he'd heard it, but now that he had days on end with no other distractions, he found himself going through everything looking for clues.

The student had been complaining that he was having trouble keeping his intent stable to filter his arcana. It was a foreign concept for Nym, that apparently some mages had to filter natural arcana to better align with the spell they wanted to create. He'd never had that problem, so he'd dismissed it from his mind and focused on what he was doing.

It took him days to realize he'd been handed the key to his problem. For weeks he'd been trying to figure out how to pull arcana from two layers at the same time without them mixing, with no success. Once he realized that he could create a filter of intent over one of the conduits to alter the arcana coming through, he remembered some of Cern's mixtures. The liquids in the jars were clearly different, and just as clearly holding themselves separate, layered on top of one another without ever combining.

Nym felt like an idiot for not realizing it sooner. It took some tinkering to figure out how to apply that filter of intent, but once he did, everything slid into place. He stood there in the middle of the forest, laughing like a madman, as he held first- and second-layer arcana in his soul well, one layered on top of the other, and they stayed that way.

Still laughing, he floated up into the air and used telekinesis to pluck a leaf off a tree twenty feet away. It sped across the clearing to land, undamaged, in his open hand. "It was so simple," he said out loud. "How did I not figure this out immediately?"

Then his soul well went dry, and he fell on his butt. His conduits were both significantly smaller than either one would be on its own, and he couldn't pull in arcana fast enough to sustain his flight spell. Nym shook his head and stood back up. His tailbone smarted, but he was still in a good mood.

He could finally harvest that patch of skywort bloom hidden behind the waterfall, but he no longer had anyone to sell it to. It was somewhat disappointing to think of how much money was just sitting there. He considered trying to cut a deal with someone in Therm's group to use them as a middleman. Rosunde or Dumont would probably be the most amicable to the idea.

It would be another week before they were out again, and he didn't want the plants going bad, so he'd hold off on grabbing them. Also, he didn't have a spare pack, and his current one was holding what was left of his food and his rolled-up cloak. But those were minor issues because he had finally succeeded in his goal!

He played with intent filtering and managed a marginal increase to his terrakinesis, but not enough that he judged it would be useful as anything other than a novelty. True pyrokinesis remained out of his reach, for now. But Nym wasn't worried. He'd added a new tool to his kit, and it was just a matter of practicing with it.

He had two new goals: increase the pull of his conduit to maintain indefinite flight while pulling from two layers at once, and brush up on the first-circle spells he'd worked out on his own but had fallen to disuse since flying was so much better, and more fun. Now he could do both, and he would.

It rained that night. Nym stretched himself to his limits using his magic to create a barrier to keep himself dry and his fire lit, which worked for about an hour. It was fascinating to watch the raindrops splatter against an invisible shell while it lasted, but the smoke from the campfire quickly filled up the sphere of hardened air. He tried to adjust it to add vents, which kind of worked, but he still found himself getting dizzy and lost his concentration.

Nym was drenched from rainwater before he managed to focus and build a new shelter. Instead of a full shell, he created a simple lean-to that protected him just as well from the rain but used a quarter of the arcana. That worked for a while, until Nym fell asleep and the spell unraveled. He was quickly woken up by a blast of cold water on his face while his campfire hissed and sputtered.

It was a long, wet, cold, miserable night. When it finally stopped raining the next morning, he was exhausted from holding the spell and not being able to sleep. Camping sucked.

CHAPTER 23

It took five days for Nym to run out of food. He supplemented what he'd brought with him by foraging, but that only took him so far. Also, a diet rich in berries had its own drawbacks, digestionally speaking. The ability to manipulate water to clean himself up was a lifesaver. He resolved never to put himself through that again.

Early on the sixth day, he returned to Zoskan. Nym debated going through his usual gate where he was well-known or circling around town to try one where they might not recognize him. Working under the assumption that he'd be able to escape either way, he decided that he would better recognize if someone was acting weird if he was talking to the gate guards he knew.

He approached the gate on foot, his soul well brimming with arcana and ready to shoot thirty feet straight up, well out of their reach. And then they just waved him through with barely more than a casual greeting and an offhand comment about him being out early today. Nym walked through practically in a daze, and more than a bit annoyed.

He'd spent the better part of a week living in the woods, wondering every night if he was going to wake up with something trying to take a bite out of him, and nobody even cared! He could have come back at any time. They probably didn't even look for him for more than an hour before they gave up. It had all been for nothing!

At least he'd had the time to internalize some new concepts and advance his magic, but that wasn't something he'd needed to go out into the woods to do. Grumbling to himself, Nym stomped down the still-empty streets in search of a food vendor who'd set up already. He forked over half of his remaining money, leaving him down to one shield two, to refill his pack, and headed over to the guildhall.

Nobody gave him a second glance, and the lack of attention itself had Nym worried. He'd been so sure that everyone knew about him, about what he'd done in Palmara. Nym wasn't given to introspection, and he'd done his best to put the event out of his mind. He didn't regret his actions, but the absolute coldness that had come over him when he did it still scared him. He didn't like thinking about it.

It was all he could think about now. Every single person he saw had to know. In every casual glance, he saw secret disgust. He knew the guards were watching him, just looking for the chance to capture him, waiting for him to walk into the guildhall so he couldn't escape. There would be a roof between him and freedom, and they could block off the doors and windows.

Panic started to overwhelm him. Quickly, he ducked into an alley and hid himself away while he struggled to get his breathing under control. His breaths came out ragged, and he clenched his hands into fists so hard that it hurt. That didn't stop the shaking. Over and over, he tried to tell himself he was overre-acting, that everything was fine.

He sat there, back leaning against a wall, chest rising and falling and so dizzy he could barely see while fear ran rampant through his mind. He tried to fight back fear with reason, to tell himself that it was fine, that he'd walked through town and nobody had stopped him. He was safe. He knew it, logically.

Cold fear twisted around his guts, fear that he couldn't rationalize his way away from. It was only after half an hour that he got his breathing back under control and was able to open his eyes again. No one had found him, thankfully. He was still safe. But there would be no going to the guildhall today. Maybe not ever again. Just the thought of stepping into a building set his heart to racing.

Nym made his way back to the gate as fast as he could and left Zoskan. It wasn't until he got back into the forest that he finally calmed down. Everything was fine, and he was vaguely disgusted with himself for panicking like that. Nothing had even happened, but just the thought of going back still made him uncomfortable. The farther he was from the guards, the better he felt. Outside of town, he was free.

Out in the forest, he was safe from people.

Nym flew deeper into the forest, deeper than he'd ever dared to go before, searching for a place of safety where he could rest.

He set up his camp on the bank of a wide, shallow stream. The canopy over-head was patchy, with plenty of space between trees to view the sky, and the underbrush was relatively sparse. It formed a thick wall on one side, mostly thorny bushes and tangled branches, but the other gave him a clear view down a number of wild game trails. Of course, the sky over the stream was clear of trees. He had quick and easy access to go airborne if something happened.

Nym spent the afternoon searching for and piling up dead wood next to a pit he'd gouged out of the ground with magic. The sun set below the tree line, and the sky took on twilight hues. First one, then two, then dozens of stars showed up overhead, and Nym finally allowed himself to stop working.

He ate sparingly from his pack, both because he wanted to make it last and because he didn't really feel up to eating. Just the thought made him queasy, but he forced a bit of food down. He went to bed early, curled up in his cloak next to the small fire he'd built. He lay there, but he didn't sleep.

At some point, he finally dozed off, only to be awakened by the night sounds of the forest. For perhaps the thousandth time, he missed that month he'd spent on the coast with Ciana. They hadn't had much, and one time his stalker shark had tried to eat his arm, but he'd been happy and worry free.

Damn Senman for ruining all that. He just couldn't take no for an answer and kept pushing to isolate Ciana, to get rid of any outside influence, to drive her to him so he could control her. Nym could have been safe, practicing new magic at his leisure for fun, and instead he was shivering next to a small fire and wishing his cloak had an extra lining on the inside. A chill mist had crept up on his little campsite at some time in the night, and his preparations were no longer enough to keep him warm.

It reminded him of his original trip through the forest, where no matter what he'd done, he couldn't stay warm. He'd attributed it to being in a new environment away from the coast, but looking back on it now, that didn't make sense. His own recent experiences of sleeping in the woods hadn't been anything like that. It was only once he'd gone deeper in that things got too cold to stand.

Something was wrong. Nym watched the mist warily, trying to peer through it to see if anything was moving in the darkness while he thought of the various dangers he'd learned about from Cern and Babkin but had never actually seen personally. One name popped out at him: frost wraith.

Cern had warned him to just run if he ever encountered one on the grounds that there was no such thing as one frost wraith. Nym considered the mist again. It might be a sign of frost wraiths, or it might just be a coincidence of the weather. He could only see a few feet through it anyway, and only because his fire was still going and pushed both the darkness and the mist back a bit.

There was a first-circle spell he'd worked out that let him see farther, but it didn't help with seeing in the dark. He'd barely ever found a reason to use it, but with his new skills in intent filtering, he wondered if he could modify it into something that let him see better at night. That would be significantly more useful, in his opinion.

No matter how he fiddled with it, he couldn't make it work. Instead, he tried taking the base spell and modifying it to accept second-layer arcana. That wasn't as easy as it sounded, and when he did finally get it working, it didn't do what he wanted. Instead of seeing through the dark, everything became white and faded. The mist grew thicker, if anything. When he waved his hand through it, he found that he was able to see its outline in the mist, but it didn't help with things farther away.

This was worse than nothing at all, so he dismissed the spell. Everything went black again except that little circle of light he was sitting in, and the more he looked at it, the surer Nym became that the mist was actually alive after all. Little swirls of it played across his limbs, reminding him uncomfortably of a snake tasting the air with its tongue. It was getting steadily colder too, so much so that his breath was starting to come out in little steam puffs.

Whatever was happening, Nym wasn't going to stick around any longer for it. He grabbed his pack and floated upward in the air. With a last look around, he took off to the stream to gain full clearance and shot up over the treetops. At least, that's what he started to do. He really only made it about ten feet before he stopped in place.

It felt like the mist was clinging to him, dragging him back down to the ground. The feeling only got stronger when he left the circle of his campfire's light, and then again when he flew out over the stream. No matter how much he strained, he couldn't fly out of the mist. The longer he fought, the more stuck he became.

Nym opened a second conduit to the first layer and used telekinesis to grab hold of the burning logs still in his fire. He pulled them across the clearing to float in the air next to him and burn the mist away. As the flames flared up, fed by the air currents he was controlling, he saw faces in the mist.

They were twisted caricatures of humans, with bizarre features and dead eyes. Each one was subtly different, a wider nose or jagged teeth pointing in a different direction. Their hair was wild around their heads, a halo of writhing strands that faded into the background blanket of mist. Hands reached out from bodies that were shapeless mist, and Nym felt a sudden surge of cold when they slipped past the ring of fire to touch him.

Cern's advice had been to run, but even with a ring of fire surrounding him, he was having difficulty gaining any altitude. Nym thought he could skim the surface of the stream, but it appeared that the mist was coming from the water itself, so he needed to get back on dry land and as far away from the stream as he could.

He pulled the burning logs closer to him, as close as he could without singeing himself. The weight of the frost wraiths clawing at his limbs fell away, but he found he still couldn't move more than a foot or so in any direction without it coming back. If he moved the fire with him, he could slowly proceed, but he was concerned that one or both spells would fail before he made it back to the ground.

It was close. He actually had to abandon about half of the wood and let it splash into the stream in order to keep the spell running, and he barely landed on grass when his flight spell gave out. Without the need to maintain it though, he was free to strengthen his telekinesis, and Nym had an idea. He grabbed all the wood he'd collected and planned to feed to the fire over the rest of the night and pulled it to him.

Then he dropped it all around him in a ring and sent the still-burning logs into it to ignite the whole thing. The pressure from the mists disappeared completely, but the chill remained. It was lessened, but served as a reminder that he hadn't escaped, only delayed. The ring of fire he'd created would last half an hour at most before it burned out, leaving him defenseless with hours to go until the light of the sun burned the mist away.

He needed to come up with something if he wanted to survive, and he needed to do it fast.

CHAPTER 24

A cold, rational calm descended on him. He needed to take action to save himself, and he couldn't allow emotions to cloud his judgement. That feeling, so alien to Nym, was something he'd pulled away from every time he'd felt it coming on since he'd killed Senman. But he knew he needed it now, and he welcomed the emotional numbness that came with it.

Analyzing the situation was the work of moments. He had a ring of fire, and his enemy was a living fogbank that had rolled in and constricted his movements. Worse, the chill he felt was obviously magical in nature. It sapped his strength far quicker than it should have. He couldn't even tell how many frost wraiths were hiding in the mist. He needed to change the situation if he was going to survive.

Nym's first thought was to pour on the pyrokinesis. His control was lacking, but if there was ever a situation where more fire was a good thing, it was this very one. The problem was that he was standing right in the middle of the source, and he couldn't get too far away from it. He was certain to be burned alive if he fueled the fire with his magic.

If he could just regain his mobility, it would be so easy to torch everything. Of course, if he had his mobility, he wouldn't be in this situation to begin with. He needed something else. Air magic was his specialty, but his attempts at blowing away the mist just punched random holes that were immediately refilled with more mist. Now that the frost wraiths weren't on top of him, it was difficult to pick them out of the background.

Air and fire were out. He couldn't think of any way earth would help him right now. That left water. Normally he would source the water he needed to work magic from the river, but in this case, he decided to try to pull it from the mist. It would be harder to gather it, but the point wasn't to do anything with it, just to get rid of the mist.

Nym sat down in the center of the circle of flames. He forged his conduit as wide open as he could and let arcana pour into his soul well. It was the work of moments to fill it completely, and then he set about grabbing hold of the water in the mist and pulling it out. It condensed into thousands of little droplets, clumping together and raining down, threatening to put out his only defense.

Nym took control of the water near him and caused it to all gather into one giant orb the size of his torso. Once it was big enough, he shot it off into the stream to splash harmlessly, then repeated the exercise. Arcana flowed into his soul well with each inhale, and out with each exhale. He worked the magic, again and again, slowly breaking down the mist that shrouded the forest.

As he did, the frost wraiths lost their cover. At first, it was only glimpses before they faded away again, but the mist continued to thin, and soon enough he could see them fluttering around him, looking for a way to breach the barrier of fire he'd surrounded himself with. The flames were weakening, running low on fuel, but their protection wasn't completely gone yet.

He split his concentration to channel arcana into his flight spell. Instead of using it on himself, he captured a frost wraith in a thin shell of hardened air, then squeezed that shell. Without a corporal body, it was easy to condense it into a tiny stone the size of his thumb. Then he did it again, and again, and again. His focus wavered, and he couldn't manage another.

As soon as he stopped concentrating on it, the spell snapped and the frost wraiths flowed back out, unharmed and full-size. There was no way he was going to stop the hundreds of wraiths swarming the area that way. Maybe he didn't have to though. He just needed to clear a path to escape. That was a gamble, since he didn't know how widespread the frost wraiths were, and if he left the circle of protection his fire offered him, he'd be feeling their icy claws on him immediately.

That was fine for a minute or two, but they could restrain him too, and drag him back down into a horde of them. If he hadn't been next to the fire when the mist first rolled in, they would have pinned him in place and frozen him to death without him ever being able to do anything about it. He might not even have woken up.

Nym shook his head. He'd have to risk it. He was fast and agile in flight. Thanks to his work thinning the mists, he could see the wraiths now. There were a lot of them, but he thought he could manage enough of them to get a clear shot at the sky and flee at top speed. As long as he got high enough up, he could escape.

How high that was and whether or not he'd freeze from the purely mundane cold of high-altitude flying was a matter of debate. What was certain was that staying on the ground was not an option. He needed a way out, the sooner the better. He was only going to get more exhausted the longer this all dragged on.

Nym stood up and plotted out his course. Working on the assumption that the higher he went, the thinner the mist would be, and the thinner the mist, the fewer frost wraiths there would be lurking in it, his plan was to go straight up. He was starting to slow down now, too tired, too drained, to think clearly. This would likely be the only chance he had to survive the night.

To start, he poured arcana into the fire and caused it to spread through the remaining wood. The fuel would burn up in less than a minute, but while it lasted, he would be as protected as he could possibly be. Then he crafted the air cushions he needed to propel himself straight up. Finally, he started picking off targets, not bothering to encase them in shells, but simply creating walls of air and swatting them away.

Nym exploded into the air, shooting past dozens of grasping hands faster than they could grab hold of him. He weaved through the frost wraiths swooping through the air, shivering as bursts of cold washed over his skin. Up he went, fifty feet, then a hundred. His blood was ice in his veins. At two hundred feet, the whole of the forest was sprawled out below him, and bare tendrils of mist reached up to him, trails for the frost wraiths to follow.

A sweep of wind severed them, leaving Nym alone in the moonlight. His limbs trembled with cold and fatigue, though he was to the point where he wasn't really feeling the chill anymore. That was probably not a good thing. He wasn't sure. It was getting harder and harder to think. He clung to his goal: escape. The frost wraiths were still below him, and even now more tendrils of mist were arching up into the night sky to reach him.

Nym flew north in a drunken line. He wove back and forth, struggling to maintain altitude and direction. The mist thinned out as he pulled away from the deep forest, and the air gradually grew warmer. Part of that was that he kept getting lower to the ground, but he didn't realize how low until he crashed into a tree he hadn't seen in front of him.

Fortunately for him, he had slowed down to barely a trudge. Unfortunately, the shock of impact broke his concentration completely, and the flight spell ended. Nym flailed about as he fell, hooking arms and legs that he could barely feel around branches. He ended up tangled up in a few of the thicker ones after falling a few feet and breaking the thinner branches near the top.

That was where Nym spent the night, cradled in a random tree's wooden clutches, shivering and barely conscious. The sun came up a few hours later, revealing a thin-limbed boy with a torn cloak half draped over him, too delirious to answer the questions of the man standing at the base of the tree, too weak to fight back when the man climbed up and freed him, and too uncoordinated to climb down himself after.

The last thing Nym remembered was being laid out on the ground and covered in another blanket while the morning sun burned away the last of the dew on the grass. Then there was darkness.

* * *

Nym woke up in a bed in a strange room. He shot upright as a surge of panic swept through him. With effort, he suppressed it and took a breath. There was no one else near him. He wasn't restrained in any way. There was a window in the room with closed shutters. He could open them and fly away.

He was not trapped. There was no need to panic.

It still took him a few minutes to calm down. Once he managed it, he was annoyed that he couldn't summon the cold calmness from last night. Something had broken in his brain when those guards from Palmara had cornered him, like every deep, dark fear he'd never dared to even give form crashed down on him all at once. And it just kept happening. He didn't feel safe anywhere anymore.

If he had the choice, he would take the cold, ruthless calculation he'd once shunned. He would live with that wrapped around him like a cloak if that meant the overwhelming fear never came back. Nym couldn't summon it at will though. It seemed to show up whenever it felt like it, not when it was convenient for him.

He climbed out of the bed on shaky legs and gave himself a once-over. He still had all his fingers and toes, but was covered in bruises, especially on his chest and arms. "Stupid tree," he muttered, though he could barely even remember hitting it.

His clothes were on a table next to the wall, dirty and torn. Of his pack, there was no sign, and his cloak was fit to be cut up for rags and not much else. That was a blow there. Now he had no food, no money, and nothing to keep him warm at night. He was back to where he'd started when he'd first come to Zoskan, except now he was injured on top of it, and he'd already burned his bridges in town.

He would thank whoever had saved him and follow the road to the next town. There didn't really seem to be any other options, and there was no point in staying anymore. He'd never get the crests he needed for that teleport to Abilanth. It would be faster to fly there himself, not that he actually knew where it was.

Nym got himself dressed, thankful that if nothing else, he'd saved his shoes and that his flight jacket was only splitting at a few seams. He could get that repaired. It wasn't a total loss. Then, just because of how paranoid he'd gotten, he forged a conduit and filled his soul well with arcana before he opened the door.

There, sitting in a pair of chairs in front of a massive hearth, were two men. The first was the man he vaguely recognized as having found him and gotten him out of the tree he'd spent the night in. He was tall and well muscled, his head shaved and a sharp goatee jutting off his chin. His bare arms were covered in scars, and he held a clay cup in his hands that had steam rising off it.

The other was Babkin. Nym groaned. Of course it would be. The big innkeeper looked over at him and nodded. "Welcome back to the land of the living, Nym."

CHAPTER 25

I imagine you are wondering why I am here," Babkin said.

"A little bit, yes."

"My friend here found you, you see. And then he came to town to get some medicine for you, as you were sick with death chills and delirious. And because he is my friend, he stopped to see me. That is what you do when you are in the neighborhood. He told me the tale of the curious boy he found in a tree looking like a busted kite, and it was not hard to figure out he was talking about you. So I am here to make sure you are alright, and to see if you are finally ready to give up this senseless fascination with this forest."

"Well that certainly explains it then."

The other man sitting next to Babkin set his drink down and said, "Hello. My name's Leaf. Uh, welcome to the forest. I can't really blame you much for wanting to be here instead of living in a town. It's much nicer out here, but yeah, little bit dangerous on occasion. Don't mind Babkin's mother henning, he does it to everyone."

Babkin scowled at his companion. "I do not mother hen everyone," he protested.

"What do you call it then?" Leaf asked.

"I am trying to keep this boy from killing himself."

"He survived a run-in with a frost wraith. Sure, he got a bit roughed up, but he's still breathing. That's not nothing."

"He would not have needed to survive it if he had stayed where it was safe."

"How did you know it was frost wraiths?" Nym asked, frowning.

Leaf shrugged. "Not hard to see. Go live in the north for a little while and eventually you'll see someone who got caught in the cold. They look a lot like you. You learn to recognize the signs and how to treat for them."

"Did you say wraiths, as in more than one?" Babkin asked. "You are extraordinarily lucky to survive a run-in with two or three."

"I don't know how many there were," Nym said. "Too many to count. Maybe a hundred? The mist was so thick I had to fly a few hundred feet up to get out of it."

Both men abruptly sobered. "Tell no lies," Leaf said, his voice hard. "You do not need to stretch your tales here. I am already convinced of your bravery."

"I'm not lying," Nym said, confused. "Why would I lie?"

"Because what you are saying cannot be the truth. No one could live through an attack of that magnitude, and frost wraiths gathering in numbers thick enough to form a fogbank that size is an impossible event."

Both men were deadly serious now, and Nym got the sense that there was something important about his encounter that he wasn't grasping. At their request, he described the events as accurately as possible, several times. By the time they were satisfied with his recollections, both men wore grave expressions.

"Do you think Ul'tuthik broke free?" Leaf asked.

Babkin shook his head. "Everybody would know. This may be a warning sign. We'll need to investigate this."

"I'll leave today. It'll take me days to get there though, especially if the frost wraiths are coming out in droves now. Unless . . . hmm . . ." Leaf gave Nym a speculative look. "How are you at passenger flight?"

"Leaf, no. Do not involve him in this any more than he already is. He is far too young to—"

"Do not try to tell me what I can and cannot do, Babkin." Leaf's voice took on a hard, dangerous edge. "I am not one of those village bumpkins who cowers when you raise your voice. Nym is just as much a part of this now as you or I. Surviving a frost wraith attack of that scale is unheard of. If he's willing and it can save me days of hard travel, I'll use that power."

"Uh, excuse me. What are we talking about?" Nym asked.

Babkin glowered but didn't say anything. He just stared daggers at Leaf while the other man ignored him. "Short version: there's a spot where a necromancer poked a hole in reality that leads to the lands of the dead. A monster got free for a little bit, but we stuffed it back through, killed the necromancer, and put a patch on the hole. It's had twenty years now to try to get free, and it looks like maybe something broke, so I'm going to go look before we call in assistance."

"Oh, and you want me to fly you out there. I get it."

"That's pretty much it. So, can you do it?"

Nym shrugged. "Depends how heavy you are and how far you need to go."

"This is a terrible idea," Babkin rumbled, but they both ignored him.

Leaf continued, "Then there's the fact that you were completely inside the fogbank created when they group up and didn't just die on the spot. That takes . . . powerful . . . magic. I believe you, but it's a mystery. You should not have survived something like that."

As far as he knew, Nym hadn't done anything special. He'd stayed near the fire, used a bit of magic to make it burn hotter, and ran for it the first chance he had. "Maybe it was because I cleared the mist away so I could see them?"

Leaf shrugged. "We don't know much about the frost wraiths. The name . . . that was actually an argument in the old group. Our mage insisted that it wasn't accurate, that they weren't actually water aspected, that it was a metaphorical 'chill of the grave' and that their touch drained life from a victim. Everyone else overruled him because getting a hug from one of the bastards was like being dunked in cold water."

"I remember that," Babkin said. "Veran had to be restrained, he was so upset."

"Gave you a black eye, if I recall," Leaf added. He laughed. "I thought you were going to break him in two."

The innkeeper did not laugh. "It was a great effort to restrain myself," he said. "Had it been anyone else, I would not have been so gentle."

"Gentle? He never did get that wheeze out of his voice after you punched him back."

Babkin appeared faintly embarrassed and quickly changed the subject. "Regardless of the past, it would be better not to involve Nym in this. The seal is our problem. It is specifically why we are still here. He should return to Zoskan."

"Why don't you ask him what he wants to do, Babkin?" Leaf said. "That's always been your problem. You think you know best, and you trample all over what anyone else has to say about it. Nym, what do you want?"

"Me?" Nym was caught flat-footed. "I guess . . . I wanted to save enough money to use the teleport platform to go to Abilanth and see about joining the Academy." Babkin looked startled, but Nym ignored him and continued, "I figure I owe you one for getting me out of that tree, so I can take you to where you need to go if you want. Then I'm heading down the road to the next town to try again. I can't make any money in this town anymore. Too many restrictions."

"You wanted to go to the Academy?" Babkin said. "Why didn't you tell me?"

Nym just stared at him for a minute. Finally, he said, "What business is it of yours what I want to do?"

He tried hard to keep the bitterness and resentment out of his voice, but it was obvious he hadn't succeeded judging by the look on the two men's faces. Leaf shot Babkin an exasperated look and said, "How much does the mage guild charge for a teleport now anyway?"

"I am not sure. I don't keep track."

"Two crests for a one-way trip to Abilanth for one person," Nym supplied.

"What! That's robbery!" Leaf yelped.

"That certainly explains your willingness to take risks for quick cash," Babkin said. He sighed. "I owe you an apology, I think. You should not have been out here, but I assumed it to be foolish childish fancy that led you to risk your life. You had a goal, an admirable goal to better yourself, and I was an obstacle to that because I did not take the time to talk to you."

Leaf's jaw dropped open. He stared at Babkin, then looked to Nym, then back to Babkin again, before sputtering, "You . . . he . . . how . . . what? You . . . what? You've never given an apology in your life!"

"I am old now, Leaf, too old to be full of fire and ready to conquer the world. In my haste to prevent a boy from flinging himself headfirst into an early grave, I never stopped to consider why he was doing the things he did. That having been said, I still have to insist that he should not be involved any further in this. The seal has held for two decades, it can hold a few extra days while you go check on it."

Leaf made a face. "Easy for you to consign me to make the trip while you go back to your inn. The boy is a scrapper, like me. He's tougher than you're giving him credit for. Tell you what, Nym, you want to go to Abilanth. Fly me to where I need to go and back here, and I'll pay your way for you. All . . . two crests, by God's saggy sack, that's a lot for a simple teleport. But yes, two crests."

"Just like that? Do you know how hard I worked to figure out double-layer casting so I could harvest those stupid plants for Cern, and then you wouldn't even let me sell them to him?" Nym asked Babkin.

"I do not know what double-layer casting is, so no, I am afraid I do not know."

"It doesn't matter! The point was it was hard work. Fine, whatever. I'll do it. But I want a meal first!"

"I think I can agree to that," Leaf said. "Babkin, are you staying?"

"No, I think I must get back soon. Nym, I will tell Cern he can buy from you if he wants. You will need a great deal more than two crests to obtain an education at the Academy. But promise me that when you are done with this foolishness with Leaf, you will stay near the edges of the forest where it is safer. I will be warning everyone away from the deep woods for the time being until we can finish investigating the frost wraith outbreak."

Nym rolled his eyes. "I'm not making any promises. I will do whatever I want to do. Stop treating me like a little kid."

"You kind of are a little kid," Leaf pointed out.

"Do you want my help or not?"

Leaf raised his hands in surrender. He walked away, laughing to himself, and started working in the little kitchenette he had sat up in one corner of the room. Meanwhile, Babkin glowered at Nym. Nym just glared back at him.

"Fine. You are obviously far more capable than I gave you credit for. Ease an old man's mind though and be careful. You are too young to meet your end in a monster's belly. Leaf will know if anything tries to sneak up on you. Do as he says and retreat to the sky while he fights, if it comes to that."

"Flying off is my default reaction to trouble," Nym told him. "No reason to change tactics now."

Babkin shook his head and sighed. He heaved himself to his feet and threw back the rest of his cup in one gulp. "Leaf, please come find me in town once you've surveyed the seal. I am holding you responsible for Nym's safety."

"Get out of here, you old worrier," Leaf said, not looking up from where he was dicing some vegetables. "I'll see you in a day or two."

The old innkeeper departed, and Nym took his chair. "This'll be fun, huh?" he said.

Leaf grunted, but he looked a lot more tired and worn out than he had a few minutes ago.

CHAPTER 26

Nym wanted to blame it on the fact that he was still recovering, but the simple truth was that he was used to lifting his own weight in flight, and Leaf was probably four times that. The man was over six feet tall to begin with and if not as heavily muscled as Therm, he was no stick.

At least it was Leaf he was ferrying and not Babkin. Nym doubted his ability to even lift the innkeeper. Carrying him for any appreciable distance was definitely out of the question. As it was, Nym had his doubts that he was actually speeding up the journey.

They had to take frequent walking breaks, and Leaf was so adept at slipping through the brush that he was almost as fast on foot as Nym was flying by himself. The problem was that Nym was slowing him down on the walking segments and not flying fast enough or far enough to make up for that.

Leaf took pity on him, and they stopped for an early break. He broke out some trail rations for them to snack on, which were honestly about as bad as the hot meal Leaf had served him. He was a man of many talents, but cooking was not one of them.

While they were eating, Leaf started casually naming off the various types of plants around them, listing some facts about each of them, including which ones had medicinal value. When they started walking again, he explained how he was moving through the underbrush so quickly, a combination of predicting thin spots to push through from experience and knowledge of local geography. Some plants were more pliable and could be pushed past easier, and Leaf was an expert at picking them out of the foliage.

Nym tried to imitate him while they walked. If anything, he thought it should be easier for him. He was so much smaller than Leaf, and he could fly. It seemed like that should provide him with many more gaps to slip through. At the very least, he should be able to keep up with the man, if not outpace him.

It didn't work out that way, of course. And Leaf laughed at him when he got annoyed that he was failing to keep up. "You have a week or two of woodcraft," he said. "You are competing against close to forty years of experience, over twenty of them in this very forest. It is not reasonable to expect to outpace me."

"But . . . the flying, and I'm smaller, and . . ."

"Yes, yes. All very reasonable. Completely incorrect, but reasonable. But come on, if you've got enough energy to argue about it, let's fly some more."

And so it went in cycles. They flew for maybe half an hour, and at a speed Nym chafed at but couldn't increase. Then they walked for an hour while he recovered his strength. When it got late, Leaf stopped them at a meadow and told Nym to rest while he gathered firewood.

They built up a roaring bonfire in preparation for frost wraiths, but none showed up. Nym was surprised, but Leaf just shrugged and said, "We are not so deep into the forest that they are a concern yet. Tomorrow night, for sure."

Then he handed Nym one of his spare cloaks, which was easily long enough to be both blanket and pillow, and bid Nym good night while he sat with his back to the fire and stared out into the darkness. A long knife was stabbed into the ground next to him, along with several arrows. The bow to go with them rested in Leaf's lap.

The next day was more of the same, but Nym was pleased to see a measure of his full strength returning. They flew longer and farther with each trip, and it was shortly after noon that they began to see fog filling the forest below them. It didn't reach over the treetops, but it was thick and spread out in every direction.

"I do not like this," Leaf said, frowning down at the forest. "Frost wraiths don't come out in the day. There should be no mist here. It is unnatural, clearly their work. We still have a few miles to go to reach the seal too. It would be bad to land in there."

Nym told him, "I'm good for a little bit still. We can do a few miles in one go."

"But can you fly us back without having to rest?"

Nym peered down into the mist and shuddered, remembering the feel of the cold claws on him, holding him down. "It might be best to take a break before we fly over it."

"I'm not sure we should go any farther," Leaf told him. "If the mist is this thick here, how bad will it be at the source? Will we even be able to approach it?"

"I can condense it into water and clear some of it up," Nym offered. "It comes back pretty fast, but it should be enough to at least get a look at the ground."

"Are you sure?" Leaf asked. "It could be the death of us both if your magic fails in the middle of this mist. The smart move would be to turn back now and go straight to Zoskan. This alone is enough evidence to call in the mage guild to investigate further."

Nym shrugged. "Up to you. As long as I get paid, I'm good either way."

Leaf scratched his chin and stared down at the forest. "No, let's go back. I did promise Babkin I'd keep you safe. Plus, you've got an Academy to conquer, and the sooner you get started, the sooner you'll be the strongest mage in the world, right?"

You will grow strong, stronger than anyone else, or you will break one day when it turns out you are too weak.

"Nym? Nym!"

Nym snapped back to the present. "Huh?"

"Come on, let's go back," Leaf said.

"Right . . ."

Nym didn't say anything as they flew back. That single memory, the only thing he had of his past, played itself on a loop in his brain, over and over again. When they stopped for the night, Leaf made another bonfire for them, but seeming to sense Nym's mood, he didn't try to talk to him.

This time, instead of falling asleep, Nym lay awake deep into the night and wondered who he was, and if going to the Academy would help him figure that out.

They reached Zoskan the next day. Leaf handed over two crests, per their agreement. The coins were gold, twice as fat as a silver shield, and stamped with some sort of glyph or sign. "What does it mean?" Nym asked as he held them up to the light.

"Not a clue. I was never much for civilization. Why do you think I live in the woods?"

"Maybe it's just better to live in the woods," Nym muttered, eyeing the gate guards as they approached the wall.

"I think so, but most people don't agree. Why do you want to go to the Academy if you don't like living in town?"

"I want to learn more magic." Nym left it unsaid that he needed to get farther away from Palmara. A few days out in the wilderness had done a lot to ease his anxiety, but seeing the guards was bringing it all back to the front of his mind.

Leaf noticed and put a hand on Nym's shoulder. "You alright there?"

"Yeah. Just fine. Everything is fine."

"If you say so." It was obvious Leaf didn't believe him, but he didn't push Nym to open up about it.

The guards let him in without a problem, just like they always had. The more he interacted with them, the easier it became to convince himself that the Palmara guards hadn't communicated with anyone in Zoskan. He was still leery about going inside though. That idea that everyone was just watching and waiting for a chance to grab him when he couldn't escape was firmly lodged in his brain.

If he couldn't get over it though, he might as well turn around and go live in the forest. There was no functioning in society if he was completely unwilling to ever set foot inside a store or an inn. He couldn't sleep in a bed under a roof if he was so afraid that someone was going to grab him the second he walked inside.

"You sure you're alright?" Leaf said again.

"Still fine."

"Okay. If you want to talk about it, I'll listen. Sometimes, when you've been by yourself for a long time, it's an adjustment to be around a lot of people again. There's nothing wrong with easing back into it."

That wasn't it at all, but Nym just thanked Leaf for the advice and changed the subject. Soon enough, they parted ways, with Leaf heading to the Trough and Saddle and Nym going straight for Cern's place. He had some money to make.

He managed to get a spare pack from Cern by knocking on the window of the alchemist's store and talking to him in the doorway. Then he flew back out to the woods and finally harvested the skywort blooms hidden behind the top of the waterfall he'd found on his first day of searching. Cern gave him three silver shields for the lot.

Walking into the guildhall and buying that teleport was nerve-racking. Even though there were no guards at all, let alone ones all the way from Palmara, he kept remembering the feeling of that hand clamped down on him. The mage at the desk assumed he was nervous about the magic and spent the entire time assuring him that the process was completely safe. Nym stepped onto the platform and waited, doing his best to keep his breathing under control. With a flash of light, he disappeared from Zoskan.

In the Trough and Saddle's common room, Ciana sat at a table and picked at the meal half-heartedly. It was delicious, far and away better than anything she'd ever prepared herself, but she was too nervous to enjoy it.

The innkeeper, Babkin, had spoken to her a few days ago after the mages at the guildhall had directed her to the Trough and Saddle. It was the last-known place Nym had stayed, and she'd arrived while Babkin was away on business. As soon as he'd come back, he'd told her that Nym was safe and should be back from a job soon.

So she'd waited, and waited. The door opened, and she looked up in anticipation, but it wasn't Nym. Instead, a tall man with a shaved head and a sharp goatee wearing forester leathers strode in. He went straight for the hall that led to Babkin's office without stopping to order anything or talk to anyone.

Ten minutes later, the stranger walked back out and disappeared just as abruptly as he'd shown up. A few seconds later, Babkin's shadow fell over her. "Have you seen Nym?" he asked her.

She shook her head, and he added, "He came to town with my associate. He should still be nearby if you'd like to go look for him. Do not worry about paying for this meal."

"Thank you," she said, scrambling to her feet. She was out the door in a flash, but Nym was nowhere to be seen. Undaunted, Ciana scoured the nearby streets looking for him. Hours passed with no trace of him. Then she checked at the guildhall to see if he'd been there and learned that he'd paid for a teleportation to Abilanth, a city that sounded vaguely familiar, but she couldn't place where she'd heard it.

What she did learn was that it was over a thousand miles away, and that there was very little hope of her reaching it on foot, given that by the time she reached the mountains splitting the country in two, it would be midwinter and they'd be completely impassible.

Once again, he'd left her behind. This time she hadn't even seen him go.

CHAPTER 27

The very first thing Nym noticed when he appeared on the platform was that Abilanth was so much colder than Zoskan. He yelped at the shock of sudden cold air, drawing a chuckle from the attendant mage. "Don't worry, that happens a lot," she said. "I can recommend a good tailor if you need."

Nym considered his limited remaining funds. "Is it going to get much colder than this?" he asked.

"Oh goodness, yes. This is the summer season. Abilanth is so high up in the mountains that it never really gets warm here. Let me guess, here for the Academy, not the city?"

"Um, yes, I guess that's true."

That was one reason at least. The other was that he sincerely doubted anyone in Abilanth had even heard of a small coastal fishing village called Palmara, let alone kept up to date on the latest happenings there. The giant knot of anxiety strangling him had instantly loosened as soon as the teleport went off. He'd made it out of Zoskan; he was safe.

"Well you're a bit late but not completely out of luck. Entry exams started a week ago, but you have today left to test in," the attendant told him. "You, er, may want to see the tailor first. You look like you lost a fight with a blade juggler."

"Ran into a tree flying away from some monsters," he admitted. "Lost my cloak and my pack then."

"That'd do it. If you still need healing, I can point out a nearby clinic. They're a bit more expensive than some of the ones in the outer ring, but the quality is there to justify it."

Nym didn't think he'd have enough for both. "Maybe after the tailor. It is freezing in here."

"Colder outside," she told him. "Come with me then."

She led him to a map framed on the wall. It showed the city's layout, including a series of walls set in concentric circles that the top had been scooped out of due to their position on the side of a mountain. The center was occupied by a sprawling castle, which was itself surrounded by a series of large estates containing nobles' manors. Outside the core was what was labeled as the inner ring. The Academy was there, taking up the top third of the circle and extending out into mountain outside the city walls.

The attendant pointed out where the guildhall was located in the middle ring, then tapped a few other spots and listed off businesses she thought he'd be interested in. That included a lot of restaurants and cafés, an inn, the tailor she'd mentioned, a barber, a postal service, the clinic, and a cobbler.

She then moved on to the outer ring and pointed out a few more clinics and a lot more taverns and bars. While the outer ring was the biggest, it also seemed to be the poorest. A lot of the city's artisans practiced their crafts in the middle ring if they could afford it. There were similar places of business in the outer ring, but the attendant warned against their quality.

She seemed to have an overinflated opinion of Nym's financial situation, but he didn't correct her. It did make him uneasy that she assumed he had money. He wasn't sure if it was because he'd come through the teleport platform, which was a prohibitively expensive way to travel, or if it was because she thought he was going to the Academy. It was nice to know that the exams ended today, but there was no chance of him getting in. He hoped that next semester, things would be different. For now, he needed time to acquire funds.

By the time she was done pointing things out on the map, he was starting to shiver. "Thanks for all the help," he said. "I'm going to go find that tailor now."

"You're quite welcome." She gave him a pleasant smile and looked him straight in the eye, like she was waiting for him to do something.

Confused, he waved goodbye and left the guildhall. The map was too big, and she'd pointed out too many places for him to remember even half of them, but he'd taken special care to commit the tailor's shop to memory and found it easily enough.

There was a bit of a line when he got there, mostly teenagers, but their orders were easily filled. When it was his turn, the tailor beckoned him over. "Oh my God, you poor thing," she said, clucking over him. "You must be freezing in those rags. Let me just get your measurements here. Do you need school robes or town clothes? Or both, hmm?"

Nym blinked. Everyone seemed to assume he was on his way to the Academy. It stung a little bit that they were all wrong. He supposed it made sense, given his age and that it was apparently the start of a new semester. "Just a set of clothes for town," he said. "I'm not going to the Academy. Not yet."

"Well I did think you looked a bit young, but there's all sorts of talent. Next year, I'm sure you'll be there. You do come back then and I'll get you some nice robes."

"I would have thought the Academy would provide them," he said. Considering how expensive everyone said the place was, it seemed like the least they could do was to house, feed, and clothe the students.

"Oh, they will. But if you want something that fits you, you'll want to come back here to have them altered. And if you want more than two of them, why, I can make you a few extras. If you want them lined to protect against the cold, and honestly, who wouldn't, I can do that for you too."

"That sounds wonderful, but for today, just a pair of pants and a shirt, please."

The tailor clucked her tongue again, but she finished the measurements and, in no time at all, had picked out a set of clothes for him. "That will be two shields six for the clothes, or three shields two with alterations."

Nym pulled out his three shields from his pocket. "This is all I've got on me, so I guess just the clothes."

"Hmm. Indeed." The woman's friendly demeanor disappeared.

"Ha, don't be like that, Aggie," the teenager in line behind him said. "Here, I'll cover the two for you, friend. How are you going to look nice and catch the eye of a cute girl if your clothes don't fit you properly?"

Nym wanted to refuse the charity. It was a nice gesture, but he needed that last four shims for food and shelter. Abilanth was way too cold for him to consider sleeping outside, and he wasn't even sure where he'd find food on his own. "No, you don't have to do that. I'll just pay the two and six."

"It's really no trouble. I insist," the teenager said.

"No, it's . . . Thank you, but no."

The tailor waited impatiently while the two boys argued about whether or not Nym would accept his charity, but finally got sick of it and stepped in. "He said no. Fool boy wants to wear baggy clothes, that's his choice. Now, two shields six, here's your four back, and your clothes. Please step to the side so I can help the next person."

Nym left the shop in his oversize pants and shirt. His old clothes were bundled up under one arm, and he had four shims left. He found a nearby café and paid a shim for lunch, which he felt was grossly overpriced. Everything in the city was more expensive than he thought it should be, but no one else blinked at the price of things.

He had three shims left to his name, and while he wanted a cloak, that seemed out of his price range considering what he'd paid for just the pants and shirt. He hoped there was enough left for a bed at an inn, or at least a spot near the hearth in the common room. If Nym had known how much more expensive everything was, he would have at least bought new clothes in Zoskan.

He considered that idea for a second. He knew that logically, it would have been a smart move, but getting out of that town was an enormous weight off his mind. He was already feeling so much better in Abilanth. It was easy to walk around again. He didn't feel like a guard was going to grab him and haul him off here.

Smiling despite how little he had left in his pocket, Nym turned his mind to finding work. His greatest advantage remained his ability to move rapidly and ignore terrain outside of town. He needed to find someone who wanted something moved from one spot to another. With that thought in mind, he decided to try what had already worked for him. He went and found an alchemist's shop.

The first one he found refused to even talk to him. As soon as the manager found out he wasn't there to buy something, he kicked Nym out. The second one was run by an older man with shaky hands that gave Nym grave concerns about his ability to mix things properly. It was irrelevant though, since his supply lines were already sorted and he didn't want to make changes. The third shop owner just laughed at him and told him to get lost.

He hit a few random stores, just to ask if they needed help with anything, but no one had work for him. Dejected, he decided to widen his search from the middle ring to the outer ring. There were three gates leading to the outer circle of the city, all of them guarded. Nym headed straight for the wall and then followed the street along until he found one.

The guards let him through without incident, and he resumed his search for gainful employment. He had hoped to avoid the outer ring since he expected the pay would be less, no matter what he found. He hadn't expected the job situation to be just as hopeless there. Nobody needed anyone. The taverns didn't want a dishwasher, or a server. They didn't need anyone to run to markets. The forges didn't need a kid to pump the bellows, and the tanner didn't need anyone to scrape hides.

It was getting late, and Nym hadn't managed to find any kind of work at all. He gave up for the day and headed back to the middle ring, only to be stopped at the gate. "Badge," the guard said, holding his hand out.

"What?" Nym asked.

"I can't let you through without your identification badge unless you pay the fee."

That was the first he'd heard of a badge. "How much is the fee?" he asked.

"Two shims."

Inwardly, he cursed. The trip to the outer ring had been a complete waste of time, and now it was costing him almost all his remaining money to get back to the nice part of town. He reached into his pocket, only to discover that it was empty.

Frowning, he patted his other pocket. That one was empty too. "I . . . seem to have lost my money," he said.

"No entry then. Step aside," the guard said. He didn't give Nym a second glance and just called out for the next person to step forward in a bored voice.

Defeated, Nym trudged away from the gate. It was a good thing he'd spent most of his money on a new set of clothes after all. It had taken less than a day to lose the rest of it to some random pickpocket. He followed his own trail back a few blocks and found a dead-end alley he'd noted when he was looking for work. It wasn't pretty or even clean, but it was mostly protected from the wind.

With a dejected sigh, he sat down in a corner and spent his first night in Abilanth shivering in the cold.

CHAPTER 28

Nym woke up in the middle of the night and walked back to the wall. He already knew that staying in the outer ring was a trap and that if he wanted to claw his way upward, he'd have much better luck in the middle. He also wanted to have some words with that attendant who'd never mentioned to him that he needed some sort of identification to move closer to the center of the city.

Since he had no money and no way to get it in the immediate future, he used magic instead. Judging that there were too many unknowns to going directly over the walls, he flew up the mountain instead. There at least he was sure he wouldn't be spotted by guards or caught by any magic that might have been placed there specifically to detect anyone trying to sneak over. He was in a city of magic, after all, and there was no telling what it was capable of.

So he skimmed the stone of the mountain, at times flying almost completely vertical, until he was a thousand feet outside the bounds of Abilanth. And then he just went a few hundred feet to the side and came right back down. His shoes touched down on the smooth stone of a middle-ring street and, just like that, he was back where he'd started. No one came running, no one started shouting at him.

At least one thing had gone right. Not much else had for him since he'd gotten to the city. Just about all his assumptions had been wrong, but he was more or less stranded now. There was no way he was getting a teleport back, even if he wanted one. He had no idea how far it was to the next closest town, he had no food or money, and living off the land wasn't really an option. Everything he'd seen indicated that he was in a barren, rocky land, not conductive to scavenging a meal.

Nym found a new alley to rest in. It wasn't as sheltered as the one he'd left, but he considered it a small price to pay if it meant he'd have the run of the middle ring for the day. He tried to go back to sleep, but it eluded him, and he was still wide-awake when the sun came up. Tired and sore from the cold, he rubbed his eyes and tried to work the kinks out of his muscles.

His stomach grumbled, but he ignored it. It wasn't the first time he'd gone hungry, and it wouldn't be the last. Of more concern was the scratchy dryness of his throat. It was getting bad to the point that he started mentally debating the merits of flying a few thousand feet up the side of the mountain to eat some of the snow painting the peak white.

It was obvious that the city survived on its magic. They probably imported all the food and raw materials they needed since they lived in such an inhospitable location. That made it a lot harder to survive on his own since there were no free resources up for grabs. The more he explored, the more he got the sinking feeling that he'd screwed up enormously coming to Abilanth.

His big advantage was his magic, but he'd come to a place where that was common. Maybe he was a better flyer than other mages, but it didn't matter here. If he was going to survive, he needed to expand his magic. He wasn't going to do that at the Academy. He'd have to teach himself, and he'd have to do it quickly before he starved to death.

With that thought in mind, he started hunting down bookstores. In a city with more concentrated magic than anywhere else in the country, maybe even in the whole world, there had to be plenty of books that he could study from. He would find them first, and then, one way or another, he'd get access to them.

Finding the bookstores wasn't hard. They were everywhere in the middle ring, and they did indeed have the kind of books Nym wanted. The issue was of course that he was broke and none of the owners were interested in trading some labor. Worse, books were three or four times more expensive in Abilanth that what he'd found at the bookstore in Zoskan.

Nym cased out eight bookstores throughout the day, all the while trying to ignore how thirsty he was. They all had interesting books that he thought he could learn from, and they all wanted way too much money. He picked out two stores to revisit that night on the basis that the owner of one was a jackass and the other looked the least defended. It was near the wall on a street that had no guards stationed nearby and had a pair of second-story windows that Nym thought he could gain easy entry from.

Once, when he was coming out of the fifth store, he almost panicked to find himself walking into a column of twenty men who looked like guards. On closer inspection, he upgraded them from town guards to professional soldiers. They looked grim and carried full packs as they marched in time. He watched them go down the street, and people scramble to get out of their way. They turned toward the mage guildhall and disappeared.

Relieved that it had nothing to do with him and his scouting completed, Nym retreated to an alley to wait for it to get dark.

* * *

The streets were empty, and the night sky was overcast. Nym couldn't ask for better cover. He floated in the air in front of the window, studying it using the spell he'd accidentally made when he'd attempted to make a dark vision spell. Everything was white, and details faded into the background after a few feet, but he could see the outline of the shutters perfectly.

He discovered that he could see through the shutters like they were glass, which made it even easier to locate the inside latch holding them closed. A precision burst of air flipped it back, giving him access to the glass beneath. That wasn't locked, and he just pushed it open to gain access to the bookstore. Nym closed the shutters behind him and paused, ears straining. Everything was silent.

Confident that he was alone, he descended to the floor. It was harder to navigate with his sight limited to a few feet around him and with the strange see-through-outline quality everything had, but eventually he found the shelf he was looking for. At least, he thought he did. The weird white vision had another drawback he hadn't initially realized: he couldn't read anything printed on the books, and that included the titles.

He let the spell go, hoping there would be enough light to at least confirm he'd found the right books. That was not the case, and he was just as blind. Mentally cursing, he grabbed one at random and brought it up to the glass window to try to read the title. That didn't provide the light he needed either. It was ironic how appreciative he was of that cloudy sky just a few minutes ago, and now that he was in the store itself, he couldn't tell what he wanted.

There was no help for it. Unless he could whip up a true dark vision spell on the fly, he was just going to have to go by memory. He closed his eyes and thought back. The snooty manager had been standing by the table holding the book Nym wanted to know the price on. When he'd found out Nym couldn't afford it, he'd put it back on the second shelf. Nym tried to mentally count how many books from the left it was.

He traced the shelf in question to the seventh book and pulled it out. It felt right, the right thickness, the right size. He remembered a gilt embossing on the title page and flipped the book open to check. It was there. Excitement coursed through him. If nothing else, he had found the one book he wanted. All he had to do now was fly back out through the window and close it behind him. Someone would eventually realize it was gone, but hopefully long after they'd forgotten Nym had ever expressed any interest in it.

If he read it fast enough, he might even return it and take another one before anyone realized. He laughed at the idea of treating the bookstore like a library. No doubt the owner would have a fit if he ever found out, but there wouldn't really be any harm done.

He reactivated his quasi-dark vision spell and spread out the books a little bit so there was no obvious gap on the shelf. Then, mission completed, he flew back up to the window and slipped through it. As soon as he passed through, the book in his arm started screaming. Nym was so startled that he dropped it, but he quickly snagged it with a cushion of air and brought it back up to his hands. An aura of magic surrounded it, emitting the ear-piercing sound.

There was no help for it. He spun in place and chucked the book back into the store, hoping that would shut it up. Then he slammed the window closed and noted that it somewhat muffled the sound, but the book was definitely still creating a racket. He considered closing the shutters too, but it would take precious time to relatch them, and he could already hear guards approaching.

Nym flew off, skimming the roofs and checking to make sure there was nobody nearby when he had to pass over streets. He spotted several patrols, but none of them noticed him in the dark. Over the next hour, he kept moving, putting distance between himself and the bookstore he'd attempted to burgle. Only once he was far enough away that he didn't see active guard patrols every few minutes did he finally slow down.

"Well, that could have gone better for you," a voice said from right next to him.

Nym just about fell off the roof in surprise. He spun in place to see a lanky man squatting down, looking out over the city. It was impossible to make out his features in the dark, and even then, Nym was almost positive he was wearing a mask under the hood of his coat. Whoever the man was, Nym hadn't seen him approach, and he seemed to know about the burglary.

There was no reason to admit to a crime though. "Who are you? What are you talking about?" he asked.

"I mean your attempts to abscond with some valuable merchandise from the Quill and Bindings. I suppose you weren't aware of the alarm spells set to go off whenever a book leaves the building without authorization. Rookie mistake, really. It could happen to anyone. Your entry and exit, however, that was good stuff. Very stable flight, and if I don't miss my guess, fine control over a lock you couldn't even see to open the shutters from the inside."

Nym's stomach dropped into his shoes. Whoever this man was, he'd seen everything. "Who are you?" he asked again.

"You can call me Valgo," the man told him. "I have a . . . let's call it a business opportunity for you. I could use someone with your talents to help with my work."

"What work is that?" Nym was skeptical. He'd been all over the city looking for work, and nobody had been impressed with him. Whatever Valgo wanted, it was doubtful that it was something Nym wanted to be a part of.

"The same kind of work you do," Valgo told him. "I know a bit of magic. You know a bit of magic. With a bit of training, we could get anywhere and take anything."

"That sounds like a bad idea."

"The bad idea was stealing from a bookstore without understanding the wards. Did you even know that they existed?"

". . . No."

"There you go then. You've got much to learn, my little lightfoot. You come work for me and I'll teach you all you need to know."

This wasn't the kind of education Nym had come to Abilanth to obtain. He wanted to learn magic, not thievery. The theft had been an act of necessity. He'd even been planning on returning the book once he was done with it! Maybe. It depended on how bad he needed money and if he could find a pawnshop to buy it.

When he didn't say anything, Valgo told him, "You take a day or two to think about it. When you get desperate, come to the Ivory Haven on the west side of the outer ring and ask for me."

Then the man was gone, disappearing into the dark while Nym fled to a new roof. He didn't stop moving until the sun was fully up and he was sure that Valgo wasn't still stalking him. How the man had seen everything and then followed him from roof to roof for over an hour after without Nym ever noticing, that scared him.

What scared him even more was that he still hungry and very, very thirsty, and with each passing hour, his options were fewer. If he didn't want to die in the streets, he might not have a choice but to work for Valgo.

CHAPTER 29

The Ivory Haven was a gambling den. With its name, Nym shouldn't have been surprised. They didn't want to let him in at first, both because of his age and because he had no money. Nobody got into a gambling den with empty pockets, and nobody got to remain when the money ran out. When he told the bouncer he was here to speak to Valgo, they changed their stance, and he was escorted to a room down a dark hallway leading away from the main gambling floor.

He was left in an empty room. There was a table with a lantern on it, unlit, and two chairs. All were made of rough, unfinished wood, the kind that he'd expect to walk away with a splinter or two just from sitting on it. They closed the door, leaving him in the dark. Nym wasn't sure if they were expecting him to light the lantern, but if so, he had no tools for it.

Maybe he was just supposed to sit in the dark until Valgo showed up. Nym wouldn't be doing that either. He channeled arcana through his soul well to form the quasi-dark vision spell, and the room came back into view, or at least it did for a few feet around him in every direction. He paced the outside of the room, noting as he did that the bouncer was still standing outside in front of the door, guarding it.

He also found a hidden exit behind a false wall, which was laughably easy to spot since he could see down the hallway it connected to. Nym leaned against the wall next to it and waited. Sure enough, Valgo came into sight, creeping along silently and pausing to put his ear to the wall for a moment before he activated the mechanical switches that caused the wall to swing open. They were completely silent on well-oiled hinges, but even without his magic enhancing his sight, Nym would have sensed the change in the air.

Valgo moved with confidence, despite the room being pitch-black. Nym suspected he had a true dark vision spell to help him navigate but didn't see the glow of arcana around him other mages had exhibited. Perhaps it was possible to hide that as well.

Valgo had obviously seen him standing next to the door but hadn't said anything as he crossed the room silently and struck a spark to the lantern. A small flame flared up, and he adjusted it to throw enough light to illuminate the table.

"You aren't surprised to see me," Valgo observed.

"Felt the change in the air when you opened the door."

"Hmm . . . excellent, but maybe only in an enclosed space. It did not seem to work for you last night."

Nym shrugged. The man obviously had a flair for the theatrical, and Nym wasn't going to get sucked into the drama. He did not trust Valgo, and he wanted to give away as little information as possible. Valgo knew he could fly, and if Nym had his way, that was all he'd ever discover about him. Every secret he gave up was a bargaining chip he lost.

Valgo studied him in the light of the flickering flames, not that he needed them. If he wanted to pretend he did though, Nym would play along. "So," he said, "you have decided to accept my offer."

"No, I've decided to hear the details of your offer. It would seem to me that it's necessary to know what the offer is before I accept it."

Valgo laughed softly. "Wise beyond your years. That is good. Though I think you did not grow up on the streets. You are only half as suspicious as you would be otherwise."

The truth was that Nym's stomach had begun to twist itself in knots when he entered the Ivory Haven, and it had only gotten worse when the bouncer had led him to the meeting room. He did not trust any of them, and the only thing that kept him from fleeing was knowing how desperate his situation was and that nobody in a gambling den was likely to try to imprison him.

Though once he thought about it, he was technically a criminal here now too. But the guards didn't know who he was, so it didn't count. They wanted someone for the bookstore break in, but not Nym specifically. Why that made a difference, he couldn't tell. Emotions weren't rational, and he was just thankful the fear wasn't as paralyzing as it had been back in Zoskan. Somehow the thought of being imprisoned and tried for Senman's murder was worse than the fear that Valgo would try to kill him right now.

That fear also existed and, in Nym's opinion, was entirely rational. But he countered it by telling himself that Valgo wanted something from him and hadn't even told him what it was yet, so he would at least have the chance to hear the man out and could pretend to accept the offer before fleeing if need be.

"Very well, let me enlighten you to the opportunities that exist in your future, my young friend," Valgo said, sweeping his hands out wide. Nym was starting to find the theatrics annoying.

"You've got a measure of natural abilities. You've reached into the second layer, what they call the Edge of the Horizon up at the Academy. And I am guessing you did it on your own, considering the condition you're in. You don't have anyone backing you up. No one is bankrolling your application. You need a place to live, a place to study, someone to tutor you and give you the resources you need to grow. I can do all of that for you."

"That all sounds great. What do you want in return?" Nym asked.

"I want you to do what you were already prepared to do, but against more valuable targets and more successfully. I will personally teach you the stealth and illusion magics I use, and I'll feed you information on soft targets."

"You want me to be a thief, and to take all the risks of being caught and then give you the profits. Why would I do that? Why not just steal things for myself and keep all the profits if I'm taking all the risks?"

Valgo grinned and said, "And who are you going to fence the goods to? Do you know which pawnshops know not to ask questions? Do you have the capital to bribe guards and servants to give you information? Do you have friends high up in the city bureaucracy to get you out of trouble?"

"Do you?" Nym asked.

"Of course I do. How do you think I got to be so successful?"

"I don't know how successful you are," Nym pointed out.

"I'm successful enough that I knew you were casing bookstores yesterday, which one you would hit, and what you were after. I watched you do it from the roof of that cute little bakery across the street. You were impressive, but rough, unrefined. Clearly an amateur. Let me make you a professional and we'll both get rich. Everyone gets what they want."

"I'm sure your victims don't feel that way."

Valgo snorted and waved a hand dismissively. "Rich tits who only know they should be outraged because someone dared to rob them. Believe me, they feel no lack of comfort at being relieved of some spare coin and jewelry."

That was probably true. Nym knew he wouldn't feel much guilt over mugging someone like Amos. That rich little prick had it coming, and he'd probably just get another purse full of crests and keep moving forward like nothing had ever happened and whine about it over his dinner that night.

That did not mean every rich kid was the same. Nym considered that teenager who had offered to pick up the difference at the tailor's shop. He would feel horrible robbing someone like that. He'd done a lot of things over the last month that Ciana wouldn't approve of, even in the last day, but he hadn't sunk that low, not yet.

"It's an interesting offer," Nym said. "I'd like some time to think about it."

Valgo knocked on the door Nym had been let in through. It opened to reveal the bouncer. "Take our young friend here back outside," he instructed. "If he comes back tonight, alone, show him back to this room. Otherwise he should be turned away at the door."

"Got it," the man said. "Come on then."

Nym was escorted back out to the streets, and the door slammed closed behind him. He walked away, thinking furiously. On the one hand, he had no interest in becoming a thief. On the other, he was very, very hungry. He'd spotted a fountain in the middle ring and managed to scoop up a few mouthfuls of water, which did a little bit to assuage his thirst, but the weird looks other people at the park gave him convinced him to move along in a hurry.

One way or another, he was going to end up stealing to survive. He'd tried finding honest work, and it just wasn't out there. What little money he had saved when he got here was gone, spent on warmer clothes and then the remainder stolen. The question in his mind was whether being independent was better than putting himself under someone like Valgo.

The thief was obviously experienced, well-connected, probably rich, and most importantly, had access to magic. Nym saw it in the meeting, just for a moment, when the lantern had been lit. Once his eyes had shifted from the white outlines that saw through objects to normal vision, and he'd noticed the aura of arcana around Valgo's face. It was like an oily black sheen surrounding his eyes, but only for a second before it disappeared.

Valgo definitely had some sort of vision-enhancing spell he used, which meant he was the real deal. He probably couldn't teach Nym a tenth of what he'd learn if he could go to the Academy, but that wasn't in the cards. The offer he had in front of him was learn to steal, make Valgo richer, and in return have food and shelter and access to magic.

Nym wasn't stupid. He knew he wasn't getting the better end of the deal. Valgo would screw him over the second he thought it was worth more than keeping him around. Worse, if Nym went down this road, he was likely sabotaging his potential future at the Academy. That was the whole reason he was here. He might come back from being a thief who stole food to survive. He wouldn't come back from being a thief who knocked off nobles' estates.

He walked the streets and alleys of the outer ring while he wrestled with his conscience. Short term, the answer was obvious: take the deal. Long term, the answer was also obvious: stay far, far away from the deal. He needed to think long-term, so he should reject Valgo's offer. The problem was that he wasn't sure he could survive in the short term if he did that.

As it got darker, he saw other kids creeping around. Some were a bit older than him; most were younger. All of them were ragged looking, with shaggy, unkempt hair and dirty, torn, and scuffed clothes. None of them had shoes.

Nym winced at that. His feet were cold even with the layer of leather protecting him from the stone streets.

"Hey," he said to one of the kids. "Where is everyone going?"

"It's bread day," the kid told him, looking at him like he was stupid. "What's a fancy kid like you need with it?"

"He's not fancy," an older boy told him. "Looks like he got lucky and stole some warm clothes. They don't fit him at all. A real noble would have it all tailored. You homeless?"

Nym nodded. "Thought I could find work here. Thought wrong. Nobody will hire me. Someone stole my money, not that I had a lot. Been sleeping outside since I got here."

The boy shook his head and sighed. "Come on, new kid. I'll show you where to get some food."

Nym followed the children to a church built up against the outer wall where a pair of priests were giving out some old, stale bread. It was not good, not at all, but it filled his stomach for the first time in days.

The kids showed him an old, abandoned warehouse they slept in. It was in such bad shape that he worried it would collapse on them, but at least it had open access to the sky in case he needed to flee. Nym settled into a corner and tried to get some sleep.

He did not go back to the Ivory Haven that night. He slept just fine.

CHAPTER 30

It turned out there were a lot of ways to scavenge in a city, once Nym knew what he was doing. He was never full, never comfortable, but he wasn't under Valgo's thumb. He could keep trying to find a way into the Academy. In the interest of not being arrested, Nym refrained from using his magic as much as possible. He didn't have a license and wasn't likely to get one any time soon.

That was not to say that everything he did was strictly legal. Some of the other children were adept pickpockets. It was entirely possible that he was now living with whoever had robbed him on his first day, but if so, nobody had admitted to recognizing him and he hadn't asked. He completely understood why they did it.

Nym was not a pickpocket. He lacked the manual dexterity and the nerves. But he wasn't above rummaging through trash for some food that was only slightly moldy. That part could be cut away easily enough. He wasn't above spying on people, and he wasn't above picking up something left unattended and scampering off with it.

Probably his biggest legal sin was hopping the wall with some regularity to explore the middle ring. Once, just once, he'd gone to the inner ring. Almost immediately he'd been accosted by guards wanting to know who he was and how he'd gotten in. He'd been unceremoniously escorted not only out of the inner ring, but through the middle ring and into the outer. The guards had not been gentle, and the entire time, his heart had been beating so hard he thought it would burst out of his chest.

If the guard holding his arm had let go for even a second, Nym would have flown off into the sky, consequences be damned. The man's hand was an unwavering vise though, and it didn't let go until Nym was being roughly thrown through the gates and he was warned not to let them catch a filthy gutter dweller in the middle or inner ring again.

As the weeks rolled by, Nym learned how to survive. He wasn't thriving by any definition, but he found food. The street kids looked out for one another, at least a little bit. They had a stash of blankets, old and ratty and thin but better than nothing, that were distributed as the weather got cold. There weren't enough for everybody, so kids huddled up with their friends to share heat.

Things were getting worse as it got colder, but so far, everyone was hanging on. Nym's problem was that he was only just getting by. There was no money to be had, and no access to training, tutors, or resources. Not for the first time, he regretted leaving Zoskan. The more weatherworn and torn up his clothing got, the more the guards noticed him, and Nym started to feel that familiar panic again. Something about guards paying attention to him scared him.

He was starting to fear going into buildings too, but that was less of an issue since nobody wanted a homeless kid in their store anyway. Everyone knew just from looking at him that he didn't have a single bent bronze wedge, and thus was not a potential customer. He could at best be a nuisance, at worse a thief, so he was blocked from even entering stores by guards or shopkeepers in the middle ring, and booted out immediately in the outer ring.

Things were slowly getting worse for him as the weather turned bad, but he was hanging on. Then the first snowfall hit Abilanth, and everything went wrong.

Nym stood in the center of an alley near the south edge of the wall, surrounded on both sides by four grown men. He shrank back toward the wall as they advanced, forming a half circle. "Well, well," the one with the club said. "Looks like it's our lucky day, huh, boys?"

"Sure does," one of them agreed. "We needed someone just like you, and you look like you need a warm place to sleep. Everybody wins."

Somehow, Nym doubted that. "I've already got a warm bed," he lied. "Sorry, but you'll have to find someone else to help with whatever you need."

"I doubt it," the man with the club said. He pointed it at Nym's shoes, then his knees, then his torso. "Shoes are coming off the soles. Holes worn out in the knees. Coat is split at the seams. The clothes aren't heavy enough for winter. You're one of the kid bums that holes up in that old warehouse."

"Even if I was, that's good enough for me. Leave me alone."

"See, I think you're one of those whoresons that got turned out onto the street. Got too big and started costing dear ol' mom some of the clients. So she cut you loose. Well, good news, you get to join the family business. You'll get a warm bed and two meals a day, and you'll be a call boy. They'll rent you by the hour."

The man leered at him and smacked the club into his hand. "Now, you don't need all your teeth to be a call boy. And bruises heal eventually. So don't think I'm afraid to rough up the merchandise. You can come easy or hard. Your choice, call boy."

The sun was behind the mountains now. The men cast long shadows in the twilight hours, and as they moved, those shadows twisted like demons. A gust of wind howled down the alley, sending up snow flurries that briefly blinded Nym. In that moment of vulnerability, one of the men lunged forward and grabbed Nym.

"Get away from me!" he screamed, opening his conduit up and filling his soul well.

Snow wasn't exactly like water, but it was close enough. Nym grabbed hold of the flakes and sharpened them into shards of ice. Then spun around in the air, cutting the man who grabbed him. Little slices appeared on his hand, causing him to flinch back, and then across his face and into his eyes. The man bellowed in pain and stumbled backward, grabbing at his eyes.

Before Nym could flee, the club struck him across the back of his head. He tumbled to the street, and his vision blackened. He knew he needed to do something, to use his magic, to run, to scream for help. All he could do was hang on while the world spun around him.

Something hit his ribs hard enough to flip him over onto his back. He saw leering faces overhead, tried to focus on them, but it was too hard. He was seeing at least triple, all of them dancing around one another, weaving in and out of his sight.

Then they disappeared. There was some yelling and some loud thumps, and a new face appeared. Hands helped him upright and held him steady. "It's okay, take your time. Just focus on my voice. You're alright now. Deep breaths. Steady now. Good, good."

Nym pulled himself back together slowly. He was still in an enormous amount of pain, but it was just pain, not nausea and dizziness. He could focus, maybe not as well as normal, but better than he could a few minutes ago. The first thing he saw was all four men slumped against the wall in front of him. They were alive but injured. There was a lot of blood in the alley, some of it probably Nym's.

"Nym, focus please," the voice said. Nym realized someone had been speaking to him for a little while now. He tried to mentally play back the conversation, but it was just noise.

"How'd . . . how'd you know my name?" he slurred out.

"Of course I know your name. I've been keeping track of you for a month now. Did you think I'd risk someone so valuable to a couple of rented thugs looking to fill empty rooms in a brothel? As for you, you idiots, go grab kids somewhere else. If you knew he was staying in my shelter, you knew better than to touch him."

Nym finally got a look at his rescuer. Even shrouded in twilight shadows, it was unmistakably Valgo. He trembled in sudden fear and wondered if it would have been better to get abducted by the body snatchers after all. Nym did *not* want to owe Valgo a favor.

Valgo pushed something into his hand, and Nym looked down at in confusion. It looked like some sort of ticket, but he couldn't read it in the dark. "Little present for you. There are three books at a pawnshop called the Stop 'n' Hock. They were pawned for four shims, with the option for the holder of the receipt to reclaim them for five shims in the next week."

"I don't have five shims," Nym mumbled.

"I'm sure a smart boy like you can find a way. Run along now. I need to have a chat with these men about the consequences of interfering in my business operations."

Valgo put a hand on Nym's back and guided him toward the end of alley. Nym stumbled forward and kicked up some snow as he staggered back out onto the street. Behind him, he could hear all four men blubbering and stammering as they made excuses. Then there was the heavy thud of metal chopping down onto meat.

Nym kept his eyes locked forward and ran as fast as his legs could carry him. He didn't slow down until he could no longer hear Valgo handing out his punishment.

The next day, Nym found the Stock 'n' Hock. Valgo hadn't been playing with him. The books really were there, confirmed by the pawnbroker and shown to him. They were his, as long as he came back with the receipt in his hand and five copper shims.

Nym clutched the receipt like his life depended on it. He knew Valgo was taunting him, trying to push him into compromising his morals. Nym wanted those books. He wanted them badly. But did he want them enough to steal money? He didn't need the books to survive. It wasn't like stealing food.

He returned to the old warehouse, what the almost two dozen homeless kids living there called the sanctuary. He bumped into Ermy, one of the older boys who was an accomplished pickpocket. There was nobody there Nym respected more. Ermy brought in the lion's share of the food that went to feeding the younger kids. Without his work, half of the children living in the sanctuary would be dead.

"Ermy, listen," Nym said. "You always have a bit of money you scrounged up. Do you have five shims?"

"Why?" Ermy asked suspiciously.

"I need it. Look, I'll . . . uh . . . sell you my coat? That's good for five shims, right?"

Ermy eyed it up, suspicion replaced by naked desire. "You sure? It's only going to get colder. You're going to regret this in a month."

"I need the money," Nym repeated. He shrugged off the coat and held it out. "Deal?"

Ermy snatched the coat out of his hands and immediately put it on. He pulled a handful of shims out of his pocket and handed them over. "Don't know what you're thinking, but good luck."

"It was worth it," Nym told him. "But hey, when you get too big for it, maybe pass it on to Dai. She needs it the most, okay?"

"Sure," Ermy agreed easily.

Nym practically ran back out into the streets, and he didn't slow down until he got to the Stop 'n' Hock. When he left, he clutched three slim tomes to his chest. He returned to the sanctuary and settled down in a corner. The other kids watched curiously, but Nym ignored them and began to read.

CHAPTER 31

There are three layers of extrareality that are wrapped around existence. By forging a conduit out of his will, a mage can pierce the veil that separates our reality from the next. The first layer is known as the Phase Shift, as it is closest to ours. By bringing back arcana, the essence of a layer, a mage is able to perform magic.

Arcana from the Phase Shift is too similar to the essence that suffuses our own reality to perform truly powerful magic. It is made for little things, and a good guiding rule is that Phase Shift arcana is good for things a person could have done himself. The most common example to illustrate this point is basic telekinesis.

A young mage may learn to channel arcana to lift objects and move them, but it feels as though he is physically moving the object. Thus he becomes tired from muscle strain, and is limited by his own physical capacity. There are some benefits to be had, such as moving an object that would not be safe to physically handle or retrieving it from a place that would be difficult to reach.

This primer concerns itself primarily with exploring the first layer and the basic spells a novice mage can practice to improve his foundational understanding of magic. It takes a certain amount of willpower both to hold a conduit open and to shape the raw arcana that fills a mage's soul well, and it is easy to become both physically and mentally exhausted.

The book wasn't exactly treading new ground for him, but now that Nym finally had something, he was determined to read every single word of it. There were some interesting facts scattered throughout the pages, though not a lot that was immediately helpful. Unfortunately, as a beginner's instruction manual, the book focused primarily on different mental exercises to help learn how to forge a conduit to the first layer and hold it steady.

Nym found the first book to be largely a waste of his time. The author was of the opinion that the first layer was good for nothing but practicing basic concepts and that a true mage should seek to advance to the second layer as quickly as possible. Considering that was how he felt about it, Nym wasn't sure why the author had written the primer in the first place.

If he'd been interested in becoming a professional soldier, the book would have been an invaluable starting point. The spells could be cast nigh instantaneously as the first layer was easily reached and often augmented physical capabilities. Nym was not truly utilizing his access to Phase Shift arcana at all, but he shifted learning more to the bottom of his priority list as the second layer was where true magic came from.

In that respect, the other two books were much more beneficial to read through. Some of it was review for him, as it appeared that an elemental understanding was a basic starting point. Many mages had an intuitive affinity to a particular element and often built on that before expanding into more complicated spells that required abstract thinking to construct.

Unfortunately, both of the other books skimmed over the topic of basic elementalism, merely noting that it was common for an affinity to exist and recommending other books to train on a specific one. The bulk of the information was on concepts that revolved around gaining better control over a conduit. According to both books, absolute mastery of the conduit was required to ever advance past the second layer, and it was the rare mage indeed who managed it.

There were some interesting mental exercises that Nym was eager to try, but what he really wanted was instruction on new spells. His magic needed to be more flexible so that he would be more valuable and could find work. Of that, there was very little. The third volume had a few starter spells to expand his repertoire, but it was just more basic elemental manipulation. There wasn't much there that he wouldn't have figured out on his own given a bit more time.

Even if it wasn't exactly what Nym had hoped for, he was happy with his new knowledge. It was a lot of fundamentals, about half of which he'd already figured out, but it pushed him to think in new ways. There was a big section that focused on how magic interacted differently when self-targeted and when sent out into the world, and again for things that were alive and things that were not. Those ideas led him to develop what he would consider to be his first truly complicated piece of magic.

He still hadn't gotten over Valgo's display of dark vision. He knew it was possible. He'd seen the evidence, but he couldn't figure out how. In his quest to duplicate that magic, he found something else. His quasi-dark vision spell that let him see everything as though it were lines sketched onto paper had a serious flaw: lack of range. Nym fixed that by modifying the spell's anchor point.

No longer did it show him the same thing he saw with his eyes. Now he could project it out as a form of rudimentary scrying. He could still only see a few feet around the anchor point, but that point was now mobile. Nym could spy on anyone, though it was limited to only sight, and it got hard to hold the spell together past a few hundred feet. Walls didn't stop it though, so it was an excellent scouting spell.

He also increased his water-manipulation abilities exponentially. Nym could easily pull water out of the air now, something he hadn't even known as possible without mist or fog previously, and pour it into a cup he formed from ice. Having a big chilled box made of ice proved popular with the other kids, as the water was invariably cleaner than whatever they managed to scavenge, plus they had fun with the chunks of ice floating in it. Nym briefly wondered if he could sell ice-making services to restaurants, but his new scrying eyes showed him that, once again, the abundance of mages from the Academy had beaten him to it.

He devoured the three books in a day, then spent a week digesting their contents and thinking up ways to apply them to what he already knew. He also brainstormed magic that would be most immediately useful, like an insulation or heating spell. His focus was on subtle magics; he didn't want to get fined for using magic without a license, but it was a lot harder to catch someone using a hand-warmer spell than someone flying around town.

As the weather got colder and snow became more frequent, he turned his attention entirely to using his magic to generate heat. Unfortunately, something about elemental fire still escaped him, and the best he managed was to heat up some scrap wood he pried out of a hole in the wall to the point that it merely smoldered instead of bursting into flame.

He kept working on it. Keeping himself from freezing to death was high on his priorities, and if Ermy had been wrong that he would regret trading his coat away, he certainly did miss it. So Nym practiced, and he failed, and he caused a few small fires, but those were easily put out. A few more weeks passed by . . .

Nym was not surprised when Valgo approached him again. He'd been working on his scry sight, trying to figure out how to expand the range and also train himself to acclimate to an unexpected nausea he got as he widened its field of vision. Humans were not meant to see in that wide a range, and everything started to get curved in a way that made him want to throw up if he moved the scry anchor too fast.

Nym was sitting on the edge of the roof of a healing clinic, watching traffic trickle in and out of the business. Despite the late hour, there was always somebody on duty and always a few people in need of emergency services. His range had expanded enough to both watch the interior and see himself sitting there, and Valgo approached from the far end, which gave him plenty of warning.

Nym dismissed the spell so that he could study the stealth magics the thief used to conceal his approach. Even knowing where he was, it was difficult to see the man. His aura was as black as the night around him, but Nym found the outline and stared at him.

Valgo paused, surprised maybe that he'd been detected. But then he continued forward, his gait still confident. He sat down next to Nym and said, "Still improving, huh? Those books were a good investment. Where did you learn the detection spell you used to see me?"

"Made it myself," Nym said. "What do you want? It's kind of creepy that you're stalking someone my age."

"Hey now. It's natural for me to look after my investments and the children living in the home I provide for them. You are both of those things. Besides, I have work for you."

"I don't do your kind of work," Nym told him flatly.

"Right, but see, I have this."

Valgo held up a pawnbroker's receipt, though it was too dark to make out the words. "More books?" Nym asked. It didn't matter how tempting the offer was, he wasn't going to steal for the man. Working for Valgo would only lead to him getting dragged deeper into a lifestyle he did not want.

"Specifically, three books. Your books. This is the receipt for the books on magic you sold when you were finished with them, or maybe when you got desperate. But I respect you, kid. My money's on you got all you could and unloaded the baggage."

Nym's brow furrowed. He had sold those books once he was done reading them, just yesterday. "How do you have that?"

When anyone sold something to a pawnshop, there were two receipts. One went to the seller, and the other went to the broker. Nym had destroyed his receipt; he didn't need the books back, but he did need the five shims he got for them, which was barely a fraction of what they cost new. So Valgo had to have the broker's copy.

"The guy who owns the shop practically considers the Ivory Haven to be his second home. He owes me all sorts of favors. More importantly, this receipt is evidence that you owned those three books, which just happen to be the same three books that were stolen from a bookstore in the east middle ring two weeks ago, which was reported to the guard.

"Now . . . you know you didn't steal them. I know you didn't steal them. But the guards, well, you have to see how suspicious it looks. Here you are, a homeless orphan, nowhere to go, no money. The guards would never believe you acquired those books legally." Valgo laughed cruelly. "I doubt they'll even investigate beyond getting your description and arresting you."

He stopped talking for a minute and mimed thinking. "Did you know that in Valtareth, they cut off a thief's right hand? Fortunately we're not so barbaric here. Still, one could argue that it's better than being indentured to the penal system while you pay off your debt. Fortunately for you, there's a third option."

"You have work for me," Nym echoed Valgo's earlier words.

"See, I knew you were a smart boy. Now, since you're here in the middle ring and I know you don't have an identification badge showing you as a citizen, that means you've got a way around the walls. That's good because you're going to need to go to the inner ring. Let me tell you all about a noble who lives there named Jaspar Feldstal."

Nym stared off into the darkness glumly. He should have known better than to think he'd dodged Valgo's play. The thief had known exactly what he'd do with those books once he was done with them. Now it was time to pay the real price for accepting help from the evil man.

CHAPTER 32

Nym regretted coming to Abilanth, Academy or no. He couldn't for the life of him figure out why he'd thought this was a good idea. It wasn't like *he* was going to get into the Academy. He was too young, too dirty, too poor, and too unknown. A part of him had thought it would be easy to waltz right in when he'd found out Amos had been admitted. After all, that twit could barely magic himself out of an empty room with an open door, so Nym should have had no problems.

He hadn't factored in Amos's family, the money, the connections, the pedigree. Sure, Nym was a better mage by far, but Amos was a known quantity. He would go to the Academy, attend his classes, *pay his tuition*, and graduate in a few years, just the way the Academy wanted. Nym would not do any of those things. Nym couldn't even get into the middle ring without sneaking in.

Teaching himself was not going so well. His experiments with fire magic had nearly gotten him kicked back out onto the streets. The other kids all hated him now, and it was only because Valgo had a use for him that the old thief had interceded to let him stay, proving once and for all that Nym was firmly in his grasp now. No one had cared enough to help with all the burns he'd gotten.

So he huddled in a corner that smelled of rotted wood and mildew and cursed the sky for giving them more snow. The roof was more holes than shingles at this point, and all the good corners were taken by other kids. Sure, Nym could bully his way in. He was bigger than most of the kids, except for a few of the oldest, and it wasn't like anyone else had magic. All it would cost was any semblance of security and yet another guilty barb in his conscience.

Street kids were vicious, and right now everybody hated him. If Nym forced someone out of one of the good corners so he could be moderately more comfortable, the most likely result was that one of them would murder him in his sleep. Valgo might be annoyed since he still had plans for Nym, might even beat whatever urchin did it to death, but that wouldn't help Nym after the fact.

No, the best option was to accept the mildewy corner for the protection it gave him from the wind and lament that his lack of control over his pyromancy had cost him the goodwill of his fellow street urchins. He needed to keep working on the internal-heat-regulation spell anyway if he was going to survive the winter. It was that or find a new place to sleep, and he was not interested in the other offer he had.

Nym shuddered just thinking about it. If Valgo hadn't come along when he did, it would have been a kidnapping, not an offer. He was not eager to peddle his ass in a brothel, no matter how warm it was or how regular the meals were. It was twelve kinds of messed up that places like that even existed, and worse that thugs went out and just rounded up random homeless kids to fill the rooms.

He was so lost in his own thoughts that it took him a minute to realize something was happening. The street kids were all running for the far end of the building, but they were excited instead of scared, so Nym knew there was no danger. Nobody could rabbit like a pack of street urchins, and they'd disappear at the mere whiff of trouble. Curious, but also knowing he wasn't welcome, Nym rose from his place and followed after them at a distance.

A young man was in the building with a pack. He was maybe sixteen or seventeen, wearing brown robes that announced his status as a student at the Academy. Nym had seen some of them around town when he'd first gotten to Abilanth, and he recognized the stitching on the border, even if this one's color was different from the ones he'd seen.

The teenager set down the pack and started calling the urchins toward him by name. They clearly knew what was happening, since they all came willingly and no one crowded him. Nym's eyebrows rose as he watched the student mage pull out jars of salves and ointments, then administer them to the kids.

Everyone got their turn; everyone waited patiently in a way he'd never seen them behave for anyone. Nym smiled to see it, then went back to his corner. It was nice to see that even here, there were some people who cared. The mage was no doubt from some rich family, but spending his dad's money on medical aid for the poor was better than what he'd seen other rich kids waste it on.

He put the student out of mind. As nice as it was to see a ray of hope in the darkness, he still had a long way to go before he climbed back out of it. Valgo was not going to relinquish his blackmail material. He was going to have to help the old thief knock over a couple of manor houses owned by rich nobles. At least it would be stealing from people who could afford to lose it.

That was just a stall though. Valgo wasn't the type of person who would just thank him for a job well done and let him go. There would always be another job as long as he had his hooks in Nym, more work that risked Nym's life to make Valgo rich. He needed to get rid of the pawnshop receipt Valgo had acquired, maybe the books too. More than that, he needed to get rid of Valgo.

The world as a whole would probably be a better place, and if he could get access to all the loot the man had stashed, there would be enough to pay for his place in the Academy and provide a place to live for the street kids currently suffering under Valgo's tyranny. Everyone would be better off if he could only think of a way to do it. Nym hadn't realized how much of the money they stole was funneled right to the old thief until he'd started asking about it.

"Hello," a voice said.

Nym started in place and looked up to see the student mage standing in front of him. The teenager smiled at him and said, "Do you need anything taken care of?"

"No," Nym said slowly, more of a question than an answer. He thought about it for a second. "No. I'm fine. Thank you."

"Are you sure? Those look like fresh burns on your hands and arms."

"Ah . . . that. No. Those are fine."

The burns were his punishment, a thing that the other kids saw and let them know that Nym was suffering for his mistake. Nobody had any blankets anymore, but Nym had it worse because he still had to deal with the burns in addition to being cold.

The student frowned at him and squatted down to sit next to him. "Want to talk about it?" he asked.

"Not much to say. I got the stupid idea that I could warm up our blanket stash so everyone would be more comfortable, but I suck at fire magic and set them on fire instead. Burned myself putting the fire out, and now everyone hates me because it's the first month of winter and we're all going to freeze to death before it gets warm again."

"Blankets," the student muttered to himself, looking around appraisingly. "Of course they need blankets. Hmm."

He turned back to Nym and said, "But you, you're very young to be using fire magic. Really, any second-circle spell is impressive. Did you have a master who took you on as an apprentice?"

Nym laughed bitterly. "Do a couple of beginner books count?"

"Fire though," the student said. "It's considered the hardest of the basic elemental manipulations because the other ones all have sources to draw on. Air is everywhere. Earth is easy to come by as soon as you leave the city, and not too difficult to gather even here. Water, well . . . just look at all the snow.

"But fire, fire is different. With fire, you can't just merge your arcana into the air or ground and enforce your will on the world. Fire needs a spark, an act of creation."

"Got that part down," Nym muttered glumly.

"And once you've formed that fire, it naturally wants to spread and consume. That is fire's nature. It's not like water or air that will settle back to a neutral state once you've finished your work. Fire is hungry, it is alive, and it fights you the whole while. It takes discipline to control fire."

The student raised a hand and showed Nym a small candle flame that floated above his palm. "I do have some small talent with fire magic. This is the exercise I recommend you practice on. It will help you refine your ability to both create fire and control it in a safe manner. The worst you can suffer is a minor burn, and the most likely result is the fire snuffing itself out if you make a mistake since it has no fuel but the arcana you feed it. It's much safer than practicing fire on a pile of flammable blankets."

The student had channeled his arcana so quickly and so effortlessly Nym hadn't even seen that he was casting a spell. That . . . that was impressive. Nym had never seen anybody able to cast magic so smoothly that it didn't even have the telltale glow of arcana filling their soul well, especially not arcana from the second layer. A sliver of fire flared up, fed on nothing but raw arcana, then died when it burned through its fuel.

"Once you've mastered that, you can start working on the basic parameters of control: amount of heat, light, size, and what it will burn. They say the greatest fire mages can melt solid rock with pinpoint accuracy. Wouldn't that be something to see?"

"Yeah, I guess it would."

The teenager stood back up and brushed some loose snow off his robes. "I'm sorry about the burns. They can be quite painful, and children can be cruel. Sometimes good intentions can have disastrous results, and all they see is what was lost, not the reasoning behind it. Are you sure you don't want me to look at them?"

Nym sighed and shook his head. "It's my punishment. They keep me safe because the other kids know that I'm cold *and* in pain."

Something pressed against his foot, and he looked down to see a tiny glass jar being pushed into him by the student's shoe. "I doubt anyone here knows exactly how fast those burns should heal or is going to be looking at what anyone else does in the dark of night," he said offhand, not looking down at the salve.

Tears welled up in Nym's eyes at the unasked-for kindness, but he willed them away. "Thank you," he whispered, and the student nodded.

"I'll be back around when I can, probably in a week or so. Be careful not to get the burns dirty. Burn infections are nasty and expensive to treat. You should look for some clean rags to wrap your hands in. Oh, and if at all possible, I would appreciate the jar back once it's emptied. Good glass can be expensive too."

The student paused to think. "Of course, if it should happen to get stolen by someone who wanted to sell it to an apothecary, why, they would probably get enough for an empty jar to have a hot meal or two. There would be nothing you could do about what's taken from you, so I wouldn't hold it against you if you couldn't return it to me later."

Then the teenager left. Nym watched him stop to talk to a few other kids, sometimes just for a few moments, sometimes longer. He seemed to know everyone and had a kind word for them all. Nym picked the jar up out of the snow and hid it under his shirt when no one was watching.

It was nice to meet a good person again. The mage reminded him of Ciana in all the best ways. There hadn't been too many of those people in his life, just giving with no expectation of return, and he vowed again to repay all of them someday.

CHAPTER 33

Nym had waited a week on Valgo's instructions. The house patriarch of the Feldstal family had left on some business in the west, something important and complicated, and he was liable to be gone for weeks dealing with it. Nym didn't get the details from Valgo, as they weren't important to his job. What was important was that a powerful noble mage was not going to be home when his house got burgled.

Getting into the upper ring was as easy as it always was. Getting to the Feldstal family manor was a lot trickier. Nym kept to the roofs and made his way slowly to his destination. Valgo had given him tons of information and even shown him a copy of the noble family's crest. It was easy to know when he'd found the place, since the nobles apparently felt the need to carve it onto every flat surface in sight.

It was easy to scry the symbols too, and Nym confirmed that they were also present all over inside the manor as well. It struck him as extremely narcissistic, but then again, they were nobles. Regardless, he wasn't there to gawk at their interior decorating. He checked the patrol routes and waited for an opening, then flew through the night to land on the manor roof. From there, it was easy enough to find a window, use basic telekinesis to open it from the inside, and slip in.

Things got more complicated once Nym was inside. There were no patrolling guards, but there were stationary ones, and despite the late hour, there were still large sections of the interior lit with what appeared to be magically enchanted orbs that floated in the air near the ceilings. Nym took a few minutes to examine one that was lit in what looked like a dining room that nobody was using.

He judged it to be an acceptable risk as the servant's hall that connected the dining room to the kitchen was dark, and his scrying had found nobody in any of the nearby rooms. It was the first time he'd seen arcana infused into a physical object, and though he wasn't familiar with the spell to create light, he was able to see the web of runes inscribed into the stone.

It was easy to pick out the flight runes. From what he understood, all runes were a physical representation of how arcana was woven into a pattern to create a spell. It wasn't enough to just copy the rune; each section had to be inscribed in the correct order. Extrapolating from there, Nym quickly divided the orb into three sections. He mentally set aside the flight runes and looked over the rest.

Those he divided into two sections. First, the runes he thought generated the light effect. They were duplicated all over the orb so that it would shine light from every direction, and though he didn't know how to write it, it was so simple that there were really only a few different ways it could possibly have been put together. Nym was sure he could replicate it.

The other section was stuff he wasn't sure on. The best he could figure was that it was a support structure to absorb and store arcana, possibly accept some sort of command input to activate the flight and light runes, and maybe a few other functions he couldn't think of. The runes themselves were foreign to him, completely removed from his own work with elemental magic.

Nym would have liked to take one with him for further study, but he wasn't sure how to control it or if it was keyed to the house in some way. The last thing he needed was another incident like the bookstore alarm. Besides, he wasn't here by choice. He'd be damned if he was going to take a single bronze wedge more than he had to.

He moved from room to room slowly, preferring those that were unlit when possible. He was wearing a mask Valgo had given him just in case someone spotted him, but the hope was that it wouldn't be necessary. Plus, it was easy enough for him to navigate even without sight and stay hidden in the dark rooms. He just floated over all the furniture and hid near the ceiling while he scouted out nearby rooms. It was tedious work, but he knew where he was going. The family had several vaults underground, and while they did hold real wealth, Valgo wanted something else.

The thief had instead provided Nym the route to a library on the third floor. Unfortunately, it wasn't near an outside edge, so Nym had to cross a few hundred feet of open yard, enter through a fourth-floor window, one of the few that opened far enough to let a person in, and sneak down to the third floor and cross a third of the manor house itself to finally reach it.

Supposedly, the library itself had a hidden room where Valgo's target was stored. Nym would find out when he got there. He wasn't even confident he'd make it that far. He was not a good thief, and despite the late hour, the interior of the manor was much better lit than he liked.

The stairs were proving to be especially problematic. There were a pair of guards stationed at the bottom, and they were not moving. Nym sat in a dark room across from the top and scried them for half an hour, and the most he'd learned was that the one on the left seemed obsessed with picking his nose. At the rate he was digging, he'd be striking buried treasure soon enough.

Everything was well lit, and he couldn't see himself managing to get past them without them moving or some kind of distraction. There was supposed to be a second set of stairs on the other end of the house, but that was a whole new set of problems just getting to them. Nym had almost resigned himself to plotting out the trek when one of the guards walked away from his post.

Nym held his breath and stared through the scry. He just needed the other guard to take a few steps to the left and he would be able to fly down and hug the ceiling. His shadow wouldn't be thrown across the man, and he could slip into another empty room just down the hall from the stairs. He waited, his eyes locked on the guard, mentally willing him to move.

And the man just stood there, digging up his nose like he had an itch on his brain. Nym was tempted to go anyway, just gamble that the guard wouldn't notice him flying by. It was a bad idea though, and he knew it. He needed to be patient, but he also knew that if that other guard came back, he'd have no chance at all.

Nym watched the guard stand there, occasionally fidgeting in place. If the guard wasn't going to leave on his own, perhaps Nym could distract him. He did a final sweep to make sure there was no one else nearby and that the second guard wasn't on his way back from wherever he'd disappeared to. Then Nym floated through the air, just out of sight of the guard but ready to shoot past him as soon as he had his opening.

He forged a second conduit with an intent filter on it and pulled first-layer arcana into his soul well. One feat of minor telekinesis later and he was holding the guard's foot down. The next time he tried to shift in place, he nearly fell over. Surprised, the guard glanced down at his foot. Nym pushed back against the recoil in his arms when the man struggled to lift his leg and mentally kicked out with a second wave of telekinesis to push against the back of the guard's knee.

He went down with a clatter of metal, cursing as he fell. Nym made sure to create enough force around him to guide the fall so that he fell forward, and then he swooped down the stairs and ducked into the empty room.

Heart hammering in his chest, he immediately recast his scrying spell and checked on the guard. The man was back on his feet and peering down at the floor. Experimentally, he lifted his foot and put it back down. Then he did the same to the other one.

"What even the hell?" he muttered, loud enough for Nym to hear him in the nearby room. The guard bent down to examine the floor, but of course there was nothing there.

"What are you doing?" the other guard asked, coming back.

"My foot got caught on something," the first guard explained. "But there's nothing there."

Rather than make fun of him like Nym had expected, the second guard took it seriously. "Go get whichever captain is in duty right now. Tell him we might have an intruder in the house with magical capabilities. Explain to him what happened to you."

Nym's face fell. It had seemed like such a good idea at the time, but he'd once again underestimated how accustomed the people of Abilanth were to magic. His whole mission was on a much tighter timetable now, and it was going to be that much harder to reach his objective, not to mention getting back out with the loot.

Nym considered his options. He could abandon the job while he still had the chance. He hadn't been discovered yet, but he'd already screwed up on not letting anyone know he was there. One busted out window wasn't going to change much at this point, especially if he was on his way out when he did it.

Valgo wasn't likely to accept that as an excuse. Nym didn't know exactly how the man would react, but whatever he chose to do, it wouldn't be anything good for Nym personally. The old thief was one problem Nym couldn't just fly away from. As long as he was trapped in Abilanth, living in an old, run-down warehouse that Valgo owned, and with those stolen books in a pawnshop attached to him, he was screwed.

At the same time, the thought of the guards catching hold of him inside the manor was terrifying. He could feel the senseless panic setting in, and no amount of rationalizing the situation was going to change that. Nym tried to control his breathing, to force himself to think clearly. He needed to move now, before someone found him.

Five minutes later, he was still frozen in place. He'd completely lost control of his scrying spell and was just sitting in a dark room, waiting for someone to find him while his mind spun out a hundred different ways everything was going to go wrong. It was only when no one opened the door and found him after half an hour that he finally managed to calm himself down.

Ashamed of himself, Nym took a moment to clean his face on his sleeve and recast his scrying spell. There were guards patrolling now in addition to the ones standing at intersections and doorways, but not a lot of them. If he could keep himself under control, he could still finish the job. He was unbelievably lucky that no one had heard him or even just opened the door to check in the room. He hadn't even made any effort to hide out of sight.

Nym took the time to scry out the rest of the floor and figure out where the rest of the guards were and what they were doing. Then he mapped out a route from his current position to the library. The timing would be tricky, as it depended on slipping past three patrolling guards with overlapping paths. In order to make it work, he needed to move ahead three rooms in the next four minutes, wait two minutes for the hole in the patrols, and slip through.

If one of the patrolling guards showed up even half a minute early, he'd catch Nym, and that would be that. Nym took a deep breath and started moving. Everything went according to plan, and he ghosted down the hallway, flying silently about a hundred feet behind a guard. If the man turned around, he'd see Nym, but it didn't happen. He slipped into another empty room, this one looking like some sort of trophy hall.

There was no real cover, but he didn't care. The room was dark and, most importantly, directly across the hall from the library. All he had to do was scry the hall to make sure it was clear, cross an empty ten feet of space, and get inside the library. He'd already confirmed that was unoccupied.

Once the hallway was clear, Nym jerked the trophy room door open, closed it behind him, and walked over to the library. He opened it, slid in, and closed it behind him. Then he got his first physical look at the place.

There were so many books. Surely some of them would be about magic. It was beautiful. The room itself was huge and had two levels, though there were no doors on the second level. It would have made everything a lot easier if there were. Dozens of light orbs floated in the air, brightening the whole place up like it was midday in there.

Nym had already scouted out the secret room behind a bookshelf. He even thought he knew how to get in. There weren't any obvious mechanical mechanisms embedded in the wall that led to a trigger of some kind, which meant unless there was something magical, he just needed to lift the shelf out of the way.

It didn't matter though because Nym floated over a bookshelf and found himself staring down at a person that his scrying spell had completely failed to detect.

CHAPTER 34

She was a girl a year or two older than Nym with long, blonde hair done in loose ringlets wearing a fancy purple nightgown embroidered with what he recognized as runic constructs. They had to be the reason his scrying spell hadn't seen her. She was protected against magical sight in some way.

The girl looked up from her book suddenly, and he realized that his shadow had fallen across the table she was reading at. Nym let the flight spell go and fell a few feet behind the bookshelf to hide, but it was no use. It was easy to see through the gaps in the shelf, and if he could see her, she could see him too.

"Who's there?" she called out. "Come out."

That was it. The whole job was a bust. He'd tripped up over a girl who was maybe twelve and just happened to have runes stitched into her clothes that blocked scrying. He'd relied too much on magic to compensate for his lack of abilities as a burglar, and it hadn't been enough.

"I said come out!"

The girl was on her feet now and stalking toward the single bookshelf that separated them. She could clearly see him, even if his form was broken up by the books in front of him. That didn't stop her from circling around it, and Nym fled the other direction.

There was no way he was getting into the vault now, but maybe if he could hand Valgo some new information about it, that might be enough to satisfy the thief. If Nym didn't make it out of the house though, he was fully prepared to tell the guards every single thing he knew about the thief who'd coerced him into this stunt.

Nym dodged backward from bookshelf to bookshelf, occasionally flying completely over top of one while the girl pursued him. "Come back here," she demanded.

Nym didn't answer, of course. He just kept putting distance between himself and the girl. His plan was to lure her to the back side of the library, as far from the exit as possible, and then zip across the room and use the lead time to escape before she alerted the guards. It was a bit of a gamble, since at any time, she could give up her pursuit and go straight to yelling for help.

Those were the only two options he was expecting her to have, so he was caught completely off guard when the misty aura of arcana appeared around her and he found himself locked in place. Fortunately, it was his own spell that kept him moving, so while his limbs were frozen, he was able to keep flying away from her.

She watched him rise up, statue-like, and dart up to the second level, and said, "If that's how you want to do this, fine by me!"

A few seconds later, she was up in the air, following him with her own flight spell. Hers seemed a bit less controlled, causing an actual current of air to whip around her and her hair to flair out wildly. The nightgown barely rippled, as if it were made of lead instead of cloth. That was probably for the best, if for no other reason than to preserve her modesty.

Nym couldn't have moved his jaw to speak even if he wanted to, but inside he was repeating every curse and swear he'd ever heard. Of course the girl was also a mage, and if she was living in a place like this, probably a better one than him. Amos was an idiot, and he'd still beaten Nym just because he actually knew what he was doing.

The paralysis spell was kind of interesting though. Parts of the spell looked like they were based in water magic, spun to be frozen, but counterbalanced with fire and earth so that it was only a muscle lock. It didn't actually chill him, which he appreciated. More importantly, it seemed to target his limbs while leaving him limited mobility in his trunk. Since he liked being able to breathe, he was a fan of not having his chest paralyzed.

But what it all pointed to was that she was capable of casting second-circle spells more advanced than anything he'd ever thought up. Fortunately, it was a universal truth that it was easier to break things than to build them. While he fled using his own flight spell, he picked at the weave of magic holding him in place. It was cleverly tucked in on itself, but once he found the ends of the knot, he slid shards of arcana in to pull it apart.

The spell broke with a thrum, and a wave of arcana burst out in all directions. The girl let out a shriek of surprise as the arcana washed over her. It broke her flight spell, and she fell to the floor, which was a good fifteen feet below her.

Without taking the time to think about what he was doing, Nym conjured up a cushion of air to catch her and set her down gently. It worked, kind of. She slowed down for a split second, enough to bleed off the momentum, then fell through the cushion the last few feet and barely landed on her feet. "That was close. Thanks!" she called out.

"You're welcome," Nym told her before he could think better of it.

"Will you come over here now?"

"Nope!"

The girl shot back up into the air, the aura of arcana covering her whole body. She raised a hand and shot out a needle of pure arcana. Nym's eyes widened in surprise, but he was not the same boy he'd been months ago when Amos had done that to him. He swatted the arcana off to the side easily. He really should figure out how to do that. It looked easy enough, just a shaped shard of arcana that was fired into an enemy mage's soul well via merging with the arcana aura. It didn't even need to be aimed as long as they were actively channeling arcana.

Now that he thought about it, that was a good way to end this game of tag they were playing. His only concern was accidentally killing her via arcana poisoning. He didn't know how much arcana her soul well could hold or how much of a gap there was between incapacitation and death. After all, he was the invader here, and it was bad enough that he'd snuck in to rob them without adding murder to his conscience.

While he was debating it, the girl hadn't been idle. Three more needles shot out of her at different speeds and angles. He deflected one, dodged a second, and took the third in his thigh. Immediately, wild arcana rampaged through his soul well. His flight spell stuttered, suddenly too difficult for him to maintain. He tumbled out of the air, clipped a bookshelf on the way down, and spun to the floor.

His muscles spasmed as arcana flooded into them, but Nym was already working on breaking it down. The girl had underestimated his soul well, and he actually managed to contain and expel over half of the arcana injection before he hit the ground. The rest had seeped out, but he'd given himself arcana poisoning so many times with his own experiments that learning how to handle it had become a necessary skill.

He was back on his feet now, one hand on a nearby table to steady himself. A gust of air blasted across his exposed skin, alerting him to the girl's presence. She hovered in front of him, scrutinizing his appearance. "Well," she began, "that was fun. It's a poor disguise though. Where did you even get these rags?"

"Rags! These are my clothes!" Nym protested.

"What class are you in? Did my brother put you up to this prank?" she continued, as if he hadn't spoken at all.

"I . . . What?"

"Come on, take off that stupid mask. I want to talk about your flight spell. It's so much more controlled than mine."

"Air is kind of my best element," he found himself saying, and immediately wondered why he was engaging the girl in conversation. She seemed happy to go along with it though, and if it gave him the time he needed to clear the arcana out of his body, he'd play along.

"I figured. That air cushion you caught me with held against my dispersion rune sequence long enough to slow me down. Which, uh . . . Thanks for that." Her cheeks flushed. "I can't believe I lost my concentration on my spell. It just got all weird for a moment, and I couldn't hold it together. What even was that?"

Nym was all of a sudden reminded that nobody else had ever shown the ability to see arcana in the world around them like he could. He wasn't about to reveal it to this strange noble girl though, and he honestly wasn't sure why the arcana backlash did that.

"Just . . . uh . . . I think from when I broke the paralysis spell you used on me."

She appeared thoughtful for a few seconds. "Ah, I see. You linked it to follow the arcana feed back to me when you dispersed the construct. That's really advanced stuff. Also, take off the mask now."

"I'd . . . rather not."

She reached out a hand to grab the top of the mask and pull it off his head. Nym flinched back out of her reach. "Come on," she told him. "I'm not going to have a conversation with nothing visible but your eyes."

Nym shied away, and she lost patience. With a spell-enhanced leap, she pounced on him, dragging the mask off his head and sending him to the ground with her landing on top of him. "Ha!" she crowed, holding up the mask in victory. Then she looked down, and her expression turned to confusion. "Who are you? I don't recognize you from any classes."

"I don't go to the Academy," Nym said, struggling to get out from under the girl. She couldn't possibly weigh that much, but she had him solidly pinned. He suspected the culprit was her nightgown, which had acted as if it was far heavier than it should be while she was flying. Something in the runes stitched into them must have increased its weight for everyone but her.

"You don't? But you can do magic. I saw you cast second-circle spells."

"Self-taught," he told her. "Get off of me."

She didn't move. "If you don't go to the Academy, then why are you here? Did my brother hire you?"

"I don't know who you are. I don't know who your brother is. I'm not here because I want to be."

"This is very confusing. How did you get in then?"

"Magic," he deadpanned.

The last of the arcana leeched back into his soul well, and Nym used it to form two air cushions. One was underneath him, and the other under the girl. He pushed hers straight up and his horizontal. She rose maybe a fraction of an inch before her nightgown dispersed it, but that was all he needed to go careening across the floor and get out from under her.

The plan worked perfectly, until he slammed headfirst into a bookshelf at full speed. Everything started spinning then, and it was an effort of will to keep from throwing up on the rich, thick, plush carpet. Things were bad enough without adding property damage to the mix.

The girl squeaked in surprise as she fell to the floor, and again when he smacked into the bookshelf. Nym barely noticed it, but several books fell off the shelf onto the floor around him. It only clicked in his head what was happening when she caught one three inches from his nose.

"Okay, that's enough. After that one, I think we need to get you to a healer. Come on, get up. I'm not carrying you there."

"Why are you helping me?" he slurred out.

"Because you're fun and you can do magic." She thought for a second. "And because I'm bored and I want to know what your story is."

CHAPTER 35

Maybe it was the concussion he undoubtably had given himself, but Nym was starting to like this strange and naive girl. Here he was, breaking into her house, and she considered her attempts to capture him a game and now wanted to provide medical aid when he'd gotten hurt.

"Bad idea," he said.

"Why's that?"

"Not supposed to be here," he admitted. "I could get in trouble."

"I hardly think getting a scolding is worth having an untreated head wound."

Nym struggled to put together a string of coherent thoughts. "No, could get put in jail, or executed. Telling them about Valgo might not be enough to save me. Better to be quiet and hidden so no one finds me. Except you found me, ruined it all. Now I need to escape."

He realized he was babbling, but it was so hard to keep track of what was going on. He tried to struggle out of the girl's grip, but he was unfocused and uncoordinated. She easily held him in place. "Easy now," she said, her voice soothing. "You're rambling, and it's all very interesting, but it doesn't make a lot of sense."

Nym tried to explain about the blackmail and the planted evidence, but he didn't do a very good job. The girl held him still while he talked, and it took him a few minutes to realize that maybe he needed to shut his mouth and that he was already in enough trouble. By then, it was far too late.

Arcana sprung up around the girl, and she wove it into a spell Nym had never seen before. At least, he was pretty sure he hadn't. "Malk, please join me in the third-floor library immediately," she said to empty air.

"Who's Malk?" Nym asked.

"That would be me," a man's voice said from behind him. "The better question is, who are you and why are you in the manor? Lady Analia, please take a step back."

"That's not why I called for you," the girl said. "This is my new friend Nym. He had an accident and bumped his head against the bookshelf. He's been babbling for a few minutes now, but he needs to be given medical treatment to make sure there are no long-lasting consequences."

"You . . . want to heal this intruder?"

"I told you, he is my friend."

"He is a criminal who broke into your family's ancestral home, no doubt with nefarious intentions. We are lucky that you were not harmed when he happened upon you."

"I have given you your instructions," the girl said. "Please carry them out."

Nym chose that moment to interrupt by falling over and throwing up on the floor. "Sorry," he said. Everything was fuzzy. Everything was spinning. He needed to escape, but he was only just barely coherent of that fact. Doing something about it was beyond him.

The next thing he knew, he was lying on a narrow cot, staring up at the ceiling. There were five people standing around him, but he only recognized two. One was the girl from the library, and the other was the man she'd summoned. Nym hadn't gotten a good look at him, and only knew it was him because he recognized the voice.

"—need to stop being so reckless. He is not a stray cat to be giving a saucer of milk. What if he'd been a stronger mage than you? What if he'd kidnapped or killed you?"

"Oh, he was a stronger mage. No doubt about it. His spells were a bit . . . basic, but he's got me outclassed in power and control."

"All the more reason to restrain him properly! Who knows what kind of spells he'll throw at us in a bid to escape!"

"He will not try to escape. I have shown my trust in him, and he will trust me in kind."

"He is awake," a new voice said.

"Thank you, Nemari," the girl replied.

"As always, it is a pleasure to serve, my lady."

Nym turned his head to look over at the people gathered around the cot. Closest to him were two guards wearing the noble family's livery. Each was lightly armored and had a sword strapped to his waist. Nym noted with some amusement that the nose picker was one of the ones guarding him, but he did not recognize the other.

Of the other three people, one was the noble lady, Analia. She was still in her nightgown. One was a man who looked like he was in his fifties but with a body like a professional soldier's less than half his age. He was incredibly handsome, with a full head of salt-and-pepper hair and a perfectly groomed beard that hugged his jawline.

The last was a tall man who wore a mask similar to the one Nym had worn. His body was concealed by a heavy cloak, only open enough to show off a pair of rugged boots. His eyes were dark and shadowed. He was watching Nym, sizing him up no doubt, and formulating the best way to take him down. Nym assumed he was Malk.

"How are you feeling, Nym?" the girl asked.

Now that he thought about it, he was surprised how good he actually did feel, physically at least. The concussion was gone, and he was now able to look back on the last half an hour of his life with mounting horror as he recalled how much he'd told Analia about why he was there and who Valgo was. He couldn't believe, even with a head injury, that he'd been so stupid.

It was a safe bet that Malk knew all of it too, and unlike her, he wasn't suicidally trustful. If Nym was the luckiest person in the world, he'd escape the manor without being handed over to the guards and survive Valgo long enough to fly straight out of Abilanth. Then he could starve to death in the mountains instead of being murdered by the city's criminal underbelly either in a jail cell or a back alley.

"Like, there's no way this ends well for me," he confessed.

Malk snorted but didn't say anything. Analia ignored him and said, "There's no reason it has to end poorly. Based on what you've already told me, you're as much a victim here as my family is."

"If we could believe a word of it," Malk muttered behind her. He raised his voice and added, "Lady Analia, please step back behind me."

The bodyguard moved to place himself between Nym and Analia, but she shoved past him. "I trust him," she said firmly. "But . . . would you consent to a truth reading?"

"I don't know what that is," Nym told her. He knew what it sounded like though, and he didn't like the idea.

"That's hardly reliable," Malk protested.

"You doubt my abilities?" the healer asked.

"There are far too many ways to get around it, and you know that."

The healer gestured at Nym. "I think I can handle a child."

"Hush, both of you," Analia said. "A truth reading is when a mage with a talent for healing uses magic to read your body, to look for signs of dishonesty. They also alter your thoughts to make you want to answer questions truthfully. It isn't always reliable, and there are many who find it to be ethically objectionable. However, in this case, where you are an intruder in my home, I believe it is necessary to set everyone's minds at ease. I will not force you to do it. You can refuse."

"And if I do?"

"Then we shall see whether you will be released out on the street or directly into the custody of the city guard."

"Guess I don't have much choice then, do I?"

"There is always a choice. You made a series of choices that led to you smacking headfirst into a heavy oak bookshelf with several hundred books on it. I made a choice to ask Nemari to make sure you didn't die from it. Malk made a choice to be a pain in my butt tonight."

"My lady, please."

Analia ignored Malk and kept talking. "So yes, you have a choice. You can choose to reach back out and trust me as I am trusting you, or you can choose to cast the die and see where your fate takes you. Either way, it has been an absolutely fascinating evening for me. Thank you for that."

Nym rolled his eyes. "Quite the speech," he said, his lips curling up into a soft smile. "What do you need me to do?"

Analia gestured to the healer. "If you would?"

Nemari stepped up next to the bed and told Nym, "Just sit up here. I'll place my hands on your shoulders. You are going to feel a kind of tingling sensation. That's just my arcana entering your body. It will fade after a bit. The spell will alter the way you regard other people and exaggerate your friendship to Lady Analia. This is normal and temporary. Some people have extremely adverse effects to this magic, and if you begin displaying any of those symptoms, the spell will end immediately."

"Got it," Nym said, sitting up. "Go ahead."

Hopefully they wouldn't ask anything he didn't want to answer, but he was more than happy to throw Valgo under the cart. Let him get trampled by the horses if it saved Nym from being turned over to the guard.

It took Nemari a minute to forge his conduit and begin filling his soul well, one long, awkward minute where Malk gave Nym a death glare and Analia studied him. The two house guards on either side of the bed watched him warily, but otherwise ignored everything going on and stood motionless. Well, one of them was motionless. Nose picker was just as fidgety now as he'd been an hour ago.

Slowly at first, but with ever-increasing intensity, he started to feel arcana creep across his skin and soaking into his body. It didn't strike at his soul well, the way an arcana injection did, but instead followed deliberate paths leading all the way through him. Nym shuddered at the feeling, but didn't try to fight it off. He was sure he could have if he wanted to though, probably using the same meditation technique he'd learned to fight arcana poisoning back in Palmara.

"He is ready," the healer announced suddenly.

Nym didn't feel any different. He opened his mouth to say something, thought better of it, and just shrugged. Analia moved to stand directly in front of Nym and said softly, "First, tell me the truth, Nym. Do you mean anyone here any harm?"

"No." That was an easy truth for him to tell.

"Would you harm anyone?"

"Sure, to save my life. If Malk attacked me like he wants to, I would fight back."

The girl laughed and said, "Understandable. But barring any attacks on your person, would you attack anyone in the house?"

"If someone attacked you, I would try to stop them."

"What if someone attacked Malk?"

"Eeeeehhhhhhh . . ."

Nose picker was laughing behind him now, trying hard to stifle it but failing. It didn't help that Analia looked like she was about to burst keeping her own laughter contained. The only ones who didn't react were Malk himself and the healer channeling the spell.

"Tell me the whole truth of why you are here, please."

Nym explained about the hidden vault in the library he'd been told to find, that Valgo had extorted him into using his magic to break in using the pawnshop receipt. He explained how he'd bought the books from another pawnbroker and sold them once he was done because he needed the money, and only learned afterward that Valgo had stolen them to set him up.

Analia waited politely until Nym was done. Then she said, "Can you please clarify what you mean about a library vault?"

Nym explained again about the vault and where he'd located it. When he was done, Analia shook her head and said, "There is no hidden room in the library. Malk, do you know anything about this?"

"No, my lady."

"But it's there," Nym said. "I saw it myself."

"Well, let's go take a look and see."

CHAPTER 36

Nose picker and his fellow house guard had been left outside the library, and Nemari had stayed behind in the infirmary. Nym, Analia, and Malk were standing in front of the bookcase that hid a secret room. "This is it," he told them.

"I've been in this library a thousand times and never noticed anything odd. I've read four different books off this shelf already," Analia said. She peered at the shelf from various angles, walking to one side and then the other.

"I don't see anything unusual. Same type of wood, same size." She started pulling books off one at a time and handing them to Nym. "Here, put these on that table."

Nym helped her empty the entire bookshelf out. Once it was bare, she resumed her investigation. She even went so far as to fly up to the top of the shelf and examine it from that angle. When she was done, she shook her head and said, "I don't see anything here."

"I can see the dimensions of the room with my scrying spell," Nym said. "The doorway stretches from here to here. But there's nothing in the walls around it. No switches or levers or anything. It's just a hole cut into the wall behind this shelf."

"Then I suppose the only way in would be to lift the entire thing up and move it out of the way."

"The intruder doesn't need to be here for this," Malk said. "If this hidden room actually exists, whatever secrets inside of it are no business of his."

"That . . . is actually a very good point. I'm sorry, Nym, but whatever is in this room—"

"If it even exists," Malk said.

"—is a family secret that I would not expose without my father's permission," Analia finished, ignoring Malk's snide comment.

Nym decided not to point out that he could already see the layout of the room and had a fairly good idea of what was in there. There were books, lots and lots of books, which probably wasn't a coincidence since the hidden room was attached to the library. He didn't know what they were about, but he imagined it would be sensitive information about any illicit activities the family was involved in, restricted or forbidden magic, stuff like that.

There were also a few trinkets and curiosities. Some of it looked like jewelry, but Nym figured there was a reason it was stored separate from the main vaults. It might be magical in some way, but he couldn't see any arcana infused into the objects through his scrying spell. He wasn't sure he'd recognize it in person either.

Finally, there were a few worktables set along the back wall with a variety of tools. Nym had never seen anything like them and couldn't even hazard a guess as to their purposes. Between them was a large cylinder, about five feet tall and three feet wide, that was completely opaque to his scrying spell. It was obviously magical in some way, and Nym was curious about what was stored in there.

"And so, I will lift this and see what is behind it. Malk, please wait over there with Nym."

At first startled, Malk nonetheless nodded and escorted Nym to a far-off table. "Have a seat," he said. Nym was sure he was just as curious, but the bodyguard took his duty seriously and didn't take his eyes off Nym while Analia worked.

Immense winds whipped through the library, scattering loose books off the tables and knocking over a few chairs. Nym endured it for a few seconds, but as the wind got stronger, the books started taking flight. He quickly formed walls of air, channeling the wind up toward the ceiling where there was nothing to blow around except the light orbs. Those swayed back and forth, but it looked like the flight runes inscribed into them were stronger than the winds Analia was wielding.

Malk started to speak, probably to tell him not to use any magic because it was suspicious or whatever, but then he gave the rest of the library a second glance and saw how much of a mess it already was. Nym could practically see him rethinking his stance.

The bookshelf lifted a few inches in the air and wobbled as it slid forward. He didn't have the angle to see into the room behind it from where he waited with Malk, but just from Analia's body language, he saw the instant she spotted the hidden door. The shelf skidded across the floor and nearly tipped over, but she caught it halfway to the ground and pushed it back upright.

"So far it appears you've been telling the truth. There is a hidden room behind this shelf."

Nym hadn't really felt anything like what the healer had described during the supposed truth-reading spell, but he figured there was no harm in going along with it. Analia wasn't anything like he'd expected her to be, and he was starting to think he might actually come out of this ahead. Valgo would lose his blackmail leverage, and Nym could see him resorting to more drastic and violent measures, but if he could get on good terms with the heir to a noble house, it might not matter.

Nym looked around the library. This place was his dream. The Academy would be ideal, but that was never going to happen. Just getting access to the Feldstal family library would help him in so many ways. He'd seen dozens of titles for beginner mages that he would love to tear through and marked a few other more advanced tomes that seemed relevant. If only half of them proved useful, he'd be significantly better off than when he got to Abilanth.

That all assumed he managed to cash in on whatever goodwill he'd built up for going along with this whole thing. He took a moment to reflect on that thought. Half an hour ago he'd thought his best option was to starve or freeze to death a few hundred miles out of the city. Now he was plotting how best to pillage the library for magical knowledge, with assumed permission.

According to what Valgo had told him, Analia's father was out of town running some big, important mission. Briefly, Nym wondered if her dad was involved with that big necromancer-seal thing he'd stumbled into back in Zoskan. Leaf had seemed pretty sure that it was serious, and they'd need some magical muscle to patch it back up, and Abilanth was a good place to get a lot of that in a very short time frame.

More importantly, if Jaspar Feldstal was out of town, that meant his daughter could be running the place in his absence. Sure, there was probably somebody acting as a governor or castellan taking care of stuff, but nobody who would dare to contradict the young lady of the house. At least, he hoped that was the case. It would be extremely convenient for him if so, since she seemed to like him for some godforsaken reason.

With the winds finally dying down, Nym dismissed his own spell and looked around. There were books everywhere, overturned chairs and tables, and half of the light orbs were wobbling around overhead, throwing weird shadows over the mess. Analia was ignoring all of it. She cast a simple spell, and light started shining out from beyond the revealed door, and she stared ahead, mouth agape.

"What . . . what is this?" The words came out a whisper, only heard because utter silence had descended back on the library.

"My lady?" Malk started forward.

"Stay where you are," she snapped.

Then she walked into the hidden room, leaving Nym and Malk to sit in silence. Nym had a general idea of what was in the room, and he knew what he was supposed to be retrieving. Jaspar Feldstal was researching something, and there were a number of journals detailing his experiments that Valgo wanted. That, and only that, was his target. But the job was already blown to hell and back again, so he might as well salvage what he could from it.

About ten minutes later, Analia still hadn't come out. Nym looked over at Malk and said, "You think we should start cleaning this up?"

"I think you should stay right where you are and keep your mouth shut."

"Yep, I guess we could do that too."

In truth, Nym had only suggested it to give him a chance to get a closer look at all the titles so he could start planning out which books he wanted to read. It didn't hurt that he figured it would score some points with Analia, and also because, just a little bit, it hurt his soul to see the books so mistreated. There were a few loose pages lying around that had been torn out, and he was itching to collect them and try to match them to whatever books were missing them.

Malk was having none of that. Every time Nym so much as shifted in place, the bodyguard perked up like a dog and stared at him. It actually became something of a game to Nym, waiting for the tension to leave the man's body, then shifting in his chair just to watch Malk snap back to attention.

Nym confirmed that the bodyguard couldn't detect him casting magic, or if he could, he was pretending otherwise for some reason. He used his scrying spell to watch Analia move around the room. She spent some time looking over the workbenches, but the majority of it was spent flipping through books. Not for the first time, Nym wished the spell would show him printed text.

She spent an hour or so in the room, and when she came back out, she shuffled forward in a daze and collapsed into the nearest chair. After a few minutes of silence, she said, "Please put the bookshelf back. Nobody is to know about this room."

Nym lifted it back into place with considerably less collateral damage and started telekinetically throwing books onto the shelves at random. He had no idea what organizational scheme they used, but he prioritized the desk they'd emptied the shelves onto. Of course, the windstorm had scattered them, but he did his best to find them.

While he worked, new strands of telekinetic force radiated out from around him, righting chairs and tables and piling up loose books onto them. It took barely a minute to restore the library to some semblance of order, and he was quite proud of his speed. When he'd first started, he could barely keep a half dozen objects rotating through a pattern. Now, he was moving upward of thirty at a time in unique trajectories.

Analia watched the work with hollow eyes. "And for all that, you're not even half spent, are you?" she asked Nym.

"It's just a first-circle spell."

"I'd have given myself arcana poisoning three times over channeling that much. Basic telekinesis is good for one or two items, maybe three or four if you've invested a lot of effort into practicing it. I don't even know how you did that."

He had spent a lot of time working on that telekinesis spell. The only one he'd worked on more was flight. Analia was of the opinion that his magic was impossible though, and he suspected she'd been exposed to a lot more magic than him.

"Can I see you cast telekinesis?" he asked.

"Maybe later," she said. "I've got . . . got a lot on my mind right now."

Nym decided to ignore the hitch in her voice. Whatever she'd found out, she wasn't happy about it. He liked the implication that there would be a later though. In his mind, that meant he wasn't about to be booted out onto the street or handed over to the city guard.

"What happens now?" he asked.

Behind him, Malk shifted subtly. Nym only knew it was happening because he had his scrying spell running and was watching in all directions using it. The man was gearing up to attack him, but unless he exhibited some magic that Nym hadn't seen from him, he wasn't worried about it.

Then again, Malk had shown up immediately when Analia had called for him, and he was a bodyguard for a very rich and very powerful nobleman's daughter. He could be incredibly dangerous.

Nym started to mentally plan out the next few seconds if things turned sour. The first thing to do would be to get some distance, then find the first window and get outside. After that, he'd disappear into the night.

"I'll have a servant show you to the guest quarters. We can talk more in the morning," Analia said. "I have a lot to think about right now."

"Oh," Nym said. That worked too.

CHAPTER 37

ym tried to count up how long it had been since his last hot bath, but he had lost track of time while living on the street. His best guess was about two months. It was every bit as enjoyable as he remembered. Unlike the wooden tub that was hauled into his room at the Trough and Saddle and then laboriously filled one bucket at a time, rich nobles had indoor plumbing and a pool-sized marble tub set into the floor.

Somebody poured hot water down a tube, or maybe they used magic to do it. Either way, the servant who'd led him to the guest quarters had asked if he wanted the bath prepared, and when he'd said yes, had promised to attend to it immediately. He supposed they were counting the buckets because they somehow knew when it was full too.

He found fresh nightclothes when he was done that were honestly better than anything else he'd worn in his entire life, as far as he could remember. The nice clothes he'd purchased from the tailor when he'd first arrived didn't compare to the pajamas left out for him, not even when they were new. And now they were more holes than clothes, but Nym didn't have the tools or knowledge, or money, to repair them. So the knees were worn out in the pants, and there were a few small tears. The shirt was in slightly better condition, but not by much.

But the clothes left out for him were clean and whole and comfortable. Surprisingly, they were a good fit as well. The servant had a sharp eye for size. And then there was the bed. It was easily big enough for ten of him to lie side by side, then another row of ten below that. He couldn't even guess why anyone would need a bed that big.

In short, the guest room was the most luxurious experience he'd ever had. The only thing missing was food and drink, and even that he had no doubt a servant would fetch from the kitchens if he only took the time to ask. It was all wonderfully decadent, and Nym couldn't really enjoy it once he compared it to how he had been living for the past month and a half.

The furniture in just this one room would have housed everyone in that busted-up, falling-down, holes-in-the-roof-and-walls warehouse that was under the control of a criminal who preyed on children. No doubt the curtains and the carpets and the expensive imported wood would have been enough to build a group home for all of them. The cost of the marble that had gone into that tub could feed them for a year.

Nym wondered how often the room even got used. It was a guest room, after all. Then again, even if the Feldstal family housed someone in the room nine days out of every ten, it still would be extravagant and wasteful. Worse, if this was the guest room, he could only just imagine what the rooms for the nobles who lived here looked like.

Then he considered how many closed doors he had passed when he was being led to the guest room and tried to remember the floor plan he'd studied. He guessed that, at minimum, there were five or six more rooms just like his.

"This place is obscene," he muttered.

Part of him was tempted to sneak right back out and flee the house. He knew he could probably get away without too much trouble, as long as he didn't run into anyone else with antiscrying runes stitched onto their bathrobe or something. What held him back was that he had failed to complete Valgo's job, which meant he was in all sorts of danger once he left. That, coupled with the fact that it wasn't too late to turn him over to the city guard, kept Nym firmly stuck in the room.

On a more personal level, he still wanted access to the library. That was opulent to the extreme, just like the rest of the house, but at least it served a practical purpose. He was eager to be let loose in that two-story room to pillage the shelves. Hopefully Analia would cooperate with that ambition.

Nym swallowed his distaste for the whole thing and settled into the bed. He felt lost in it until he piled up a few pillows next to him to make it seem smaller. Even then, it was impossible to get comfortable. He tossed and turned and sighed, unable to sleep until late into the night. Thoughts and plans and worries chased one another around and around behind his eyelids. When sleep did come, it was troubled and ended all too quickly.

The servants woke Nym up by barging into the guest room. His eyes snapped open to the rattle of the door handle, and by the time the servant entered the room, he was already out of the bed and pulling arcana into his soul well. The servant pulled back in surprise when he saw Nym floating in the air.

"Good . . . morning, sir."

"You guys don't believe in knocking around here?"

"Ah, pardon, sir. I did knock, but you did not answer."

Nym was suspicious about that. He was an extremely light sleeper, and getting an hour or two at a time had become his normal sleep pattern. It was never really safe out on the street, not even in the sanctuary, especially not after he'd accidentally set the blanket closet on fire.

"Did you need something?"

"I am to escort you to breakfast with Lord Bardin and Lady Amalia."

"What time is it?"

"Half an hour past dawn, sir."

Nym groaned. "Why are we up so early?"

"Lord Bardin has always been an early riser, and more so since he began his responsibilities at the Academy," the servant explained.

Nym shot him a venomous glare. "I did not need you to answer that question."

"As you say, sir."

"Just give me a minute," Nym said. He ducked into the bathroom to take care of his business, then followed the servant across the manor to where Analia was seated at a table with an older teenager, maybe eighteen or nineteen. The family resemblance was obvious, from the hair color to the facial structure to the vivid green eyes.

They were sitting in a room with walls made out of glass, watching the morning sun peek up between the mountains and chatting quietly while servants trooped in one after another to load the table with various dishes.

"Ah, our guest," the man said. "Come, have a seat and join us. Nym, was it?"

"That's right," Nym said, pulling out a chair. Ironically, the room put him at ease. Freedom was at hand if he needed to flee. A chair through the window and a flight spell would get him out into open air, and he already knew he could outfly Analia. He eyed the food being piled up in front of him. There was far more than three people could eat. It smelled amazing though.

Nym decided that he believed the leftovers would go to the servants and not be thrown out. Even if the official decree was to toss it, he didn't think the servants would follow the order. At least, he hoped they wouldn't. Even between three people, they wouldn't eat a quarter of the food on the table.

"My name is Bardin Feldstal. I am an adjunct at the Academy. I understand that you are a mage who was coerced into using your magic to break into our home to raid a secret room that we weren't aware existed. Please, tell me more about that."

Nym laid it all out while he ate a breakfast of ham, eggs, sausage, thick bread, fresh fruit, and chilled milk. It wasn't often he got a chance to load up, and he wasn't about to waste it now. Analia looked slightly nauseous as she watched him pack it away, but Bardin wasn't fazed.

"How are you still eating?" she asked, aghast.

Her brother started laughing. "He's paying back an energy debt. You're going to see this a lot when you're an upperclassman, twig-skinny mages eating four times as much food as a grown man in a single sitting. Nym's reserves have been empty for a while. If you cast a medical diagnostics spell on him, you'll see that he's actually malnourished and has been using arcana to keep from wasting away."

Nym had to grudgingly admit that maybe the table wasn't as overfull as he'd initially judged it to be. He wasn't quite sure what Bardin was talking about though. All he knew was that he hadn't gotten enough to eat in weeks and weeks, and now that the food was in front of him, his stomach was a bottomless pit.

"My sister is quite taken with your abilities," Bardin said.

Analia shoved him so hard he fell out of his chair. "That is not how I would phrase it," she told him.

From his new position on the floor, Bardin laughed. "To be honest, I'm curious too. She said your telekinesis spell allows you to control dozens of objects individually. If that's true, you'll be famous for beating the current Academy record of nineteen. And the record holder was an archmage who died about fifty years ago."

Nym looked over the table, pulled arcana into his soul well, and started lifting the cutlery and flatware. He focused on empty plates first and ended up with a respectable fourteen items floating around him. Then he ran out of empty plates.

"Not quite a record then, but still very respectable, especially for someone . . . so . . . young . . ."

Bardin trailed off as the remaining six plates, these ones still containing food, rose to join the dishes floating in the air. Nym was starting to feel the weight now, but he was sure he could still manage a few more small items. Unfortunately, he couldn't spot anything else small enough to be moved that wasn't also currently being worn by one of them.

So instead he set them to dancing, plates whirling around forks while knives slipped between them. All of it rotated in a hypnotic pattern, in and out and around, spin and return, then start again. The Feldstal scions watched the display, Analia with rapt attention and Bardin with quiet disbelief.

Nym caught the glow of arcana around the older brother as he shot off a number of detection spells. Nym wasn't sure what they did, but Bardin looked satisfied with the results. Deciding the show was over, he set the remains of their breakfast back down on the table, all except a bowl of strawberries he'd been eyeing up but hadn't gotten to as they were on the opposite side from where he was seated.

"That is the most efficient telekinesis spell I have ever seen," Bardin admitted. "I'm not sure it actually qualifies as discrete control of the objects, since a few of them were banded together on a single wave of force, but it's still a sight to see."

"Quit buttering him up," Analia said. "Let's talk about the offer now. You want to ransack our library, right? Books on magic? I want to know how you built your telekinesis spell and how you do your flight spell. Trade?"

Nym didn't have to think about it very hard. "I think I can agree to that. What kind of time frame are you thinking?"

"An immediate one," she said.

"No," Bardin vetoed the idea. "I want to see this too, but I have a first-year conduit-shaping class I have to teach this morning. Why don't the two of you work on cleaning the library back up for now, and he can pick out a few books. When I'm back in the afternoon, he can awe us with his magic."

Analia pouted but acquiesced in the end. Bardin said his goodbyes, shook Nym's hand, and strode out of the room. He whistled a merry tune as he walked down the hallway, leaving the two of them behind.

"This is going to be fun," Nym said.

"We'll see. Maybe. There's a lot of cleaning up to do. My brother was not happy about the mess." She paused and stared off into space for a second. "Malk! We're going to the library."

"Of course, my lady," Malk said from behind Nym, causing him to leap out of chair in surprise.

"How long have you been standing there?" he sputtered.

The bodyguard didn't bother to answer.

Nym glared daggers at his back as he followed the pair to the library but did his best to put Malk out of mind. This was going to be his first real step into the world of magic, where he could find answers to all the questions he hadn't even thought to ask yet. Malk wasn't going to ruin that for him.

By the time they got to the library, Nym was all smiles.

CHAPTER 38

The library was more of a mess than Nym was expecting. When they walked in, Analia took one look and said, "We'll be lucky to get through this today."

"Maybe you shouldn't have made such a mess," Nym said.

She at least had the decency to look embarrassed, but Malk turned to snap at him, "She is the lady of the house. If she decides to tear the walls down, your place is to keep your mouth shut and get to work when your betters tell you it's time to fix it."

The sudden fury in Malk's voice shocked Nym, and for a moment he was afraid the man was going to attack him. When that didn't happen, Nym said, "You can do that if you want. I don't work for House Feldstal though. I'll help pick up the mess for two reasons: because Analia was nice to me, and because I want a chance to read some of these books."

Malk snorted. "You should be sitting in a dungeon right now. No, you should be in a mage cell, not that I think you're dangerous enough to warrant one."

Nym had no clue what a mage cell was, but he resolved to research that some other time. It sounded nasty and did absolutely nothing good for his ever-present fear of being captured by the city guards. If a mage cell was some sort of box that kept him from using magic like he assumed, he'd go completely mad in it.

Analia ignored Malk's comments, or maybe she just didn't feel like he'd said anything out of line. For all her casual disregard of the social hierarchy, she was after all a nobleman's daughter. She could probably count on her fingers the number of people she'd actually have to listen to if they tried to give her an order. Nym was not on that very, very short list, of course.

She had some magical training already, so he just hoped she'd apply a similar mindset to learning from him. He wasn't an Academy professor though, so he was missing a lot of the gravitas that came with the position, plus she was older than him. He was fighting the always-uphill battle against that.

Analia surveyed the mess her wind spell had made with her hands on her hips. "Alright, you two, time to get to work. First, I want any books with pages ripped out piled on this table. Loose pages next to them. If it's obvious which book the page belongs to, set it over on the second table with the page on top. I will work on rebinding them while you sort through."

That was what they did for the better part of an hour. Analia knew a spell that could repair torn pages as long as she had the book and the page that was missing. Nym watched curiously as she cast it repeatedly, noting the burst of arcana that popped between her hands each time. It looked like the spell had a complicated base that took her about thirty seconds to set up, followed by a sudden surge of arcana to connect everything at once.

He was itching to try the spell out himself but didn't want to explain how he'd learned it. As far as he knew, the ability to see arcana as other mages cast spells was something unique to him, and he'd kept it a secret to everybody. Someday, it was going to pay off big time, and he was going to learn some mighty fine magic on the sly from someone who had no idea what he was doing.

There was also the fact that if he ever ended up dueling another mage again, which was seeming more and more likely to happen, being able to cold read their spells as they were being cast could be a literal lifesaver. What he could do didn't seem comparable in any way to an aura-reading spell, which simply functioned to help show if someone was holding arcana in their soul well and get a rough idea of whether that amount was increasing or decreasing.

The book-restoration project went well, in Nym's opinion. There were hundreds of loose pages that had been torn out, and by the time they were done, they only had seven pages left needing homes. Analia didn't recognize them and set them aside for her brother to look at.

"Okay, next project. We need to properly reshelve these, but unfortunately, *we* mostly means *me*, as Nym has no idea where anything is supposed to be, and I'm pretty sure Malk has never touched a single one of these books before today."

"I think one of them hit him in the head last night," Nym offered up helpfully.

Analia let out a great, exaggerated sigh. "Doesn't count," she said sadly.

"So how are we supposed to help you then?"

She picked up a book, looked at it, and set it on an empty table. "This is now the table for all things legal and tax related."

A different book went onto a new table. "This table is for alchemy texts. That one is for metalworking." She pointed at one table after another. "Medical. Engineering. Elementalism. Agriculture. Transport and logistics. House records. Spell books."

Nym cast that last table a long, lingering glance. There were already three books on it with many more likely to come. He wanted to spend as much of his time as possible going through them while he still had the chance. It was too bad he wasn't setting the rules for his trade with the Feldstal scions. All he could do was watch the pile grow larger as the three of them sorted through the books.

He wasn't ashamed to admit that Analia did all the heavy lifting. She sorted through books ten times faster than he did, both from familiarity and the speed at which she could read. That was fine. It was her library after all. But he was a little embarrassed that in the time it took him to skim through one book and determine which table it belonged on, Malk did three.

Finally, with many errors on his part, it was done. Analia directed the reshelving of the upper shelves to Nym for his telekinesis and did the lower shelves herself. Malk stood off to the side and glowered at Nym's back while he worked, which he found extremely uncomfortable.

After a quick break for lunch, they returned to the library. Since Bardin still wasn't back yet, they both chose books and settled into overly large chairs stuffed to bursting. Nym chose a book that described different techniques for arcana control needed in various spells.

The book referred to his own personal style as conducting, where he simultaneously held open his conduit to allow new arcana to pour into his soul well and spun it out into the world to create magic. The pinnacle of conducting was to balance the input and output perfectly so that it flowed in a never-ending stream. That seemed like an unnecessary goal to him, but the book recommended the style for those whose soul wells were underdeveloped and unable to hold large quantities of arcana.

Nym didn't think he had that problem, though if he was being honest, he didn't have much to compare to. His magical stamina was steadily growing and showing no signs of slowing down, which led him to the second chapter.

The book referred to casting by using a massive pool of arcana all at once as erupting, which someone apparently thought was a stupid name, judging by the crude jokes scribbled into the margins of the page. He had to agree, but regardless of the author's nomenclature, the style itself was important to master. Some spells simply had to be done in a hurry or required too much focus to work the magic and hold a conduit at the same time.

For those spells, eruption was the answer. The style focused on building up the soul well to hold absolutely massive amounts of arcana, and then burning it in a short window. It was the preferred style for combat specialists who often couldn't afford to take things slowly, and was generally paired with huge conduits that were difficult to hold in place but that could refill the mage's soul well. The mage would then alternate between refilling and draining his soul well.

Nym could see the usefulness, but he'd never had an issue keeping a conduit open when things had been tense, so he didn't think it was a style he would be pursuing.

Most mages fell somewhere between those two extremes and covered for their weaknesses with a variety of other techniques. The book recommended learning leaching, the act of pulling arcana out of the environment, and intercepting, the act of stealing arcana being woven into a spell by another mage.

It took Nym a bit to figure out what the book meant by leaching, as he'd never really noticed any sources of arcana in the world around him. There were occasional exceptions, such as the light orbs, but such enchanted objects obviously weren't what the book meant. Finally it dawned on him that it was talking about tapping into the soul wells of other living beings to take their arcana.

The final recommendation was to use what was known as ritual magic. This involved the mage slowly building up arcana in a large, complicated spell. Generally speaking, the amount needed was far greater than a single mage could draw in through a conduit in any reasonable amount of time, and multiple mages often collaborated to accomplish a goal.

There were lots of props and tools that went into ritual magic, necessary if for no other reason than to temporarily house the excess arcana the mage generated, and of all the techniques described in the book, Nym felt it was the least relevant to him personally. He couldn't see himself working hand in hand with other mages, nor did he have the finances to afford the trappings of ritual magic. For now, he'd settle for increasing his own repertoire and leave group castings for a future date.

Bardin had excellent timing. He showed up just as Nym was putting the book back on the shelf, having finished it from cover to cover. He strode into the library and made a show of looking around, paying special attention to the places that Analia had reshelved herself.

"Like it never happened," he said. "Wait, no . . ."

He switched two books around and nodded to himself. "There we go. Like it never happened."

Analia rolled her eyes at his antics, but it was easy to see she was excited. "Finally. Does it always take you this long?"

"To do my job? Yes. We have a schedule and everything. Same time, every day."

"Why do you even bother? It's not like you need the money."

Bardin gestured toward the library around them. "This right here? This is nothing compared to what the Academy keeps just in the restricted sections. I teach first-years simple stuff that the actual professors don't have the patience for. In return, I get unlimited access to stuff you can't even imagine yet. And between you and me, there are more restricted sections even I don't get to see."

"You haven't even read half the books in this library," Analia told him.

"So? Most of them are boring. Like this whole shelf here is nothing but tax ledgers. Who wants to read that?"

There was really no arguing there. All of them, with the possible exception of Malk, were interested in magic above all else. Nym still wasn't sure if the bodyguard was a mage or not, but he wasn't going to rule the possibility out.

"Anyway, I am here now, so let's get to it. I am just dying to know. Plus, I'm totally going to swindle Professor Lakridge out of some reagents he's hoarding when I bet him on how many objects I can lift independent of each other at the same time." Bardin rubbed his hands together eagerly and led them to an open space in the center of the library. "Nym, please describe your telekinesis spell to us."

CHAPTER 39

I don't get it," Analia said.

"I'll be honest . . . Me neither." Bardin gestured to the spell book on the table between the three of them. "This can't possibly be right."

"I developed this myself, and I didn't have any spells to study from, so it was a lot of trial and error, but this spell appears to be more or less the same one I use," Nym said.

They'd gone over it. Nym had demonstrated his telekinesis spell. He'd broken down the movement of the arcana, and Bardin had announced that what he was using was a basic telekinesis spell with no frills or twists. He'd even pulled a beginner's spell book off the shelves and pointed it out. If anything, the standard telekinesis spell actually did a slightly better job at weight transferal by spreading it out to impact all muscles instead of focusing on the arms and torso like Nym's version did.

"So the real problem is the mind can really only keep track of so many things at once. It's not hard to pick up ten or twenty objects in a bundle just by wrapping them in one big telekinetic grip, but then they all move as one. That's not what you're doing."

Nym was holding twenty books in the air individually, each one rotating around him in a different pattern. It was a bit of a strain to keep them steady, but no one was grading him on the smoothness of their flight. "I'm not sure what to tell you. The only thing I'm really doing different than how the book describes it is how I handle the weight."

"What does it mean then?" Analia asked her brother.

"Well, he's also using less arcana than he should need by cutting the even spread of the weight out of the spell. Maybe that's the key? Using less arcana makes it easier to run parallel discrete processes?"

Bardin lifted up seven books and set them to floating around. They trembled in the air and, one by one, fell back to the floor until he only had three left. "I could probably hold four steady indefinitely if I really put my mind to it, but I'd need to forge a tier-three conduit just to keep the arcana flow in the positive," he mused out loud.

The rest of the books landed in a stack on the table in front of him. The glow of arcana around him intensified, and he cast a new telekinesis spell using Nym's variations. All seven books rose back up into the air again. He lost control of two of them before they even stabilized, and the other five shook in place. One more thumped down, and the last four stabilized.

"I don't think that's the reason." Bardin let out a loud, defeated sigh and returned the rest of the books to the table. Nym picked up the books off the floor with his own telekinesis spell and added them to the pile, while keeping up the orbit of the twenty books that were already spinning around overhead.

"Incredible," Bardin said. "How are you keeping track of so many individual objects? Are you just that brilliant, Nym? Just doing the same thing as the rest of us but five times better?"

"What's to keep track of? I set the path, and now it's just going to do it until I tell it to do something else or I run out of arcana."

"Huh . . . Kind of like ritual magic but without the instruments. Your mind is just maintaining all of it at once without tying any of it to an object. But still . . . to keep that running for as long as you have, I can't even calculate the tier that conduit is."

Nym shrugged. He didn't have a problem with running out of arcana. The limiting factor to his magic was usually his own exhaustion. A soul well could be filled and drained many, many times in a single day, but eventually all the arcana would poison him. The better his control, the longer he could go without suffering the symptoms.

"I guess if I couldn't pull in new arcana fast enough, I'd just make a second conduit to the same layer," he said. "But I've never had to do that. I only need to make two conduits if I want to do something like fly and use telekinesis at the same time."

"What?" Analia came up out of her chair. She looked back and forth between Nym and Bardin. "It's possible to have multiple conduits open at the same time?"

"You'll learn about it in your third year. It's not easy to do at all. Nym, how did you ever figure it out on your own?"

"Two conduits wasn't the hard part. Keeping the arcana from mixing in my soul well was where it got tricky."

Bardin started laughing. "Oh God, you really are just fumbling through all of this, aren't you? You make multiple conduits based on . . . I don't even know . . . instinct and raw talent, and intent filtering is the stumbling block?

That makes me feel a lot better about all of this, you know? Less inadequate at being shown up by a twelve-year-old."

"Ten-year-old," Nym corrected.

"Sure, sorry. You're very tall for your age then. Either way, so young that you should barely be doing anything beyond instinctive magic. Somehow, you're doing things that are incredibly advanced or outright impossible based on what I know. I really don't even know what to say. You're going to be an archmage by the time you finish your Academy training."

"I'm not going to the Academy," Nym said. "I wanted to, but . . . I can't even walk around the inner ring without getting hassled by the guards. They'll throw me out as soon as they catch me. It's happened a few times in the middle ring too."

"Right, sorry. I'm getting ahead of myself. That's something I was planning on talking to you about a little bit later. Noble houses sometimes take in talented commoners and sponsor their education in exchange for a contract of servitude. This is usually for trade professions like craftsmen, but your obvious magical talent would be an easy sell to our father. Every noble house needs more mages."

Nym could already tell he wasn't interested just from the description of the contract. He'd rather be free and figure his magic out on his own than owe years of service to someone else. He didn't want to be rude though, especially since he'd barely gotten a chance to look at the Feldstal library. Also, he was an intruder turned guest, so he still needed to be on his best behavior.

"You would pay for me to attend the Academy?" Nym said. "How much would that cost?"

"The standard contract for craftsmen is ten years, but their training is usually only two years. The Academy is a six-year curriculum, and even if we had you stay here instead of in on-campus housing, it's quite expensive. There are a lot of factors that determine tuition, mainly which classes you end up taking, but conservatively, a thousand crests would be my guess. I would have to speak with the accountants to run the numbers, but I am guessing your contract will need to be for twenty years. The terms would be laid out to include an additional year of service for every hundred crests you go over."

The number was overwhelming. He would spend years making that back in Zoskan, and it was a complete impossibility here. He was never going to attend the Academy unless he sold himself into servitude. He'd be an old man by the time he was free again, and that assumed the Feldstals didn't find some other way to keep their hooks in him.

"That is a really long time," he said, dazed just thinking about it.

"It's just a guess. Don't take anything I said as a guarantee. It could be less, could be more. Promise to consider it though. No offense Nym . . . but you're in a really bad position. This could literally save your life."

That was also true. He was homeless and being pressured by a thief who wouldn't think twice about disposing of him if Nym became too inconvenient. He had no way to make any money to afford food and shelter. Really, when he considered it, his best options were to either swipe something valuable on his way out, pawn it for two crests, and take a teleport to literally anywhere else, or to sign the contract, no matter how bad the terms were.

"What about a contract to just keep access to your library? I could teach myself a lot from the books here."

Bardin nodded. "I'm sure you could. You have managed some amazing things already teaching yourself, but this library is a fraction of the size of the Academy's, and everyone benefits from having actual teachers. I'm not saying you couldn't get there eventually on your own, but you will be a master mage by the time you graduate from the Academy."

That was probably true, but Nym didn't like the deal. He didn't want to take it. "I guess we can hammer out the details once the actual contract is drawn up," he said.

Analia had been silent throughout the conversation, but she interjected there. "Exactly! Nym's right. That's a conversation for another day. Right now, I want to know how he does his flight spell. That was the deal we have already."

Bardin held his hands up in mock surrender. "You heard the lady, Nym. Let's move on with today's agenda."

"Okay, so for how I fly, I am using basic air manipulation to create cushions that hold me up. I actually did spend a week or so with a master mage who did the same thing, so I'm pretty sure there's not anything new for you guys here."

"Oh? Who was it? I know most of the masters who've come out of the Academy in the last decade."

"His name was Brogan," Nym said.

"Brogan . . . Brogan . . . Hmm . . . Older man? Very military when he's on the ground, borderline insane in the air?"

"That's him."

"Who's that?" Analia asked.

"He does flight training for mages going into the military. I've heard he used to teach at the Academy thirty years ago, but he . . . uh . . . left . . . due to differences of opinion with the administration of the time."

"That sounds like a fancy way of saying he got fired," Analia said.

"Well," Bardin began, "Yeah . . . pretty much. I guess he didn't care to follow the curriculum agreed upon by the other professors. Told them they were a bunch of incompetent idiots. There's a few stories that float around the classrooms, even today, about the fights he got into with some of the other professors."

"So, if you trained with this Brogan fellow, you must be pretty good," Analia told Nym.

"Brogan is a horrible old monster," Nym said flatly. "He let me use the training grounds, but I wasn't part of his classes. It . . . didn't go well when we tried that."

"Sounds like there's a story there."

"Nothing I want to think about too much," Nym said.

"But still," Bardin said. "If you're using the same flight technique as Master Brogan, that must be a good one. I've never heard of an air-cushion method."

"What does the Academy teach for flight spells?" Nym asked, curious.

"We don't. There's a slow-falling spell we learn just in case, but flight is generally considered to be very difficult and dangerous to practice with. It's very easy to have a fatal accident. The fact that Analia not only is proficient with a flight spell, but that she's only thirteen, is quite the feather in our house's cap."

Analia didn't look proud though. If anything, Nym thought she looked extremely uncomfortable all of a sudden. He wouldn't have guessed that she was the type of person to be embarrassed by some praise, but he supposed everyone had their quirks.

"Mine is a bit different than hers. I started using telekinesis as a base. Basically instead of picking up other things, I wanted to be able to pick up myself. So I solidified the air around me and use magic to move it while it holds on to me. Here, let me show you what I mean . . ."

CHAPTER 40

The lessons went fine, as far as Nym could tell. They agreed to continue tomorrow, and Nym was given access to a few other books. Bardin recommended them to him after telling him that they covered a broad spectrum of basic topics. The goal was to identify holes in Nym's self-taught skills so they could recommend new books to help catch up on those.

This was the same idea Nym had been using while they waited for Bardin to get home, but it was easier when there was someone to point out exactly which books were designed to give general overviews of various magical disciplines. It was all useful information, but it wasn't instructions for new spells, which was what he needed.

There was no way he was signing that contract, no matter how short the terms were for. He needed to squeeze as much magic as he could out of that library while it was still open to him. No doubt when he refused Bardin's offer, that would be the end of his stay. In fact, it would be better if he disappeared before that offer showed up, just in case the Feldstal family didn't take the rejection well.

The new goal was to learn enough spells to make him versatile, find some work if possible, and scrape together enough money to get out of Abilanth. The city was a death trap for people like him. There were too many destitute people living in the outer ring under a system designed to keep them there. Even getting enough food into the city to keep people fed required constant magic, never mind luxury goods. Everything was so expensive, and so many people had nothing at all.

Worse for him, once he left the Feldstal estate, he would have to deal with Valgo's attentions again. Nym wasn't sure if that was going to be in the form of the old thief making good on his blackmail threats or just stabbing him in a dark alley. Either way, once he walked out the front door of the manor house, he had a limited amount of time to make himself scarce.

So when he finished the book Bardin recommended, he immediately wanted another one. He wasn't precisely a prisoner in the guest room, but he didn't figure he was likely to be welcomed to walk around on his own. There was a man posted outside the door, after all. Nym wasn't particularly offended by the lack of trust, considering the circumstances with which he'd started his association with the Feldstals.

There was only one thing to do. He opened the door, and the guard snapped to attention. "Hi," Nym said. "Am I allowed to go to the library to get a new book?"

"My orders are to escort you wherever you want to go."

"Perfect. Let's go then?"

Nym still had to use his scrying spell to find his way around, but with that helping him he walked around as confidently as if he'd been born there. The guard passed a quick message to a servant they passed, and Nym noted the servant hurrying off toward the nobles' bedrooms.

He entered the library to find it empty, though he doubted it would stay that way for long. The real question was who exactly would show up to keep an eye on him. He was betting on Bardin, assuming the man hadn't left the manor house to attend to something. Analia was probably too inexperienced to know what to steer him away from.

Perhaps he'd overestimated them. Nym spent five minutes searching the shelves. That turned into ten, then thirty, and still no one showed up to shepherd him. He picked out several books and piled them up on a table. For another half an hour, he read about strengthening elemental aspects he struggled with. Specifically, he continued to work on his fire magic. The Academy student had given him advice that he hadn't had the time to really experiment with, but there was no reason not to check it against something a bit more official.

He skimmed through that book and started on one that talked about basic rune structure. After reading for a bit, Nym got curious. It seemed easy enough, just an investment of arcana into specifically prepared channels that mimicked magical effects. As long as the runes were constructed properly, the only real limitation was the material used. A rune drawn on a piece of paper would burn itself off quickly, whereas one made using metal threads and sewn into a nightgown could last for months or years.

Nym practiced tracing some of the runes out on a spare sheet of paper, then strung them together in the pattern he'd seen on Analia's nightgown. It had stopped his scrying spell from even realizing she was there. If he did it right, it would prevent anyone from spying on him. It might even help hide him from Valgo. There had to be some way the man kept finding Nym, and magic seemed like the most reasonable culprit to him.

The runes shimmered in his sight, weaker than the ones on the light orbs.

That made sense to him. His was made of ink on a paper instead of being carved into stone. The amount of arcana he could pump into the runes was a bare sliver. But the important thing was that it worked. At least, it did something, presumably what it was supposed to.

He smirked to himself when a few minutes later, the door to the library opened and Bardin walked in. The noble affected surprise at seeing Nym there, but Nym thought the real reason no one had shown up was because they were already watching him. He'd foiled that by successfully duplicating the runes he'd seen on Analia's nightgown.

It hadn't been that hard. By no means was he proficient in rune structure. He was a long way from inventing his own runes or even understanding what they did. All he'd done was copy what he'd seen while referencing the book to make sure each rune was drawn properly, then empowered the whole sequence. The only reason he even knew what the runes did was that they'd stopped his own scrying spell.

Even his suspicions that Bardin was magically spying on him were just that: suspicions. It truly could be a coincidence that the man had come into the library right after Nym activated the antiscrying runes, but he doubted it. Still, the easiest way to find out was to talk to him.

"Perfect timing," he told the nobleman. "Do you have a minute to advise me on where to look for a few books?"

"Of course. What are you studying?" Bardin asked curiously. The man was either authentic or a fabulous actor.

"I've been looking at runes. I didn't even know they existed and had only a basic idea of what wards are, but they seem so useful and intertwined that it seemed like a good field to study."

"Runes, hmm. That's a very, very complex field. Even the basics aren't generally something done in the first or second year of study. Are you sure that's what you want to invest your time in?"

"I just think they're interesting. They don't seem so bad. I've sketched out a few already and empowered them."

Nym was sure Bardin already knew that, but he showed off his work anyway. The nobleman studied it for a moment, his eyebrows rising as he looked it over. "Nym, this rune sequence has seven structures and nine linking runes. There are even two contingency structures and an ambient-resonance structure. Where did you even find this? I know it's not in that book."

"It was stitched onto your sister's clothes," Nym said.

"Ah! Of course. Do you know what it does?"

"I am not sure," Nym said. He had his guesses, but it could and probably did have a lot of effects he wasn't aware of.

"It's an advanced privacy sequence, very common among nobles to keep people from spying on them. But to do this . . . and on a sheet of paper no less. This should have burned out before you empowered even half of it."

Bardin was flummoxed. He just stared at the paper, occasionally shaking his head as he mouthed words that Nym thought might be the runes read out loud. Finally, he set the paper aside and fixed Nym with a serious look. A glow of arcana appeared around him.

"Be honest with me, Nym. Who are you? How are you doing this? Why are you here? There is no way you are a self-taught novice who's been working with magic for a few months. All of this . . . the telekinesis, multiple conduits, rune sequences, this is not beginner work. One thing would have been astounding, but everything together . . . no. I don't believe it."

"I don't know who I am," Nym told him, trying to keep his gaze steady while he examined Bardin's aura. "I swear. I washed up on a beach one day with no memories. My theory is that I already knew magic prior to whatever happened to me and I'm just kind of . . . relearning it now."

"That still doesn't explain your age. I've met mages who've been working magic for a decade that would struggle to do some of the things you've casually demonstrated today."

"Well I don't know, Bardin." Nym waved his hands at all the books around them. "Is there a spell in here to restore lost memories?"

"Here? No. That would solidly fall under third-circle magic. I'm so curious about this though that I'd almost consider paying for it myself just to see the results."

The aura reminded him of the truth spell they'd used on him, only far simpler. It lacked all the compulsion elements, not that Nym really felt like they'd worked on him. In a moment of insight, he realized that one of the reasons they'd been so friendly and trusting is that they thought he'd agreed to a magical compulsion to regard Analia as a friend.

Bardin's aura was some sort of divining spell. If Nym had to guess, he'd say it was for detecting falsehoods somehow. It probably wasn't very reliable considering how much easier it was for him to cast it, or maybe Bardin was simply a better mage than the healer who'd fixed up his concussion. Perhaps *better* wasn't the right word. The healer was probably significantly specialized for his job.

"How much would that cost?" Nym honestly wanted to know. The one single memory he'd unlocked had been enormously helpful in pushing his abilities forward to the second layer. He couldn't even guess how much he'd lost. He had years more between his age in that memory and his current age. That wasn't even considering the room he'd seen in the memory. It looked like something out of the Feldstal's home, only even more opulent.

"Depends what they find. Just for the diagnostics, not too much. That's a second-circle spell. Fixing whatever happened is another matter."

"Someone did a diagnostic spell on me once when I first washed up on the shore. He said I was faking and there was nothing wrong with me. But I'm not!"

Bardin was silent while he thought. Minutes stretched on, and Nym started to speak several times. Each time, he stopped himself and waited. He knew he was at a disadvantage, that he needed Bardin and his family's resources far more than they needed another mage on retainer, no matter how talented he might be.

"I have a friend who owes me a favor. We will pay them a visit tomorrow, and they will do a proper diagnostics spell, not whatever crap version some backwater magister performed. Once we have the results, we'll revisit this issue."

Nym was instantly suspicious. Bardin's motivations were entirely transparent. He saw Nym as a resource, something to tie to his family to be used to further enrich the nobles. He was friendly enough, to be sure, but in the same way he was friendly and polite with the servants. He didn't consider Nym an equal, and even though that was the naked reality of their respective stations, it still grated on Nym to be looked down on.

For the chance to recover his lost memories though, he'd put up with a lot. Nym forced himself to grin and said, "I can't wait."

CHAPTER 41

Nym spent the night reading through the books Bardin had recommended, as well as a few he picked for himself. He skimmed through a lot of it, as all the books were for beginner mages and most of it overlapped what he'd already read. There were a lot of competing schools of thought for how a mage's foundational understanding should be built, which mostly stemmed from arguments over which kind of mage was the best.

In Nym's opinion, each method had its own advantages and drawbacks, and there was no real reason to limit himself to just one. Of course, there were only so many hours in a day, and there was probably some optimal route to learning it all that he hadn't even begun to tease out yet. It didn't matter, since the reality of his situation was that as soon as he refused to sign a contract indenturing himself to the noble family, he'd go back to scrounging for whatever he could get.

As long as he had access though, he needed to skip past the beginner books and find a few actual spell books in the library. He'd flipped through a few, but Bardin had done too good of a job loading him down with books that talked about magic without actually explaining how to do it. Nym had a lot of new ideas floating around in his head that he planned to test out when he got the chance, but not a lot in terms of actual useful spells.

They left the house together with a few guards in a carriage, which was a novel experience for Nym. He was grateful to travel that way, as the carriage had the same privacy rune sequence that he'd seen before inscribed onto it and had curtains. With any luck, Valgo's spies wouldn't realize Nym was in it. With a little more luck, they'd think he'd been killed doing the job and write him off.

Nym didn't feel like he had any luck at all.

The carriage took them to the Academy, which in hindsight was an obvious destination. He had been expecting a personal residence, but of course most of Bardin's contacts in the magical community would be based out of the school that he was employed at that probably trained almost every single mage in the city.

The Academy was a series of large buildings that butted up against the mountain cradling Abilanth, and then continued right up its surface. The stone was shaped into stairs and wide shelves to allow for more buildings. All of them, even the ones in the city proper, looked like they'd been grown out of the stone rather than built. Everything was too smooth with no mortar to hold the stones together. Instead, it was as if a series of enormous granite cubes had been hollowed out, except with no seam where they met the ground.

That wasn't to say that the Academy was plain or lifeless. Metal rails lined the stairs, light orbs floated in delicate wrought iron cages mounted on poles, and various signs announced the uses of the buildings. Nym caught sight of a large, grassy courtyard situated between a ring of buildings with several marble statues featured prominently in the center.

Bardin wasn't interested in touring the place, and instead led him directly to a five-story tower that had more glass windows than Nym had ever seen in a single building. The posted sign let him know that the tower was the home of the various professors and instructors who molded the young minds that attended the Academy.

"You don't live here?" Nym asked.

Bardin shook his head. "I'm not a full-time professor. I only teach low-level classes for first-and second-years, and like I said, I mostly do it to keep access to the Academy library. Even for nobles, nonfaculty just doesn't get the same unrestricted access."

They were allowed in once Bardin showed off a silver-and-gold bracelet marked with the Academy's symbol and explained that they were visiting a Professor Langdon. Nym followed behind, curious about the bracelet. When Bardin presented it for verification, it had some kind of arcana reaction, and Nym wondered if he could duplicate it.

That was a mystery for another time though, as they only went up two floors before stopping to knock on a wooden door with the symbol of a closed eye carved into it. Several rune series sprawled out from the center symbol, looping around in a way that didn't seem like it should work according to Nym's admittedly limited knowledge of runes. He doubted they were there for decoration.

The door opened before Bardin could knock on it to reveal an androgenous person who looked maybe forty. Honestly, it was hard to tell. Their hair was long and braided, and their skin was an odd mixture of smooth and wrinkled. The robes around their body were loose enough to obscure any potential curves or bulges, leaving Nym uncertain how to place the professor.

"Ah, young Bardin. And with you is the strange boy you spoke of?" the professor said. Their voice did nothing to help Nym's confusion.

"Yes, this is Nym. He is a true magical savant. I can't even explain some of the things he's shown me, and he can't either. He doesn't remember anything from before a few months ago."

"A most unusual case. Come in, come in! This way please."

Professor Langdon led them through a rather spacious room that had two padded couches, four chairs, a table, and a dozen six-foot-tall shelves all overflowing with books, scrolls, pamphlets, and loose papers. Nym looked around in confusion. The room itself was too big.

The doors in the hallway where only ten feet apart. At maximum, the room could be a bit over twenty feet wide including the width of the professor's own door. And that assumed that the suites on either side had doors right up against the walls, which meant they'd be half the size of the one Nym was in. Even then, it didn't seem like everything could possibly fit in one room, and there were three other doors leading off the main room.

"This room doesn't fit," he said, looking around. "It can't."

Professor Langdon cackled. "Oh, he is a quick one. You must be wrong, since here we are. How do you explain that?"

"Magic?"

"Maybe not so clever as I was led to believe then. Obviously, it's magic. This is the Academy!"

"Some type of shrinking spell? No, it might work for objects, but I think I would realize if I'd been targeted by something like that. Wards of some sort would be necessary to maintain it. There are wards here, but not for that. If we're not smaller, then . . . perhaps the doorway is a teleportation to another location, and the tower is just a collection of doorways."

Nym immediately dismissed that idea. "The maintenance costs would be incredible for that many teleportation platforms, plus, again, I didn't feel like I was targeted by that. And I could see you through the theoretical teleport when you opened the door. Perhaps a more advanced gateway might work, but . . . No, something spatial though. I want to say spatial expansion, but wouldn't that be incredibly dangerous to live in? If the spell failed, you could be killed."

"Ah, see, you got there in the end. You are correct, it is a spatial expansion, and it would in fact be dangerous to live inside something like that without the proper wards set up. Believe me, I'll have plenty of warning before this place collapses. I'm surprised you recognized them though. Bardin was not lying about how puzzling you are."

Bardin started explaining more about the things he'd seen Nym do, but Nym ignored him to study the wards. If not for his ability to see arcana, he probably wouldn't have noticed them, but unlike other wards he'd run across, these were active and showing no signs of powering down. His understanding of wards was that they needed a trigger before they were empowered, but in this case that didn't seem to be true.

His best guess was that the wards also served as a framework to stabilize the extradimensional space. In fact, the more he thought about it, the more he thought that he wasn't looking at wards at all, but a rune sequence writ large. The entire suite was a giant enchanted object. He wanted to ask, but given the location of the runes, he couldn't think of a way to explain that he'd seen them without giving away that he could see the arcana embedded into them.

Reluctantly, he dragged his focus back to the conversation, only to find Professor Langdon laughing at him. "What?" he asked.

"Looks like he's back now. Does he get lost in his own head often?"

"I don't know him that well," Bardin said. He smiled at Nym. "But a few times I've given him a piece of magic to chew on and he's gotten that glazed-over look. Just wait, tomorrow I'm going to be sending you another message saying he's enchanted a box to hold a thousand books."

"If he does, I'm stealing him as my apprentice. Second-circle magic is already impressive for his age, third-circle would make him a once-in-several-generations genius. But enough of that, come, to the lab. Let's see if we can figure out what's going on with this young man's memories."

The lab was, if anything, even more crowded than the professor's sitting room. The things inside also looked insanely expensive. There were a lot of mirrors inscribed with complex rune sequences hanging on the walls. In between them were tables filled with crystals of various sizes, shapes, and colors, as well as hundreds of jars filled mostly with powders that came in just as many shades as the crystals themselves.

A barrel in one corner glowed brightly in Nym's sight and hummed audibly. Professor Langdon noted his gaze and waved a hand at it. "Nothing too fancy. It's just helping to round out some crystals to be used in my third-year divination class. Come, come, sit here in the center of this circle."

The circle in question was made of semiclear powder. It looked suspiciously like a block of quartz he'd noted on one of the tables, only ground down fine. Being careful not to disturb it, he stepped over the line and sat down where he'd been told.

"Good, good. Capable of following basic instructions. You'd be surprised how many would-be apprentices can't do that. Too many rich nobles' brats who aren't used to being told what to do." Professor Langdon cackled again and poked a bony finger at Bardin, whose cheeks flushed red.

"Alright, this is the hard part. Bardin, please wait by the door. Nym, just relax. You're going to be in there for about ten minutes. You may start to develop a headache. Please let me know if it gets too severe. Are you ready?"

Nym nodded and settled in for a miserable time. He watched the aura of arcana surround the professor and condense around their hands. The arcana jumped out to the circle of quartz powder, which ignited with light, revealing a set of ward runes underneath. Those lit up in waves, pulsing slowly from bright to dim without shedding any actual light.

The professor maintained the connection without talking for the entire time. Nym kept waiting for the headache to start, but it never did. Instead, the professor's frown kept deepening. Finally, the spell ended, and the professor regarded him with a puzzled expression.

"What's the word, Professor Langdon?" Bardin asked.

"I honestly don't know," the professor said. "I've never gotten results like this before."

"Results like what?" Nym asked.

"It's like . . . like you didn't exist prior to four months ago. Strangest thing I've ever seen," the professor explained. "You are obviously not four months old, and yet, nothing."

"What does that mean?" Nym was trying not to worry just yet, but this was somehow worse than the magister thinking he was lying about his memory loss.

"Damned if I know," the professor announced. "But I love a good mystery. Let's find out more!"

CHAPTER 42

The testing continued for another hour, though Professor Langdon didn't feel the need to explain much of what they were doing for Nym's benefit. He followed their instructions to the letter and did his best to keep control of his fears and his temper. It did not help that the professor often chatted with Bardin about him, both of them acting as if he wasn't even in the room.

He gritted his teeth and forced himself to play along. Even for just the chance of recovering his missing memories, he cooperated. There were a lot of technical terms being thrown around that Nym didn't really understand, but eventually Professor Langdon ran out of tests and invited them back to the sitting room to go over the results.

"This is quite an unusual case," they said, for probably the eighth time. Nym felt a twinge in his eyelid.

"What were you able to determine, professor?" Bardin asked.

"First, as I said during the original diagnostic spell, you seem to be four months old. Do you know about object-reading spells? They interact with items in a temporal fashion to see history related to them. We can do the same for people, but it's a lot less reliable, especially with mages. For you, it comes up with some random scattered moments in your timeline, but nothing older than a few months."

"What does that mean?" Nym asked, again. He'd been asking variations of that question for an hour while the professor babbled in circles.

"Obviously it means that the spell is wrong, unless you have reason to believe that you are a baby stuck in a preteen's body." The professor paused and gave Nym an intent stare. "No? Well, it's always best to rule out all possibilities."

"Naturally I wanted to test this magically as well, so the next set of tests was to determine your actual age. The results were . . . inconsistent. Biologically, you're eleven years old. If I had to guess, I'd say you have a birthday coming up in the next two months. However, your body shows signs of rapid aging, maybe as much as four or five times as fast as normal."

"Wait, what's this now?" Bardin cut in. "Are you saying that he's actually a toddler who grew up too fast?"

"Well, no, not necessarily," the professor said. "I was not able to determine how long he's been under this effect. It could have started a month ago, or a year. Or yes, perhaps it's been going on his whole life. I don't know."

"What does it mean?" Nym asked.

"No idea," the professor told him, their eyes sparkling. "It's fascinating though. Anyway, in regard to your memories from before the incident, I can't find anything. There is no evidence of tampering, no signs you've been attacked by anything that devours thoughts, dreams, or memories. In fact, the cutoff is so clean that it's suspicious itself.

"Whatever happened to you did too good a job of cleaning up after itself. It doesn't look natural. There's this sharp cutoff in your past where everything just . . . stops happening. It's like you were spun wholesale out of arcana and dumped onto this world, like you didn't exist at all prior to waking up on the beach you told me about."

That wasn't exactly true. He did have one single memory from when he was younger, but he hadn't shared it with anyone since Ciana, and he didn't want to start now. It indicated that he belonged to a family that was important, which meant that maybe he was vulnerable to that family's enemies, which meant he didn't want to be found by those enemies without the aegis of his family. Nym considered sharing the information briefly, but he didn't trust Bardin not to find a way to use the information against him, and he didn't trust Professor Langdon not to tell Bardin even if Nym found a way to pass the information on without the nobleman hearing it.

"Do you know how to fix me?" Nym asked instead.

"I don't have a clue. Whatever happened to you isn't something I've ever seen before. I fully believe that you have no memories older than a few months though, so I can confirm that at least. I know that doesn't help you much person-ally, but it should help lay to rest any concerns about the veracity of your claim."

"It's still kind of worrisome though, professor," Bardin said. "You are a master mage, capable of casting third-circle spells, who specializes in divination. If you don't know how to proceed, who else could? Even worse, if you can't even diagnose what happened to him, let alone fix it, how powerful is whoever did this? And why would anyone do any of this to a child?"

Professor Langdon started laughing. "Oh, I forget how young you are some-times. Third-circle magic is respectable, but you don't make it to archmage without reaching the fifth layer. They are capable of magics I can't even dream of. There are stories of a mythical sixth layer past that, the realm of God, but who could say if it's real. Personally, I think the idea serves to give archmages something to strive for, to let them keep reaching for that next plateau."

"Why don't I know about any of this?" Bardin demanded, bewilderment plain on his face. "I work for the Academy!"

The professor just shrugged. "I'm not responsible for anything other than divination classes. This seems like something that would be under the field of general knowledge to me. I really couldn't say why we don't teach new mages about the five layers of extrareality from which we can draw arcana."

"But . . . the Astral Sea . . . it's endless. That's why it's the Astral Sea. It's impossible to forge a conduit that transcends an endless distance . . . isn't it?"

"Eeeehhhh . . . technically, yes? You're a bright boy, I'm sure you'll figure it out someday. And if not, there's no shame in that. Almost nobody ever actually makes it to the fourth layer, and even the ones that find it, only a fraction of a fraction manage to pierce it. Maybe build up some clout with the school and ask Headmaster Veran to explain it. He is an archmage, after all."

The professor turned away from the nobleman, who stood there flummoxed, and resumed examining Nym. "Back on topic, shall we? Now, I did say that there's this clean cut four months ago, but imagine your life as a string. It proceeds forward in a straight line from the day you're born to the day you die. That's the flow of time. Some people describe it as a river with a current because you can only go one way, and with magic you can try swim against the current to slow time down, or with it to speed time up. But you can't ever go backward, you can only change the speed you go forward.

"But for the purposes of this discussion, time is a string stretching across your life. Except, you don't have a string beyond a few months ago. It leads into the future normally enough, but nothing behind it. It just vanishes. There's no birth event at the beginning. What there is . . . are little knots. Seven of them, if I've counted correctly, stacked on top of one another, all taking place in a fraction of a second.

"I have no idea what these knots are, other than to tell you that they are a snarl in your memories. I tried to pick one open and see what was in there, but it was too complicated for me to unravel. So that's the best advice I can offer you. Figure out what those seven knots are, find someone who can work with them, and see if they can give you any clues."

That was annoyingly vague. Once he cut through the long-winded explanation, the professor's advice wasn't really anything better than "find someone who is better than me to try to help you." Nym didn't have a clue where he was going to find someone like that. He wouldn't even be at the Academy now if not for Bardin's connections.

"Do you know anyone who could do that?" Nym asked.

"Not anyone who's still breathing. Samric Olethal was arguably better than me at divinations, but he's been dead for twenty years now, and I was spot-on in predicting that, so I guess I won in the end. There are a few prognosticators among the Glacial Valley tribes who tend to have some pretty unique abilities, but they're all trolls, and they are not friendly toward humans. Not at all. Nope. They will definitely try to eat you if you go there."

Nym bit back some harsh words and did his best to remain polite. "Is there anything you can tell me at all to help?"

"Sure. All sorts of things. If you keep screwing around with your problems instead of taking care of them, you're going to get struck by a bolt of lightning. You've got a family reunion coming up soon, though it's a small one. And, um . . . I'm not really clear on this one, but something to do with a necromancer? It's kind of foggy. Still a ways off, I think. It's kind of in a bit of a feedback loop. The less you divine about it, the less likely you are to interact with that future event."

"Oh . . . I don't know what any of that means."

He didn't have any family, at least not that he could remember. Maybe they meant he'd meet someone he was related to but not know it.

Professor Langdon snorted. "Well of course you don't. You're not supposed to. It's the future! Took me sixty years to get to this level of skill. If you did it at your age, well, I'd just die of embarrassment. Might take you with me on my way out too."

"What do I do next then?" Nym asked, dreading the answer.

"I don't have a clue! But good luck. Come back someday and let me know how it all turned out, won't you?"

Nym had learned a lot of vulgar words in his time being homeless. He used all of them in the next few minutes, and when he started running out, he mixed them into new combinations to keep going.

"So that could have gone better," Bardin said once they were back in the carriage.

"I know. I'm sorry. It was a very frustrating conversation."

"Yes, but still. The professor was doing us a favor, after all."

Nym stared out the window through the crack in the curtains and watched houses go by. After a few blocks, he said, "What would you do, if you were me?"

"Well that's easy. I'd come back to my estate, have dinner with my sister and me, and work on rounding out your basics some more so that you'll be ready to enter the Academy as a student when the next term starts."

In other words, Bardin still expected him to sign that contract and become indentured to his family for twenty years or more. Nym had just days to extract as much information from the Feldstal library as he could. Hopefully they would let him look at the actual spell books instead of just going over theory.

He didn't know what he'd do after that. He couldn't imagine himself signing that contract, and once he left the estate, it would be back to taking care of himself, scrounging for food, trying to dodge the guards and Valgo. He might just try his luck filling a bag with as much food as he could get his hands on and flying toward warmer weather. If he was fast enough, he wouldn't freeze or starve.

"I guess we'll just take it one day at a time," he said out loud. Bardin nodded in agreement, thinking that Nym was going along with the future he'd laid out for the boy.

CHAPTER 43

That night, Nym managed to slip an actual spell book into his stack of reading to take to bed with him. He also scribed a new rune sequence to prevent scrying but delayed activating it until he returned to the guest room he'd been given. Even then, he studied the Bardin-approved books for several hours until it was well after midnight.

The guard outside his door stayed there all night, but Nym wasn't worried about him. He doubted the man knew any magic at all, not even first-circle stuff that some soldiers sometimes dabbled in. What he was really waiting for was to confirm that the actual mages had gone to sleep and weren't going to be spying on him.

That was why Nym turned out the lights and spent an hour in bed, pretending to be asleep. There were only so many hours he could devote to the plan though, and he wasn't willing to waste all of them on caution. Heart hammering in his chest, he opened a conduit and filled his soul well with arcana. Then he sent a tendril out to activate the rune sequence on the table next to the bed. It flared to life in his sight, and Nym climbed back out of bed.

His clothes for the day were wedged into the bottom of the doorframe before he turned back to the light orbs sitting at rest in their holders. They were easy enough to operate, once he knew how. He turned one of them back on, but set to dim, and pulled the spell book out of the middle of the pile.

Then Nym sat cross-legged on the middle of the bed, naked, and began to read. He skipped over the first-circle spells and the elemental-manipulation exercises, though he did make a note to come back and look at the earth and fire ones if he had time, and started on the second-circle section. Unfortunately, it only took up thirty pages at the end, but there were still seven spells there that he didn't know how to cast, and he was determined to fix that before the sun came up.

The first was the basic arcana-injection spell that Amos had used on him months ago. Once he read the breakdown of how the spell functioned and went over the steps, it was trivially easy to put together. Nym practiced a few times, though without a willing target, he couldn't work on the timing.

The second spell was the aura-reading spell that Lathia had told him about, the one she said Amos had used to know when to fire the injection off. Nym skimmed over it, and it looked straightforward, but his ability to see arcana was superior from what he could tell. He marked it a low priority to come back and learn properly if time permitted.

He started getting frustrated with the third spell. It was the slow-falling spell Bardin had described to him, and it was utterly useless considering his mastery over elemental air. The structured spells the book described were inferior in a lot of ways to the flexibility of elemental mastery. They were very narrow and defined in their purpose, making them less versatile, and they also took longer to cast. Sometimes they used less arcana, but even that was just a matter of practice before elemental casting won out.

Finally, at the fourth spell, he found something useful. It was an improvement on a first-circle spell that helped see farther. Nym had to flip back to an earlier section to find the spell being referenced. That was easy enough to do, though the spell had a problem with feedback in the form of splitting headaches if used for too long or in too-bright areas. The second-circle version was similar, except it worked in bright or dark areas.

Finally, Nym could use magic to see in the dark.

He immediately set to practicing the original first-circle spell. Once he felt he had sufficient control over it, he upgraded to arcana from the second layer and enhanced the spell's structure using the modifications the spell book described. It took him a few tries to get it right, but eventually the spell took hold.

It took a surprising amount of effort to hold it in place, but it worked. He dismissed the light orb and looked down at the book. Even with no light at all, he could still make out the words on the page. It all ran a bit together since he got more of the idea of color than actual colors, but it was legible. Excitement lanced through Nym. With this spell, he could "borrow" from bookstores, study, and put the books back on the shelves. He wasn't completely screwed when he lost access to the Feldstal library.

Nym dismissed the spell and recast it another dozen times, just to make sure he could do it from memory. With each attempt, it got easier to cast, and easier to maintain. It might have been his imagination, but he thought everything was a bit less blurry and colors more themselves too.

The remaining three spells were useful in a different way. They provided a measure of safety in the form of a kinetic barrier that would bounce physical attacks away from him, an upgraded version of the first-circle telekinetic cutting edge, and a mind-scrambling spell that would daze his victim for a minute or so at maximum power, a few seconds at minimum.

Nym practiced them as best he could, though once again, without a target, it was hard to determine how successful he was. Despite that, he was happy with his progress. He had a way to defend himself beyond merely flying away from trouble, and a way to fight back if he absolutely had to, though he couldn't really think of much use for the mind-scrambling spell. One day though, he might need it, probably when he least expected it. So he practiced weaving arcana together into the pattern for it.

The guest room didn't have any windows in it, but it did have a magical clock with a faceplate that brightened slowly as the sun rose. With that to alert him, he stowed away the book, used telekinesis to pull the dirty laundry back to the hamper, and laid down with the intent to pretend to be sleeping.

Three hours later, he woke up confused and disoriented at the time. It took him a few moments to even figure out what day it was, and he only grew more confused as his mind caught up. There was a tray sitting on the table with food on it, and just the sight of it was enough to make him realize how ravenous he was. He scarfed half of it down before he even saw the note placed on the tray.

Analia is always starving after she stays up all night practicing. This should tide you over until the next meal. Please be sure to return all *the books to the library today.*

It wasn't signed, but then, it didn't have to be. There weren't very many people who could arrange the surprise for him. He grimaced anyway as he read it. After all the preparations he'd taken, Bardin had seen right through him.

He ate and bathed and got dressed in yet another set of clothes that had been tailored to fit him. After more than a month of wearing the same clothes, he had a new set for every day of the week. Nym knew what was happening. They wanted him to sign the contract, so they were showing him the high life. Unlimited food, access to knowledge and training, shelter and comfort, and all for the low cost of signing decades of his life away to their service.

In a way, he supposed it was flattering. He wasn't sure how this kind of thing usually worked, but there was probably a lot more work on the would-be mage's part to convince a noble house that he was special, that he was worth the time and effort and money. Nym had fallen face-first into this deal, after breaking into their house to rob them no less. It was ridiculous how lucky he was.

And all he wanted was to find a way out.

The contract was coming down on him at any time. He tried not to bring it up, but he knew Bardin was working on it in the background. Or rather, some clerk somewhere was working on it, making projections and judgments about how much he was worth, how many years they'd need to recoup the expense, how many more to turn a profit. They were calculating food and education and charting out how they would run his life to best suit their needs.

Nym expected he had at best a day or two left, and most of his time was taken up working with Analia on her elemental-air-manipulation abilities. She was determined to turn her flight from riding a storm to something controlled, and it forced him to be vigilant at all times. Already he'd saved her from nasty spills that would have resulted in a trip to the infirmary twice.

She was getting better, and that was probably in large part thanks to his advice. If he could figure out how to tell her what she was doing wrong without giving away that he could see the arcana in her spells, he could probably have her flight stable in a few hours. That wasn't an option however, so he was reduced to generic recommendations and talking about how he did it, hoping she'd pick up the tips she needed from his commentary.

It was a slow, tedious process. If it were anything other than flight, he could just give her some help, let her practice, and check on her. But because she couldn't cast her own flight spell quickly enough to save herself if she fell, which she did, often, he was forced to watch and catch her.

The evening at least was spent digging through the library for written treasures. Bardin still showed up and prodded him toward more beginner books. He didn't seem to believe Nym when he said he'd read enough and that the new books were just repeating information he'd already absorbed.

"It's because he teaches beginner classes," Analia told Nym. "He has to cater to the slowest in the classes, and he has a hard time recalibrating for smart students like us."

"Still annoying. I've read this exact passage in another book already. It was lifted out word for word."

Bardin was sitting at a nearby table grading a stack of reports from his students, a pained expression on his face. "What even does this mean?" he muttered. "None of this works the way you think it does. This is literally impossible. Did you even read the material? Fail."

"Does that happen often?" Nym asked.

"About six weeks after the start of each term when they have to turn in their first major projects. Every single time, he gets himself worked up like this. It was funny the first few times, but now it's just kind of sad," Analia told him.

"It is somewhat disturbing to see the same thing happen over and over again," Malk observed from his place near the table. "Still, your brother sacrifices much for the good of the house. It is not right to mock him for it."

Analia didn't deliver the expected retort. Nym felt he'd gotten to know her quite well over the last few days, and she loved to banter. Malk was a bit of a hard target as he took himself far too seriously in Nym's opinion, but Analia had known him for years and knew just how to keep him going.

Instead, she looked hesitant and afraid, and maybe tired. Her eyes roamed around the library, suspiciously looking everywhere except the shelf that blocked the entrance to the hidden vault. She never spoke of it after the first night, and Nym never did get a chance to find out what exactly was in there.

Whatever it was, it was obviously still weighing on her mind, and he found his curiosity reignited. It wasn't any of his business though, so he shoved all thoughts of it aside and went back to the increasingly frustrating process of trying to pry new nuggets of knowledge out of the beginner manuals Bardin kept forcing on him.

With a sigh, he set his book aside and reached for a new one. Maybe the next one would tell him something new.

CHAPTER 44

The next morning, Nym met Analia for practice. Instead of the garden they'd been using, she led him back to the library. "Are we working on something else today?" he asked.

"Sort of," she hedged.

She sat down at a table and gestured for him to take the seat opposite of her. "This is . . . delicate. Promise me you won't repeat anything I tell you here."

"I promise," he said. He wasn't even sure whom he could tell.

"I know that you're self-taught, but you're really, really good," she said. "I work hard. I have all the advantages of wealth and station. I've been learning magic for five years now, and the only reason I'm not enrolled in regular classes at the Academy is that I get a whole slew of private tutors instead. But you . . . You've got a few months of memories, basically nothing besides the clothes on your back, and those have seen better days. And somehow, you're better than me."

"Where are you going with this?"

"I need help figuring some stuff out, and I can't take it to Bardin. I want you to help me."

Nym's eyebrows shot up. "This is about the room, isn't it?" he asked softly.

She nodded and stared straight ahead, fear plain on her face.

"What's in it?"

"I don't know," she whispered. "Something horrible, I think. I don't understand most of it."

"Why do you need me?"

"Bardin looked at it with me. He wasn't surprised. I think he was already in on this secret of my father's, and they didn't want me to know. It's something about me, I know it. I read parts of the journals he kept. I need help figuring out what he did."

The journals were what Valgo had wanted him to steal. Nym probably wasn't going to get a better opportunity to abscond with them, but at the same time, it would be betraying the trust Analia and Bardin had placed in him. It seemed like Bardin genuinely wanted what was best for Nym, or at least he wanted to help Nym by helping his own family more. He didn't see anything wrong with the contract, and probably most of the people working in the manor had something similar.

If Nym helped Analia, Bardin wouldn't be happy with him. He would probably revoke his offer of a contract, which wasn't a real loss in Nym's mind. Sooner or later he was going to end up out on the street anyway. If he went this route, at least he might get to study some secret research not available anywhere else in the world.

Losing the library would be a blow, but now that Nym finally had a spell to see in the dark, and now that he'd learned a bit more about wards, he was confident he could treat Abilanth's bookstores as after-hours libraries. He had a lot fewer moral qualms about that than he did about stealing from them. More than that, he had actually learned a fair bit about the basics of magic, enough that he had some ideas for how to construct his own spells rather than learning someone else's.

Really, he didn't have much to lose compared to what he might gain. From a purely logical perspective, helping Analia was the right move. On a more emotional level, he liked Analia, and he owed her a favor. If not for her actions when he'd first broken into the library, he likely would be in a mage cell. She'd caught him, and when he'd hurt himself trying to escape, it had only been her mercy that had kept him free.

"How do you want to do this?" he asked.

"I'm not good enough with air cushions to move that shelf. And I don't think anyone wants to pick up the library after another wind spell. I need you to get me in."

"I can do that," Nym said. "And then what?"

"There's a lot of equipment in there. I recognize a few things, but I don't know what most of it is for. There are books in there too with a lot of weird stuff I can't figure out. It's at least third-circle magic. But I figured between the two of us, even if we can't cast it, we could at least work out the theory behind it so we know what it's for."

"Is Malk going to just let us do this?"

Analia looked surprised at the idea that her bodyguard would have any sort of independent desires that would contradict her own. "He . . . I think so. His job is to keep me safe."

"Sure, but you're talking about going against your brother's wishes and, presumably, your father's. He knows who fills his pockets. If he does try to stop us, can he?"

"He knows a lot of first-circle magic. He's very fast, very strong. If he took the initiative in a fight, he could drop either of us before we had a chance to react. But if we knew he was coming and had some distance, well . . . I don't think he could catch me, but he could maybe prevent me from getting into the room. But I don't think he would try!"

Nym didn't like the sound of any of that. Malk had always registered as a threat in his mind. The man made no secret of his dislike and that he considered Nym a criminal. To be fair, he was right, so Nym tried not to hold it against him. If Malk set his mind to it, he could be a fairly large problem to deal with.

Nym considered his new kinetic-barrier spell. It was primarily designed to be used against small, fast-moving things, like arrows or thrown weapons. He thought that if he powered it enough, he might be able to keep Malk out, but that would be exhausting in minutes. And this was all just speculation, since he hadn't had a chance to stress test it. It was easy enough to hold when nothing was hitting it, but he imagined it would be a different story holding the barrier when someone like Malk was attacking it.

"If we can get into the room, I think I can keep him out, for a little while at least. But if I'm doing that, it's going to be hard to focus on anything else. If this is going to go right, he needs to be on board with the plan or far enough away that he can't interfere. This whole thing is your idea, so you should decide."

"I don't think he'll fight us. He only argues with me if he thinks I'm going to do something that's not safe. We're not doing anything but looking at books. As long as we don't make another mess, I think we'll be fine. Do you think you can lift the whole bookshelf without unloading it?"

"Yeah, that shouldn't be an issue."

"So you'll help?"

He made a brief show of considering it before flashing her a grin and saying, "I'm in. When are we doing this?"

"Right now," Analia said.

"If you're sure," Nym said. Analia nodded, and he filled his soul well. Cushions of air wrapped around the whole shelf, tight around the front to hold the books in place. The shelf lifted a fraction of an inch off the floor, just enough for it to slide forward and swing to the side. It did it without a whisper of sound too; Malk didn't even notice until the two kids stood up and walked over to it.

"When did that happen?" he yelped, scrambling to catch up.

"I asked Nym to open it up for me. I want to do a bit of reading here."

"Are you sure you should?" Malk asked.

"I am quite sure that I should do whatever I please," she told him loftily.

"Of course, my lady. I will keep watch on the door and keep the outsider away."

"No," Analia said. "He'll be coming with me and acting as my assistant for the day."

"But . . . this is a hidden vault of knowledge belonging to your family. Surely you aren't going to share those secrets with this miscreant."

"I've made my decision, Malk. Please keep anyone from bothering us while we work."

The man shot Nym the most hate-filled glare he'd ever seen in his life. With visible effort, he forced out through clenched teeth, "As you wish, my lady."

They entered the hidden room. As soon as Analia passed the threshold, wards lit up in Nym's sight, though they didn't seem to do anything but connect to a series of panels set high up on the walls that all glowed a soft green. The room was laid out exactly as Nym's divinations showed it to be.

"I was wondering why this room doesn't have the same antiscrying rune sequences on it as your wardrobe," he said idly. "If it's so secret, you'd think it would."

"Hmm?" Analia looked over at him from the book she'd grabbed from the shelf. "I'm not sure. It might be a power issue, or that the arcana in the runes would interfere with the research. Maybe we'll find the answer in all of this. Here, this is what I want your opinion on. It seems to be a book of spells designed to make permanent changes to a person."

Nym took the book from her and flipped through it. It was as she said, although the spells were vastly more complicated than anything else he'd ever seen. "This is going to take a while to work through," he said. "And this is just one book out of . . . what . . . sixty?"

"Like I said, I'm not trying to cast these. I want to know what my father was working on. These six journals here are his. The ten before that are my grandfather's. Here, read this entry. It'll clear it all up."

Finally! Something's gone right.

The incubation tank is fully functional, and the newborn is still young enough to undergo the procedure. I missed this opportunity with Bardin, but I won't let it slip past me again.

If my father's theory is correct, an ascendant isn't born. They are made. What little lore we have regarding them tells of limitless arcana flowing through them like a raging river, while man licks rivulets of water from a cave wall. The soul well must be the key.

This first experiment should serve to cause it to grow exponentially as the subject ages. It will be years until I know if it worked, but if so, my new daughter will have the potential to be the most powerful mage of her generation. If it works, I can go public with the research, and we can adapt it to work outside of just my own bloodline.

Everything is ready. The tank will keep her alive while the magic works on her. Tomorrow, I will begin the ritual. This will work. It has to.

Please, God, let this work.

"What the hell is this?" Nym whispered. He looked up at Analia, who had tears in her eyes.

"I don't know. What did he do to me?"

"Did he risk your life in that . . . that thing there?"

Nym turned to look at the cylinder. It was made of glass, and empty. Elaborate rune sequences were etched into the glass, looping around and around its surface from top to bottom. It was almost impossible to read because a second set of rune sequences had been carved onto the inside of the glass. Nym couldn't even begin to guess what any of it was for.

"Did it work?" he asked, looking at it in sick fascination.

"You know how we have ways of measuring how much arcana your soul well can hold?"

Nym remembered reading something about it. The criteria for testing didn't make a lot of sense to him, but the gist of it was the soul well grew with the body, and at a predictable rate. An average mage should score a ten on the scale, regardless of when they took the test.

"What did you get?" he asked.

"Last time they measured me six months ago, I scored a twenty-six."

CHAPTER 45

Nym flipped through a few more of the journal entries, but there was very little that was meaningful to him. It seemed that Jaspar Feldstal wasn't entirely happy with the results of the experiment, as he often lamented that he hadn't managed to push the bounds of human possibility. The journal showed a man swinging between erratic and depressed as time stole away the chance he had to continue experimenting on his daughter.

"How much of this have you gone through already?" Nym asked her.

"I didn't have a lot of time when I got it in here, and it's been kept closed off. But I have spent the last few days thinking about this. It's so hard to know, is my control below average because that's just who I am, or is it a side effect from one of these experiments? I work hard. I'm smart. Why do I always struggle to keep spells stable? And it's the same for so many things. How much is me, how much is what was done to me?"

Analia's identity crisis aside, Nym had other questions. "What is this thing he keeps mentioning, what he was trying to turn you into. An ascendant? I've never heard of them."

"I'm not sure, either. I guess maybe it's a term for someone who's really good at magic, or maybe someone who has the potential to be. The experiments I understand seem focused on increasing my potential to beyond-human levels."

"Maybe there's something in some of these other books that explains it," Nym said. "It might help us understand exactly what these experiments were designed to do if we know what the end result is supposed to be."

Nym went through book after book, but very little of it meant anything to him. There was a ton of stuff on anatomy, including some illustrations that made him blush, but he didn't understand the annotations, other than that they were some sort of supposed circulatory system for arcana. He hadn't read anything like that in the other books. As far as Nym understood it, arcana accumulated in the soul well and went directly out of the body to create the magical effect.

But if he was reading the books right, the soul well was just the base that most mages used. By creating veins for arcana, a mage could increase the amount they could hold at once, though it made them more susceptible to arcana poisoning since it meant they were housing arcana in their entire body instead of focusing it to just the soul well, which was naturally built to hold arcana in.

The veins weren't natural, and only experienced mages could, slowly, start to build them using magic to modify themselves. One of the primary goals of Jaspar Feldstal's experiments was to create this network in his infant daughter's body, something that he grafted onto her soul well and that would grow naturally with her throughout her life.

Prior to going over the research, Nym's understanding was that the soul well's size was fixed, and that it grew as the mage grew. There were no artificial ways to inflate it, and the path to more power was through enhanced conduit control combined with learning how to dump an entire soul well's worth of arcana in an instant. Then again, it seemed like the more he learned, the more he realized how little he knew, and how there was so much that was deliberately kept from lower-ranked mages.

They worked for hours, with Analia giving him topics to find that she pulled from the journals, and Nym scouring the reference texts so that they could try to figure out exactly what the journal entries were talking about. He wasn't necessarily successful, but he sometimes found information for Analia, and her noble's education gave her a much better foundation to understand what she was reading.

There were gaps, but the overall picture was grotesque. Her father had done numerous experiments on her, most of them dangerous, painful, or risky. She'd practically lived in the incubation tank for the first year of her life, its magic the only thing that kept her alive. Jaspar hadn't limited his experiments to just her magical abilities either. He'd gone to work on her physical appearance, her voice, her brain, her musculature, everything he could.

That was bad enough on its own, but the real kicker came when Nym realized the age gap between Analia and her brother. "Bardin was nine when this all happened," he said. "He knew something was up. Maybe they didn't give him the details, but he had to question where his baby sister disappeared to for nearly a year!"

"He didn't seem surprised when I confronted him about this," Analia said wretchedly. Tears ran down her face freely; she'd given up trying to surreptitiously keep her face clean after the first hour. Her dress across her lap was wrinkled from her clutching it so tightly while she read, and her hair had started to come undone, leaving long strands falling over her face.

The two fell silent after that. Nym idly flipped through some of the spell books, but the magic was useless to him. For one thing, everything was from the third circle, and he hadn't breached that barrier. For another, it was all made to interact specifically with the Feldstal bloodline. There were some base theories on body manipulation that he might one day find useful, but the spells themselves weren't worth the effort to remember.

Analia was lost in her own thoughts, no doubt trying to come to terms with everything she'd learned about herself. Once they'd finished combing through the journals, she'd spent a lot of time staring blankly ahead. Nym wisely gave her time and space.

Early morning stretched into afternoon, and while it would take months to even read everything hidden in the room, let alone comprehend more than a tiny fraction of it, there wasn't really much left to be learned in general. He put the last journal back on the shelf and considered what he'd learned. Valgo wanted those journals for some reason, and Nym suspected it wasn't so that he could modify them to work on his own kids. More likely, it was blackmail material.

What Lord Feldstal had done in that room seemed highly unethical. It might even be illegal, but Nym didn't know the laws well enough to guess. He wasn't even sure if there were laws to cover something like this. Either way, the journals made it clear that Analia had almost died multiple times during the experiments, but her father managed to preserve his research subject, which was what he cared about the most, especially since her mother had passed away soon after she was born. He'd viewed Analia as his last chance.

Experimenting on strangers without their consent was surely illegal, but doing it to his own family might be different. Then there was the fact that laws for nobles weren't the same as laws for commoners, and mages had a whole other set besides that. Nym didn't know if the fact that the experiments were designed to be beneficial even changed anything. It certainly didn't seem to set Analia's mind at ease, though that might have been more the fact that her father's journals showed almost no interest in her well-being coupled with an apparent willingness to risk her life repeatedly.

"I think it's time to go," he said. "There's nothing left to learn here but the details. And I don't think you want to ever replicate this magic."

"I want to burn everything in this room," she said. "This shouldn't have been done to anyone. How could he think this was alright?"

"I don't know. But come on, let's get out of here. I'm sure it's about time for lunch."

Together, they walked out of the hidden room, and Nym placed the bookshelf back in front of it. The row of journals that Valgo wanted was left behind.

* * *

"I want to go with you," Analia said suddenly.

"What?" Nym asked around a mouthful of scone.

"When you leave, I want to go too."

Nym swallowed the scone, cleared his throat, and said, "What makes you think I'm leaving?"

"Oh come on, it's obvious. Every time Bardin brings up that stupid indentured servant contract, you visibly cringe. Were you trying to hide that reaction? We all know you don't want to sign it. Bardin still thinks he's going to bring you around if he just dazzles you with enough gold and knowledge, but you're not going to stay, are you?"

"No, probably not," Nym admitted.

"You know that contract's been ready for three days, right? The only reason Bardin hasn't given it to you is he's still working you over until he's confident you'll agree to it."

"Unless he can remove all the years of servitude from it, I'm not going to sign it," Nym said. "And since that's kind of the whole point, it didn't seem like something that we could negotiate."

"No, definitely not. So you're not going to sign it, and then you'll leave, and when you do, I want to go with you," Analia said.

"That seems like a terrible idea, no offense. I get that you're mad at your dad, and I don't blame you, but if you disappear, your family isn't just going to shrug and move on. People will be looking for you, and they won't hesitate to use force to find you."

"So we take a teleport somewhere else, where they can't find us."

Nym started laughing. "You have no idea how expensive that is, do you? How much do you think this meal, half of which isn't even going to be eaten, would cost you anywhere in this city?"

"Why does that matter? It's not like I don't have money!"

"For now, sure. Let's assume you manage to sneak out with a big sack of gold crests. How long is it going to last you? Are you willing to eat plain bread, maybe an apple or a slice of cheese? Are you willing to sleep in trees and under bushes to keep the rain off? Can you wear the same clothes for weeks straight?"

He was probably exaggerating. A hundred crests would no doubt set Analia up for life in moderate comfort, but nothing about the manor was moderate. It was all luxurious, opulent, and wasteful. She'd lived her entire life like that.

"Plus," he continued, "what about Malk? He's your personal bodyguard. At some point, he's going to realize what you're doing and stop you. There is no way his orders are 'let Analia do whatever she wants, up to and including risking her life.' How are you going to get away from him when he tries to bring you home?"

"That's . . . I hadn't thought of that." She frowned and looked down at the pastry on her plate. She'd barely nibbled it, and that right there told Nym all he needed to know about her survival abilities. Any kid back at the warehouse would have scarfed that down in two bites, just to be sure no one else got it first.

"Look, I like you, but the streets will eat you alive, and that's where I'm going back to. Stay here and enjoy your life of luxury, where you have a clean bed and clean clothes and all the food you could want and no one is going to try to kill you in your sleep for your shoes. You don't have to worry about freezing to death at night, or guards hitting you so hard they break bones just because you're in the wrong part of town."

"It can't be that bad if you'd take that over working for my family," she said.

"Well it's possible that I'm not making the best choice, right? And for me, that's choosing an entire life of servitude. You notice that none of the staff is eating at this table with us, don't you? So you're going to be giving up a lot better of a deal than I would be."

Analia crossed her arms and glared at him. "Don't try to talk me out of this. My mind's made up."

"Well mine's not!"

"Fine, how about this. I'll hire you. I've got enough money to get us both out of here. You teach me how to survive, and I'll teach you all the fancy magic stuff I learned through years of having private tutors."

That brought Nym up short. It was a terrible idea. He knew it was, but he could leave Abilanth if he took Analia with him. He could get away from Valgo, go back somewhere warmer, and learn more magic. If he could convince Analia to make reasonable purchases, they could both live off whatever modest sum she managed to abscond with.

He was going to regret this.

"How are you planning to sneak out?" he asked.

CHAPTER 46

There was a lot of hushed whispering going on to make sure Malk didn't overhear them. He was on the far side of the room by the door, but it was better to be safe. He could bring the whole plan down before it even got started. Fortunately, the man had to sleep just as much as anyone else, and he commonly slept on the same schedule Analia did.

Their basic plan was simple. They would leave more or less the same way Nym had gotten in, by sneaking by the guards using his scrying spell and flying out through a window. Analia would prepare a pack with clothes and valuables they could pawn, plus any hard cash she could get her hands on. Nym would be in charge once they left, and they would go straight to the mage guildhall as soon as the sun came up, before anyone noticed they were missing.

There were so many ways it could go wrong, but there weren't actually a lot of options. Analia wasn't getting out of the house without Malk, and there was only so much she could take with her without it becoming suspicious. Trying to lose him in the city was a bad bet, so they settled on stealth and disappearing before anyone could bring her back.

Nym wasn't really comfortable with the amount of risk he was taking in the plan. If they got caught, Analia would get in trouble, but he could be executed for kidnapping a noble. The fact that she was leaving voluntarily probably wouldn't factor into that decision. He tried to keep in mind the rewards if they succeeded. Analia's money would make his life significantly better, and more importantly, her shared knowledge would finish rounding out his foundation so that he could begin creating his own magic instead of scrambling to steal scraps from books.

All he had to do was pull it off and get them both out of town.

"What are you studying tonight?" Bardin asked. "That doesn't look like magic."

"I needed a break from magic," Nym explained. "I mean, I'll have years to learn all of that, but there are so many other topics here. I wanted to read about something else."

"And you chose . . . geography?" Bardin asked, his brow furrowed as he looked at the title on the spine of the book.

"Also some history. I wanted to see if the names and places meant anything to me."

"Any luck?"

Nym shook his head. "I'll keep trying."

Bardin tapped a finger against his chin as he thought. "If you're looking for triggers to lost memories, it would probably help to have more recent study material. That country you're reading about, Saldoral, doesn't even exist anymore. It dissolved thirty years ago when the Korshic Empire successfully blocked all their trade routes in an attempt to starve them out. They were both shipping highland silks, but Saldoral had the better market share and better land to produce them."

Bardin recommended Nym a few books that had historical information on events that had happened in the last few years, which Nym gladly switched to. In truth, he was looking for his next destination, and finding out that the country he was considering didn't even exist anymore was a rather large problem.

Analia left early, merely stating that she was tired of studying every night and wanted to relax. Bardin waved her off and returned to grading papers, which seemed to be going about as well for him as it had the night before. And Nym was left to his own devices, within reason.

After an hour, Bardin set aside his work and set down across the table. "Nym, can we talk?"

"We are talking right now," Nym said, not looking up. He was afraid of having a conversation with the man. Bardin was more perceptive than he let on. He might already know about their escape plans somehow, or maybe he was ready to push the contract finally. Either way, Nym wasn't going to like this conversation.

"I'm going to have the contract for you to look over tomorrow, but I wanted to go over some stuff tonight, get a feel for what you're looking to get out of all of this. That way, any last-minute changes can be made before I give you the whole thing."

Nym tried not to show any reaction. Of the two biggest possible topics, this was the safer one. He was leaving in the next six hours, so all he had to do was play along. He could do that. Analia's words from lunch came back to him. Bardin already had the contract ready, and he knew Nym was reluctant to sign it, so this was another pass at making it more palatable, an attempt to convince Nym that it was the best deal he'd ever get and would be worth all the years of servitude.

"Well alright," he said, putting the book aside. "I guess first let me start by thanking you for letting me stay here this past week. I think I've gotten a lot more out of it than you have."

"It's been no trouble at all. You've provided some unique insights into alternative ways to do magic, and honestly, I'm still scratching my head over your telekinesis spell. It's worth it to have you here just so I can keep trying to crack that one.

"But let's talk about the future. I understand that it's intimidating to sign on for something for so many years, but maybe it would help to reframe that. You're going to go to one of the most prestigious schools on the continent to learn magic from experienced and powerful mages who have decades of experience as instructors. A magical education really does not get much better than this. That's the immediate benefit.

"After that comes the work. I want you to understand that we don't expect you to slave away every second of the day for the house's benefit. Mages do important work, and you'll be paid a monthly stipend. Think of it as having a job waiting for you as soon as you finish your studies."

Nym wondered if that stipend was even a fraction of what he'd make on his own. It didn't matter. Even if they were offering three times that much, he still didn't want it. He wanted freedom. He needed it. Nym refused to be tied down, beholden to anyone, forced to do someone else's bidding. He might make an agreement, and he'd honor his side if he wasn't coerced into it, but he was never going to be someone else's servant.

He didn't really know why he felt that way. Lots of people answered to someone. Kids answered to parents. Workers had bosses. Nobles ruled over all of them. The king, if this country had one, he wasn't really sure, told the nobles how it was going to be. Or maybe it was a council, or the church. It didn't matter who was in charge. The point was that Nym wasn't going to voluntarily place himself under anyone else's power. He was a free agent.

"That does make it feel better," he lied. "Where did your team land on length of time?"

"It's flexible. We've got a few paths for you to take through the Academy depending on what you want to specialize in that we need someone for. Some take longer than others, so of course they cost more. The shortest one we came up with is fifteen years, highest is twenty-three."

"And that's years after graduation, right?"

"Correct."

"Would I be staying here?"

"That depends on what the house needs. You might end up on assignment somewhere, though of course the Feldstal family is based in Abilanth, so this is where you would return to after finishing a job. We will be covering the cost to keep you fed and housed, no matter where your work takes you."

It wasn't a horrible deal, all things considered, but it wasn't what Nym wanted. All he could say was, "I think I understand. I'll have to read over the actual contract to see if I have any more questions."

"Great!" Bardin stood up and clapped a hand onto Nym's shoulder. "I'll leave you to it then. Enjoy learning about . . . uh . . . the Republic of Galthala? Nym, no offense, but your skin is a little light to be associated with them. And they are not friendly toward foreigners. Maybe look for memory triggers a bit closer to home."

"Right. Thanks."

Finding a new place to live was harder than he thought it would be.

The hardest part about sneaking out was the guard who spent all night in front of his door. Nym silently laughed to himself as he used the mind-scrambling spell he'd learned "just in case" almost immediately. It only worked for a few seconds, but that was all he needed to slip away.

Nym wasn't completely clear on the aftereffects of the spell, other than that they weren't permanent. It was designed to make someone groggy and unfocused in a combat scenario, so that they couldn't defend themselves, and he knew that the guard would understand something was wrong once he snapped out of it. He just didn't know if the man would realize what happened and set off an alarm.

Not willing to risk it, Nym sped along through the air. He was back in his old clothes, though he did have one set of the nicer clothes they'd provided him stashed away in a bundle he'd made by piling everything up on a shirt, folding it over, and tying it together with the sleeves.

All Analia's clothes had the antiscrying runes stitched into them, which meant he couldn't be sure she was at the agreed-upon meeting point. He would just have to show up and hope she'd made it. If not, he'd wait for a little bit, but one way or another, he was leaving before the sun came up.

After so many days of staying in the manor house, Nym was extremely familiar with its layout and had a passing notion of the guard checkpoints. They mostly avoided the personal quarters of the nobles, with only a few stationed here and there so as not to be walking around making too much noise. That did mean it was off-limits to Nym, but when he'd asked Analia how she was going to get out, she'd told him that was her problem and not to worry about it.

Nym made it to the fourth floor without getting caught and slipped into the parlor they'd arranged to meet in. "Empty," he muttered under his breath. Of course, she still had a few minutes before their designated time, but he'd been expecting she'd be there and waiting.

He floated up to the ceiling and hid in the corner by the door, hoping that if anyone poked their head in to look around, they wouldn't think to look up.

Long, tense minutes went by as the meeting time came and went, and just when he was about to give up, the door creaked open and Analia stuck her head in.

"Nym," she hissed. "Are you in here?"

"Yes," he whispered back.

She jumped and looked up. "Why are you on the ceiling?"

"In case someone who wasn't you looked into the room."

"That's . . . a good idea, I guess. Are you ready?"

"You're late! I've been ready for ten minutes."

She entered the parlor, hauling a large trunk behind her that floated on a cushion of air. Nym stared at it, aghast. "Are you out of your mind? You can't bring that much stuff with you!"

"It's not optional. All the money is in there, plus my clothes and some books we absolutely need to have."

"How are you going to fit that through the window?" he said.

She looked back at the trunk, a look of dawning comprehension on her face. "Oh."

"Yeah. Oh."

CHAPTER 47

What are we going to do?" Analia asked.

"Leave the trunk behind! Obviously!"

"But . . . my stuff."

"We're not going on vacation," he snarled. "Ditch everything but the money. You can buy new stuff somewhere else."

He was really curious how she managed to sneak an entire trunkful of stuff past the guards. Admittedly, her air cushions had gotten much more stable, though not to the point where she could support herself for long-distance flights. The sheer size of the thing should have made it impossible to sneak around though.

"You didn't . . . didn't just walk this past everybody, did you?"

"I told them I was putting it into storage," she said.

Nym winced. Of course she hadn't actually snuck out. Why would she sneak anywhere? She could go wherever she wanted, whenever she wanted. "What about Malk?"

"He's still sleeping."

"But wouldn't someone go wake him up if you're going to be moving around?"

"That . . . I don't know. We should hurry, just to be safe."

"I agree. Unlock the trunk so we can get the money out."

"Only if you promise to carry my things."

Nym glared at her. "I'm not doing that!"

"Well I can't do it myself. I'm not as good with elemental air manipulation as you are. And I'm not leaving it all behind."

"Maybe I'll leave you behind," he muttered darkly.

"You wouldn't."

Nym was doing his best not to explode, but he could feel his temper fraying. "We do not have time for this. Do you understand that if we get caught, you get a slap on the wrist and maybe an extra guard assigned to you? I end up in prison at best, or executed for kidnapping a noble at worst. This is not a game. We cannot bring all of this with us. Now open the damn trunk, get out what's actually important, and let's go. Or yes, I am leaving without you."

Part of him thought he should feel bad for yelling at her, but he could practically feel the rope around his neck tightening. They hadn't even taken the first step yet, and she was already fighting him about the best way forward. Nym didn't expect her to follow orders without question, no matter that she had agreed to do exactly that, but he was surprised everything was falling apart thirty seconds into their joint escape attempt.

Her lip curled, and she opened her mouth to start shouting at him, but at the last second thought better of it. Nym was deadly serious, and he wasn't going to be budged on this. With an exasperated sigh, she flipped open the trunk and revealed its contents.

More than half of it was clothes. Nym immediately ruled them out, not only because she didn't need them, but because they were completely impractical for the kind of life he was envisioning. There were gowns that shimmered, even in the dark, and slippers that sparkled with embedded gems. There were dresses and nightgowns, but he didn't see a single pair of pants or sturdy shoes in there.

The books were harder to give up. They were valuable in and of themselves, plus he always wanted more knowledge. The unfortunate reality of their situation was they had no way to transport them, and Analia had picked twenty of her favorites and packed them into the trunk. Depending on what they were, he figured that he could probably pawn the whole stack for a crest, maybe one crest five if any of them happened to be rare.

After that were a variety of things he couldn't even put names to. There were combs and brushes, little glass vials with some sort of pump on them to spray out the liquid inside, and other things that he'd never seen. It all looked fairly expensive and compact, and he thought they might go for a good amount if he could convince Analia to sell them. They had the mark of personal possessions that she wouldn't part with easily though, so he thought it was better to cut it all away now rather than fight to get rid of each one individually when it became too much to carry or they needed the money.

The coin pouch was surprisingly big and heavy, and even if it was all shields, there was still enough to keep them going for a few months, assuming he could keep Analia's spending to a reasonable level. He foresaw many upcoming fights about money, and their definitions of what exactly a reasonable purchase was clashed.

He grabbed that and set it aside. Then he displayed his own bundle. "Here. Get yourself dressed in something appropriate to wear outside, then make a small bundle out of a shirt to contain just the things you absolutely have to have.

That's one book at most, none of the extra clothes. I'll keep watch for guards, but we need to move as soon as possible."

Analia's eyes promised murder, but she did as she was told. Nym ignored her and sank into his scrying spell. He did laps as far as he could reach, paying particular attention to anything coming from Analia's personal chambers and his own guest bedroom. The guard there must have decided he'd dozed off for a second because, as far as Nym could tell, nobody was looking for them yet.

Analia finished, and they scurried off to the nearest window. It was inside a dusty room full of furniture covered with sheets. It certainly didn't look like anyone had used it in years. Nym spotted the window, which now that he got a good look at it, might actually have been big enough for Analia's trunk. He decided not to tell her that. Turning back to face her, he said, "Let's get go— wait, why are there two sets of footprints in the dust?"

Malk's hand closed around his throat and lifted him off the floor. "I knew it would come down to this. You came in a thief, and you're leaving the same way."

Then he threw Nym across the room with more strength than any human could possess naturally. Nym saw a brief flash of arcana surge through Malk's limbs before the room was spinning around him. Pain flared across his back when he hit the wall, then his knees when he hit the floor. It was all he could do to keep from collapsing right there.

"Stop!" Analia shouted. "Stop this right now!"

"I don't think so. Once I'm done with him, you're going back to your room. I don't care what Bardin has to say about it. You'll be under house arrest until your father gets back from dealing with that mess they dragged him into."

"How . . . how did you know?" Nym slurred out the words.

"I've been watching for days, kid. When you opened up that room, I knew you had what you wanted finally, you'd conned Analia into trusting you enough to let you in, that you'd make your exit real quick. It wasn't hard to figure out, to listen in on the plans. You made them right in front of me. What, you thought just because you were whispering that I wouldn't know what you were saying?"

Nym got his first good look at him. He had some sort of paper talisman pinned to his shirt. It was too hard to read it with the man moving, but Nym knew it had the antiscrying rune sequence printed on it. The bodyguard had prepared well for the encounter.

Malk leaped across the room, clearing a couch in one smooth motion and bringing a foot up to kick Nym just under his ribs. Nym let out a hoarse cry of pain and flipped over onto his back. The bodyguard raised a foot and brought it down on Nym's face. Before it could reach him, arcana flooded into his soul well, and he cast the kinetic-barrier spell he'd learned.

Malk's stomp rebounded off the barrier. The upward force pushed him back, and he was forced to stagger a few steps just to keep his balance. Before he could recover, he was hit with a blast of wind. Malk gave a cry of surprise that turned into a hacking cough as the air was filled with sheets and a cloud of swirling dust.

The kinetic barrier did absolutely nothing to stop the dust, and Nym started coughing just as hard. Blinded, he activated his scrying spell to find Malk, only to confirm his suspicions. He hadn't missed anything on his first pass. As far as the spell revealed, he was alone in the room.

Nym deactivated it and made his way over to the blue glow of arcana that he knew was Analia. "Come on, let's go while he's dealing with this."

There was a blur of motion through the billowing dust cloud, and Malk appeared in front of him. Fortunately for Nym, he'd kept the kinetic barrier up. Unfortunately for him, this time Malk put his whole body into the strike, and the stress of it was overwhelming. Nym felt the arcana in his soul well gutter out, and he desperately opened a new conduit to try to sustain it.

Analia wasn't standing around helpless though, and while he was fending off the bodyguard's attacks, she cast her own spell. A burst of magical force erupted out of her and struck Malk's hip, causing the man to yelp in pain and spin to the floor. He was back on his feet immediately and limped back over to where they were retreating toward the window.

Arcana flared around Malk, and with a flurry of strikes, he broke through the kinetic barrier. Nym was struck four times before he could react, and it was so hard to keep up his concentration while he was being pummeled that he couldn't even think of a spell to cast.

He reacted on pure instinct and fed his arcana into a burst of fire. It scorched the air between them, forcing Malk back and burning away some of the dust still rolling through the room. "Come on," he said, grabbing Analia. He pulled first-layer arcana in to grab the bag of coins and jerk open the window, then they both jumped through it. Nym's air cushions caught them, and they started to rise.

Malk's hand clamped around his ankle. "Where do you think you're going?" he snarled as he jerked Nym down. The air cushions resisted the pull, but it felt like he was going to be torn in two as his own magic tugged him up. Nym kicked at the man's hand with his free foot, but it did him no good. Somehow, Malk was in the air next to them, having jumped six feet straight up to drag him out of the embrace of his spell.

The air cushion no longer supported him, and he came back down onto the third-floor roof in front of the fourth-floor window. Malk pummeled him with blow after blow, and for a brief moment, Nym was sure he was going to die. He reached for arcana, trying to ignite the air again, but what he'd done on instinct, he couldn't replicate consciously.

He forced himself to focus. Barriers made of air sprung up between them, but air wasn't meant to be solid. It was probably the worst element to defend himself with. Malk broke through them without really trying, and all Nym had gained himself was a single second of time.

That was enough for him to cast the second-circle cutting spell he'd learned. Blood blossomed from Malk's chest, and he fell back with a cry. That was the room Nym needed to escape, and he wrapped himself in a full cocoon of air to slip away. With a moment to breathe finally, he scooped up Analia too, and the two of them flew off over dark rooftops into the city.

CHAPTER 48

Nym flew them around the wall instead of over it, despite Analia's insistence that it didn't make a difference. "They'll be looking for us now. We've already failed at getting away without anyone noticing. At least we can make some effort to not walk past every guard in the city."

In truth, all he wanted to do was crawl into a warm bed and go to sleep. His ribs were bruised from the kick; every breath was painful. His whole body ached from the all-over pummeling Malk had given him, especially his jaw where he'd taken a punch to the face. There would be a set of spectacular bruises all over by the time the sun came up, which would make him even more conspicuous.

He'd lost the spare set of clothes he'd taken, which made him curse the idea of wearing his old ones out. For all that the clothes they'd given him were much higher quality, they weren't actually thicker or warmer than the set he'd bought on his first day in Abilanth. Even with them getting threadbare and holey, the old clothes were warmer and drew less attention on the street. But the new set was worth way more and was more comfortable. Once they'd gotten away from the city, he'd planned to switch over to them.

It was still late at night, though in an hour or so he'd have to start thinking of it as very early in the morning instead, and the middle ring didn't have all the places to hide that the outer ring did. It was better maintained, better patrolled, with no abandoned buildings or convenient unguarded warehouses. Nym set them down in an alley outside the market district where he figured nobody would disturb them.

"I should have focused more on learning healing magic," he said once their feet were back on the ground. "I don't suppose you know any?"

"Sorry," Analia said. "We could go to one of the clinics in the city?"

As much as Nym wanted to say it wasn't worth the money, the fact of the matter was that he was really hurting. Besides, he didn't even know how much money they had. While he doubted the pouch was full of copper or brass coins, that didn't mean it was gold crests all the way up to the top either. He expected it to be a mix of mostly shields with a few crests and maybe a handful of shims.

"How much would that cost us? Both in time and money?"

"It depends on how badly you're hurt. I think we should go though. Better to do it now while we're ahead of everyone."

"How much do we have?" he asked, dreading the answer but hoping it was more than they needed.

"I don't know. I didn't stop to count it."

"I guess we should figure that out first."

They didn't count all of it, but Nym was pleased to see that he'd been wrong. It was mostly shields, but about a third of the pouch was crests, with no shims or wedges to be found. That actually worked out well for them as they could use the crests for big purchases, and it wouldn't be hard to break a few shields down into pocket change.

"We need to secure this. This is too tempting a target and it's too easy for a pickpocket to get into. As soon as someone robs us the first time and pulls out silver or gold, they'll be all over us. We could end up mugged and dead if the wrong people find out about this," he warned her. "For now, hold on to it and keep it close to your stomach. Once we get out of here, we'll get some travel clothes and packs, and we can divide it up so that even if we get hit, we don't lose it all in one go."

Now that they were out in the city, Analia was much more willing to follow his lead. She was smart enough to know that she was out of her depth, or at least realized it quickly enough when he started warning her about the many dangers of being even moderately wealthy in the poorer sections of town where the guards weren't a friendly force.

They set off on foot, Nym limping behind Analia while she led the way to the nearest clinic. "I'm surprised you know your way around the middle ring," he said.

She shook her head. "We come here often enough for the markets. I've passed this clinic in the carriage a hundred times."

They crossed an open square with a pair of guards who gave them a funny look, but upon seeing them heading straight for the still-open clinic and Nym's limping gait, neither made a move to stop them. The clinic itself was a modest, single-story building with three rooms in it. Nym's scrying revealed a man and a teenage girl inside sitting at a table in the back. He didn't recognize either of them, or the guards who'd watched them walk over.

Some of his nervousness about being inside buildings started to creep back into his mind, but he firmly pushed it away. He was fine. This was not the same situation. The more he fought that feeling off, the more it seemed to intensify, but Nym didn't have much of a choice. He was starting to think he was really hurt in a life-threatening manner. That kick Malk had planted on him was just hurting more and more.

When they walked in, the man came out of the back room and took one look at the bruise forming on Nym's face. An aura of arcana came up around him, his a warm yellow with wisps of green in it, and Nym saw him weave it into some sort of diagnostic spell. "Mehta," he called out. "We have an emergency patient. Come here."

"Lost a fight," Nym explained, though the healer hadn't asked. "I took a hard kick to the ribs. I think that's the worst of it. Getting harder to breathe."

"Follow me," the healer said. They got him into the exam room and laid him down on the raised bench that was the centerpiece.

"My name is Jorak, and this is my daughter and apprentice, Mehta. I will be helping guide her through your treatment today. Don't worry, you are in good hands."

Analia waited at the door, one hand clutching the pouch to her stomach like Nym had instructed and the other worrying at her dress, leaving the fabric wrinkled all over as she squeezed and twisted it. She appeared more distressed than Nym was, but he had the distraction of watching the spell work that she couldn't see.

Nym didn't get a lot of opportunities to watch other mages work, especially not this close. He wasn't planning on wasting this one. They went through a few diagnostic spells, one of which was actually first circle and seemed to mimic doing a physical exam, from what he could tell. The other ones were designed to look at his innards, at least according to the healer's guidance of his apprentice as she cast the spells.

He also did his own diagnostics, assuring Nym as he cast them that his apprentice's work was excellent but that he would always double-check it, and thanked Nym for his patience. Since Nym was getting a free lesson from it too, he didn't mind. He managed to squeeze a few questions of his own in there about what the spells were designed to do, which the healer seemed delighted to answer.

"It's rare to get someone in who cares about this stuff!" Jorak said. "Usually they just want to be patched up as quickly as possible so they can get out of here."

As soon as Nym showed interest, Jorak started fleshing out his explanations to be more than just instructions for his daughter. Nym took it all in as best he could, which was easier to do since as soon as the diagnostics spells started revealing the extent of the damages, Jorak had asked Nym if he'd like a pain-relief spell to see him through treatment. Nym had gratefully accepted.

The healing spells weren't terribly complicated, even for the internal bleeding

Jorak told him he had. What they were was arcana intensive. Mehta used two or three times as much arcana for each spell as Nym did to fly for the same time, and it took about five minutes total to fix everything up once they were done figuring out what was wrong.

"There we go. I'm going to dismiss the pain-numbing spell now. You let me know if anything still hurts."

"Everything feels fine," Nym said, sitting up. "That's amazing. I think I want to learn healing magic too."

"Well I support that decision. God knows we never have enough healers. Maybe we'll get some new ones from the Academy soon and I can get off the night shift. But be warned that it's not just splashing arcana at the problem, young man. You'll be studying anatomy and medicine for years so that you can understand what the diagnostics spells tell you and know what needs to be done to fix the damage."

"Oh I didn't mean today," Nym rushed to say. "Just . . . it seems like a really useful skill set to have."

"Useful, he says," Jorak muttered. "What do you think, Mehta? Has it been worth it?"

"Ask me again once you start paying me, Dad," she shot back.

"Ouch! By my own flesh and blood, no less. But fair. In addition to the joy of occasionally snatching a human life back from the jaws of death, healers are paid quite well. Speaking of . . ." Jorak gave him a pointed look.

"Ah, right. The not fun part. The bill. How much do we owe you?"

"Eight shields." Jorak looked down at the ratty clothes he was wearing and reconsidered. "Let's say seven shields five."

Nym winced internally. He knew it wasn't going to be cheap, but at that price, he was surprised they hadn't had to pay up front. It was a good thing they'd recovered the money pouch, even if they'd been forced to leave everything else behind. Analia didn't seem fazed by the price tag, but Nym wasn't sure if that was because it was reasonable for the services or because she had no idea how much money was actually worth.

Either way, she counted out eight shields and said, "And let's say the extra five is for your daughter doing such an excellent job, shall we?"

"That seems like a good idea to me," Jorak said. He flipped one of the shields over to Mehta and said, "Here, and another five from me makes a full shield for your work."

"Well thanks, Dad. Not like I did all the work," she said sarcastically, but there was a smile on both their faces, and Nym took it as friendly joking.

The pair made their goodbyes, and Nym walked back onto the street in much better condition. His limp was gone completely, as was the tightness in his chest. Analia followed him, and they got moving again. "Okay, our best chance to get out of the city is as soon as the mage guildhall opens for business," Nym said. "We'll stake it out and make sure Malk didn't get there first. As soon as we know it's clear, we'll go and buy a teleport out of here, though . . . maybe we should pick a new location. I don't know how much of our plans he overheard."

Making sure no one saw them, Nym lifted them up onto a roof opposite the guildhall and started scrying as thoroughly as possible while Analia watched for threats that resisted his scrying spells. The sky slowly lightened as the sun rose, and Nym didn't see anything suspicious. Opening his eyes, he told Analia, "I think we're safe. They should be open soon and we'll be out of here. Analia?"

When she didn't answer, he turned to look at her, only to see three men standing there. Analia was unconscious, held upright by one of the men. "I see you've learned some new tricks," a new voice said from behind him.

Valgo stepped out of the darkness right next to Nym, causing him to flinch back. "You're not the only one with tricks though," the thief said. He stabbed a thin needle into the side of Nym's neck. Immediately, Nym's whole body went numb, and he went down bonelessly to sprawl on the roof.

"Bring them both. The boy failed his mission, but it looks like he brought me something better," Valgo said.

The last thing Nym saw in the predawn light was one of them reaching down to put a black bag over his head, then everything went dark.

CHAPTER 49

Nym came to in a dark room with his arms tied behind his back and the bag still over his head. Every part of him tingled painfully, especially his hands. He could hear the sound of people talking nearby, but it was muffled, as though in another room.

For all Nym knew, Valgo could be standing right next to him, and he needed every advantage he could get. So he didn't move. He didn't groan. He didn't do anything to give away the fact that he was awake. Instead, he forged a conduit and filled his soul well, then cast his scrying spell. He was thankful that he'd never developed the habits some mages had where they required words or moved their hands around when they used magic.

He saw the room in his mind, saw that it was empty but for him. He was in a building somewhere, a large one that stretched out in every direction. The first thing he checked was the location by sending his scry straight off in a random direction until he passed the exterior walls. He didn't recognize the street, but he definitely knew an outer-ring alleyway when he saw it. It was some sort of gang hideout, and Nym felt he could allow himself a few assumptions about where in the city that was based on his knowledge of where the bad neighborhoods of the outer ring were.

His scrying spell was only good for about a hundred feet, maybe a hundred twenty on a good day. The building was bigger than that, but he was at least able to map out the rooms directly around him. There were thirty-two people that he could detect in that radius, but he knew Valgo was now employing antiscrying rune sequences too. There must have been spies in the Feldstal house staff who'd alerted him that Nym's scrying couldn't see through the runes.

For all he knew, Valgo could be standing right behind him, waiting like a spider, ready to bite as soon as he moved. Worse, he didn't know where Analia was. Her own rune-threaded outfit was working against him now. He needed to get free and find her before it was too late.

That cutting spell was already coming in handy. It had extremely fine control, and he was able to slice through the ropes tying his hands together without so much as scratching his own skin. Then, using the scrying spell to see, he flew straight up to the ceiling where he would be out of reach of anyone trying to grab him and jerked the hood off.

The room was empty.

Nym felt a bit silly but justified it to himself as sensible precautions. He knew there were people invisible to his scrying; it was only smart to keep that in mind when he made his plans. Every move he made, he needed to keep in mind that he was acting on incomplete information.

He had a couple ways to proceed. First, he could try to escape and get reinforcements somehow, whether that was the city guard or people directly from House Feldstal. He doubted he could convince the city guard of anything, so that meant making contact with people like Malk. Nym was not a fan of that for obvious reasons, plus if he looked at it long-term, he would be putting himself in a position of vulnerability. There was absolutely no way Analia was going to get away from them like she wanted if he went running back to her family for help.

Another option was to find and rescue her himself. That had a much lower chance of success with a much higher chance of personal injury, but if he pulled it off, they would be in a better position if her family wasn't involved. If he knew where she was, he could plan to save her. It would be nice if she'd come save him instead, but he suspected that Analia was the real prize of the night. Valgo no doubt planned on demanding a huge ransom to return her to her family.

Nym spent a few minutes going over the building again. From what he could tell, it had been a huge, sprawling three-story inn at one point. He found rooms that were being used as offices, rooms for storage, rooms for sleeping; the kitchen and common room were still in use on the ground floor. A pair of hallways ran parallel to each other about thirty feet apart on the second floor, with stairs on either end that led up and down.

Below all of that was a cellar. There were barrels and kegs stacked on one wall and, in one corner, a wooden framework filled with bars. The bars had a door built into them, which was closed. Three people stood outside of it, none of them really moving too much. There was no one inside the cell, as far as Nym could tell from his room on the third floor.

If Analia was a captive and they were in the same building, that was most likely where she was. Nym started plotting his route there. There weren't a lot of options, if he stayed in the building. But there were some shuttered windows in a nearby office that he thought he could reach without being spotted by anyone.

His way back in was through the window in the kitchen, and then down the stairs. There were two people at work in the kitchen that he was hoping he could avoid if he timed it correctly since one of them was constantly going back and forth to the common room hauling plates of food. The other seemed to be thoroughly distracted with preparing the food.

Getting through the kitchen without being noticed was the most important part of his plan because, if he got caught there, it was likely that he'd end up being chased by the dozen or so people in the common room currently eating. His hope was to just sneak through, with his mind-scrambler spell on standby just in case the cook looked up at exactly the wrong time.

All of that still left him with the problem of three people guarding a hope-fully-not-empty cell, and any scrying-blocked surprises that might come up along the way. For that, he needed magic and the element of surprise. The kinetic-barrier spell worked best against arrows or thrown objects—anything with low weight and high speed was deflected quite easily, according to the book he's gotten it from. He could use the cutting spell offensively, though it had done only superficial damage to Malk. He had concerns about its effectiveness.

"This is a bad idea," he said out loud. He nodded to himself. "Can't believe I'm doing this."

Then he got up, grabbed the rope and mask so that anyone who looked in would hopefully think he'd just been moved instead of escaped, walked out into the hall, and headed over to the office with the window. He ran into his first snag there; it was locked. That was fine; he could try a different room. There were a few windows on the third floor, and nobody up there seemed to be awake. The second room was locked too. So was the third. Finally, he found a storage room that wasn't locked, but that was packed full.

Nym managed to scoot over the top by way of flight and use telekinesis to undo the latch. That left him with a gap of maybe eight or nine inches to squeeze through between the top of the window frame and the rack sitting in front of it. There was no way he was moving that rack, so he carefully inched his way out. It was just lucky that the windows were shuttered with no glass, or he wouldn't have been able to get through at all. The hood and rope were left behind, buried in the back of the room.

The sun was up, but it was still early morning, and there wasn't a lot of activity outside. At least, no one started pointing at him and yelling. Nym thought lost an hour or two of time from whatever the thing they'd stabbed him with did. If he could find Analia quickly, they might still be able to buy a teleport out of Abilanth.

Nym flew down to the ground, hugging the side of the building as he went, and skimmed over to the kitchen window, which was thankfully still open. If the cook had decided to close it, he would have had no choice but to use a mind scramble on him and hope for the best.

The server came back in and picked up some more plates, then left again.

The cook stood at the stove, probably facing at a far enough away angle for Nym to slip in, but he didn't want to risk it. The man was alternating back and forth between the stove and a cauldron over an open flame in the hearth on a different wall, and as soon as he went back to check on that, Nym would have his opening.

He crouched outside the wall, waiting and hoping that no one saw him or came to check on him and found the room he'd been tied up in empty. The server came back in and out another three times, and Nym was starting to think he'd have to risk it when the cook finally moved.

Nym floated up and through the window, his body held stiff with his arms over his head like he was diving into water. He slid soundlessly into the kitchen and, in a single smooth, continuous motion, flowed down the stairs into the cellar. Only when he was halfway down did he change his direction to hug the ceiling and move into a corner.

Luck was with him. Analia was sitting in the cell, awake and looking extremely miserable. That was as far as his luck went though because, in addition to the three thugs guarding her, there were another three. Nym recognized them from the roof as the ones who'd also been using antiscrying rune sequences.

Three was already a long shot. Now he had six of Valgo's minions to deal with, and he didn't have a clue how he was going to do it. The only thing going right for him now was that the cellar was big and they hadn't bothered to keep most of it lit. There were two lanterns hanging from hooks on the walls near where the cage was, and the rest was dark. There was plenty of room for Nym to hide.

As he saw it, he had two problems. The first was subduing Valgo's crew in some way, or finding a way to make them leave. The second was getting the key to the cell Analia was locked in. He didn't see it anywhere, either with his eyes or by scrying. That meant it was either in the pocket of one of the three he couldn't scry, or it wasn't in the cellar at all. He took a few minutes to comb through the rest of the hideout but didn't see it anywhere.

His best guess was that Valgo had it. It made sense, in a way. Analia was valuable; he wouldn't want just anybody having access to her. So he took the key with him. It was smart, a lot smarter than what they'd done with Nym, just dumping him into an unlocked room with nothing more than a foot of rope wrapped around his wrists and a sack on his head.

Nym didn't fancy his odds of fighting through six people, especially not when he needed to hit them quickly and quietly enough that they couldn't raise the alarm. He thought he could probably get through the locked door without a key by using some extremely fine-tuned telekinesis. Keys weren't that complicated, after all. He'd just force the internal mechanism to turn in the lock.

He sure hoped that worked because, if his idea to get rid of the guards worked, they would not have a lot of time. Nym reached out to the air in the kitchen above him and, using his scrying to direct his efforts, scattered the burning logs across the kitchen floor.

CHAPTER 50

The reaction was immediate. The cook started bellowing in surprise, and all six guards looked toward the stairs. Nym watched the man grab hold of a fireplace poker and try to flick the logs back into the hearth. While he was doing that, Nym used a cushion of air to push the contents of the stove onto the floor and stoked the fire inside with an influx of air. Flames started shooting up through the seams in the metal, causing the cook to yell again.

"The hell is going on up there?" one of the thugs asked.

Nym wasn't good at controlling fire. He could make it spread, but he couldn't stop it. He'd gotten some good advice, and he'd practiced a bit, but compared to his skill with air or even water, he was laughably bad. For his purposes right now though, all he needed was to make it spread. So he did.

Fire raced across the floor, and the yells became more panicked. Men from the common room abandoned their meals to rush into the kitchen and help try to put it out, but Nym fed the flames more arcana whenever it looked like they were about to be overwhelmed.

The guards were all looking at one another and muttering, trying to decide what to do. It was easy to hear the shouts and stomping around above their heads even from Nym's position in the back corner. It looked like there was a short but harsh argument going on between them, which ended with one of the rune-protected ones saying, "Screw that. I'm not waiting for the damn ceiling to collapse."

Then he left. Another one followed him after announcing, "She's in a cage. It's locked, she's not going anywhere. I'll be back once we get this taken care of."

The distraction had worked, but only partially. Nym kept it up, hoping the pressure would force the rest to abandon the cellar. The fire kept spreading, urged on by his magic, and was now climbing up the walls and making its way into the common room. Most of the people had fled the building, though there were a stubborn few still trying to smother it.

One of the guards poked his head back down the stairs and said, "This place is going up. The fire . . . It's not natural. We checked, and that little mage Valgo was playing with is gone. We think he started it somehow. Come on, let's go."

"How the hell is that kid gone? His magic is supposed to be blocked! Did someone come rescue him?"

"I don't know! Does it matter right now? You want to burn alive down here?"

"What about the girl?" another guard protested. "She's worth a fortune. Valgo'll kill us if we leave her here."

"What are we supposed to do? You got a key?"

"Well, no."

"Then it sounds like you can get the hell out of here while you can, or you can stay and burn with her. I'm going now before the fire blocks off the door."

And with that, the man was gone, and the remaining guards went with him. Nym's distraction was a success. He just needed to get a now-terrified Analia out of the cage so they could make their own escape. She had kept quiet while the guards argued, but once they left, she climbed to her feet and started looking around.

Nym had to admire her for that. She wasn't going to just sit there and die, but he didn't know how she planned on getting out. She didn't have his proficiency with telekinesis or with elemental air manipulation. Hopefully she knew some spells tailored to the situation.

Once he was sure all the guards had exited the hideout, at least all the ones who weren't protected from his scrying, he moved out of the darkness. "Analia," he whispered. "Can you get this door open?"

"What? No, of course not. How would I?"

"I don't know. I thought maybe you knew a spell."

"No, they got me with something when we were on that roof. I can barely hold a conduit open, and any arcana I try to draw in goes right out of my soul well and starts poisoning me."

"Really? They stabbed me with something that knocked me out for a bit, but I feel fine now."

She gave him a hard look through the bars. "Are you really bragging right now?"

"No! I'm just saying . . . maybe try again?"

"I've been trying, Nym! Even to save my own life, I can't cast a thing. I'm surprised they didn't do the same thing to you."

"Okay, okay. This is fine. I'll just go back to my original plan."

Locks were complicated, but his scrying spell let him literally see inside them. Nym had never used magic to pick one before, but he was confident he could figure it out. He used telekinesis to move stuff around and kept trying to turn the mechanism holding it, but it resisted turning. Scowling, he played with the pins until he figured out where they all needed to be and turned the lock.

"Ha!" he crowed as the door swung open. "Okay, next question. Do you know what they did with our money? We're not getting a teleport without some funds, and I couldn't find it anywhere in their hideout."

"Who cares about the money?! We'll get more," Analia said, pushing her way past him.

"Unless you're planning on going back home, I really doubt we're going to replace it easily."

"Nym! Worry about it later. This place is on fire. Do you not smell the smoke?"

"Well of course I know that," he said. "I'm the one who lit it."

"You . . . what? What if you couldn't get the door open?" Her voice rose into a screech at the end.

"What did you want me to do? Ask them to go one-on-one with me until I'd knocked them all out? They're twice my size!"

"As adorable as this bickering is, I'm going to have to insist that you put out the fires you started on my property," Valgo said.

Nym jerked away from him where he'd appeared out of the darkness. Somehow, the thief had entered from the back half of the cellar. Nym knew for a fact that there were no hidden passages leading in. Valgo obviously knew some magic himself, but teleportation was third-circle stuff. If Valgo was that good, they were completely screwed.

The thief took a threatening step forward and brandished the metal rod he'd jabbed Nym with earlier. "Let me be perfectly clear with you. The girl is a payday. Her father will drop a thousand crests to get her back, and she'll be returned unharmed. She has nothing to fear. You, on the other hand, have annoyed me greatly. I am trying to decide on the best way to proceed with you. My thoughts are as follows:

"First option. I kill you. You've cost me money and time and proven unwilling or unable to do the work I assigned you. Second option. I knock you out, again, and sell you to a group of Byramese flesh carvers who occasionally contact me needing new samples for their work. They would love to experiment on you since you seem to defy several standard laws of magic. Third option. You put out the fires and start cooperating with me. You'll work for me until you've repaid the cost of all the damages, at which point I'll determine your future."

Nym just stared at the man while he ranted in an oddly precise and coherent manner. Then, once Valgo was done, Nym smacked him with a fully powered mind scrambler. At maximum strength, it was supposed to leave its victim dazed and confused for up to a minute, assuming they had no magic of their own. That obviously was not the case here, and Nym was just hoping it gave him fifteen seconds to get away.

"Come on, we've got to go," he said as he scrambled for the stairs. Hopefully

Analia would be right behind him because they really did not have time to argue. Cinders were already falling from the ceiling as the floor over them started to burn through. The heat rolling down the stairs was awful, so much so that Nym harnessed the air just to push it away.

The fire covered the entire kitchen, and smoke obscured his vision. Fortunately, his magic was still going strong. Nym pulled the air out of the room, and the back door exploded open to belch thick smoke into the air. There were probably three dozen people there watching their hideout burn when Nym and Analia emerged into the open on cushions of air.

Most of them stared in shock at the pair, but before Nym could fly off, he was tackled by one of the guards with the antiscrying outfit. Analia let out a huff of surprise as she hit the ground, only to be grabbed as well. Nym struggled to push the man away, but he was too heavy for telekinesis, and picking him up with air cushions didn't work so well when the target refused to let go of him. Sure, Nym could pick them both up at once, but that didn't get him free.

He was about to lift all four of them into the air and try to bluff his way into convincing Valgo's thugs to let them go, but the old thief himself emerged from the shadows of the building. He took in the situation at a glance and started snapping out orders.

"Get the girl out of here. Gag her and bag her. No one can recognize who she is. You, grab the boy's other arm before he tries to fly off."

Valgo stalked forward with the metal rod. "I decided on the first option, kid. You're too damn annoying to let you live."

His arm flashed forward like a striking snake. Just before the tip stabbed into Nym, there was a deafening boom, and the world went white.

Omarin went over the construct again while Nym's face scrunched up in concentration. He repeated the weaving, only to have it unravel.

"Your intent is not clear enough. You are attempting to mix three different elemental properties, and they do not want to. You need to convince them, and you need to hold them apart until it is time for them to all collapse into one. It is not enough to mimic the final pattern. You must hold the framework just so."

"The fire won't listen to me!" Nym said. "Even by itself, it doesn't want to. I can't make it do what I want and control air and water at the same time."

"You do not need to make the fire do what you want. You need to convince it that following the path you've laid out is what it wants," Omarin told him.

"How do I do that? Fire's not alive, and if it was, it would just do what I told it because it has to!"

"You tell it with your arcana, foolish child. You know this. You must bait the fire into following your will."

Nym tried again, painfully, slowly reconstructing the framework for the spell.

He wove in elemental air and water, framed in a matrix of his own arcana, his will given form, and carefully, so carefully, threaded gossamer strands of arcana through the construct. He ignited it with a wisp of fire, and in a flash it wound its way through the construct.

Nym pulled the supports away, and the whole construct collapsed onto itself. A boom rolled through the air, and a burst of lightning arced away from him. Thirty feet away, a scorched patch of earth five feet wide appeared.

"Not bad," Omarin said, "but let's work on your aim some more."

"Yes, sir. I'll try again."

"Good, now remember, lightning inherits from fire a desire to follow its own path, so you must create the path that it most wants to take in order to aim this spell properly."

Nym's face scrunched up again, and he slowly started to rebuild the framework. He was a little bit faster this time, and faster again the time after.

Sight returned, and nine people lay dead around him. Their charred corpses were twisted and scorched, with smoke rolling off their limbs. Valgo was not one of them, but he was considerably charred himself and seemed to be unconscious.

"What was it that professor friend of Bardin's said?" Nym mused out loud, his voice cold and hard. "Oh, right. 'If you keep screwing around with your problems instead of taking care of them, you're going to get struck by a bolt of lightning.' I guess they were right about that."

CHAPTER 51

Nym hadn't felt that cold numbness descend on him once since he'd reached Abilanth. He'd thought he'd finally put it behind him, and he'd welcomed that for two reasons. First, it only ever seemed to happen when his life was in danger, which was never a position he wanted to be in. Second, it scared the hell out of him afterward.

But in that moment, with the specter of death looming over him, Nym embraced the change. The fear drained away, and with it the indecision and the hesitation. He was ruthless, and he knew what he needed to do.

"Leave," he told the people who were still upright and capable of moving. The ones on the ground were dead already or would be soon. They were not a concern. Valgo was, but he couldn't kill the thief, not yet. If nothing else, Nym needed the money they'd taken from the Feldstal manor, and he hadn't seen it in the hideout.

He hadn't found any real treasury there, but since Valgo was definitely loaded, that meant it was somewhere else. If he was lucky, he'd come out considerably ahead. All he had to do was get the information out of Valgo and loot the stash.

He was embarrassed to think that he'd ever been afraid of the man. Valgo knew some magic, sure. He had minions and spies and money. But Nym just needed to remember a single midlevel spell, just one complex offensive piece of magic, and he'd easily beaten the thief. It had been the work of a moment to smite the courtyard.

The strike had been wild and unfocused, but he could forgive himself considering how close he'd cut it. The girl was still alive, which was a good thing. She seemed a lot less valuable now that he was about to come into his own financial windfall once he discerned the location of Valgo's treasures, but still, she'd done nothing to wrong him, and it would be a shame if he'd accidentally killed her.

The minions weren't leaving like he'd told them to. Instead, a variety of small crossbows were being revealed and aimed at him. A few of the bolder ones had pulled blades and were advancing. Nym cast his kinetic-barrier spell to protect himself from ranged attacks and flew fifteen feet into the air. With the burning hideout to his back, he stared down at the minions and contemplated the best way to break their morale.

It would be hardest and probably least productive to kill them all. A few more well-placed lightning bolts would thin the crowd, and the few who survived would surely flee, but the spell was complicated and difficult to aim. Valgo and Analia were close enough to the action that he risked hitting them, so he decided against that particular bit of magic unless they forced his hand.

Fire was another possibility. His control wasn't spectacular, but with his recent insights, he was finally starting to get the hang of it. It wouldn't be too difficult to light a few of them up, though he doubted he'd be able to put them back out again. There was still enough snow in the yard that he was sure it wouldn't be a problem.

While he considered, the first volley of crossbow bolts struck his barrier and rebounded everywhere. A few of the minions cried out when they were pierced by them, but Nym was too distracted to pay much attention. The barrier held, but the sudden drain to his soul well was larger than he'd anticipated. He needed a second conduit dedicated exclusively to keeping the barrier going.

The rest of his options were intimidations at best. Blasts of air could knock them over. He could try to freeze them. The spell that cut through things worked, but it was limited. In the end, he decided his lack of control over elemental fire manipulation wasn't an issue in this scenario. Rather than reach out to the burning building to borrow fire, he threaded arcana over his chosen targets like a spiderweb, then ignited them all at once.

Theatrics were an important part of intimidation. Even though he didn't need to, Nym pointed a finger at each of his victims. The four people he selected lit up and started screaming. They quickly abandoned their weapons and dove to the ground to roll around, trying to smother the flames.

Nym could have fought to keep the fire going. That was much easier than trying to extinguish it, but in this case, he didn't see any reason to. Instead, he turned to point at a new person and layered him with more webs of arcana. The man's eyes widened, and he turned to run but only made it a few steps before Nym ignited him.

Slowly, he panned a pointed finger across the gathering. Nobody was attacking him now, and tension hung thick in the air. It was like they were afraid to move, that the first one would attract his notice. He paused for a second, his finger pointing straight up.

"Leave," he said again.

With Valgo still on the ground and showing no signs of regaining control of the situation, or even that he was conscious, his minions finally broke. Those that were capable fled. Those that needed help crawled off as best they could. A few people stopped to help them, but most of them were left to hobble away under their own power.

After a minute, the only ones left were Nym, Analia, Valgo, a few groaning thieves who hadn't managed to clear the yard thanks to their injuries, and a bunch of corpses. The smell of charred flesh from the initial lightning strike was strong in the air, and much of the snow in the yard itself had vaporized into steaming mist thanks to Nym's magic.

He considered the hideout behind him and decided it would be best to put the flames out so there was no risk of them spreading. Elemental water magic rippled out from him in a big, inelegant mass that collected loose snow and hurled it at the building. At the same time, he ripped the air away from the fire and channeled it straight up in an attempt to both smother it and starve it.

The flames dimmed but didn't disappear completely. He thought he could probably do it though, if given enough time, and assuming he didn't give himself arcana poisoning first. The elemental spells were brute-force magic, akin to heavy lifting, and he was getting tired surprisingly quickly. It must have been all the magic he'd used throughout the night, possibly coupled with the healing he'd needed for his physical injuries.

Suppressing the fire wasn't a high enough priority for him to continue to dump arcana into it. What he needed was a safe place to transport Analia and Valgo, and a surefire way to restrain the old thief. Neither were conscious now, both heavily injured. Analia had survived because Nym had deliberately tried not to hit her; Valgo because of his own magics. Nym needed a healer for her and an interrogation room for him.

If he'd been able to recover the money, he would have turned Valgo over to the Feldstals and let them handle him, but the coins were nowhere to be found. He needed that pouch if he was going to get Analia fixed up without returning her to her family, which meant he needed Valgo to wake up and tell him where it was. His spell list was still very limited though, and he didn't think he had anything that could restrain a normal person, let alone a mage who had shown an ability to do as least limited teleportation.

Then he spotted the small metal rod Valgo had used on him. He scooped it up and examined it. It was maybe six inches long, about as thick as a finger, made of something that might have been silver, with one flat end and one that tapered to a blunted point. It was covered in runes that were tiny, very difficult to read.

He didn't recognize a lot of the individual runes, but he knew it knocked people out, and he guessed it was supposed to do something like an arcana injection to disable a mage's ability to cast spells. The most important part was that it looked like all he had to do was channel some arcana into it to activate it, and then jab the pointed end into the intended victim to discharge the spells.

That seemed simple enough. Nym charged it and stabbed it into Valgo's leg. Arcana punched into him, then faded away. It seemed like nothing had happened. Nym wasn't sure if it had worked or if he'd done something wrong. Just to be safe, and because he wasn't particularly concerned about Valgo's well-being, he charged it a second time and poked the man again.

It had the same results. Nym shrugged and pocketed the enchanted rod. If it worked, great. For now, he'd proceed as though it didn't and be as careful as he could. He needed first to wake Valgo up, and then to find a way to get truthful answers out of the thief. Nym had half an answer for the second problem, at least. He'd copied Bardin's truth-seeking spell and was pleased to see that it was easy enough to get up and running, and also didn't have any real impact on the amount of arcana he was holding in his soul well.

He did not have time to wait for Valgo to wake up on his own. The sun was already up, and even though it was the outer rings, somebody would show up soon to investigate the burning building. Nym wove cushions of air to pick up Analia and Valgo and, using his scrying spell to lead the way, threaded through the city streets while avoiding its citizens. There really was only one place he felt safe enough to go.

The kids didn't spend a lot of time on the second floor of the warehouse. The stairs were rickety where they still existed, and even the weight of a child was enough to make them creak and sway. The space wasn't really needed anyway, and being higher up just meant being exposed to more wind. In short, it gave Nym all the privacy he needed.

It was the work of a moment to blast the accumulated snow away and lay Analia down in a relatively sheltered corner. Valgo got tossed into the snowbank. He was still unconscious by the time Nym made it there, but Analia was awake, judging by her quiet, pained weeping. She'd been caught in more of the lightning strike than he'd thought, he just hadn't realized it until he got a look at her back and saw the shredded clothing and burns.

She was breathing hard too, which actually concerned him more than the more visible injuries. He considered taking her to a clinic and trying to use her family name to direct the bill to them. Unfortunately, he didn't know if they'd work on the promise of payment, and if he left Valgo alone, there was every possibility that the old thief would work his magic and escape somewhere. Nym needed him alive and controlled if there was going to be any chance of recovering the missing money.

He didn't think there was much choice. The longer he waited, the worse

Analia was getting. He picked her up again with his magic, gave Valgo's still but unconscious form one last bitter look, and flew off toward the middle ring.

He took her to the clinic that had patched him up a few hours earlier and told her that they'd been attacked and lost their money, and she'd been struck by lightning magic. He then told Jorak that her name was Analia Feldstal and that her family would no doubt pay whatever the price was to have her healed. Before the healer could protest, Nym was back out the door and in the sky again.

He ignored the shouts from a nearby city guard commanding him to get back down on the street and flew as fast as he could back to the warehouse. It had taken him less than five minutes to drop Analia off and return. When he got there, Valgo was nowhere to be found.

CHAPTER 52

Nym didn't want to say the last week was a total waste. He'd learned a lot about magic fundamentals and a few new spells. More importantly, he'd recovered a second memory that had showed him the importance of structuring his magic not only in the correct order, but also with the correct timing and in such a way that it would be altered. Learning how to essentially pin part of the spell in place to weave other elements around it would no doubt be invaluable in the future.

Being gifted with such a powerful offensive spell was also a boon he couldn't afford to underestimate. For the first time since he'd woken up on that beach, he felt like he had a real option besides running away from problems. It wasn't a perfect solution, as he'd already demonstrated by accidentally hitting Analia with it, but it worked very well.

He wasn't sure it was worth it though. Valgo was a bad enough enemy, but after everything that had happened in the last few hours, he was sure House Feldstal would want him too. If they didn't find him, the city guard would. He had murdered a dozen people and committed arson after all.

He absolutely had to get out of Abilanth now. There was no way around it. Even without the money, he needed to go. At this point, it was probably too late to use the guildhall's teleportation platforms anyway.

Without the threat of imminent danger, the cold numbness fell away. All that was left was Nym, and he felt paralyzed by indecision. He almost wanted that other personality back just so he could feel like he was in control and the decisions were easy. But then he remembered how transactional he'd considered his relationship with Analia while he acted that way, how coldly he'd weighed her life and safety against the potential gains he could make by letting her die.

It scared him. He didn't like who he was and the things he did when his life was on the line. He didn't like that when he saw survivors among the bodies he'd made, the first thing he did was weigh whether it was worth the effort to the finish the job. He'd left enemies alive behind him, people who might recover and want revenge.

Since he couldn't just summon the numbness whenever he wanted, he'd have to solve his own problems. Leaving Abilanth was still insurmountable though. He didn't have the funds to take a teleport or buy supplies. He barely knew which direction to go if he left, but none of that mattered at this point. Thanks to Nym's greed, Valgo was still alive and would no doubt have a healer of his own patch him back up, a hundred people had seen him flying over the city, and both the Feldstals and the guard would be coming for him. If he stayed, the only question was who would get to him first.

The plan was to wait for nightfall and sneak out. He only had to stay ahead of everyone for one day. It was sorely tempting to leave immediately, and if it were anywhere else, he would. But if there was any city in the world that could catch someone who was flying away, it was Abilanth, home of the Academy and hundreds of full-fledged mages.

Nym slunk around back alleys and hid from sight as the hours passed by at a crawl. Every time he saw another person, he flinched away. Every time he spotted a guard on the street, he fought down a feeling of panic. Eventually he found a dead-end alley with some garbage piled up that he was able to hide behind. He settled into place and started scrying the whole length of the alley, watching to see if anyone approached.

Hours and hours went by, with his throat getting dry and his stomach rumbling, but Nym refused to leave his hiding spot. Morning turned into noon, and noon into evening. In another hour or two, the sun would be hidden completely behind the mountain, and he would leave.

It was the obsessive, even paranoid, scrying that saved him. He saw hands emerging out of the shadows behind him, saw them reach out to grab him. He jerked forward just in time to avoid being caught, but not fast enough to avoid fingers snagging onto his shirt. With a cry, Nym was pulled off his feet into the darkness.

He landed inside a pitch-black room and lashed out wildly with bursts of telekinetic energy. It slapped against a person but wasn't strong enough to do more than elicit a grunt. Nym's scrying spell snapped, the distance between the alley and wherever he'd been taken too great. He cast a night vision spell, and the room lit up just in time to see Valgo limping toward him with a knife in one hand. The burns across his body were half-healed, but the old thief was still crispy and obviously in great pain.

There was no time to build up the delicate construct of a lightning bolt, not when Valgo was already lunging at him. The only thing Nym could do was hurl himself back and to the side. He could see the aura of a night vision spell on

Valgo's face too and knew he couldn't rely on the darkness to shield him from getting stabbed.

This time there were no clever comments or banter. Valgo didn't go for theatrics or speeches. He just came at Nym, relentlessly, with murder in his eyes. Nym reviewed his options while he maneuvered to keep his distance. The ceiling was too low to fly out of reach, and while Nym could rely on his air manipulation to dart around and stay away from the older man, Valgo had prepared well. There was no furniture to use as a shield, the only door was locked, and there were no windows. Nym was well and truly trapped.

One of them wasn't walking out of the room alive, and Nym needed an uninterrupted second if he didn't want to be the corpse left cooling on the floor. He was faster while he was flying, and he could use telekinesis to try to trip Valgo up, but that was pushing him to his limits, and the thief hadn't even started to use his own magic yet.

Valgo reached into his coat and produced a smaller, oddly shaped knife. Nym had an instant to wonder why it looked so different than the other one the thief was holding, and then it was flying through the air at him. Panicked, Nym snapped his kinetic barrier up to deflect it and released his air cushions to try to dodge.

He had his flight back under control before he hit the ground, but in that one frozen moment where he tumbled, vulnerable, Valgo's arm disappeared at the shoulder. It emerged from the darkness next to Nym, and the blade of the knife slid into Nym's stomach. It came back out, bloody up to the hilt, and Nym screamed.

The barrier collapsed, and he crashed to the floor, holding his gut as blood poured out between his fingers. The old thief sneered and disappeared, only to show back up in the room kneeling next to Nym. He reached down and grabbed Nym's hair to jerk his face up and expose his neck.

Frantically, Nym formed a solid barrier of air between him and the knife, with a kinetic barrier behind it. The knife punched through one, then the other, barely slowing down. A dozen telekinetic hands caught Valgo's arm and held him back for a bare moment. Then the strain overloaded Nym's arms, and his muscles tore from the feedback.

That was all the time he needed though. It was sloppy, but the spark of elemental fire ignited in the spell, and the construct collapsed on itself. Lightning bloomed in the air between the two of them, scorching Nym from his face to his feet and throwing Valgo across the room. The knife flashed as it went tumbling through the air to stick point first in the ceiling.

Nym tried to move, but every part of him was in agonizing pain. If Valgo wasn't dead now, then Nym was only going to live long enough for the thief to finish the job. He waited, too hurt to move, too weak to focus on making new magic, and stared into the darkness. His night vision spell had failed him when the lightning bolt went off.

He closed his eyes and tried to remember the spell the healer had cast on him to numb pain. It wasn't terribly complicated compared to the rest of the healing magic, but it was still hellishly delicate, and Nym had only seen it cast once. He put it together slowly over the next ten minutes as arcana trickled through him. It was all he could do to hold a conduit open and weave the magic into something coherent. Halfway through, it collapsed.

Nym nearly gave up, but no one was going to come rescue him. He started over. And over. And over. On the fifth attempt, he pulled it all together, and the spell went off. Whatever it did though, it didn't work. He was in just as much pain as before he'd started. Nym would have sighed if he could have moved his face.

An hour later, he managed to successfully cast the spell. If the lightning bolt hadn't cauterized the knife wound in his stomach, he probably would have bled out long before he managed to pull it off. Once the pain receded, he realized that he'd stopped even putting pressure on it.

Slowly, he climbed to his feet. With his night vision spell back up, he looked down at himself. His clothes were in tatters, his skin blistered and burnt in a pattern that reminded him of roots or tree branches. It started on his cheek and spread out to cover his whole chest and curled down onto his right leg. A second pattern started at his left knee and traveled down to his feet.

It looked similar to the wounds Analia had, only with far more thorough coverage. Just looking at it sent new aches through him. If not for the pain-suppression spell, he thought he would have collapsed again. With a broken laugh, he realized he'd been wrong before. He thought Professor Langdon's off-the-cuff prophecy had been fulfilled with the initial strike, but if he'd finished Valgo off when he'd had the chance, he wouldn't be in the shape he was in. He'd been struck by his own lightning because he kept screwing around instead of acting decisively.

Valgo was now thoroughly dead. Nym triple-checked and even used magic to pull all the air away from the body for five minutes just to make sure the thief wasn't faking. The only way to verify it any further would be to dismember Valgo, which Nym lacked the tools, time, energy, and willpower to do. Instead, he turned to the locked door and summoned up enough arcana to unlock it with scrying and telekinesis.

It didn't take long to find a way out, but he had to stop for a quick detour. It seemed Valgo had retreated back to a secret base in the outer ring, which included his own personal vault. Nym found it casually with scrying magic while mapping out the interior to find an exit and noted a plethora of mechanical traps in the room. Once he reached it, he dropped the scrying and checked to confirm there were a few wards set up as well.

The weakness of any ward was the material it was inscribed on. In this case, they were hidden behind panels that created false walls surrounding the room. It was easy enough to tear those down as they weren't actually anchored to anything. Nym assumed they were made to be pulled away so that the wards could be serviced when needed, but for him, it just meant that he didn't have to try very hard to get a knife in there to deface them.

He had no clue what the wards did, but it was easy enough to break them. Once that was accomplished, he floated over to a giant safe that stood up against the back wall and forced it open. Inside were a small fortune in gems and coins all conveniently packaged in a bag, along with a dozen different forms of identification for various cities, most of which Nym had never heard of.

Then he let himself out a second-story window, marked the location, and dragged himself through the air to the closest outer-circle clinic. The healers on staff regarded him with blank horror when he staggered through the door, but he flashed enough gold around to be seen immediately.

They weren't as good as Jorak and Mehta, but two hours later, he was able to walk back out under his own power. He was covered in new scars, especially a wide, puckered one on his stomach, which had been the hardest wound to treat. The healer told him he'd need to come back for follow-up treatments to make sure infection hadn't gotten into him. Nym agreed, though he had no intention of doing so.

It was deep into the night now. He was suddenly rich, and down one enemy, but he still needed to deal with the Feldstals if he wanted to stay in the city, assuming that was even an option. If Analia could defend him, he might save himself from being jailed for murdering their kidnappers. Otherwise the new plan was to use some of his stolen money to supply himself for the journey and leave as soon as possible. Nym snuck into the middle ring to visit the clinic he'd dropped Analia off at and check if he still had an ally among the nobles.

CHAPTER 53

Jorak was once again manning the clinic, and Nym was silently thankful both that the man always worked the same shift and that every time he'd needed healing, it had been at night. The healer gave him a sour grimace when he came in. "You're back," he said.

Nym was wearing an oversize-shirt-and-pants combo he'd bought off the outer-ring healer, meant for adults. He was practically swimming in it, but his old clothes hadn't held together after the lightning strike, plus there was a lot of blood on the scraps. On the bright side, it was easy to hold the money pouch to his stomach and disguise it as him just trying to hold the pants up. A belt hadn't been part of the deal.

"I came to make sure my friend is alright and that you were paid for your services."

"Yes, and yes, though the men her family sent to collect her were not pleasant."

"She went with them?" Nym asked.

"Yes."

"Willingly?"

"Maybe not happily, but yes. No one carried her out through the door."

Nym let out a sigh of relief. "That's good. I'm glad she's safe. Thank you for helping her."

"Listen, I understand that you had an emergency, and that her life was in danger. But never, ever, ever do something like that again. I was under no obligation to treat her. Any healer could have refused to help and been well within their rights. The only reason I worked on that girl is because the two of you had already come through hours earlier for healing."

"We got att—" Nym started to say, but Jorak cut him off.

"And whatever game you two are playing at, stop before you get yourselves killed. She looked like she'd lost a mage duel, and teenage girls *should not be having mage duels.* You don't look so good yourself. You've been to another healer in the last hour, just barely a day after I patched you up. And whoever worked on you was sloppy. I can tell you were under a pain-suppression spell for hours."

"How do you know that?"

"It messes with your brain. The longer you have one on, the worse it gets. A good healer will fix that as part of your treatment, but whoever worked on you didn't bother. It'll go away on its own after a few days, as long as you don't have a new one cast on you. The longer it stays active, the worse it gets."

"Okay, but how do you know what my brain looks like?" Nym asked.

The healer hesitated a second before elaborating. "Spotting signs is just kind of a thing you develop with enough experience. I could go on about your unfocused eyes and posture and the shuffle you're walking with, but let's just leave it at I know what to look for, and you've got all the flags."

"Can you do anything about it?" Nym asked. The first healer he'd seen hadn't even bothered with a pain-suppression spell, and Nym wasn't sure if that was because they were low-skill outer-ring healers or because he already had his own spell running.

"All things considered, I'll want to see cash up front. But yes, I can fix it and anything else that might be wrong with you."

Nym pulled out a gold crest and set it on the table. Then he flew up in the air and landed on the examination bench. "If you can make me good as new, it'll be well worth it."

Jorak grumbled, but the money was good, and he got to work. If Nym hadn't had the extra cash, which was at least twice as much as Analia had taken from her home, he would never have wasted it on a second round of healing. He didn't really feel like he needed it, but he wanted to get another chance to study healing spells. He'd seen them twice now, and would have stuck around for Analia's healing except that he didn't have any money and was deliberating dumping her on the healer's lap in hopes that he'd do it anyway.

Unfortunately, Jorak did not offer him the pain-suppression spell, so once again he was unable to see a professional craft it. He'd really wanted the outside perspective since he'd mostly fumbled through it and wasn't confident he could replicate it. He did get to look at a few of the diagnostic spells and solidified the patterns in his mind, and Jorak was able to smooth out a lot of the leftover scarring from the lightning strike.

"Someone stabbed you?" he asked, surprised. He poked at the puckered scar. "Deeply too. You're lucky you had someone with you to get you to a healer."

"I . . . yeah . . ."

"The cauterization pattern is weird though. It's more like it's part of this lightning scarring . . . What were you even doing?"

"Someone tried to stab me," Nym said. "Well . . . did stab me. And then he was going to, you know . . . and I zapped him, but since he was so close, it also hit me."

Jorak pulled back, aghast. "Are you telling me you nearly killed yourself with your own spell? Wait, back up. Are you telling me that a kid like you can create a lightning bolt out of magic? I can't do that, and I'm a retired army mage! I mean, I specialize in healing, but I still know my fair share of combat and utility magic."

The healer just kind of stared off at nothing for a minute while Nym fidgeted in uncomfortable silence. When it got to be too much, he said, "So can you fix it? Or heal it? Or I don't know. I guess it's okay if the scar is permanent. Most people don't get scars healed. But the other healer said there could be infections."

Jorak snorted. "Third-rate charlatan," he muttered. "If he'd done his job right, no, that wouldn't be a risk. I can smooth out the scar a bit, but it's never going to go away completely. Maybe if your friend had gotten you to me when it was still an open wound instead of cauterizing it."

Nym debated telling him about using his own version of pain suppression and walking himself to the nearest clinic, but decided he didn't want to answer any questions about how he'd learned it. He glossed over that and let the healer continue his work.

Surprisingly, he did feel significantly better once Jorak was finished. He wasn't expecting to, but a lot of soreness he hadn't realized he had disappeared, and the tightness in his muscles relaxed. The experienced healer had muttered to himself the entire time he was working on them, something about incompetent cut-rate scabs who couldn't heal a papercut without growing the blood vessels in backward.

When he was done, Nym hopped off the table and snatched up the pouch. He tucked it back under his oversized shirt and grabbed his pants with one hand to hold them up. "Thanks for the fix up," he said. "Hopefully I won't be back tomorrow."

"Wait, don't you want your change?" Jorak said, holding up the crest.

"Eh, you keep it. If anyone asks, you never saw me."

The healer frowned and considered it. Then he sighed and shook his head. "I get enough gray hairs from my own kid. I don't need them from you too. Look, when your friend left with her bodyguard and the soldiers, she asked me to tell you something. 'Go with plan D and I'll meet you there in a month' were her exact words. She said you'd know what that meant."

"I do," Nym said. "Thanks again."

That plan confirmed his worst fears. It was their final reserve plan in the event that they couldn't get away from the manor clean and the city guard was looking for them. It meant he couldn't access the teleportation platform and would have to physically travel to another city to try to use theirs. The closest city to Abilanth was over five hundred miles away and would take weeks to reach on foot. Worse, the route was extremely dangerous. Worse still, that wasn't the final destination.

They'd made the plan on the assumption that they would be flying, which would cut down both the danger and the travel time significantly. However, it also assumed a full kit, which would be absolutely essential for him to acquire, and that might not be so easy now. Nym needed a new pack, clothes, a coat and cloak, shoes, and food that would keep for weeks, and he was hoping to find some sort of mask designed for flying. He'd found that as he got faster, and especially as it got colder, the wind was becoming a real problem.

Dawn was only an hour or so off, and Nym prioritized the warmer clothing in the middle ring. He wasn't sure how much interference to expect from the city guard outside of choke points like gates and the mage guildhall, and if he was forced to flee, he wanted to be warm when he went. He could survive a lot longer on an empty stomach than he could wearing clothes that he had to physically hold to his body to keep them from falling off.

For all the bad luck he'd had in the past few days, Nym completed his shopping list without a problem. He even paid extra to get his new winter outfit tailored to fit him, got a new, thick leather coat, shoes, gloves, and pack, and a wool aviator's mask that not only covered his whole face, but had a pair of built-in goggles with glass lenses.

Once his pack was full, including the still-hefty money pouch, he returned to Valgo's hideout and spent the rest of the day looting it. Between his scrying and his ability to see magic, he thought he found every last valuable. When he was done, he returned to the warehouse and started handing out coins. If anyone deserved Valgo's ill-gotten gains, it was the street children he'd kept under his heel.

Nym kept the crests, if for no other reason than it would be extremely suspicious to have a bunch of kids between the ages of five and ten running around with gold, but in less than an hour, he'd emptied out every last wedge and shim into their hands. To the older kids, the responsible ones who'd done their best to take care of everyone, he handed the majority of the silver shields with instructions to buy new clothes and maybe rent a place to live that was better protected from the weather.

Nym was about to leave when someone walked into the warehouse. It was the Academy student he'd seen a few weeks ago, the one who'd been handing out bandages and salves. The teenager studied him curiously, a soft smile on his face.

"You got out," he said as he approached, motioning toward the new clothes and pack. "You're leaving."

"I did, and I am."

"Good for you," the student said. "Did you practice your fire magic?"

"A bit," Nym said. "I'm still working on it. Thank you for showing me where to start."

They watched the kids scamper around, some of them disappearing for a bit and coming back with warm food. "Where did the money for this all come from?" the student asked after a bit.

"The thief who was using them to pickpocket for him died. I looted his hideout and distributed all the smaller coins to them. The older kids got the shields to spend on blankets, food, medicine, shelter, whatever they need."

"Hmm, that's good. I guess my services won't be needed any longer."

"Why didn't you just hand some money to them in the first place?" Nym asked.

"Me? How would I do that?"

"What? Your family would notice if you took that much money?"

The student laughed. "I don't have any money. I make this stuff myself."

Nym's jaw fell open. "What? But . . . how? You go to the Academy."

"Well, just between you and me, I got a scholarship. It almost never happens, I'm told. I'm not from here, and I had a letter of recommendation. It's . . . very high-pressure. If I don't graduate, I'll have to repay it all. That would ruin me, financially speaking, for the rest of my life."

Nym regarded him quietly. He never would have guessed. "So, every time you visit, all the medicine you bring, how do you get the herbs and the jars?"

"There's work at the Academy for those of us willing to do it. The student body is made up of a lot of kids with very rich parents who would never stoop to doing any sort of manual labor."

"You're crazy," Nym told him bluntly.

"Maybe. But look around. How much did you just give away? I guess that makes us both crazy."

"I suppose."

Nym opened his pack and dug around in it until he came up with a handful of crests. He held them out. "Here, take these. Promise me you won't waste them. Keep an eye on these guys for me, keep them out of trouble if you can."

"Are you sure? That's a fortune right there. You don't even know me."

Nym smiled. "You were kind to me when I needed it. That counts for a lot to me."

He pressed the coins into the student's hand, hefted his pack back onto his shoulders, and walked away. As the sun settled low into the mountains and the shadows stretched out over Abilanth, Nym reached out to the arcana and flew off over the snow. It was going to be a long journey, and the sooner he got started, the sooner he'd see the next town.

CHAPTER 54

The road leading away from Abilanth was treacherous, deliberately so. In his studies of geography, Nym had learned that he'd been living in a capital city, one that they'd built on the side of a mountain to protect themselves from the neighboring country. He didn't feel the politics or history of it was all that interesting, but the short version was that he was living inside a country called Delvros, and they were not on friendly terms with Nordram to the east.

In the event that he and Analia were barred from using the Delvros teleport network, their new goal was to travel on foot and cross Nordram's border far enough away from any checkpoints that they could slip in unnoticed. The plan relied heavily on Nym's growing ability for overland flight.

That was all well and good, but he didn't see how Analia was going to catch up to him. Her original flight spell taxed her so heavily that she'd exhaust herself in minutes, and she was nowhere near proficient enough after only a few days of practice with his version to safely fly hundreds of miles. All of that assumed she was able to get away from her family, who were surely watching her much more closely.

Still, he owed Analia a lot, and if she'd said to go with this plan, it wasn't like he had anywhere better to be. So Nym flew south, bypassing the many twists and turns of the road below him as it snaked around. He saved hours by being able to fly over ravines and canyons or bypassing narrow, treacherous stretches that hugged sheer walls and were exposed to thousand-foot drops. For Nym, it was background scenery as he flew.

By the time morning came, he was twenty miles away, and the steep mountain slopes started to flatten out. It was still a barren landscape of snow framed by craggy peaks, but he'd gone probably three times farther than he would have on foot. Nym kept an eye out for a sheltered place to rest with an eye toward caves or even just nooks in the stone, anywhere that he could get out of the eternal winds and the snow swirling through the air. It had been coming down, all night, thicker and thicker.

Eventually, he found a wide ridge of stone about ten feet tall that had a thick overhang. There was a spot where the ridge curved around and made a pocket that protected from the wind in three directions. Nym landed nearby and scried out the nearby landscape for anything living. When he found nothing, he entered and settled down to rest.

It was cold, but there wasn't any snow built up, and it was dim enough that he felt he could get at least a quick nap. Nym wrapped himself in his cloak, snacked on some of the rations he'd purchased, and settled in the back, facing toward the entrance. He was so tired that he didn't even realize he was drifting off before his eyes closed and he slumped over.

The sound of snuffling woke him up. It was fully dark when he opened his eyes, and he could hear some sort of animal nearby. A quick night vision spell showed him a creature with white fur pawing at his pack, trying to get it open. He was about two feet tall at the shoulder and vaguely wolflike, but with a short bushy tail and a narrow muzzle that was currently wedged under the flap of his pack. His paws were huge relative to the size of its body, and Nym could see scrapes on the rock where the animal had paced around his pack trying to get at it.

"Hey!" Nym protested. "That's not yours!"

The animal, whatever he was, looked up at him calmly, then shoved his snout back into Nym's pack. Nym climbed to his feet, filled his soul well, and pulled the pack away with telekinesis. The animal hopped after it, but Nym held it overhead out of its reach. He stood there underneath, staring up at the pack, then looked to Nym expectantly.

"What? I told you it wasn't yours," he said.

A sparkling sheen of arcana started forming around the wolf, and a tendril lanced out to strike Nym before he had a chance to react. Instead of an attack, words formed in his mind.

[Food?]

Nym jumped in surprise. "You can talk?"

[Yes talk. Food?]

With a sigh, Nym grabbed the pack out of the air, opened it, and pulled out a piece of jerky. He tossed it over, and the creature snapped it out of the air. He chewed happily while Nym watched with a bemused expression. The chunk of meat was soon gone, and the wolf resumed staring at the bag.

"Sorry, but I need the rest. I've got a long way to go," Nym said.

[Go where? No path.]

Nym turned to the exit, only to find it blocked by a wall of frozen snow. It was stacked higher than the overhang, and he realized with a start that the lack of light was not because he'd slept through the entire day, but rather that he'd been entombed by the weather. There was a single tunnel dug through the snow, narrow enough to be uncomfortable for him to pass through, but perfect for his uninvited guest.

Nym pushed at the wall with hydrokinesis and ripped the ice supporting it out. It resisted, but fortunately wasn't too thick for him to overpower it. Snow fell into the nook, and with a second push, he blew a hole open all the way to the surface. The makeshift tunnel immediately collapsed, and it took him a few more rounds before he'd widened it enough to pass through.

Nym flew up into open air, only to find that he couldn't see anything more than a few feet away. The snow was coming down so thick, and with so much wind behind it, that there was no visibility at all. He could only make a guess as to which direction he wanted to go, even if he was willing to fly in it.

Already, he could feel the chill starting to seep through his pants. Nym had no choice but to wait for the blizzard to pass by. He retreated back under the ridge where, while it was still cold, at least it wasn't a total whiteout. The wolf thing sat near the hole Nym had made and watched him come back in. He let out a huffing sneeze as snow powder dislodged by Nym's passage sprayed his face.

"Guess I'm stuck here for a bit," he told the creature.

[Share food?]

"You've got a one-track mind, don't you?" Nym hugged the bag close, keeping his precious food supply safe from the wolf. "I told you I don't have enough to share."

The blizzard was a major problem. He had no firewood, and despite his new, insulated clothing, it was freezing out. If ever there was a time and place to finish figuring out that internal-heating spell, it was now. But even if he figured out the spell, that only solved one problem. There was no telling when he'd be able to travel again, and he didn't have unlimited food. He could starve, leaving nothing but a half-frozen corpse that someone would eventually find months from now when the weather turned and everything started to melt.

Nym rested against the back wall, as far from the snow and ice as he could get, and focused on channeling his arcana. He'd figured out how to use it as fuel and make lines for it to follow when he ignited it, but short of setting himself on fire, that wasn't going to warm him up. He needed to practice modulating it so that he could wrap himself in arcana that was warm instead of burning.

He started with the intent filter he'd used to lay out lines of flammable arcana, then tried to mellow it down. He wanted arcana that would radiate heat slowly instead of something that would burn up in an instant. Nym sprayed it across the wall and ignited it, but instead of the wall releasing warmth out into the makeshift cave, one single spot in the arcana heated up. The rest remained inert.

Nym wasn't disappointed though. He'd been working on this for close to two months now, and this was the first time he'd gotten his magic to generate any sort of heat that wasn't at maximum strength. He'd come a long way from his early attempts where it took all his focus to get kindling to ignite.

Nym tried a few configurations while the wolf watched. Eventually, he got bored and started trying to get into Nym's pack again. Nym shooed him off a few times before giving up and splitting his concentration to hold the pack overhead on a cushion of air. The animal sat underneath the floating pack and stared straight up at it, all the while whining piteously.

"Stupid thing," Nym muttered, not sure if he meant himself or the animal. He fetched another scrap of jerky out and tossed it over. The wolf gulped it down happily, then resumed staring at Nym.

"What's your name anyway?"

A jumble of images came through the telepathic link, mostly memories of snow flying through the air as the wolf dug through it at top speed. Nym couldn't find a name anywhere in there, just a lot of sensory information about smell and the feeling of snow on the wolf's paws.

"Uh . . . Dig? Snow? I don't know how to translate this. Cold Paw? How about that? Can we go with Cold Paw?"

[Cold Paw], the wolf repeated. *[Is good.]*

After another hour of fiddling, he finally figured out how to get the heat spell to spread properly. The key was in the arcana he'd used as a fuel. It didn't want to spread properly when he made it slow-burning, and while it was possible to manually ignite a hundred different spots, it was tedious and slow. Once he'd altered his intent and lowered the threshold needed for the ignition to spread, he was able to pick a few random points, and soon the entire wall was radiating heat.

Cold Paw was fascinated by that for a few minutes, but eventually he must have decided it was too warm. He went over to the ice wall and rolled around in the loose snow, then stood up and shook the flakes out of his coat. Then he resumed staring at the pack. Nym rolled his eyes and went back to experimenting.

The rock wall was still too hot to touch, which meant that he couldn't coat himself in arcana. That wasn't really what he was ultimately trying to accomplish anyway, but it would be a step in the right direction. His current use of pyrokinesis was only working because the wall was rock. He was sure if he tried it on a wooden building, the heat would quickly build up until the material it was stuck to ignited.

He wondered if he was going about it completely backward. Perhaps instead of trying to add heat to his body, he needed to be pushing cold away from himself. As long as he never let the spell drop, it would be functionally the same thing, only without the risk of spontaneously combusting if he didn't cast the spell perfectly.

Or maybe the whole concept was just too complicated to be performed with basic elementalism. Every theory he came up with, even the ones he couldn't make work, relied on constant input from him. If his focus wavered, things would start to fall apart. If he didn't hold the exact right amount of focus, he could put too much arcana into the spell, and it would overload.

A large part of the appeal of the more complex spells that didn't rely on elemental control was that they were less effort to maintain. If he'd done the spell right in the first place, it would last as long as it was designed to. He had no doubt there were spells that were designed to do exactly what he was trying to accomplish, but he hadn't found them in the short time he'd had access to an actual library.

It took a few more hours of experimentation, but eventually Nym had a thermal barrier that blocked out all sources of warmth or cold. He pressed his bare hand up against the ice and held it there for ten minutes, then dismissed the spell and examined his fingers. They felt fine. None of the cold had gotten through. The spell did the same thing for his heated wall, though after a few minutes, it became more of a strain to hold the barrier in place.

"I guess I just needed the proper motivation," he told his new friend. "And that was being stuck in a frozen hole during a blizzard, where I'd either figure it out or freeze to death."

With that one problem solved, Nym turned to the next issue. He didn't know how long he would be stuck here, and while he did have extra supplies, he didn't want to run out before he'd gotten a single day's travel away from Abilanth. He especially couldn't afford to keep giving away his meat, no matter how pathetic Cold Paw's whining was.

New snow had filled in the hole Nym had made to the surface, so he had to punch it back out again to check on the weather. The blizzard was still going strong, with at least another three feet of snow built up just in the last few hours. Visibility was even worse, if anything.

When he came back down, the wolf was gone. Nym just sighed and sat down, his back against the ice wall. "It's going to be a long few days," he said out loud.

Suddenly Cold Paw's head popped up right next to him and he let out a yip. With a startled yell, Nym leaped to his feet. The wolf just sniffed at him, stubby little tail wagging, and pulled at his sleeve. Bemused, Nym let him drag him over to the hole he had dug through the snow and ice.

"What, you want me to come with you?"

[Follow. Meet family.]

Nym wasn't really in any danger from the cold now, and if he needed a break, he could always blast his way down to the stone below and create a new heated shelter on the floor while using hydrokinesis to freeze the snow into a ceiling overhead. The weather wasn't really getting any better, and the idea of meeting more talking animals had him curious.

"Okay, I guess let's see what's out here under the ice."

He crawled into the hole after his new friend.

CHAPTER 55

As it turned out, Cold Paw had more going for him than just telepathy. In hindsight, it was obvious, but watching him plow through hard-packed snow faster than Nym could crawl after him would have been enough of a tip-off even if he couldn't see arcana gathering around Cold Paw. Nym just wished his magic extended to the snow he was pushing out of the way. That all flew backward, and Nym quickly learned to give the animal a spacious twenty feet lead if he wanted to avoid being constantly pelted with loose snow.

He had no clue what Cold Paw was, and so he added researching local magical creatures to his list of things to learn about. The wolf seemed friendly though, so Nym followed, slowly at first, but then faster when they connected to a snow tunnel that was twice as wide as the ones Cold Paw made.

He wasn't sure how far they traveled, not being used to crawling or walking hunched over, and not even really sure Cold Paw's tunnels went in a straight line. He was getting tired though and decided it was time for a rest. "Hold on," he said to the wolf. "I want a break from holding this thermal barrier. I'm going to melt down to the ground and make a little camp."

Cold Paw yipped and scampered off up the tunnel a bit while Nym used his elemental water manipulation to push down the snow and compact it tighter. When that stopped working, he shifted to pushing it sideways instead. Eventually, he dug his way through about ten feet of snow to the frozen ground and laid out his heating spell.

Nym let himself relax for a few minutes, enjoying the rising heat and not having the mental strain of holding up the barrier. He used hydrokinesis to melt some of the snow and let it warm up for a bit before having a drink of cool, clean water. By the time he was done, the ground was getting soft from the spell, but Nym would be gone long before it turned muddy.

He stood up to leave but got distracted by a whining sound overhead. Cold

Paw stood at the edge of the tunnel, looking down at Nym's impromptu camp, and scratching at the snow. He looked nervous, and when he saw Nym looking back at him, he started growling.

"In that much of a hurry?" he asked. "What's wrong?"

[Danger], the wolf projected.

Before he could say anything else, ice and snow exploded out of one wall, and a long, sinuous form crashed down onto the ground. It looked something like a snake formed from living ice, only twice as thick as Nym's shoulders, and with a long series of scrabbling legs that ended in pointed, chitinous tips. They sunk into the soft ground, but the monster easily pulled itself out and shot forward.

A head that had no eyes, just a round hole full of teeth and extended mandibles that presumably pulled in prey, lunged at Nym, who shot up straight into the air and smacked against the icy roof of his campsite. The monster below, some unholy mixture of a centipede, worm, and snake, undulated across the ground, tearing it up into a muddy pit as the loose dirt mixed with the melting snow.

It didn't pay Nym much heed once it was on the ground, which he found strange considering it had lunged straight at him. Before he could consider it, he felt a rumbling in the ice behind him. Nym flew to the side just in time to avoid a second monster bursting through the ceiling and falling to join its brethren on the ground.

Everything was getting colder quickly, so Nym reactivated his thermal barrier. The combination of flight, insulation, and night vision was enough to tie his arcana up completely. Even forging a second conduit merely equalized the arcana going into his soul well with how much was coming out.

The monsters weren't paying any attention to him now, so he flew over to where Cold Paw was growling down at them. "Come on," he hissed. "Let's get out of here before another one shows up."

The wolf stopped growling and looked hesitantly at Nym. His head kept shifting back and forth, like he was expecting Nym to do something. "What?" he asked. "I'm not fighting those if we don't have to. I run away from my problems."

[No kill heat hunters?]

"Heat hunters?" Nym shuddered. "No thanks. They look dangerous."

Reluctantly, Cold Paw turned away and started down the tunnel. No longer willing to crawl at a slow speed, Nym stretched out horizontally on a cushion of air and flew after him. The sound of the monsters thrashing around behind him echoed down the tunnel, motivating him to fly closer than he otherwise would have. Fortunately, the tunnels were already dug, so he wasn't getting blasted with all the loose snow Cold Paw had been sending his way earlier.

They didn't get very far before the monsters finished up whatever they were doing. The sudden lack of noise was more nerve-racking than listening to them thrash around, if only because now Nym had no clue where they were. They could be heading straight for him, about to burst out of a wall and tear a limb off. Maybe Cold Paw had been right and he should have attacked the worms.

Nym wished he'd taken the time to see if he could scry through snow. As it stood, he didn't dare dismiss his night vision spell to check. That would be the instant the monster popped up, and he'd be blind and unable to react in time. He could dismiss the flight or thermal-barrier spells, but he'd already determined that things didn't quite work right when he was trying to run night vision and scrying at the same time. They interfered with each other, and Nym mostly just got sick from the feedback.

He kept one hand on the wall as they flew, trying to feel for any rumbling that might indicate the monsters digging. He didn't feel anything, but Nym wouldn't be surprised to have one pop out in front of him anyway. He'd only felt the one that had come through the ceiling because his whole back was to ice, which was considerably more solid than packed snow. Even with that advantage, he'd only had a fraction of a second's warning to get out of the way before the monster had pierced the roof and dropped onto his camp.

A few minutes passed with nothing happening, and Nym decided it was worth the risk to look around with scrying. He dismissed his night vision spell and poured arcana into scrying instead, then swept it around him in expanding circles. The good news was that he could in fact see various things embedded in the snow around him, mostly loose rocks. The bad news was that since the monsters could appear from any direction, it wasn't great odds that he'd see them since he still only saw a few feet before everything faded to white.

Even if he perched the anchor for his scrying spell on his forehead, he was only going to get a split second's warning, and for that he was trading his ability to see down the tunnel. Cold Paw was far enough away that Nym couldn't keep track of him without moving the scrying anchor.

He swept the area one more time, following the curve of the tunnel, before he dismissed the scrying spell and recast night vision instead. "Should have stayed back at my original camp," he muttered. Cold Paw gave a quiet woof that Nym took as agreement.

Snow exploded into the tunnel, and a white, sinuous body filled his vision. It slammed into him as it flashed by, heading straight for Cold Paw. Nym was stunned for a second, but the wolf wasn't defenseless. He leaped at the worm monster, nimbly skipping over its mouth face and landing on its body. Sharp claws dug into icy flesh, scoring the scales deeply and staining its hide with some sort of greyish-blue ichor.

The second monster burst into the tunnel, also ignoring Nym. He wasn't sure why, but he immediately focused on it as it went by and dismissed his flight and thermal barrier. With only his night vision to assist him in aiming, Nym built a lightning-bolt spell. The worm monster must have sensed something because it curled up on itself and shot backward, crystalline flesh scraping against its own body as it lunged, mouth open, at Nym.

Lightning boomed down the tunnel in an instant of brilliant light and loose snow. The worm monster practically swallowed the attack, and it crashed to the packed-snow ground to thrash about in obvious agony. Smoke billowed out of its open mouth, and it started to sink into the snow, its body superheated from the lightning strike. Cracks appeared all over it, weeping ichor.

Then the other worm crashed into it and started tearing it apart. It savaged the dead body, pointed legs dissecting it and mouth tearing chunks of flesh out. Nym didn't really know why, but he was more than happy to fry the second worm if it was just going to stand there and let him. He built the spell back up, checked to make sure Cold Paw was clear, and let loose again.

With both worms dead and slowly sinking as they melted through the snow, Nym reactivated his flight and thermal barrier. He flew over the corpses to meet Cold Paw on the other side. The wolf stared at him with big, wide eyes, then hopped about in excitement. *[Boom!]*

"Yeah. What was that all about? I thought we'd left them behind."

Cold Paw tugged on his sleeve and started dragging him down the tunnel again.

"Hey! Stop. Stop that!"

But eventually Nym just let himself be dragged off as Cold Paw excitedly led the way. They didn't encounter more of the worm monsters, but Nym kept a sharp eye out anyway. After another hour of significantly more stressful traveling, Nym decided to punch through to the surface and check on the blizzard. The tunnel kept trying to collapse on him, prompting him to just unleash a huge blast of air that spat snow dozens of feet into the open air.

Nym flew up and looked around. The blizzard was still going, but it appeared to have calmed down somewhat. Snow was coming down in sheets, but with the thermal barrier up, it wasn't so bad topside. It was definitely harder to hold it though. Nym thought that, in an emergency, he could probably manage an hour or so of flight before he'd need to find shelter to rest.

Cold Paw popped up next to him from his own hole and started exploring eagerly, his nose to the snow. Somehow, despite it all being fresh, the wolf slid across it smoothly. When Nym bent down to examine his trail, he found a thin layer of ice coating the paw prints the wolf left behind. Once he thought about it, it made sense. His own efforts at tunneling had involved a lot of loose snow trying to fall on him when he dug, but Cold Paw's tunnel was solid, despite the weight on top of it that should have buried them both.

"Well, come on," he said. "Might as well get back under the snow. This stupid blizzard isn't going to blow itself out any time soon, and the thermal barrier is draining me too quickly to maintain up here."

Nym scooped up the wolf with an air cushion and flew the both of them down the tunnel, Cold Paw yipping excitedly and wiggling around the whole time. When they were back in the tunnels, he ran around Nym several times in a circle, drawing a smile from the tired boy.

[Fun! Do again?]

"Alright, alright. Calm down. Maybe later. For now, where are we going?"

Cold Paw started running down the tunnel, then stopped and barked at Nym until he followed. Together, with Nym having no idea what was going on but amused by the wolf's antics anyway, the two of them continued their journey under the frozen landscape. Unseen over their heads, the sky mercilessly punished the land with more and more snow.

CHAPTER 56

Nym needed to take a break, but he was afraid of a repeat of the worm-monster incident. Cold Paw seemed to be getting more anxious as they traveled too, coming back to tug at his sleeve every time Nym stopped for any reason. Reluctantly, but aware of the danger, he forced himself to keep moving. The strain of keeping up the thermal barrier and night vision was wearing him out, so much so that he was long past even considering casting a flight spell as well.

He rounded a bend in the tunnel and stumbled forward when they were abruptly out in the open, in a spacious cavern made entirely of snow and ice. The ceiling was at least fifty feet overhead, made of solid ice with who knew how many feet of snow piled on it. And there were dozens of wolves there. Small ones scampered around, playing with one another. Large ones lazed in little holes they'd dug in the walls, sometimes half-buried in loose snow.

And then there were the monster-sized ones. He saw two of them immediately, both four or five times the size of Cold Paw, and both noticing him as soon as he entered. One of them stood up, shaking off loose snow and three different pups, and started walking the length of the cavern toward them.

"Um, am I allowed to be here?" Nym asked Cold Paw. The wolf just huffed at him, then sat down next to him to wait for the big one to approach.

It reached them and crouched down to Nym's eye level, sniffing at him. Nym could feel its growl in his bones, but the wolf looked at him with intelligence. It wasn't a wild animal, whatever it was. It turned its attention to Cold Paw, and the two made various noises. Arcana flashed between them in silent communication.

Cold Paw must have vouched for him because the old monster turned away with a sniff and walked back to the middle of the cavern, where it plopped down in an explosion of snow that sent several pups rolling away from it. They all leaped back to their feet and raced forward to crawl all over the old one again.

"What have you gotten me into?" he asked the wolf, who just grinned up at him, tongue hanging out of his mouth. "Well, come on then. Where are we going?"

Nym felt a lot of wary eyes on him as he walked through the cavern, mostly from the adult wolves. The pups, Cold Paw just barely not fitting into that category, mostly romped around or watched him, their little tails ablur. The more Nym looked around, the more he realized that a lot of the wolves were injured in some way or another, and that there were suspiciously few adults compared to the number of pups playing in the middle of the cavern.

Cold Paw led Nym to a wide-mouthed cavern near the back. He followed the young wolf inside, thankful once again that he'd figured out night vision. Otherwise he'd be completely blind and would have missed a positively ancient-looking wolf curled up in the back. When they entered, he stood up on shaky legs and hobbled forward.

[You are a human mage? My progeny has brought you here, claiming you can aid us.]

"I am only an apprentice mage. I don't know what help you need, or if I can do it."

[The pup says you slew two of the heat hunters on your way here.]

"The worm monsters? I guess so, yeah. They didn't seem very interested in me."

The heat of his campsite must have attracted them. Once he'd put his thermal barrier back up, they'd lost interest in him. Somehow, they tracked heat and, apparently, hated it. As long as he wasn't losing any warmth, they either didn't see him or didn't care. That made him feel a lot better about traveling the tunnels.

[A new hive has appeared near our hunting grounds. They are voracious, implacable. Many of our best hunters have fallen to them. If they are not stopped, we will have to flee.]

"And you want me to do it? You know I'm just a kid, right?"

[Do human children often have the ability to summon lightning?]

"Well . . . no. But still."

[If you do not think you can help, or do not wish to, then please depart.]

Nym looked over at Cold Paw, who regarded him with too-smart eyes. "First you try to steal my food, now this? You're lucky you're cute."

He took a deep breath and asked the wolf, "What do I need to do?"

Nym spent a few hours resting in a small circle of heat, which fascinated all the pups endlessly. They were not shy about crawling all over him, and once they found out he gave out pets, he was practically buried under them until a few of the adults showed up to herd them away. Nym was left alone with Cold Paw, who'd flopped down in the snow just outside the heat circle and patiently waited for him to recover.

Mostly he thought about what the matriarch wanted him to do, which was to kill hundreds of worms in their nests and, more specifically, their queen. That was the priority target. Even if he couldn't kill the other worms, killing the queen would ensure the eventual end of the hive as it was needed to maintain the cold environment and replenish their numbers.

According to the matriarch, the worms were magical creatures, so magical in fact that the queen itself generated immense amounts of snow and kept the area cold. They were weak to extreme heat, and while the queen was much bigger than the ones Nym had seen, it shared its progeny's weaknesses. That included crystalline hearts that kept their icelike bodies alive and moving.

If he hadn't been terribly motivated to help before, finding out how much of his current weather troubles could be blamed on magical ice worms certainly changed that. Nym idly wondered if he'd have avoided the whole problem simply by following the roads that curved away from the mountains instead of flying straight through them.

"I can't believe I let you drag me into this," Nym told Cold Paw, who just wagged his stubby little tail back.

[Boom!] the wolf said in his mind. Nym rolled his eyes.

"Okay, I've taken enough of a break. Just give me a minute to get ready."

He finished getting the thermal barrier up and extended it to cover Cold Paw too. The wolf did not like that, not at all. He rolled around in the snow repeatedly, trying to dispel the barrier, but Nym held it steady. As long as they were covered, the worms wouldn't see them, at least if his theory about them only seeing heat was right. And it seemed pretty obvious, so he was confident about that.

The two left together, heading into tunnels that were bigger and curved randomly. They were probably dug by the worm monsters instead of the wolves. The walls were rimed with ice instead of merely being hard-packed, crunchy snow like Cold Paw's tunnels had been. Somehow, that made Nym more nervous. Invisible or not, he could easily picture some worm running him over.

That didn't happen, thankfully, but Nym found that extending the thermal barrier to cover a second person made it three times harder to hold active. The trip was boring, but also exhausting. The exotic nature of traveling via under-snow ice tunnels had long since lost its appeal. Hours went by, with the tunnels widening and narrowing for no discernable reason. Without Cold Paw's guidance, Nym would have gotten hopelessly lost once they started intersecting with one another.

The tunnels started growing lighter. At first, Nym thought he was mistaken, but soon it was unarguable. He dismissed his night vision spell and found that he could see the world around him in shades of white and blue. A thousand more feet traveled down the tunnel revealed the source.

They'd reached their destination. Unlike the wolf cavern, the hive was open to the air. Solid ice walls stretched up to the sky, easily a hundred feet high. Frigid-cold air radiated out of an enormous lump of quivering ice in the center of what Nym could only describe as a pit, rolling across the floor and up the walls.

The whole thing was washed in an aura of arcana. Nym could practically see the snowflakes forming out of thin air and being swept up the walls to burst into the open sky above. Writhing around on the floor were dozens and dozens of the worm monsters. Nym watched as the ones coming in crawled all over the fleshy lump, and then, infused with frigid arcana, raced off into new tunnels.

One of them started heading toward the tunnel they were observing from. "Good time to test, I suppose," he told Cold Paw. "If this goes wrong, I'm going to fly us both straight up."

Then he wove together a lightning-bolt spell. He took his time, made sure he had it right, and watched the worm approach. When it was twenty feet away, he unleashed the magic. Lightning boomed, sending the snow rolling away in a wave, and the worm writhed in agony. He hadn't struck it directly, unable to forge a path for the lightning in the ever-shifting currents of air, snow, and arcana. Unlike the ones in the tunnel he'd fried earlier, it didn't die right away.

That didn't happen until eight other worms converged on it and started eating it alive. Nym could only assume that they didn't differentiate between sources of heat. Anything that was warm was fair game. If that was true, Nym thought he might have a rather easy solution to the whole mess. The mound of ice was obviously important to the whole operation, but if he coated it with arcana and ignited it, would the worms turn on it?

"Come on, I don't want to leave you here," he told Cold Paw.

The two of them rose into the air, which immediately put a lot of stress on Nym's soul well. The wind was incredibly cold and fast, stressing both his thermal barrier and his flight spell. It would have been significantly harder to maintain the thermal barrier, but Cold Paw didn't need it once they were off the ground. Nym worked quickly, fighting his way into the center of the ice-infused arcana maelstrom, and started laying out lines of arcana.

Once he had a solid net, he tried to ignite it, only to find that no matter how big of a spark he generated, the frigid coldness of the ice lump doused it immediately. Nym didn't think he had enough left in him to try a second time. His conduits were struggling to keep his soul well from going dry, and if he lost the thermal barrier, he'd freeze in moments. If he lost his flight spell, it would be even worse.

Nym needed to protect the ignition spark from the cold, and now that he thought about it, he had a perfect spell for that. He encased a small piece of the web in a thermal barrier, fought off the wave of sickness that came from overextending even further, and ignited the arcana web.

The resulting inferno was brilliant, but brief. When the fire cleared away, a pattern of scorch marks marred the lump's surface, but it seemed otherwise unharmed. A few of the worms had paused for a second and focused on the lump, but were already resuming whatever they'd been doing.

He had one more option left, but he was hesitant to waste the arcana on it. Slowly, painfully, he constructed a new lightning bolt and sent it toward the lump. It didn't hit where he was aiming, but the lump was so big that even a few feet off, it still connected. Unfortunately, it had no more effect than to leave a pockmarked scar on the ice.

"Okay, we need to get out of here," he told Cold Paw. "I have to find a place to recover before we try something else."

Not really sure where else to go, Nym flew straight up into the open air. They touched down in the snow, and he asked, "Can you make us a little cave under the snow, just something to protect us from the wind?"

The little wolf immediately started digging a burrow, and Nym gratefully followed him in. He was getting tired again, and it was getting hard to think. Once he was settled in, he let everything go except his personal thermal barrier and tried to steady his breathing. He had no idea how he was going to destroy that lump.

Nym rested, and he plotted. He discarded a few ideas, filed a few more as maybes, and then he had an idea. He grinned. It was beautifully simple, and he was reasonably confident it would work, as long as he could make it big enough.

CHAPTER 57

The plan was simple. Nym was going to hit it with an arcana injection. For something that size, and the amount of arcana it was putting out constantly, it would have to be a massive attack, but he had time to build it up. Casting it with a ritual would be best, but he lacked the equipment or practice. So, instead, he was going to do a sustained and channeled arcana injection and hopefully poison whatever that crystalline lump was.

Nym took his time setting it up. He'd never actually used the spell against a living target before, but to his knowledge, the hardest part was getting the timing right. In this case, the target was always channeling arcana, so that shouldn't be an issue. The real concern was whether he could inject enough of his own arcana into its body to have a noticeable impact.

"Wait here," he told Cold Paw. "If I don't come back, you'll have to make it back on your own. You can dig back down, right?"

[No come back?]

The wolf regarded him somberly, no yips or tail wagging this time. "Ah, don't worry. I'm sure I'll be back in a few minutes," Nym told him.

He started building his spell slowly, widening the base of the construct to four times the size he'd practiced with. Everything about it was bigger, more draining, harder to keep stable. What he was doing would never have worked in a fight with another mage. But the lump just sat there, being lumpy as worm monsters crawled over and around it.

In his sight, the arcana-injection spell was massive, taller than he was, a needle of pure arcana poised over the middle of the ice-coated pit. With a thought, he willed it down. It flashed through the air and pierced the ice lump at speeds too fast for mortal eyes to follow. Without slowing, it vanished into the monstrous lump's soul well.

The reaction was immediate. The whole thing convulsed, which was somewhat sickening to look at, and the worm monsters crawling on it were bucked off in every direction. As one, every single worm that Nym could see began writhing in agitation. A deafening wail, so loud that it drowned out the howling blizzard winds around him, rose from the pit.

Worms burst out of the ice all around the pit, waving wildly and searching for the source of the attack. Hundreds of new worms thrashed about, barely anchored to the ice as ten or fifteen feet of sinuous living body lashed through the air. They couldn't see him through the thermal barrier, and even if they could, he was floating directly over the center of the pit. Nym was safe.

He cast a scrying spell to check on Cold Paw, whom the worms could actually reach if they knew where to find him. The wolf was curled up in the den he had dug out for them, ice crusting over the walls and providing an extra layer of protection from the worms' heat-finding senses. For the time being, Cold Paw was safe. Nym resumed his assault.

More and more worms were pouring into the pit now, called back by the overmind that controlled the hive. He considered throwing down fire, just to see what would happen, but the last time he'd attempted that, it had been a waste of time and arcana. Lightning at least damaged the lump, even if it was incredibly difficult to aim.

He fired a bolt, then a second, and watched as cracks spread through the ice. The damage wasn't significant, but it did attract the attention of the smaller worms. They started swarming over the lump, hacking at the ice he'd superheated with his spell. Their mandibles tore into it, ripping out chunks of crystalline flesh and destroying it.

The ice below him rippled. Nym blinked and peered down through the snow. Visibility was bad, but he was sure ice didn't do that. Something else was going on. Before he could figure out what, the floor of the pit shattered and was pushed upward amid a sudden hailstorm of broken ice shards.

It wasn't just the floor either. Huge chunks of the walls were blasted out as something enormous flexed beneath them. Worms and ice chunks the size of horses were scattered through the air, smacking into one another at high speeds and breaking apart.

It was pure luck that saved him in that initial explosion. The largest chunks that burst from the wall went flying mostly horizontally, with the smaller pieces that broke off from collisions scattering in every direction. He was struck repeatedly by fist-sized chunks of ice that flew hundreds of feet up. Between the deafening noise of exploding ice and the pain of being struck by dozens of small, heavy objects, Nym lost track of his surroundings.

He felt his flight spell start to unravel, and desperately scrambled to shore it up. The last thing he needed was to fall into the chaos below him. He would be ripped apart in seconds. In fact, he decided a tactical retreat was the best plan of action. Before he could get moving, something rose out of the cloud of snow blanketing the bottom of the pit.

It shot up, and up, and up, so high that Nym barely managed to fly out of the way before it rose past him. It looked similar to the worm monsters he'd already dealt with, except a thousand times bigger, and its body was covered in seven more icy lumps, each one a few hundred feet apart. The one Nym had been attacking was somewhere near the middle of its body, and in light of the creature's full size, Nym was amazed at his own stupidity.

There was no way he was killing that thing. He wasn't even willing to fight it. The new plan was to grab Cold Paw and fly far, far away. Then the wolf could make them a new tunnel, and they could get back to the rest of his pack, where Nym was going to tell that matriarch that she was out of her mind, and then he'd flee the area, blizzard be damned.

The worm hive queen had other ideas. Nym didn't know if it had other ways to sense him that the smaller worms didn't or if it was just a consequence of mass, but either way its many, many legs started scratching at the air as it undulated in place. Nym was struck a glancing blow by one, which felt a lot like what he assumed getting run over by a horse would feel like, and he tumbled through the air to crash into the snow.

It was a good thing there was a blizzard going, or the impact of the fall could have killed him. It still smarted, though not nearly as much as the actual hit from the hive queen had. He got buried so far down that it actually took an application of hydrokinesis to dig himself back out. He was shivering by the time he got back in the air. The hit had disrupted his concentration on everything he'd been holding, and without the thermal barrier to protect him, his clothes just didn't do enough.

Worse, without the thermal barrier, the worms could see him. They came boiling up out of the snow right behind him, lunging upward to impressive heights that he just barely managed to outpace. He ignited a ball of arcana inside the mouth of the closest one, charring it and causing several of the nearby worms to turn on it and attack.

With that moment's reprieve, he got his thermal barrier back up. It was too late to save him from the cold, but hopefully it would still render him invisible. It seemed to be working, from what he could tell. The worms below were in a frenzy, but they were lashing out randomly now instead of leaping out of the snow at him. He counted himself extremely lucky that they only had one real sense for spotting him, and seemed to be extremely stupid.

He was out of the range of the queen now, so he just needed to get his bearings, figure out where Cold Paw was, hope that the wolf was safe from all the worms, and get away from the pit. He immediately sent out his scrying anchor to sweep around the outskirts, trying to find the den. The landscape had been so drastically changed in just the last few minutes that he'd lost track of where he was and could only guess which way he needed to go.

A shadow fell over him. Nym looked up. The hive queen loomed above him, blocking out the sun, its enormous body aimed his way as it descended. Nym had a moment to realize how stupid and careless he'd been, assuming that the queen was the same as the regular worms. Of course it would be smarter, or have better senses.

There was no way he was going to outpace it, so he pushed every bit of arcana he had into flying sideways. If he was fast, he thought he could avoid the trunk of the main body, but it would be dicey getting between the hive queen's legs. They were long enough and spread wide enough that he didn't think it was possible to fly past them.

An instant-movement spell would be perfect, even if it was just a hundred feet in the blink of an eye. He didn't know any spells like that, but twice now his magic had come through in a life-and-death situation. He'd unlocked a new memory at the last moment and recalled some bit of magic he once knew. If there was ever a time for that to happen again, it was right now. He had less than a second to save himself. Surely the world would fade to white and he'd see a vision of himself teleporting around a training yard.

The hive queen descended on Nym like the vengeful finger of God as he darted out of the way, left to save himself under his own power. He would have liked to claim credit for deftly dodging between the legs when everything slammed down into the snow, but the truth was that it was sheer luck. Surviving everything since the queen emerged from beneath the ice had been nothing but luck.

His luck ran out there, since there was no dodging the wall of snow and ice that exploded out from underneath the queen's body when it body-slammed the ground below where Nym had been flying. It smacked into him, hurling him forward and carrying him along a hundred feet or more until he came to a stop, buried deep in the snow.

Nym took a moment to think. His first priority was keeping up the thermal barrier. It was the only thing protecting him from being spotted, at least by the regular worms. It hadn't worked against the queen for some reason, but that was a problem for another time.

He needed to unbury himself from the snow, but he wasn't even sure which way to go, or if his hydrokinesis was up to the task. There was nowhere for him to push the snow to, and he had no idea how far down he was. A simple scrying spell would fix that. If his luck continued to hold, he wouldn't be too far from the surface.

Before he could cast that, the snow around him started rumbling. Nym mentally scrambled to shift from escaping to fighting, to begin the process of weaving together another lightning-bolt spell. Before he could put it together, the snow to his left disappeared completely, and a twitching black nose appeared.

Cold Paw regarded him, head cocked. *[Go now?]*

Nym let out a huge sigh of relief and let the lightning-bolt spell fall apart. That wolf was getting all the jerky when they got out of here. Nym reached up and ruffled his ears, causing Cold Paw to let out an excited little yip. "Yeah. Leaving sounds good. Let's go."

CHAPTER 58

Nym didn't remember much of the trip back. There was flying, and Cold Paw getting them back under the snow, and after that, he mostly just followed the wolf in a daze until they were back to the pack's cavern. He vaguely recalled throwing heated arcana all over a section of the floor and collapsing on it before he passed out.

When he woke up, everything ached. He definitely had arcana poisoning, which he supposed he couldn't complain about, all things considered. It was relatively mild, considering how much magic he'd tossed about and how sloppy some of his spells had been while he was frantically trying to avoid being crushed to death.

He did nothing but make himself comfortable and eat some of his dwindling supply of rations. They were going suspiciously fast, probably because Cold Paw had helped himself to Nym's pack while he was sleeping. If so, the wolf was even more clever than Nym thought, since he'd specifically shaped a hook out of ice to keep it out of Cold Paw's reach, and the pack was still hanging from it when he woke up.

The stone beneath him was a poor substitute for a bed, but it still had lingering heat from the spell he'd cast hours ago, which Nym was grateful for. He had no desire at all to use any sort of magic, even though he was effectively blind without it. In fact, once his belly was full and his thirst was sated, the only thing Nym wanted was to use his pack as a pillow and go back to sleep.

That didn't happen, of course. The old matriarch found him soon after he woke up and started pestering him for the details. With a wince, Nym forced himself to sit up and cast night vision on himself so that he could at least see the wolf thing.

[You are a little roughed up, but in remarkably good shape for a day spent fighting the heat hunters.]

"I didn't actually fight too many of those. Mostly it was the hive queen I was dealing with."

[Did you kill it?]

Nym thought he detected some excitement in her tone. He hated to disappoint, but there was no point in lying. "Sadly, no. It took everything I had just to stay alive. But I did notice something strange. Fire didn't really work against it. It was too cold to keep anything going, but I hit a part of the queen with lightning, and the worms went crazy attacking it."

[They attacked their own queen?]

"Yeah. I think that whole heat-hunting thing is really the only thing they do. They don't care what the source is or whether it might damage them. There's no instinct for self-preservation. They see anything warm, they attack it."

[And you think this strategy of heating the queen up will allow you to turn its brood against it?] the matriarch asked. *[Will that be enough to kill it?]*

Nym shrugged. "I have no idea. I can wound it. But I'm one person, and it's . . . enormous. Maybe if we could heat up where its heart is and get them to attack that?"

[Will you try?]

"Honestly, I don't know. It was way stronger than I thought it would be. I don't think I can kill it, not with the magic I know."

[Come with me, human pup. I will teach you new magics. Then you will be strong enough, and you will kill this thing for us?]

He certainly wasn't expecting that. The wolves obviously used magic, but it seemed to be instinctual, something ingrained into the species. Nym didn't think he could learn it like he learned human magic. If he could though, this might be a once-in-a-lifetime opportunity to learn spells no one else had ever known.

Of course, the price for such instruction was steep, perhaps impossible to pay. Nym was not confident that he had anything in his current repertoire that would cause serious injury to the hive queen, and he doubted the matriarch was going to teach him something world shattering.

"What if I can't kill them, even with your magic?"

[Then you return to us, and we will keep trying. But perhaps you worry over nothing. You do not know our history, do not know where my kind comes from. Come, let us discuss what magics I can teach you, the powers that kept my people safe when I was still young and strong enough to wield them.]

Nym's mouth curled into a grin. "Lead the way," he said.

Nym finished carving the runes into an orb of ice he'd shaped with magic and poured arcana into them. It took a surprisingly long time for him to finish empowering it, but once it was full, he willed it into activation, and it floated up into the air. Light shone gently on the cave, soft, but amplified by the ice-covered walls.

"Ha, my first-ever enchanted item," he said proudly. "Probably won't last too long once winter passes, but it'll do for now."

[Congratulations], the matriarch projected into his head. *[Now are you ready to listen?]*

"Yes, of course."

The light orb was a necessary step, as it was much easier to see arcana when he wasn't casting his own spells, and it was impossible to see anything but arcana otherwise since there was no light. That might not slow down the magic wolves living in a giant cavern buried under the ice, but Nym liked being able to see.

He wasn't sure exactly what he was supposed to learn though. He'd seen Cold Paw use magic to add ice to his tunnels for extra stability, and the rate at which he dug was obviously magical, but it was closer to raw elemental magic than a defined construct that Nym could copy. He suspected he might be able to do something that had a similar effect with hydrokinesis if he practiced enough, but he wouldn't be learning the fine points from Cold Paw.

Their ability to see in the dark wasn't even magical, as far as he could tell. Nor was their extreme cold resistance. That was all biological, the same way thumbs were for Nym. Their telepathy was so instinctual that he couldn't even find a spell construct in it. It was just pure arcana cast out with thought imbued into it.

[Let us begin. Understand first that we are limited in many ways compared to your magic, which is itself inferior to the Creator's. The Creator taught many spells to the first generation, but he had to adapt them so that we can use them. And unfortunately, the ability to cast spells rarely passed down to the next generation, and almost none after that. When I die, the last of our ability to use magic likely dies with me, and you will be the sole successor.]

"First question. Who or what is the Creator?"

The matriarch let out a massive huff and bumped her head against Nym. *[It was long ago. Suffice it to say that he was a being of such magic as has never been seen before, and though he looked human, he was not. He spun us out of primordial ice and the spirit of the wolf, made us into something more, and breathed life into the first of us. He has been gone for many generations now, and I am the last of the first.]*

"But what was he if not human?"

[Something that looked like a human, but immortal, all-powerful. And then he was gone, no words of goodbye.]

"I'm sorry," Nym said. "This Creator person sounds like a parent to you. I don't remember mine at all. It . . . it's not fair."

[Life is not fair, human pup. Now, no more questions. Watch.]

Arcana flared up around the matriarch and wove itself into a terribly complicated construct. It was simultaneously more complex and bigger than anything Nym had ever created, and the speed at which the matriarch wove it was beyond impressive. It wasn't collapsing either. Nym examined it curiously, trying to figure out what it did.

Snow started swirling through the air, filling the cavern. Annoyed, Nym pushed it away and went back to looking at the construct. More snow drifted past him, obscuring his vision again. Nym went to brush it back with a wave of hydrokinesis, but he stopped short of casting the spell. "You're doing this," he said. "This magic makes it cold, makes snow."

[Correct. We all carry a spark of this in us at all times. It helps keep us comfortable and, if enough of us gather, will make the snow that we live under. Only I am able to make an external construct, which produces a much stronger version of the effect. Soon, you will be able to make it as well.]

"I don't know if I could hold this stable," Nym said doubtfully. "Even if I could pull it all together, how would I keep so many pieces from falling apart?"

[The arcana freezes itself into place. Your task is merely to power it and weave it quickly enough that it does not freeze before you have finished.]

That sounded like intent filtering to Nym, but he felt like he'd gotten pretty good at it while working on various ways to warm things up without accidentally immolating himself. He needed to flavor the arcana, for lack of a better term, to make it cold. Fortunately for him, that was something he had plenty of experience with.

He forged a new conduit, filtered it with memories of being cold, huddled up under ratty blankets and watching snow fall from the sky, knowing that it would be a long night and hoping it didn't get worse before dawn broke. Nym strained second-layer arcana through that memory and started weaving as he'd seen the matriarch do.

He wasn't even halfway before the threads froze together and got stuck. Nym let the whole thing dissolve and started over while the matriarch watched. He didn't do any better the second time, or the third. "Are they sticking together too fast, or am I just too slow?" he asked.

[Both. Your thoughts of freezing are too strong, but you are also too slow to weave them. Speed will come as you learn how to make the construct, and you may find that having a strong intent helps you at that point. You should lessen your intent for now so you can practice.]

Nym expelled the arcana he'd filtered with frozen memories and thought instead of the nights he'd spent in the forest outside Palmara. Those were cold, but in an uncomfortable way. He'd been at no risk of dying from exposure, at least not most nights. He didn't like that filter though. It reminded him of Ciana, of fleeing Palmara and the overwhelming whirlwind of emotions that had pounded at his thoughts, of the horrifying, comfortable numbness that banished the whirlwind.

It was a harder filter to hold in place, but he did it anyway and started weaving the construct again. Now it was half-complete, but the arcana was getting harder to hold in place with just his will. It was cold, but it wasn't solid enough to exist on its own without his support, and there were too many pieces for him to keep track of.

[Perhaps a little stronger intent. Try again.]

"Hey, wait," Nym said in sudden realization. "You can see my arcana!"

The matriarch titled her head quizzically, like she didn't understand. *[Of course I can. How else would I instruct you on what you're doing wrong?]*

"Humans can't do that," he said. "I've never met another one that can see arcana like me."

[Perhaps you are not human then. Maybe the Creator made you too.]

CHAPTER 59

There were enough unexplained anomalies in Nym's life that he couldn't honestly rule out the idea that he might not be human. If that was true, he was even more confused about where he came from than before. He doubted the Creator who'd made the magic ice wolves had much to do with him though. If the matriarch hadn't insisted that she'd known him personally, Nym would have dismissed the whole thing as some pagan creation myth.

So maybe it wasn't the Creator who'd made him, but it could be something else. Sure, he had memories of a whole three people, some of whom had taught him things, but he knew enough about the possibilities of magic to know those kinds of memories could well be fake. Any mage capable of casting a third-circle spell could do it.

Considering all the mysteries with his past, with the signs of rapid aging Professor Langdon had found, with his ability to see arcana that no one else seemed to have, it wouldn't surprise Nym at this point if he wasn't even an actual person. Maybe Analia wasn't the only one grown in a glass tank. At least she was sure she started out human, despite whatever modifications her father made.

The fact that the matriarch's offhand comment that he might have been made rather than born could quite possibly be correct was somewhat distressing. Nym wasn't really sure how he was supposed to feel about that idea. Analia had probably gone through something similar when she'd learned the truth about herself.

With a shake of his head, Nym pushed it aside. It was just a theory, and he didn't have any reason to think it was any more correct than any other theory. "I don't want to think about this right now. Let's go back to talking about the magic."

Nym strengthened his intent and started weaving arcana again. Eventually he produced filtered arcana that was strong enough to hold its shape on its own, but still pliable enough for him to work with without ruining the construct. It was a monstrously hefty working, requiring him to forge a second conduit just to supply his soul well with enough arcana to complete it.

"Well, that's neat," he said, examining it with the matriarch. "It looks like it's working. I can now make snow in a land that's currently under fifty feet of it with an active blizzard making more even as we speak. What do I do with this?"

[With this? Nothing. You needed to understand how it works so that you can understand how to take it apart.]

"The hive queen," Nym realized. "It's casting a huge version of this all the time. That's where all this snow is coming from. Hey, how long has this been going on? I've been freezing my ass off for a month in a nearby human city!"

[The heat hunters followed us down from the mountains. We do not feel the flow of time the same way humans do, measuring it with the sky fire. Most of us have never even seen the sky fire. I could not say how long it has been since we arrived in a way that would have any meaning to you.]

"You use this too though. You're contributing to what's happening here."

The matriarch shook her head. *[Do not be stupid. You have cast this spell yourself. How much snow did you add to the world around us? Our version is localized, but the heat hunters are creatures of instinct and hunger. They destroy anything that is not frozen, and they spread the cold endlessly.]*

"How endlessly do you mean? If we don't kill the hive queen, is the entire world going to be covered in snow? Is that even possible?"

[I do not know. This land is the warmest we have ever traveled to, but it was not warm enough to fight against the heat hunter queen's magic.]

As far as Nym understood things, Abilanth wasn't that warm in the best of times. There was some solace in that, knowing that even if things spiraled out of control, at some point it would probably just be too warm for the worms to keep expanding. It didn't much help him now, but it was comforting to know he wasn't trying to prevent the entire world from being plunged into an ice age.

Still, he wished he could shove this off on someone older and stronger. There was a reason he hadn't gotten involved with that undead business near Zoskan once he'd narrowly escaped the frost wraiths. For that matter, why did the disasters he got dragged into always involve him freezing his toes off? That didn't seem fair.

"Okay, back on topic. I can cast this weather-altering spell, at least a small version of it. I've got a few ideas for break points I could attack it at to cause the whole thing to unravel, but then what? I already tried killing the hive queen, and it swatted me down like I was nothing. What can you show me that will let me take that thing down?"

Nym hadn't really seen any overt weak points that he could exploit on the outside. Even the worms it spawned seemed like mere annoyances. The queen had flicked them off and crushed them like they were meaningless. Considering how many of them there were, maybe that was true.

The old wolf matriarch grinned at him, and Nym felt a chill down his spine. That was not a fun look. That was the kind of look that meant someone had something for him that he didn't want anything to do with. "Why are you looking at me like that?" he asked, taking an involuntary step back.

[Tell me, young maybe human, what do you know about the art of breathing life into the unliving?]

It took Nym two days to successfully cast what he was tentatively calling his ice-golem spell. The matriarch made it look easy, almost as if she was simply willing them into existence. Beautifully detailed living copies of her sculpted out of ice appeared, rising out of the snow. Nym's version was not nearly as pretty.

It was shaped like a person in that it had the correct number of limbs and a trunk with a head on top. That was as far as the similarities went at first. Unlike the matriarch's multiple copies, which were lifelike in their movements, the single copy he managed to conjure up was stilted and often failed to do things like hold its balance when it tried to walk.

He spent a lot of time practicing to refine the spell into something useful while the matriarch lay down, head on her paws, and watched. It turned out that her stamina was awful, and she was really only good for a handful of demonstrations a day before she had to rest. That wasn't to say that her coaching wasn't useful because the spells she was showing him were so much more complicated than the beginner spells he'd picked up in Abilanth or anything he'd worked out for himself.

Nym did not understand half of what he was doing or why the arcana was behaving in the way it did. He just wove it together under the matriarch's direction and made the corrections and adjustments as he was instructed. Eventually he got something workable. It wasn't a beautiful statue of ice, but it could walk without falling over and collapsing.

[Now that the easy part is done, we can move on to the next step], the matriarch told him after his fiftieth or sixtieth golem.

They'd come up with a simple, relatively safe plan. As long as Nym could work the magic, he could essentially send golems into the hive queen to bait in worms. He had the golem part down, and he had the heating spell down, but now he needed to form the golem around a heated core that would slowly melt the golem from the inside and draw in the worms.

They'd tried ripping out rocks from the ground, which was still just about the total extent of Nym's ability with elemental earth manipulation, and having the golems carry the rocks covered in the heated arcana. Unfortunately, the tests showed that the worms were too quick to jump in and destroy the golems. They didn't make it even five feet if there was a worm anywhere near it.

Encasing the heated stones in the golem would hopefully shield the heat source until it was far enough in the queen that the worms would deal some damage to it while they burrowed in to attack. It would be a death of a thousand cuts, at least it would be if he could figure out how to get the golem to form around a stone core. The spell was designed to form one entirely out of cold-aspected arcana, and would only use water in various flavors as raw materials.

Of course, layering a chunk of ice with heated arcana had predictable results. They'd worked on the problem for quite a while, trying to think of some way to modify the ice golems to carry a heated core inside them long enough to get into the hive queen before the worms noticed the heat. Nym just couldn't find an intensity that wouldn't melt its way free too fast, but also wouldn't extinguish itself without ever breaking through at all.

"This would be so much easier if I knew even a little bit more about writing rune sequences," he said. "If I could write them myself instead of just copying ones I've seen, I could just make something that does exactly what we want, but delayed by a minute before it activates."

[I cannot help you with this. I know nothing of human writing techniques.]

"I know. I know. It's just frustrating that I can't get this to work," he said. "I know what needs to be done, but not how to do it."

If Analia were there, she could have done it easily. He was sure a basic rune sequence that just delayed the activation of a spell by a minute wasn't that hard. He took a few cracks at it while the matriarch rested, but his lack of knowledge about how runes were actually built stopped him from making anything useful. The closest he got was a cobbled-together sequence that used the light orb's activation runes but edited to hold the ignition portion of his heating spell.

It blew up.

"Okay, this isn't going to work! We need to take a step back and figure something else out," he said.

[You may be correct. This is my fault. I did not consider the limitations of your melting spell and how it would interact with the frozen reflection of your spirit.]

"We'll think of something." He wished he felt as confident as he sounded. The truth was that they were no closer to figuring out how to kill the hive queen, and it had reached the point where worms were starting to make regular intrusions into the pack's home. Nym had killed dozens of them in between his practice sessions with the matriarch.

There had to be some way to get heated arcana inside the hive queen, but Nym was not keen on the obvious option of taking it in himself. The whole point of the ice golems was to be a mobile, disposable unit that carried that arcana for him. "Wait . . . Carrying the arcana," he muttered. "I think we've been looking at this all wrong. What if instead of embedding the core inside the golem, I just wrap the stone in a thermal barrier for a minute and have the golem carry it?"

CHAPTER 60

It took a week total, from the time Nym had first woken up and caught Cold Paw raiding his pack for food to where he currently stood, at the top of the now-shattered pit, looking down at what he now recognized as an enormous version of the spell the matriarch had taught him to generate a blizzard. It was so huge that it took a conscious effort to distinguish it as individual strands of arcana and not just a massive aura. He understood how the spell worked now, and despite the size, he was sure he could put pressure on vulnerable portions of the construct to break it.

In order for the plan to be any sort of effective, he couldn't limit himself to just one golem at a time. He could make four now, albeit at the cost of them being considerably less effective and durable. That was fine; he didn't care if a worm shattered the golem in one blow, just that it could keep walking until it was ready to deposit the heat source he'd given it.

Nym stood at the top of the pit, resting and recovering from the trip. He didn't dare bring Cold Paw along this time, and it took him much longer than he expected it to find the place again. Nym had no interest at all in trying to navigate worm-filled tunnels by himself, so even though he'd worked out a basic snow-burrowing spell with the matriarch's help, he'd opted to fly through the blizzard despite having only a vague understanding of where he needed to go.

He lifted off the ground and flew to the floor of the pit. Here, in the center of the hive queen's magic, he couldn't hope to breach its flesh with fire, but he could trace the road that was its body as it disappeared into the ice. The pit was no longer a smooth, icy-walled hole, and even though new ice had grown over the broken slabs that had shattered when the hive queen moved, it was still easy to follow the trail of destruction.

Nym followed along the length of the queen's body, scrying when he could to make sure he was heading in the right direction. Eventually, he found the mouth of the creature buried under tons of ice and snow. It was hard work digging down to it, but the task was made much easier by the fact that the hive queen had already broken through the ice layer. Nym liked to think that he'd learned from past mistakes and wanted contingencies in place to flee into the sky if there was even the slightest chance of the enormous monster coming after him again.

All the preparations were done. He'd made himself as safe as he could. It was time to begin.

The hardest part was going to be maintaining so many spells at once, but Nym thought he could do it. He had already compressed clumps of dirt into balls and covered them in a layer of ice so that they'd hold their shape. He set them out next to him and cast the heating spell on each one, then wrapped them all in a thermal barrier.

The first golem coalesced into existence from loose snow and ice. It grabbed a ball and dropped down the tunnel to the hive queen and walked into its open mouth. None of the worms seemed to actually close their mouths unless they were using their teeth to tear into something, which Nym found weird, but when he considered that they didn't actually need to eat and that the teeth were just another weapon, he guessed it made sense.

Or maybe it didn't. Whoever had created the ice worms must have been crazy to begin with. He couldn't divine a single reason a species like that needed to exist. Maybe they were created through some bizarre natural phenomenon of arcana somewhere in the deep, frozen northlands. It would certainly explain their physiology and weird instincts. Either way, he was happy to capitalize on the fact that every worm he'd seen, including the queen, always had its mouth open.

A second golem picked up another heated ball and followed the first one down to the hive queen. The arcana tether connecting him to the golem and allowing him to control it got harder to maintain, but Nym's goal was to get them to walk far enough down to reach the frozen ice crystal heart of the hive queen and set off his heat bombs there. That was looking less and less likely as the first golem got out of range and the tether snapped.

He wouldn't be able to maintain the thermal barrier around the balls for much longer either. Though they were relatively tiny, both the amount of heat they were putting off and the distance they'd been carried away from Nym made it extraordinarily difficult to hold the spell. Nym knew where the hive queen's heart was, but it looked like he was going to have to move with the golems if he wanted to keep them walking.

He created the last two golems and sent them down into the queen's maw, then slowly flew back toward the pit, trying to keep within a decent range of all three golems as they tried to burrow deeper inside the monster. Nym had a basic idea of what the queen's guts looked like from scrying it, and though he didn't really understand what the spell was showing him, he was hoping to bait enough worms into attacking around where the heart was that it would be vulnerable to attack.

The thermal barriers went down soon after the fourth golem entered the maw. It was just too much work trying to hold them and his own barrier, keep his three remaining golems going, and fly along with them so they didn't get out of range. The ice shells holding the dirt were already melting anyway, and he hoped that the heat sources would do their job.

It was time for the next portion of the plan. He was hesitant to start this section, since he was sure it would get the hive queen's attention, but breaking the source of the blizzard should allow him to heat up the outer ice shell of the queen's body and help direct the worms he was hoping to sic on her to the right spot.

He guided the golems as far as he could before they started to break down, and then abandoned them to conserve arcana. There were four major points of attack on the blizzard-generating construct, two on the outer edges of it, one in the middle layer, and one at the center. His hope was that by attacking the arcana directly, he could do enough damage to cause the whole thing to collapse.

To do that, he was using a modified arcana injection. Instead of blasting arcana directly into the hive queen's soul well, he struck at the construct directly. The first and easiest point wasn't hard to pry open, as it was already under strain from supporting other parts of the construct. Once it started to collapse, Nym was able to move on to the second spot.

That proved to be significantly more difficult just from the sheer volume of arcana he needed to shift, but without the golems and the thermal barriers on his heat bombs to maintain, he managed to pry the arcana out of position. This gave him access to the interior of the construct, which he attacked mercilessly. The inner workings of the spell were much more delicate, and the whole construct fell apart practically the moment he reached the center.

There was an instant and noticeable change in the air around the pit. The wind died down and with that, the snow that was still floating settled to the ground. No new snow replaced it, and for the first time since he'd woken up to Cold Paw burrowing into his campsite, Nym got a good look at the world around him.

Other than the pit itself, there was nothing to see but miles and miles of snow leading back up the mountains. Occasional lone peaks poked up out of the frozen landscape, but they seemed stunted with so much snow built up around them. Near the pit itself, the snow was much rougher. Icy remnants of his last encounter with the queen created hills in the snow where they'd been buried after erupting out of the pit, but even those were starting to smooth back out as the snow got deeper and deeper.

It was a beautiful scene, but it lasted only a few moments before the frozen countryside around the pit started bucking wildly as the queen started moving. Ice cracked and ground against itself, then was thrown into the air. Coils of the hive queen's body were revealed as they emerged from the snow, leading up to its monstrous head. Mandibles thirty feet long swung through the air as the queen searched for him, and Nym made sure to keep his distance.

He swooped around to where its body still lay in the snow and started coating it with flammable arcana. Without the cold-inducing blizzard spell running, it was easy to ignite it, and he flew the length of its body doing so. Behind him, worms started popping up and attacking the queen.

That was all well and good, but he needed to focus the damage where the heart was. For that, he needed to get closer to the mouth. Now that the blizzard was clear, it was much easier to aim, and he fired off a pair of lightning bolts back-to-back into the queen's icy hide. Cracks appeared in it, and he saw steam hiss away into open air before cooling down.

So far, the plan was going well. He'd deposited heat sources inside the queen, which hopefully its spawn would dig their way toward. He'd broken the weather-controlling spell that prevented him from heating up its surface and gotten the worms to attack it. And he'd started pummeling approximately where he thought the heart would be on the monstrous creature, though it was too vertical for the smaller worms to get at it easily.

Below him, hundreds of worms were crushed into piles of fine powder by the thrashing of their queen. That wasn't the main goal of the attack, but Nym wasn't going to complain about it. He laid down more arcana where the worms were already digging into the queen, hoping they'd go deep enough to get all the way inside and go after the heated balls he'd left there.

He spotted an opening in the queen's hide. It looked like nothing so much as a narrow gap in a wall of ice, but the worms disappearing into it weren't coming back out. Nym flung out tracer lines of arcana onto the worms and let them pull it in deeper, then ignited it. Fire flashed in the open sky as the lines burned down to the queen and ignited inside her, which drew in even more worms to the wound.

Nym let out new lines and attached them to random worms burrowing their way in. He was well away from the queen's thrashing and high enough up that he'd be out of its reach. Even if this didn't kill it, he was definitely doing damage, and it was costing him relatively little arcana. He was content to whittle away at the hive queen for as long as possible.

The queen curled up on itself and lunged toward its own flank. Nym thought for a second it was killing the worms invading it, and it certainly did scrape many of them off its body. Then arcana flashed up the threads he'd spun out to the burrowing worms. It flowed up his own spell, homing in on him despite his thermal barrier making him invisible.

Nym had just an instant to sever the threads before it hit him, and he managed to cut almost all of them. Then the arcana slammed into him through the remaining few, and everything went dark. He lost control of all his spells and started falling, but he couldn't focus his mind enough to get them going again. The fall itself could kill him, and if it didn't, the worms would. Somewhere in the back of his mind, that knowledge scratched at him desperately, trying to get his attention.

He came back to himself a moment later and immediately cast his flight spell. The world slowed down around him, but it was dark now for some reason. There was a single white circle of light that he had only a moment to see, and then he crashed into a jagged shelf of ice.

Everything started moving, and Nym found himself plastered to a wall. The circle of light disappeared, and a blast of cold air rolled across him, followed moments later by tons of ice and snow. It rolled over him, sweeping him up and pushing him farther away from the light, which was bad enough on its own.

Then the walls started moving, and more of those jagged ice shelves gnashed together, chewing up the ice.

CHAPTER 61

Nym was tossed around in the snow. He layered a kinetic barrier over a thermal barrier and tried to escape the maelstrom, but there was nowhere to go. If he got caught between those icy teeth, he'd be ground into nothing. His only hope was to go deeper, past the teeth. He couldn't fly now, but he could use the burrowing spell to push himself through the snow he was stuck in.

His path was nothing even remotely close to a straight line, and he wasn't entirely sure which direction he needed to move in. As the snow shifted around him, he just focused on keeping away from the teeth. It was perhaps the most chaotic and confusing thirty seconds of his life. All the snow and ice was steadily being pulled deeper in, and Nym with it.

The walls compressed around him, squeezing him and pressing a bunch of smaller ice chunks into him. For a second, Nym thought he was caught between two teeth, and then the pressure vanished and he was pushed through the other side. Everything calmed down, giving him a chance to breathe again. Nym dug his way free of the snow and let the kinetic barrier drop. A quick night vision spell revealed his surroundings to him.

It looked like he was inside an ice-coated tunnel. Side passages branched out from the main tunnel in every direction, including through the floor and ceiling. Hesitantly, Nym took to the air and moved away from the piled-up snow and ice, which was still churning somewhat as new material came in from behind and pushed it all forward.

He felt awful, and not just because he was pretty sure he'd been eaten. Something in that arcana attack the hive queen hit him with was lingering. If he didn't know better, he'd have said he'd overstrained himself and had arcana poisoning again. That would mean the hive queen had hit him with an arcana injection though, which had disturbing implications.

If it could do something like that, it might not be as mindless as he'd assumed.

Most of its actions had appeared instinctive though, and the smaller worms were driven by nothing but instinct. Perhaps its attack had just been a natural reaction to being targeted by arcana. If the wolf matriarch could see it, there was no reason to assume the hive queen couldn't. Nym made a mental note to be more careful about assuming he was the only thing around that could see spells being cast.

Weirdly, the air was actually a bit warmer inside the hive queen than it had been outside. Perhaps the blizzard itself had contributed so much to the temperature, but either way, once he got out of the snow, the thermal barrier took less arcana to keep active.

That was good because his soul well was already protesting the additional draw of the flight spell, and the dull ache in his body started to grow. Nym needed to find a way out, and fast. Things were going to get worse for him though because without magic he was both lost and blind. He had two objectives: spread flammable arcana all over everything, but especially all over the hive queen's heart, and light it up, and find a way to that wound the smaller worms had chewed in its flank so he could escape.

He flew forward slowly, using a scrying spell that he flicked back and forth between seeing what was directly in front of him and scanning for his target. What he found instead was one of the lumps like the ones that were at the bottom of the pit. Inside were little crystalline ice spheres, each one maybe a half a foot wide. Larvae were curled up inside them, barely a few feet long and with their legs and mandibles more stub that anything.

Those weren't what he was here for, but he wondered if they would attack the queen from the inside if he heated things up. Experimentally, he coated the eggs with arcana, then made a trail of it leading deeper into the queen's body. He sparked the arcana and watched it burn. Ice splintered and cracked, very unlike what real ice would do. He supposed it was different because the ice was alive and made up the monsters' bodies.

After a bit, the eggs started to split open, and the larvae spilled out. They twitched a bit, but weren't a very impressive strike force. Mostly they just ended up attacking one another instead of the queen. Nym vaguely regretted wasting the arcana on the experiment when he was already feeling weak from the hive queen's counterattack. He'd learned something, but didn't see any value to it.

He gave up on flying after that. He had to prioritize the thermal barrier above all else, and scrying for his targets was more important than flying around aimlessly. Walking sucked for a few different reasons, mainly that the "floor" of the inside of the queen's body radiated cold and made it harder to keep the thermal barrier going. It was still less expensive than flight.

The other reason was that the hive queen wasn't done moving. It seemed to have settled more or less back into place, coiled around the pit or however it rested, but there were still occasional shifts and adjustments. Whenever that happened, it was a guarantee that Nym would be thrown from his feet.

Still, the queen was only a few thousand feet long. That was a few minutes of walking in a straight line, and its insides were surprisingly open, not like a flesh-and-blood creature at all. There was air to breathe, though it smelled off. He couldn't quite place why, just that it wasn't clean. It was pitch-black in there, but that hadn't been a problem for Nym for weeks now. At least, it wasn't on a normal day.

It was gentler on his soul well to hold the scrying spell and frequently move the anchor back and forth between plotting out his own course and searching for the heart than it was to switch between night vision and scrying. That didn't mean it was easy, and holding both spells was a constant gnawing ache. He needed to wrap this up soon, but he still hadn't found the hive queen's heart.

A hissing sound filled the air, followed by loud pops that echoed around inside of the queen. At first, Nym thought it must be something he was hearing from outside, even though he hadn't heard anything since being eaten. There was nothing else inside the queen except the larvae, and those were tucked away in their eggs.

His scrying anchor found it a moment later. One of the egg clutches had hatched. The ice forming their shells lay on the ground, shattered as the larvae twitched. They were bigger than the first clutch of eggs Nym had found, maybe two or three times the size. Unlike the ones he'd seen up close, these ones had fully formed mandibles and legs.

It didn't take long for them to escalate from twitching to writhing, and within a minute or two, the larvae were fully mobile. Fortunately, his thermal barrier was working the same as it did with the fully grown version, and the worms didn't seem to realize he was nearby. Instead, they piled back into the lump that had held their eggs and started attacking it.

Nym watched, confused. He hadn't done anything to heat that area up, but they were acting like he had. Even stranger, his scrying showed him more worms swarming over the outside of the lump, also chewing on it. It looked like they would eventually tear through it, perhaps providing him with an exit once the larvae had all escaped.

He could only assume this was part of the normal life cycle, since as far as he knew, he'd done nothing to influence it. That might explain why the worms were so willing to attack their own queen once he'd started heating it up. They'd mistaken the hot spots as some sort of signal to release the hatched young. That was a nice stroke of luck for Nym. It meant he didn't need to keep looking for that wound the worms had dug into the queen's flank and could fly through the hole a hundred feet away once the worms finished enlarging it.

In the meantime, he went back to looking for the heart. He knew it was in the top half of the worm, and thought it was close enough to the mouth that he should have already passed it. It was easy to miss things when scrying since he only saw things in a roughly ten-foot-wide sphere. Either he hadn't gone as far as he thought, or he'd already passed it and missed it.

Nym decided to backtrack a bit and check behind him again. At this point, escape was a higher priority, and he didn't want to get too far away from his exit strategy. He shot a line of arcana toward the clutch of larvae to mark the trail and retreated back the way he came. The scrying anchor swept out around him in circles, searching for the heart. It occurred to him that he might not even realize if he saw it.

For all he knew, it was just another giant lump of ice. It could blend right in with the rest of the hive queen's innards. He wished he knew anything about the anatomy of these monsters. The queen was just so hard to search due to its size, and the smaller worms appeared to be more or less solid ice when he scried them. There were little pockets with no ice that he suspected aided in the articulation of their bodies, but nothing like a flesh-and-blood creature.

By his best guess, Nym had been in the hive queen for about fifteen minutes. It felt like he should have been able to walk from one end to the other by now, but he had to admit he was going much slower than normal since he was creeping forward blind and getting weaker by the minute. He gave himself two more minutes to find the heart before he bailed, and it was only two minutes because the worms were still working on getting through the lump. If they'd already chewed their way to freedom, he'd leave without hesitation.

Scrying revealed nothing new. It was the same egg clutches he'd already passed, the same empty tunnels that wound through the queen for some inexplicable reason. There were dozens of tunnels large enough for him to pass through that twisted around one another, and hundreds of smaller tunnels that branched off from them. Nym wondered if it was a weight thing. Since its outer shell was so heavy, the inside might need to be hollow so it could lift its own bulk.

The time was up. Nym confirmed his route back and dropped the scrying spell so he could start building up arcana to fly away. It was only once he let go and everything went black that he realized the truth. The tunnels in the hive queen were a sort of cardiovascular system that pumped arcana through its body. The arcana seemed to infuse itself in the queen, meaning it wasn't even fully circular. He could see it becoming visibly thinner as it swept past him.

It would be a delicate process, but he was confident he could find the source of the arcana. The real question was whether he was in good enough shape to enact the final step of the plan he'd cooked up with the wolf matriarch. If he left now, he might not be able to get back inside without allowing himself to be eaten again, and the golem stage of their current plan hadn't really worked out.

Nym turned to track the flow of arcana upstream to what he hoped was a heart that wasn't too far away.

CHAPTER 62

Arcana dribbled along behind him as he trudged forward, leaving a trail from the larvae clutch to his current position. Nym tracked through the hive queen's body blind, taking turns seemingly at random as he tried to narrow down the source of the arcana. It got trickier where the larger arteries intersected one another, especially if there were smaller tunnels looping around and connecting them, but he was making progress.

He bounced off a wall of ice and tumbled backward. "Ow!" he said. Somehow, the arcana was flowing through what he was sensing as an exit, but he couldn't get through. Left with no choice, he conjured up a new scrying anchor to see what the problem was.

Nym stifled a groan when he got a look at it. The wall was relatively thin and perforated with hundreds of holes no wider than his finger that let the arcana pass through. Nym finally understood why he couldn't find the heart. It wasn't a big lump of ice sitting inside a chamber. It was the chamber itself, which had eight spots like the one in front of him, some sort of sieve that let arcana come out from it to be distributed throughout the hive queen.

The ice wall was maybe a foot thick. A single lightning bolt would probably break it. Nym hesitated, both because he would drain almost all his recovered arcana in addition to it hurting like crazy, and also because the hive queen so far didn't seem to have noticed him creeping along inside of it, still alive and unchewed.

But he didn't think he could get his own arcana into the room through the pinholes, and a single lightning strike seemed less risky than igniting his arcana and drawing a pack of worms to the wall so they could chew it while he waited around. Nym took a deep breath, gritted his teeth, and started pulling more arcana through his soul well.

The lightning bolt arced through the air, twisted somewhat farther to the side than he wanted, and struck the ice. It exploded in a cloud of hailstones, many of which struck Nym. He raised an arm to shield his face, mentally cursing that he hadn't stood farther back. Before he could check on the damage, the queen shifted, and he was thrown into a wall. Another shift sent him sprawling in the other direction.

Finally it settled back down, and Nym was able to enter its heart. That was a misnomer, of course. The queen didn't have any internal organs, as far as he could tell. But enormous amounts of arcana appeared in the chamber and pushed outward. He'd disturbed the balance of something, and now the arcana was rushing out of the hole he'd busted open instead of flowing evenly through each exit.

Standing in the heart chamber, he could actually feel the arcana on his skin. It was so thick and so much stronger than the arcana he was used to, it was seeping into his body. If he hadn't already had arcana poisoning, he thought he could get it just from exposure to the hive queen's heart. Shaking his head and working quickly, Nym started layering his own arcana throughout the chamber. He took some time, probably more than he should, to visit each sieve-like exit and shoot arcana into them.

Then he cast a heated-wall spell on the floor he was standing on just to make sure the worms found the place. It was probably overkill, and he groaned under the strain of the arcana expenditure, but he wasn't interested in ever coming back. He wanted the hive queen dead, the blizzard cleared up, and to fly so far south that they didn't know what snow looked like.

Nym trudged back out and retraced his steps, leaving as much arcana as he could force out of his body behind him. It was a good thing he could follow the trail and no longer needed to scry because he didn't think he could maintain the thermal barrier and lay down arcana to ignite if he had to use magic to navigate too.

The larvae were somehow still chewing at the ice separating them from freedom, though holes had started to appear. Nym was surprised, considering how easily the adults had torn through a random spot on the queen, but then again, there were relatively few adults on the outside of the queen compared to the wound he'd incited them to make.

Nym closed his eyes tight and cursed silently. He was at the end of his stamina. All he needed to do was light the match and fly away, but there was one last log fallen on the road. The smart thing to do was wait for them to finish and slip out. Using more arcana to speed the process up would just make it harder to fly after.

Standing there holding the thermal barrier and watching light trickle in from the tears in the hive queen's skin would cost him too. It was hard to say which was going to drain him more, so he decided to take the middle ground and cast another heated-wall spell on the lump of flesh. Hopefully it would attract more adult worms to tear through it faster. As soon as they showed up, he was going to light up the arcana trail and fly away.

It didn't take long after that. More worms showed up, and within thirty seconds, he could see the sky. Snow filled the air again, but not as thick as it had been when the blizzard was going at full strength. Perhaps his sabotage of the heart chamber had weakened the hive queen's magic. He hoped so. It would be easier to fly away if the blizzard was weaker.

Worms spilled through the torn flesh into the hive queen's body, and Nym ignited the trail of arcana. It flared up in sudden flames and started to burn away, alleviating his biggest fear, that the intensity of the cold and wind would prevent it from catching again. That didn't happen, but Nym almost got run over by the first worm to rush past him to attack the hive queen's body.

Nym pulled together his flagging strength and flew up through the hole before it became completely clogged with worms. They were coming from every direction, scrambling over the ice and swarming over the queen. Many of them were heading for the open cavity in its side, but many more were tearing at it, trying to dig straight down.

He flew slowly, barely as fast as his first attempts had been. Nym wanted to fly faster, wanted to do better than limping through the air, but it hurt too much to pull more arcana through his soul well. The spell was barely getting enough to function, and the thermal barrier was starting to fall apart as the much colder air outside the hive queen hit him.

Below him, the hive queen let out a roar that shook the snow and caused it to jump. Nym spun and flew backward so he could watch it spasm as its children ate it from the inside out. His lips curled up into a grim smile. "That's what you get for trapping me in your stupid blizzard," he said.

The hive queen rose to its full height, but Nym was too far away for it to reach him. There was no trailing arcana for it to chase, and though he imagined he was visible through his failing thermal barrier, he didn't think he needed to be concerned unless it started chasing him.

That didn't happen thankfully. It thrashed about, sending tremors through the ground and throwing snow up into the air. A large part of him wanted to stay and watch it die, but his practical side urged him to find a place to rest. He searched out one of the mountain peaks that poked up through the snow, wanting something that would both accept a heated-wall spell and would hopefully be far away from any worms that were still roaming around.

Nym practically dragged himself up the last fifty feet of the mountain he picked out, all his spells having given out. His limbs were so heavy and his soul well ached so badly that he spent several long minutes weighing the pros and cons between casting one last heated-wall spell or just hoping his clothes would keep him from freezing to death. It was close, but in the end, he powered through and collapsed on the now-warm stone to sleep.

It was the middle of the night when Nym woke back up. Everything hurt, but the sky was clear for the first time in a week. He took that as a good sign that the hive queen was dead. Not desiring in any way to go another round with that monster, Nym could only breathe out a sigh of relief.

Now that he was awake and relatively safe, he needed to figure out exactly how injured he was. Physically, he was bruised from top to bottom. Most of it came from being swallowed, he thought. He'd be tender for a while, but he'd heal. He didn't think anything was broken, and as far as he could tell, he'd escaped the ravages of frostbite.

Magically speaking, things were a different story. The arcana injection, if that's what it was, had hit him hard. He'd made very little progress in clearing that out, and his soul well was strained to the point that it still hurt when he woke up. Since there was no way Nym could just not use magic if he expected to survive, he was in for an unpleasant few days while he healed up.

The last problem was that he was ravenous but had no food on him. His pack was safely stored near the roof of the matriarch's cave, far away from Cold Paw's bottomless pit of a stomach. It was probably safe. Definitely.

Nym groaned. There had better be some food left when he got back.

There was nothing he could do about that now. Instead, he sat down and tried to cleanse the arcana poisoning in his body. Nym normally found this relatively easy, easy enough that he could do it in combat. The arcana the hive queen had hit him with was fighting him like nothing he'd ever experienced. He chipped away at it, but it didn't want to break down.

All things considered, his best guess was that he'd had his first brush with third-layer arcana. It was unfortunate that it was an arcana injection, but then again, an offensive third-circle spell probably would have outright killed him. He was sure the arcana lodged in his body would break down given enough time, even if he did nothing to speed up the process.

It made it difficult to function, but when the sun came up, Nym forced himself to get back in the air and confirm the hive queen's death. He found it easily enough, all its massive length splayed out in the snow and ice, torn open in multiple places, and with its crystalline body no longer glinting in the light. The icy flesh was dull now, more mud-colored than the natural ice around it.

That was dead enough for him. Nym could still see a few worms crawling around the carcass, but he was in no condition to fight them. He flew off, still far slower than he wanted, and found his way back to the wolves' den.

That was harder to find, but he knew approximately where it was, and through some judicious use of scrying, he found the tunnels leading to it and dug his way down. He was met by three full-grown beasts all standing at alert when he entered the den, followed by a dozen excited pups that swarmed all over him.

Normally Nym would have been happy to be buried in a wolf-pup avalanche, but as sore as he was, he had to escape their affections by flying overhead. That didn't stop them from chasing after him, but when he approached the matriarch's den, they gave up. She met him at the entrance and took in his condition at a single glance.

[It is done?]

"It is," he said.

[Fine work, wolf's friend. Come in and regale me with the tales of your victory.]

CHAPTER 63

Nym told the matriarch all about his fight with the hive queen, and when he got to the part where it had attacked him through his arcana, he asked, "Do you think it could use third-layer arcana?"

[I don't know what that is. It is a very powerful monster though. Was a very powerful monster.]

"Right." Nym blew out a sigh. That was the trouble with the wolves. They were intelligent, but they just didn't have some words and concepts that he took for granted. "Well, either way I'm having trouble cleaning it out of my system. It's probably going to be a few days before I can get moving again."

[A few days is no trouble. We will be leaving soon ourselves, probably around the same time.]

"You are?" Nym asked, surprised. "Why did you want me to wipe out the hive then?"

[Lack of food, more than anything. The only upside to so many of our pack being slain is that we need significantly less food than usual, but there still isn't enough here. The heat hunters kill everything living they find, and don't even have the decency to provide a meal when they are hunted in turn. This land needs time to recover, and my pack cannot wait that long.]

Nym looked over at his own pack, which had miraculously survived unmolested. It wasn't as full as he would have liked, but there was still enough for him to eat for a week or so if he was strict on his rationing. It would be a hungry and uncomfortable week, but he wouldn't starve. After that, things would get desperate.

The matriarch followed his gaze and said, *[You understand. You need to continue your own migration.]*

"Yeah," Nym agreed. "It's going to be tight. I brought extra food with me, but then all of this happened. Certain young wolves who shall not be named have helped themselves to some of it as well."

[I wish we could offer you more, but even the strongest of our pack have been reduced to hunting for small game like pups. Many of us are going hungry so that the young may still eat.]

Nym couldn't see much of a difference in the wolves from when he first arrived, but he supposed there was no reason to assume missing meals was a new event for them. If anything, it made it all the more impressive that his food supply was still intact. "If I had more to give," he started.

[You have done more than anyone could reasonably ask], the matriarch cut him off. *[Do not starve yourself so that one of mine may have one more meal. We will survive as we always have.]*

The conversation changed from there to more pleasant topics. The matriarch told stories of a particularly adventurous and troublesome young pup that it took Nym far too long to realize was her, and talked of the Creator and his wondrously impossible magics. Cold Paw came to visit, and lay next to Nym with his head in Nym's lap while he received ear scratches.

Nym's body ached, and his belly grumbled. It still hurt to renew the heated-wall enchantment that kept him from freezing, but a little less each time he did it. He couldn't afford to spend too much time recovering, but just the idea of channeling arcana for hours and hours made him want to throw up.

By the end of the third day, he knew he no longer had a choice. He wasn't recovered yet, but if he waited any longer, his only remaining choice would be to return to Abilanth to resupply. Nym spent an hour or so seriously considering it. He might be able to slip in, buy what he needed from somewhere in the outer ring where the guards were less plentiful and more susceptible to bribes.

In the end, he did a few experimental flights and found that while it was a generally miserable experience, he could maintain his flight spell for the long periods needed to fly. If he left immediately, he could still make the distance without having to risk Abilanth. So he gathered his things and prepared to go.

Before that, he had one last task. He sought out Cold Paw, who was not hard to find as the wolf had been sticking close lately. He seemed to sense something because, as Nym approached, he cocked his head and said, *[Time to go?]*

"Yeah, I think so," Nym said.

[Go with?]

"I don't think so. I need to go where it's warmer. There's no snow. I don't think you'd like it there."

[Stay with pack. Come with?]

"Same problem, buddy. It's too cold for me to live here. And I have a friend I need to meet. You'd like her, I think. She'd definitely like you."

Cold paw considered that for a second, then said, *[Bring friend and visit!]*

Nym smiled. "That sounds like an excellent idea. I'll work hard to learn the magic I need so that I can find you again. It might take me a little while though, okay?"

He finished saying his goodbyes and left the wolf pack behind, flying south toward civilization.

A winter fox sat in the air on a platform made of snow. The snow wanted to fall, but it was leashed to her magic, and she would not let it. She had come to investigate the strange twist she'd felt in the season in this area, and been surprised to find a tecula hive, of all things. The monsters rarely left the far north, where they thrived under an eternal blanket of ice and snow, destroying all living things that crossed their paths.

They were an infestation, forever spreading, spawning more and more of them. Since they weren't alive in a traditional sense and consumed arcana instead of food to survive, they could grow to unbelievable numbers if they weren't culled. This hive had been, fortunately. There were still a fair number of the lesser monsters hidden in the snow, but without their queen to protect them from the heat of the sun, they would eventually kill themselves off.

That wasn't what interested the fox though. It sensed something else hidden beneath the endless white landscape, something she hadn't seen since she was a kit: a pack of snow wolves. When she was young, they would have preyed on her, and she would avoid a pack of them at any cost.

She wasn't young anymore.

The snow held aloft by her will broke apart, and she dove through the air, slipping through the white fields like they were water. Soon enough, she landed in one of the tunnels the wolves had burrowed and followed it to catch up to the migrating pack. They traveled in a loose clump, with their very young and very old in the center, and with the few healthy adults remaining on the outside edges.

The first wolf saw her and growled, crouched down and ready to lunge. She regarded him, amusement playing on her face, then breezed past him before he knew what was happening. The wolf, confused, spun to find her. By then, she had already ghosted past the perimeter guard and was among the pups that were closer to her own size.

Alarmed barks came from the adults, followed by confused yips from the pups. A single ancient wolf calmed them all with that strange telepathic ability they used to communicate, then dropped back to walk next to the fox.

[Greetings], the wolf said.

"Hello," the fox replied. "I don't mean to bother you. I'm just looking into what happened here. Do you mind talking?"

[Not at all. In fact, I wish you'd come by two weeks ago. Let me tell you about our troubles with heat hunters.]

The fox had forgotten that old name for the tecula, the name she'd known them by as a child. Too much time among humans had buried many of her memories from before she'd gained her magic and become something more. It felt good to be reminded of when she was still young, back when things were simple, before she found her humans and they made things complicated. Still, they were worth it.

The wolf matriarch spun her a fascinating story, one that she was sure would interest and delight her humans. No doubt they'd feel the need to tell the other humans who sometimes made them do things they didn't want to, but which they did anyway in exchange for chunks of metal. The fox had always thought the concept was foolish, but it did allow her humans to buy that ever so delicious invention of theirs: ice cream.

In return for the story, the fox reached into her magic, following its connection to the place beyond the world, and opened up the door. Inside that place were many, many things that were important to her, and many other things that were merely convenient. Her magic knew what she wanted at the moment, and it pulled the carcass of an elk back from the beyond and dropped it in front of her.

"Here," she told the wolf. "My thanks for the story."

Then the fox left, her curiosity sated, and found her humans miles and miles away. They were seated around a small fire, a thing that had once annoyed her to no end but that she'd gradually come to accept. There were two of them, one big and strong with blond hair that he kept short, and the other shorter and smaller, but with blazing red hair that reminded the fox of fire. They were not perfect, but they were hers.

"Would you like to hear a true story?" the fox asked slyly. "I might be willing to trade it if you have any of that chocolate-flavored ice cream left."

Abdun picked through the memories of hundreds of humans he had turned into unknowing informants. This particular tidbit had come from some sort of human military commander who'd gotten it from a subordinate who coordinated with other humans who weren't officially part of the military but sometimes worked with them anyway. Humans were very much obsessed with their hierarchies and organizations, probably because there were so damn many of them.

This hive queen thing didn't seem very strong to him, but then, nothing living down on the ground truly did. He doubted it would take even two spells to kill it. That sense of scale was the problem though. It was so hard to pick out the exceptional from the mundane when it was all just so pathetic.

The humans were certainly excited about it, and he trusted their judgment more than his own when it came to determining what was unusual in their worthless, muddy, little lives. With a thought, he pierced the fifth layer of reality and molded the arcana into the magic he desired. His visage appeared half a world away and examined the carcass of the big worm thing himself.

The conduit extended through the sixth layer, what his kind knew as Transcendence, and drew upon magics so impossible that humans couldn't even comprehend them. He watched the battle backward, reviewing the worms, and the boy with a pathetic assortment of weak first- and second-layer arcana shapings, not even strong enough to be considered true spells.

If that boy was a hidden exarch, Abdun would spend the next hundred years living as a human. With a snort of disgust, the visage disappeared, and he went back to monitoring his human informants. This job was so. Damn. Boring. But if he could find Exarch Niramyn and deliver him to his own master, he'd be rewarded beyond his wildest dreams. He might even finally learn the conduit-forging techniques needed to pull arcana from the Crushing Void. He'd been working on piercing the seventh layer for two centuries with no luck.

As much as it pained him, Abdun got back to work. It was only a matter of time until someone found the missing exarch, and he was going to make sure it was him.

CHAPTER 64

Thrakus was not what Nym expected in a city. He'd pictured something like Abilanth, just scaled down to a smaller population and a lot flatter since it wasn't built on the side of a mountain. Instead, it sprawled miles in every direction. It was a trading city with agriculture to the south and lumber to the north. Three different major roads ran directly to it, one coming in from the west coast, though far north of Palmara, one from the east to the kingdom's border, and one from the south, carrying all sorts of traders, craftsmen, and caravans.

Nym entered from a smaller road from the north, connecting Thrakus and Abilanth together. It was less traveled in large part due to how difficult it was to reach the city hidden in the mountains, but it wasn't empty by any means. Nym saw more than one caravan traveling north. Each one was enormous, with upward of forty or fifty wagons being pulled by thick, sturdy, shaggy-haired oxen.

And that was Nym's problem with Thrakus. The city stank. There were so many animals in it that it perpetually smelled of manure and livestock. Coming from the frozen north, where the cold kept the smell of everything down, it was especially strong. The natives didn't even seem to notice. Nym was horrified to realize that after a few days, he stopped smelling it too.

It had taken him almost five days to reach Thrakus after his little detour under the snow, thanks mostly to his slow flying speed. He still felt awful, but having spent the last week at a little inn on the outskirts of the city called the Lucky Barrel and doing his best to eat his own body weight in food while casting absolutely no spells whatsoever, he was recovering quickly.

Nym paid for a whole week up front, and a second week after the first had passed, and it felt weird to not have to scrounge for money to do that. He'd broken a single crest down into a few shields and a lot of shims by first visiting a leatherworker to have his coat repaired, then used that as spending money for food.

Even after all that, he had more money than he knew what to do with. Mindful of the fact that it would probably have to last him for a long, long time, and that he had no idea what funds Analia would arrive with, he refrained from spending it frivolously. Nym paid for lodging and food at the Lucky Barrel, and a private bathroom and laundering at the bathhouse a few blocks away.

Then he rested and tried to stay inconspicuous. As far as he knew, nobody was looking for him in Thrakus, and he'd finally realized that telling people his actual name everywhere he went was doing him no favors. The innkeeper and his family knew him as Ermy, a name he'd shamelessly stolen from his homeless friend back in Abilanth. He hoped his old coat was still keeping the real Ermy warm, and that all the street kids found better shelter before the blizzard hit the city.

He'd done a lot of sleeping over those first two days, but now Nym was up, well rested, well-fed, and ready to see the sights of the new city. The pain of arcana poisoning in his body had completely faded, and as long as he didn't do any magic, his soul well didn't ache either. So he spent his second week exploring Thrakus. He found open-air markets outside the city where caravanners bought and sold out of their wagons parked next to farmers selling off some of their excess preserved food, though the prices were a little high this late into the winter season.

Nym wandered them, browsing and listening to people. He knew very little about other lands and their cultures and was planning on learning through immersion. Unfortunately, the merchants didn't like having a kid browsing through their wares and not buying anything, and after an hour, he started getting dirty looks. Nym decided it was time to find somewhere to be.

One good thing about his time on the streets was that he had learned a lot about pickpocketing, and consequently a lot about how to protect himself from pickpockets. The first step was not to appear to be a mark. A lot of would-be thieves would pass him by for easier targets as long as he wasn't obviously wealthy, flashing around a lot of coin, with a heavy pouch hanging off his belt or coins clinking in his pocket while he walked.

After that, Nym kept his coat buttoned up and his money inside a pocket sewn on the inside, which was itself also buttoned. No pickpocket was getting into that without a knife to cut through some seams or ties, and while small finger-mounted blades did exist and there were many, many thieves skilled in their use, no one was going to target a kid who was sensibly dressed for the weather but whose clothes were far from new.

He wandered around aimlessly for a while, just kind of mentally mapping out the city and noting the locations of important buildings. Very few of them were more than two stories tall, with the local mage guildhall being a prominent exception. Nym noted the location in case he needed it for some reason, but otherwise stayed far, far away from it. The mages guild and the city guard were the two most likely groups to have a description of him.

While he was wandering, he found himself running into the back of a crowd of people all standing around watching something. Curious, Nym threaded his way through until he reached the front of the crowd. That got him a few more dirty looks, but nobody said anything.

Four mages were working together, the glow of arcana surrounding all of them. Their auras were hues of brown, green, and yellow, all nature colors, and it was obvious why. All of them were casting earth-manipulation spells. The two younger ones, a set of identical twins, were using basic terrakinesis to excavate the foundation for a new building, while a middle-aged one with a beard was transmuting the loose earth into solid bricks, and the last, a woman who looked to be in her late twenties, was keeping the whole thing organized as she slowly put it all back together.

It was the fourth mage who interested Nym the most, since her work was a compilation of using magic to move the bricks into place and carving rune sequences across their surfaces as she did. He couldn't see them very well from so far away, but his immediate guess was that she was binding the bricks together to form a solid foundation for the building they were raising.

Just based on the dimensions, he guessed it was some sort of warehouse or store. Unlike Abilanth's middle and inner rings, Thrakus was not well organized. There were districts, sure, but he'd seen plenty of homes near the market squares, and more than a few businesses being run out of other homes in the middle of residential areas. All the roads were wide, even if most of them were made of hard-packed earth occasionally worn down with wagon ruts. The city had grown organically, with people putting up new buildings wherever it was most convenient at the time and very little thought given to long-term planning.

Not everyone was happy to see the mages working though. A handful of men were scowling at the scene, muttering to one another and shooting dark looks at the mages. Nym missed most of what they were saying due to the noise, but the bits and pieces he did catch made him think that the men felt they'd lost money over not being awarded the contract to build the foundation.

Other workers waited nearby with a pile of lumber and various tools, apparently planning to get started on the framework of the building immediately. And just judging from the few minutes Nym spent watching the magic, the four-mage crew would have the entire foundation completed in the next half an hour.

"—lose another contract to their crew, we're gonna go under," one of the men said.

"I know! What do you want me to do? We can't compete with their prices."

The mutterings faded back out again as Nym focused on the mage who was taking the loose earth and compacting it down, then transmuting it into stone. He didn't understand a lot of the spell, mostly because he couldn't get his own arcana to flow that way. The pattern would be easy enough to draw, but in practice, everything had to be put together just right. There was a sense of finality to each piece when it was slotted in, that it wasn't going to move again.

His own techniques were different. He quite often crafted a piece of the spell, only to stretch or bend it around another later on. It worked fine for all his elemental-air- and water-based magics, but he supposed earth manipulation was different. That was probably why he'd struggled so long. The books had tried to explain it to him, but it wasn't until he watched the mage work that things really started to click. It wasn't enough to have an intent of solidity. He needed to cast that way too.

"—how well they'd work with a few broken bones," the man muttered to his companions.

"Don't do anything stupid, Jakwen. You try anything, they'll be putting you in the ground next."

"Well someone has to! Not like you're getting anything done. Whole guild is falling apart, and you just stand there wringing your hands and apologizing."

"Boss said he was handling it. Just wait for him to work his magic."

"Meanwhile they're working their magic, and we're going broke!"

Nym tried to ignore the conversation. It wasn't his problem. He just wanted to watch the mages work, maybe get a few insights into his own earth spells. He really wished he could see what those runes the lady mage was drawing looked like. The urge to cast a scrying spell to get a better look at them was almost overpowering, but he resisted. He was still recovering, no magic allowed.

"—told me they always hit the Quarterhouse after a job. We can catch them on their way out. They'll be too drunk to fight back, it'll look like a random mugging. There's twelve of us to four of them!"

The idiot was actually discussing his plan to assault a quartet of mages easily capable of casting second-circle spells out in the open, surrounded by people, and making very little effort to lower his voice. Nym was sure he wasn't the only one who was overhearing this. The sensible one continued to try to reason with the idiot, but it wasn't going well. Nym went back to trying to ignore all of them. He wondered if he could get a better look at the rune work if he stood on the far end of the crowd, where he would be technically farther away but would also have a much better angle to read them.

As a side benefit, it would get him away from the idiot. Nym decided to do just that, but the crowd that he'd slid through to make it to the front had gained even more people, and it was now too thick to push back into. He tried, but someone shoved him back. Nym didn't quite see who it was, but the person was clearly an adult and clearly stronger than him.

Arms flailing to try to keep his balance as he staggered back a few steps, Nym's heel caught on a clump of dirt, and he ended up sprawled out on his back staring up at the sky. A few laughs and snorts came from the crowd, and then his vision was filled with the bearded face of the third mage, the one who was making bricks. He extended a hand for Nym to grab and pulled him to his feet.

"Alright there?" he asked, even as his aura flared up with some basic terrakinesis and the dirt was pulled from Nym's clothes.

"Yeah, sorry. I'm fine. I was just trying to move through the crowd, and well . . . it's kind of packed now. Thanks for the help."

"Not a problem. Best be on your way now though. There's a lot of heavy stuff moving around here; it's not a place to just be standing in the middle of."

"Right, sorry again." Nym hesitated for a second, then leaned closer to the mage. "I overheard a bunch of guys talking about jumping your crew after you leave the Quarterhouse tonight. I think they're business rivals who're sick of losing work to you. I'm not sure if they'll do it or if they're all talk though."

"That right?" the mage said. "Well thank you for the warning, young sir. What's your name?"

"Ermy," Nym lied.

"I'll tell you what, Ermy, why don't you meet us at the Quarterhouse in three hours, and I'll buy you a steak. I'll even let you pester Ophelia about the runes you've been watching her draw for the last ten minutes."

"How did you . . . ?"

"Noticed you mouthing the names, though you got a few of them wrong. But enough for now. I've got to get back to work."

"Oy!" one of the excavating mages yelled. "You're getting backed up!"

"See what I mean?" the bearded mage said. "You'd think they were in charge instead of me. I'll see you in a few hours, son?"

"Sure," Nym said, eager for the opportunity to score some free food and talk to some earth mages about magic.

CHAPTER 65

The Quarterhouse was probably the largest restaurant Nym had ever seen. It wasn't as fancy as the inside of the Feldstal manor, but it was plenty expensive. In fact, it was too expensive. Nym could afford a meal there, but he would never waste his money on something so frivolous. He really only came to see if he could actually learn more about elemental earth magic, and also because the bearded mage had promised him a free steak.

Nym didn't know what steak tasted like, but he figured if a place like the Quarterhouse served it, it was probably delicious. He was eager to find out, and eager to learn more about their magical construction company, the Earth Shapers. And since he didn't have anything better to do, Nym meandered through town until he arrived early, and then he found a nice, shady, out-of-the-way spot to wait.

It did not take long for the four mages to arrive, chatting happily with one another and their pockets jingling with each step. No pickpocket would be stupid enough to target a mage, as the four clearly were, so their coin was safe. Of course, he would have thought a common mason or carpenter would be smarter than to try to ambush them, so he supposed there was no accounting for the bad decisions of stupid and desperate people.

Nym hopped off the barrel he'd been sitting on next to a water trough meant for horses and approached the group of mages. The bearded one spotted him and said, "Oho! There he is. Come, my young friend, tonight you dine in style."

The inside of the restaurant was every bit as impressive as its exterior. There were three different bars set up around the walls and two doors leading back to the kitchen. At least twenty girls ran in and out, delivering food to the dozens of tables and booths scattered around the floor. A young man waited at a desk near the door, and when he saw them, he said, "Your usual table?"

"Plus one more. We've got a guest with us tonight," the bearded mage said.

"Very good. Would you like me to show you to the table?"

"Nah. We remember where it is. Thanks though."

The mage led the group to a table in the middle, one of six tables Nym counted that were empty. Apparently, it really was a standing appointment because none of the staff so much as blinked at them seating themselves. Once they had all taken their places, the bearded mage said, "Alright, introductions are in order. Everyone, this young man is Ermy. Going around the table, I'm Bildar, this is my sister Ophelia, and the twins over here are Nomick and Monick."

"Don't worry if you can't tell us apart," one of the twins told him. "No one else can either."

"Maybe if you'd stop dressing and acting the exact same," Ophelia said.

"But that's what makes it fun!" the other twin protested.

Once Bildar mentioned it, Nym could see the family resemblance to Ophelia. Their hair was the same color. They shared the same wide nose, and if Bildar's face was obscured by his thick beard, Nym could still see the same lip structure. Ophelia was about half a foot shorter than Bildar, but she was just as solid looking.

The twins, on the other hand, looked nothing like their boss. Their skin was darker, so dark actually that Nym didn't think he'd ever seen anyone quite that color. They had black hair that they'd each pulled back into a bun using some sort of elaborate knot and a simple leather tie. Each had fine facial features with pronounced cheekbones and was clean-shaven, and as Ophelia had said, they were dressed in the exact same outfit.

"I told them what you told me," Bildar said to Nym. "Awfully decent thing to do, giving us a warning like that."

Ophelia scowled. "Damn contractors guild has been glaring at us all month. Are you surprised one of them finally found the balls to take a swing at us?"

"Not really," Bildar said mildly. "It'll end badly for them, and there will be guards and paperwork, and it'll be a giant headache. It would be much easier if it just didn't happen."

"We all knew it was a matter of time," one of the twins said. Nym thought it was Monick.

"There's a reason we don't work town jobs, boss," the other added.

"I know! But what was I supposed to do?" Bildar turned to Nym and explained, "Normally we do big, big, big projects. Think new castles and fortresses. We were supposed to start on the new keep for the border crossing into Nordram, but a whole bunch of resources got diverted out west. I guess it's getting bad over there. Some big damn disaster, so the project is on indefinite hold, and I didn't line us up anything else to get through the rest of the year because why would I when we already had work?"

"I heard there were a bunch of undead that popped up out of nowhere, and the king's army is calling for all the help they can get keeping it under control," Nomick said.

"Where'd you hear something like that?" Ophelia scoffed.

"Just something I heard," Nomick muttered.

"How drunk were you at the time?"

"Enough," Bildar cut in. "It doesn't matter why. The fact of the matter is we're here trying to make the best of it, and if that means stepping on some locals' toes, so be it. Now, Ermy, I invited you here for two reasons. One, I want to thank you for the tip.

"Two, you know some runes, so I'm guessing you know some magic. And you're a bit on the young side for second-circle spells, but that just means you must be smart as well as bold. Now, I'm guessing you're about thirteen, give or take a year."

"Around that, sir," Nym said. He wasn't, but it seemed like every time someone guessed his age, the number went up, and he didn't think it was a good idea to explain.

"Right, so like I said, that's a bit on the young side for second-circle spells, but you can do them?"

"Yes," Nym admitted.

"What are you thinking, Bildar?" Ophelia asked.

"Well don't interrupt me and you'll find out! Now . . . where was I? Oh, right! So since you seem to be a smart fellow with a good head on your shoulders and a strong moral compass, I thought I'd see if you wanted to make a bit of coin for as long as we're here in Thrakus."

Nym had almost forgotten what it was like to be in demand. No one needed a little kid to do magic in Abilanth, but other towns and cities valued mages highly enough to overlook his age. "I'm afraid I'm not very good at earth magic," he said.

"The basic stuff is not terribly difficult, but it is terribly useful. Good field to invest some time and effort into," Bildar told him.

They hashed out the details, taking a break first to order food, and then again once it came to the table. The waiter didn't look surprised to see them other than a briefly raised eyebrow at Nym having joined them. The food was delivered quickly, and Nym had to admit that it would have been right at home in the dining room table of the Feldstal's manor. That meant it was undoubtably expensive, and Nym was glad he wasn't paying for it.

They stayed after dinner, drinking both ale and wine. Ophelia refused to touch the wine, which got her some teasing from the twins, but not as much as Bildar, who refused to drink anything but wine. Both of the twins would drink whatever was placed in front of them, which included a few shots of something they called elderfury, and which had such a strong smell that it made Nym's eyes water.

"Ermy," Bildar said, his face flushed and his words slurred, "the thing you gotta know about earth magic is that you have to plan it all out in advance. You can't fix it halfway through. It's got to be solid. It's like putting together one of those puzzle boxes. But it's worse because you have to figure out the dimensions yourself."

"Quit filling the boy's head with lessons," Ophelia scolded her brother. "It's not even his first day yet."

Nym, who'd also been served a few cups of wine and whose nose was just about as red as Bildar's, said, "No, it's fine. I like learning about magic. And this is so different from air magic."

"You can do air magic?" Bildar asked.

"Yes?" Nym asked back. He was pretty sure he could at least. Maybe not right now.

"That's great! I could never get the hang of it. It always felt like the arcana just wanted to float away when I needed it to stay put and do some work."

"You have to want to go with it," Nym confided, leaning over so far to whisper that he almost fell out of his chair. "You start at the bottom and keep working your way up as it goes. The timing is tricky sometimes. But it always made sense to me."

"That's no way to cast a spell!"

"It's okay. Maybe you're just not cut out for air magic. You're doing just fine with earth magic though."

"Ha! We'll see how cocky you are tomorrow. There's no floating away when you're working on earth spells!"

Meanwhile, on the other side of the table, Ophelia was arguing with the twins. "I'm telling you, there's no damn undead plague!"

"Why can't there be?" one of them shot back.

"You don't think we'd all know about it if there was one?"

"Maybe they're keeping it secret."

Ophelia snorted in derision. "Yeah, it's so secret you only found out because of your shadowy connections at a local tavern a thousand miles away."

"You just don't want to admit that I know something that you didn't!"

"You just don't want to admit that you're an idiot!"

Nym looked over at Bildar. "Should you break that up or something?"

He shrugged and took another drink.

There was a resounding whack as Ophelia decked someone who Nym decided was probably Nomick. "Okay, I think that's enough for the night," she declared. "Let's get your dumb asses home so I can sleep through tomorrow's hangover."

It was a bit of work to get everyone vertical, but they managed it. In some cases, that was only because they could lean against one another, but the important part was that everyone was on their feet. The table was covered in empty and overturned flagons, cups, and bottles, and Bildar carefully set a stack of six shields in the middle. Then they staggered out into the night air, all more or less walking in the same direction at the same speed.

Two minutes later, a group of seven men all holding hammers and clubs stomped out of an alley they'd just walked past and closed in on the group of earth mages. "Oh, right," Bildar said. "I forgot about this part."

A wall of dirt four feet high shot up so quickly that the leading ambushers bounced off it. "Now just watch, Ermy, and I'll show you why earth is better than air."

The ambushers had climbed over or circled around the wall and closed in on the drunk mages. There was no talking, or boasting, or posturing. They came at the mages with hard looks in their eyes and violence in their hearts. Each one was wearing a scarf or mask, or even just had shirts pulled up to cover the bottom half of their faces.

As one, they fell on the mages and attacked.

CHAPTER 66

Apparently, in Thrakus they called the local guard constables. Nym had no clue why. Everywhere else he'd been, the guard was just the guard. Also, apparently in Thrakus the constables were quite annoyed with the group for beating up a bunch of men, even if those men had been the ones to start it.

Even so drunk they could barely stand, it was no contest. The ground just opened up around the thugs, swallowing them whole and then closing again. Six of them were buried up to their necks in the first few seconds of their attempted ambush. The other one did manage to jump away in time to avoid being captured by that spell, but as soon as he landed, he fell victim to the same fate. The only difference was that it was Ophelia's spell that caught them instead of Bildar's.

And then the guards, er, constables got involved, and the whole group had to produce licenses, which Nym of course didn't have, but Bildar assured them that the magic all came from the adults anyway, so it wasn't relevant. That also annoyed the constables, who were already annoyed at being forced to deal with the whole situation, and who were especially annoyed at how drunk all the mages were.

"Can you at least get them out of the ground?" the exasperated constable asked.

Bildar stared at the man dumbly. "Maybe," he said. "Not sure if I could do it without hurting them."

"And once again God teabags my beer," the constable muttered. "Fine, we'll dig them out ourselves. You will be fined two shields per man."

"That's outrageous!" Bildar shouted. "Why should I pay sixteen, wait . . . six, seven, no, fourteen shields just because they attacked us and we defended ourselves?"

"I'm not fining you for defending yourselves. I'm fining you because you made a public nuisance of yourselves. Now if you can get them out and fix the road, you won't have to pay."

While Bildar argued with the constable, Ophelia put a hand on Nym's shoulder. "Do you think you can make it back home on your own, or should one of us go with you?"

Nym considered. It was late in the evening but not truly dark yet. There hadn't been any troubling incidents other than the failed ambush just now, and that wasn't even aimed at him. And the perpetrators were idiots who'd openly discussed their plans not fifty feet away from their would-be victims in the middle of a crowd.

"I'll be fine. It's only a twenty-minute walk," he said seriously.

"You be careful then. I'll expect you to meet us at the Boot and Strap by noon tomorrow, if you're serious about this."

Nym had only a vague idea where the inn they were staying at even was, but he was sure he could find it, especially with that much time. "I will be there," he promised.

"Good. See that you are. Now get out of here while we deal with this mess."

Nym had arcana poisoning again, but only in his head. He wasn't sure how he'd gotten it, since he didn't remember doing any magic at all, but it hurt so bad that the sunlight streaming into his room stabbed clear through to the back of his eyeballs. With a groan, he rolled over and pulled the blanket over his face.

Suddenly he sat up. The sun was already up, and he was still in bed! He had no idea what time it was or how long he had to find the Boot and Strap. He thought his arcana poisoning was getting better, hoped it was at least, because he was going to have to do magic today. Now everything was ruined.

He scrambled out of bed and ran downstairs, where one of the innkeeper's kids was wiping down some tables. A nearby table had a wooden tub piled high with dishes. Nym breathed out a sigh of relief at the sight of it because it meant they were just now cleaning up from breakfast. He still had an hour or two.

"Sorry, Ermy," the boy said. "You missed breakfast."

"That's okay. I'm just relieved that I only missed it by a bit. I have to meet some people today at noon, and I thought I was late."

"Your friend that you're waiting for is finally coming?" the boy asked.

"No, different people. I should get going though. Hey, do you know where the Boot and Strap is? I'm supposed to meet them there."

"Sure, I know where all the competition is."

Nym got his directions, thanked the boy again, and rushed out the door. He navigated his way through the streets of Thrakus, head throbbing in pain the whole way, and entered the Boot and Strap, only to find it empty. "Oh no, I'm too late after all," he moaned quietly.

"Wass'at?" a voice asked from behind him, causing Nym to jump and spin around.

An old man, all leathery faced and covered in liver spots, sat in the back corner, nursing a tall wooden mug with dried foam down the side. His hands shook, but that didn't stop him from cradling the mug close to his chest. There was perhaps more hair on his eyebrows than there was on his head, and either way, the amount on his ears took third place.

"I said, 'wass'at?' Speak up!"

"I . . . I'm sorry. I was just supposed to meet some friends here, but I think I missed them."

"You the magic boy? Here for the builder mages?"

"I guess so?"

The old man nodded to himself and took a long pull from his mug. When he set it back down on the table, beer slopped out of the top and splashed across the wood. "Right, the girlie one had a message. What was it now. What was it. Let me think. Something about fighting with the constabulary, and half of them spending the night in the drunk tank. And that she wasn't going to be here today, to try back tomorrow."

On the one hand, it was a relief. He wasn't late, he hadn't missed them, and he could go back to his own inn and go back to bed. On the other hand, it was kind of annoying, and he wasn't sure he wanted to be working with the crew of earth mages if they were going to get so obliterated that they ended up arrested on his first night of meeting them. It was not the best first impression.

"Okay," he said with a sigh. "I'll try again tomorrow I guess. Thank you for telling me."

He made his way back to his own room, stopping only to get something to drink, and then gratefully crawled back into bed for another four hours. Everything would be better when he woke back up, he hoped.

The next day found him feeling much better. He felt so good, in fact, that he thought he could start casting spells again. He tried a few small first-circle spells in his room, just to make sure there were no residual problems, but it seemed like more than a week of using no magic at all was what he really needed to finally recover from the massive arcana injection he'd been hit with.

Nym caught breakfast this time, and with plenty of time to spare. He vaguely remembered some of what Bildar had told him about the correct mindset for using elemental earth magic, and how everything had to be planned out in advance and slotted together to fit perfectly, with no room for errors or imperfections. With nothing else to do while he waited, he decided to give that a try.

Nym found an out-of-the-way spot where no one would bother him and tried to think about the deliberate placement of each piece of arcana needed for a simple earth construct he'd seen over and over in the books he'd read. If it worked correctly, nearby dirt would collect into a hard-packed sphere of earth.

It was not a complicated spell, but halfway through he realized he hadn't left himself enough space to put the arcana into the center of the construct after he built the framework. He let the spell fizzle out and started over again. Next time, he left the space, but because he left so much space, the framework didn't connect together properly.

The third try saw all the pieces in there, probably correct, but when he went to actually activate the arcana construct, one half twisted to the right while the other twisted to the left, and the whole thing tore itself apart instead of doing anything useful. That caused a small explosion of arcana that thankfully was undetectable by nonmages, or probably any actual mages either, now that he thought about it.

The sun rose toward noon, and Nym gave up practicing. He was sure that it would come under the tutelage of four skilled earth mages, assuming they hadn't gotten arrested again. He was happily surprised to find the whole crew sitting at a table at the Boot and Strap when he arrived, looking none the worse for wear, though Bildar was decidedly grouchy and was stabbing at his lunch like it had personally offended him.

"So things did not go well with the constabulary?" he asked after they'd exchanged greetings.

"Cost us three crests, all said and done," Ophelia explained. "Bildar is not happy about it."

"Those bastards at the contractors guild aren't any better off, at least," the bearded mage said. "Half their crew is still in lockup. Soon as we're done eating, we'll be off on the next job. Sorry, Ermy, but I don't think I have time to teach you with this setback, plus I was going to have you working under my license, but you can only do that officially if you're my apprentice. Nobody would have looked at it too closely last week, but with this whole thing with the contractors guild escalating, they'll be looking for a way to hit us. We would have to make it official and register the paperwork with the mage guild in order to hire you unless you can get your own license."

Nym was considering taking the licensing exam anyway. He had the money for it finally, and even if he didn't pass, it would at least let him know which areas he was deficient in. Unfortunately, he wasn't sure if it was safe to even walk into the mage guildhall. Analia's message had indicated that he shouldn't use the teleportation platforms in Abilanth, and Thrakus might not be any better.

He also imagined that even if he could pass it, he would need to supply his name at least so they knew whom to issue the license to. The Thrakus guildhall might not know who he was, but he assumed there were people somewhere in their system who would check his name against a list of wanted criminals. He could just take his assumed identify even further, he supposed, and become Ermy in truth.

The more he thought about it, the more he liked that idea. The whole personage of Nym needed to disappear for a while, at least until he knew exactly where he stood with the government and its law enforcement. Part of plan D assumed he and Analia would be fleeing across the border if necessary, but Thrakus was the meeting point if they got separated leaving Abilanth. The escape attempt had gone just about as wrong as was possible, so leaving the kingdom was the next logical step.

In the meantime though, it might be time for Ermy to figure out what exactly he still needed to learn to pass a licensing exam. By good fortune, there were four earth mages seated at the table with him who all happened to have licenses and were predisposed to helping him. It would just be foolish to ignore that opportunity for information.

"What exactly do you have to be able to do in order to get a license?" Nym asked.

CHAPTER 67

The twins took the lead on the conversation, as they were the youngest and had most recently obtained their licenses. That was still six years ago, but Bildar had been a licensed mage for two decades and Ophelia for almost as long. Both of them readily admitted that they barely remembered their own exams and had no idea if they could even pass a current-day one.

"So there's the written exam," Monick said. "And it's not all magic stuff. There's a lot of stuff about knowing the law, what kind of spells are allowed, which are restricted, what you need special permits for, the punishments for breaking the law, and so on. For example, pretty much nobody wants necromancers around. There are very few good reasons for it, and it's ripe for abuse."

"And it's icky," Nomick added.

"That too. But also, did you know that the whole region around Vharn outright bans fire magic? Sure, it's plenty useful, but they grow a lot of food, and if a wildfire got out of control, it could starve the entire kingdom. So even if you have a license, you're not allowed to use fire magic anywhere within a hundred miles of Vharn."

"What about after the harvest?" Nym asked.

Monick shrugged. "For the purposes of the licensing exam, no fire in Vharn. If you ever visit the place, maybe find out about the local customs."

"So that's one part of the written exam. Then there's a lot of questions about the proper and safe ways to conduct spells, lab safety, research ethics," Nomick started counting off topics on his fingers. "Really, the whole thing focuses on the responsible use of magic. It's just asking you to show that you know how to use magic without endangering other people."

Monick picked up the explanation. "Then there's the practicals. Demonstrate that you can control whatever your elemental affinity is, that you have mastery and precision. They'll have you perform a few dozen spells in various disciplines to show that you know what you're doing and can be trusted to work independently in fields that require those kinds of magic. Every category you can pass will get you an endorsement on your license."

"We have endorsements for earth magic, obviously. Monick and I also have a spatial endorsement showing we've proven we have a mastery of the basics of spatial magic. I, additionally, have an endorsement for alchemy that Monick doesn't have."

"Only because you took the test first! By the time you were done, the proctor was so sick of you that she went extra hard on me."

Bildar told Nym, "I also have an alchemy endorsement on my license. Unlike the basic license, those have to be renewed if you want to keep them. I'm actually due to renew mine next year."

Nym took a few minutes to process that while the group finished up their meal. Finally, he said, "I can't pass the written. I could do the practical for at least two elemental types, maybe three. Depending on which spells they asked me to do, I might be able to pass the practical. I don't think I could get any endorsements."

"There's nothing wrong with that," Ophelia told him. "Most mages are just starting their training at your age. But unfortunately, none of us have the time or spare funds right now to take on an apprentice. The busy season is just starting up for us, and we're going to be scrambling all year to find replacement jobs for the big one that got canceled."

The short version of it then was that there was no money at the table for Nym. Once he stopped to consider it, he was fine with that. He still had a sizable amount left over from his raid on Valgo's treasury, even after he'd given more than half of it away to the orphans he'd been living with. More than that, Thrakus wasn't a long-term home for him. He was just waiting for Analia to show up, which if things went as scheduled would be in the next few days. It was for the best that he not be tied down with the group of earth mages long-term.

"Can I tag along anyway just to watch? Maybe I'll learn something from observation."

"It's mighty boring to watch after the novelty wears off," Bildar said, "But sure, if you want. As long as you can stay out of the way when we start moving stuff and don't get me too distracted with questions."

"That's good enough for me," Nym said seriously. "In the meantime, maybe I can do some studying to pass the written licensing exam and find some spell books that cover the kind of magic I need to be able to showcase to get licensed."

"You'll have a good start if you can," Nomick said. "The Academy is expensive, and the more of it you can teach yourself before you go there to get shined up, the easier it'll be."

"Aren't there any mages who don't graduate from the Academy?" Nym asked. He already knew he wasn't ever going to attend.

"Sure, but they're mostly the kids of rich merchants or nobles who are getting a better private education. You don't strike me as a noble's son, so you're probably better off going to the Academy."

"Even if it is so cold that certain sensitive parts of your anatomy could fall off," Bildar muttered.

"At least your nickname wasn't Jewel Thief at school," Ophelia added.

The twins burst into laughter, only to fall silent when Ophelia turned her glare on them. "And if you ever call me that, I will rip your spleens out through your assholes," she warned them. "Both of you, no matter who says it, just to be sure I've punished the correct person."

Their side of the table devolved into good-natured bickering while Bildar told Nym, "We've got a job on the other side of the city in an hour. You can come along, but you can't do any magic under my license. I'd like to say I'll answer all your questions, but the fact of the matter is that it's busy work, and I can't promise I'll have time. Just observing isn't going to help much, but I won't stop you if that's how you want to spend your time."

"That's okay. I'm sure I'll learn plenty," Nym said. It wouldn't be as good as having it explained to him, but Nym could pick up plenty of tricks just spending some time watching them cast spells, especially since by the very nature of their work, they would be casting the same spells repeatedly for a few hours.

"Erm, I should have asked this before, but your parents are fine with this?" Bildar said.

"Oh . . . that. I don't have parents."

The table went silent. Nym looked around, noted various degrees of pity on their faces, and shook his head. "It's fine. I never had any, as far as I can remember. Sometimes I get some help from nice people; usually I do stuff on my own. I'm not dead yet, so I think I do alright."

"That's incredibly depressing," the twins said in unison.

"A little bit, yes," Ophelia agreed.

"Never would have guessed though. You must be doing something right."

The others turned to look at Bildar. "What?" he said. "He is! Look at him!"

"My brother is an idiot, Ermy. Please ignore him," Ophelia said.

"It's . . . fine?"

"Right, well, anyway, I guess let's finish this up so we can get on-site and do our jobs today."

Nym passed the afternoon off in a corner of the construction site, watching the earth-mage crew cast the same seven or eight spells repeatedly. The twins used a few earth-shaping spells to excavate the foundation, separate it into composite types, and finally to relocate it to Bildar. His spells were the most complicated as he had to tailor them specifically for each type of dirt he used as well as measuring out certain ratios.

Nym felt he learned the least from Bildar. He observed a lot of spell constructs, but they were all highly specialized depending on which materials he was working with, and Nym lacked the knowledge to figure that out. The twins had perhaps the most labor-intensive job, but also the one that Nym thought he could copy the most easily.

Ophelia was surprisingly the one who was willing to entertain questions while she worked, provided they stayed on topic. It actually got to the point where it became more of a live demonstration as she explained the rune sequences she was building and the logic behind how they were structured. Nym came away with a far more nuanced understanding of runes than he'd had before, albeit in a very narrow slice of the field. Still, the lecture gave him some ideas for practical applications on the few other runes he already knew.

While they worked, a crowd gathered to watch. The citizens that made up the crowd changed regularly as people got bored and left, while new people drifted in. The only constants were a few of the constables keeping things relatively orderly and holding the crowd back from wandering into the construction site, and a few extremely angry-looking men. Nym recognized one of them as the contractor from the other day who'd tried to talk down his guildmates.

"The competition is back to glare at you again," he said to Bildar softly.

"Yeah, I saw them come in an hour or so ago. It's fine. They got fined even more heavily than we did for 'disturbing the peace' the other night, and the ones that attacked us are still in jail. They won't try anything again."

True to Bildar's predictions, the group left without anything happening. The four earth mages went to the Quarterhouse, but Nym had something else to take care of. Part of the plan with Analia if they got separated involved meeting in Thrakus at a particular inn in a very expensive district of the city. It was, not surprisingly, on the opposite side as the stockyards. Nym had scouted it out when he'd first arrived and located his target, a massive palatial place called the Silk Box. He'd held off on scrying it until he'd felt better, but giving it a once-over needed to become part of his daily routine.

Nym found himself a nice alleyway nearby where he thought he was unlikely to be noticed and cast a scrying spell. He swept over the building as quickly as he could, but it was four stories tall and rented out whole suites as opposed to individual rooms. It took him a little time, and there was no sign of Analia.

That was slightly disappointing, but if he took her message literally, it would still be a few days until she arrived. If she was delayed for any reason, it could be another week or two of waiting. That honestly wouldn't be terrible, as Thrakus was considerably warmer than Abilanth, and he was much more comfortable now that he was flush with cash.

He also liked the earth mages and was looking forward to learning more from them. While they were having dinner, Nym finished up his chore and headed out of the city. Exactly how far he needed to go was a bit hazy as, unlike Zoskan or Abilanth, there was no wall, but eventually he figured he was far enough away that nobody would complain, and even if something went wrong, he couldn't hurt anyone.

Then he started practicing some of the spells he'd seen. Ripping up chunks of dirt was easy enough, though his came out looking like a giant hand had sunk its fingers into the dirt and tore out whatever it could reach. Transmuting the dirt to anything was completely off the table as he had no idea what he was looking at. Even though he replicated the sorting spell the twins were using, he couldn't tell much of a difference between the three piles the dirt pulled itself into. It all just looked like dirt to him.

He could still compact them into blocks though and stack them up, which allowed him to practice the basic runes Ophelia had taught him. That took nearly two hours before he managed to get it right, and even then it was only enough to anchor two blocks together. If he did three, the whole thing fell apart, and he couldn't quite figure out why.

Satisfied with his progress for the day, Nym returned to the Lucky Barrel to get a good night's sleep and continue in the morning. Therefore, he was quite surprised to walk into the common room and find Ophelia sitting there.

CHAPTER 68

Nym approached the table Ophelia had claimed cautiously. He couldn't remember if he'd ever told them where he was staying, and the whole crew liked to drink after they finished a project, so he wasn't sure how sober she would be. This conversation probably wasn't going to be fun.

"Ermy," Ophelia called out, having noticed him noticing her. "Come, sit, talk to me."

Nym slid into the seat opposite the earth mage. "Is something wrong?" he asked.

"Wrong? No, why would there be something wrong?"

"Because you're here? You went out of your way to come talk to me instead of waiting until tomorrow?"

"Oh, I see. No, no, nothing is wrong. I just wanted to talk to you about something."

"Is it about my lack of parents?"

"No! Well, kind of. But not really. Bildar was right when he said we're too busy to take on apprentices right now, but you really seemed to get runes, you know? Some of the stuff we touched on in an afternoon took me weeks to wrap my brain around."

"Speaking of that," Nym said, "Why can't I get more than two blocks to stick together? Every time I try to add a third one, the whole sequence falls apart."

"Huh? You're already writing them out? And empowering them? Where are you getting the blocks from?"

Too late, Nym realized that he wasn't supposed to know how to do the spells the crew had been casting. He was only supposed to be able to see the results, not the actual constructs. "I kind of brute forced some dirt into shape with raw terrakinesis," he lied. "But I made sure to get the size right so they'd all line up nicely."

"That's probably your problem right there. Too many different types of dirt and the rune sequence I showed you is designed to work with refined blocks. That's why Bildar has to transmute them out of raw materials first."

"Of course that's why. I'm such an idiot," Nym said. "That's so obvious."

Ophelia laughed. "You might just be a magical genius if you made it that far in one day. Which brings me back around to my point. How much do you know about the Academy?"

"Some, but not much. I know it's really, really, really expensive."

"Too damn right it is. Not every mage goes to the Academy, and not every mage who gets a license manages to graduate first. We generally call dropouts who learn enough to get a license but can't manage any endorsements magisters, and they are . . . not well paid. It's much better to find a specialty that interests you and get an endorsement for it. That's where the money is. If you can manage two or three subjects that synergize well, even better."

"Why are you telling me this?" Nym asked.

"Because I was impressed with you today, and I noticed when we talked about your future as a mage, you didn't seem too keen on the idea of going to the Academy. I don't blame you. It is, as you said, really, really, really expensive. I won't pry into your financial situation, but a kid your age making it on your own? That's impressive enough. It would be more surprising if going to the Academy was in your reach."

"Rub it in why don't you?"

Ophelia rolled her eyes. "You know what I mean. Anyway, to bring a long-winded explanation to a close, how would you feel about doing an apprenticeship with me in about six months? We're coming into the busy season now, but once it starts getting cold again next year, I would have the time to teach you properly. I'm not the richest person in the world, so don't expect me to have a full library of books for you or anything, but I could teach you to be a master earth mage."

Nym just kind of sat there, mouth agape, and considered the possibilities. He'd be able to learn magic from an expert. When he had questions, he could just ask instead of scrounging around, trying to find a book that discussed the topic or doing meticulous trial-and-error experiments until he found something that worked.

Then his mind turned from opportunities to costs. Apprentices didn't just live on their master's good graces. He would have to work for Ophelia so she could recoup the financial burden he'd place on her. He'd be tied to her for perhaps years, and he'd just met her a few days ago. She didn't even know his real name! Plus, he was a criminal in Abilanth and Palmara, possibly Zoskan too.

He wasn't even sure he could use a teleportation platform without getting arrested. That would be a fun conversation to have with his new master when he was in a mage cell having to explain to her that he'd murdered twenty or so people. No, the idea didn't float. No matter which way he looked at it, all he saw were problems.

"Can I think about it for a bit?" Nym asked, even though he already knew his answer.

"Of course," she told him. "Like I said, we're going into our busy season, so this is something in the future. Take as much time as you need."

"Thank you," he said quietly. "I'll see you all tomorrow?"

"Yes. Come on by. We'll see you at noon."

Nym waved goodbye and walked up to his room. He tried to ignore the earth mage staring at the back of his head, and the puzzled look he could see on her face with his scrying spell. He went upstairs and locked his door, then lay face down on his bed and tried not to be overwhelmed by how much his life had spiraled out of control.

The next day, Nym made his way across Thrakus to scry the Silk Box for any signs of Analia. That failed to yield results again, but he wasn't about to give up yet. He wandered the city for a little while and then, when it got close to noon, went to meet the earth-mage crew, albeit with considerably more trepidation than usual.

But nobody said anything or treated him differently. He wasn't sure if that was because it wasn't as much of a big deal as he'd turned it into in his head or if Ophelia hadn't told anybody. They finished up their meal and went to the new jobsite.

Nym spent most of the afternoon with the twins as they explained the difference between soil types and how to recognize them, then advised that separating them out with magic was mostly an application of the same spell cast with different intent filters on their conduits. At one point, one of them even took the time to draw a diagram in the dirt showing the construct they were using. Nym dutifully studied it, even though he'd seen it being built in three dimensions in real time.

"Now don't go casting that here," Monick said. "You're not licensed, but if you wanted to get some practice in outside the city's boundaries, this is a good place to start."

"Right, of course!"

Monick winked at him and then slapped his brother on the back. "Come on now, my half of this foundation is at least a foot deeper than yours. What's the holdup?"

"Well mine's mostly clay, now isn't it!" Nomick said. "Plus all these damn rocks I keep running into."

"Excuses," his brother said with a sniff. "Just put that fancy alchemy endorsement you're so proud of to work."

Nomick sputtered something unintelligible and chucked a chunk of dirt at Monick's face. Nym stifled a laugh and scrambled out of the pit the twins were digging before he got caught in the inevitable cross fire. Bildar looked over at him when he popped up, then raised an eyebrow and peered over the lip of the pit.

"Of course they are," he muttered. "Come on over, I wanted a chance to talk to you anyway."

"About what?" he asked.

"I just wanted to apologize for my sister," Bildar told him. "We talked about offering you an apprenticeship, but we agreed not to spring it on you right away. I don't want you to think you're not welcome here. The whole crew likes having you around. You're smart as a whip and as helpful as we could ask for. Ophelia didn't mean anything by it, and we're not going to kick you to the curb if you don't want to apprentice with us. It's fine to say no."

What hurt was that it wasn't that he was even all that opposed to the idea. It was nothing like the contract Bardin had tried to get him to sign back in Abilanth. In a lot of ways, it would be nice to have a master who could solve problems for him. He was in a good position today, but the money wouldn't last forever. Being a legitimate, trained mage would solve that problem before it even became a problem. It just wasn't feasible.

Nym sighed and said, "Can I be honest with you?"

"Always," Bildar told him.

"I don't have parents. I've been taking care of myself. And sometimes that means doing things that are not exactly legal. What I mean to say is, the offer sounds wonderful, and I would love to explore it, but Ermy isn't even my real name, you know?"

Bildar stopped working and turned to face him. "Son, we've all done things we've regretted after. That's the thing about growing up. You can do whatever you want, but you have to deal with the consequences. You're young, and you probably grew up too fast, but you've still got a lot of years left ahead of you. Don't plan the rest of your life around the idea of running away forever."

"But they'll throw me in a mage cell if they catch me."

"I doubt that. Those things are damned expensive to keep running, if nothing else. But what could you have possibly done that's so bad as all of that? Did you try to assassinate King Maleotrak?"

"No."

"Get caught in bed with his daughter?"

"No!"

"I'd say you're probably fine. They're not going to lock you away for the rest of your life for stealing a bit to feed yourself. And even if they would, you just give it a few years, and they won't even recognize you. You can be Ermy for the rest of your life if that's what you want."

"Well, maybe not Ermy," Nym said. "He doesn't deserve me stealing his name from him."

"Whatever name you pick then," Bildar laughed. "What I'm trying to tell you is you don't have to go through the rest of your life alone, always looking over your shoulder, always afraid. It's not a good way to live. Find some friends, make a new family. It doesn't have to be us, but we're happy to help you along the way."

"Oy! You're falling behind again, old man!" Nomick shouted up from the pit.

"Go back to slinging mud at each other, you idiots! We're having a moment up here!"

A mud pie came flying out of the pit and splattered against the side of Bildar's head. The bearded mage took a deep breath and wiped it away. Then he took another breath. Then a third. "Right, that's it then."

The whole pile of loose dirt the twins had been building up while Nym and Bildar talked rose into the air and hurtled itself into the pit. There was a pair of startled yelps followed by an extremely loud thump. Nym looked over to the edge to see both of them buried in dirt, with random limbs sticking out from various points.

"Might be the saner option to keep looking elsewhere for family," Bildar told Nym. "But I bet it won't be quite as much fun if you do."

CHAPTER 69

ice," Nym said.

Bildar looked up from where he was cleaning dirt out of his ear. "Sorry, what was that?"

"Nothing. Just felt like the right thing to say in the moment."

"Ugh, why do they always use wet, sloppy mud?" Bildar complained. "Well this isn't coming out easily."

He cast a quick spell, and all the dirt sloughed off him but left the water behind. When the earth mage didn't make a move to dry himself back out, Nym cast a small hydrokinesis spell and flicked the water away. Bildar smirked and shook his head. "Casting without a license," he said, clicking his tongue. "God bless you for that, young sir."

"I think I'm going to take off early today," Nym told him. "I . . . I've got a lot to think about."

"You do that. Keep your practicing outside of the city too. We'll see you tomorrow?"

Nym didn't hesitate. "Definitely."

"Good. Go on then. See you tomorrow."

Nym waved goodbye to Ophelia and the twins, then set out through the city. He did another lap past the Silk Box—still nothing—and headed out of town. Thrakus was significantly warmer than Abilanth, but it was still the end of winter. Things were just starting to thaw, and he didn't want to stay out quite so long this time.

Instead of practicing the spells he'd seen the earth-mage crew use, Nym decided to try using his newfound understanding of elemental earth intent and construct building to repurpose another spell. He started with the basic framework for an ice golem, but altered to be solid, full of arcana flavored with unyielding strength.

The construct remained the same, except for the parts that targeted snow and ice as the base materials, but the order in which he constructed it was completely different. His experience from his attempts to fuse stone cores into the ice golems gave him a good starting point to expand on, and once he thought about it, he was pretty sure he could make that work now that he better understood elemental earth manipulation.

Nym expected he'd have it figured out in a few hours. That was usually all it took to experiment, refine, test, and settle on a finalized construct when he was working on a spell. It had taken days to learn the original spell with an instructor dedicating all her time to help him, but this was just a modification to use earth and stone instead of ice and snow. It should be easy.

Six hours later, he was forced to admit the truth. It wasn't easy, and none of his ideas worked.

He gave up for the day but was determined to figure it out. Maybe Bildar or Ophelia could point him in the right direction. Ice golems were useful in the winter, but it was fast turning into spring now, and if he wanted to get any further use out of all the work he'd put into learning how to cast the spell, he needed to figure out the modification.

He was trudging back through Thrakus, muttering to himself and counting out steps on his fingers as he mentally reconfigured how each piece of the pattern needed to be placed, when a hand settled on his shoulders. "Hey, aren't you that boy working for the Earth Shapers?"

Nym looked up and was surprised to find himself surrounded by three men. None of them looked familiar, but his first thought was that they were from the contractors guild and looking for trouble. Their guildmates getting tossed in the slammer apparently wasn't enough of a message.

"Leave me alone," he said, trying to jerk away from the man holding his shoulder. The man didn't let go though. In fact, he squeezed harder to prevent Nym from escaping.

"That's him. I recognize him from the crowd the other day."

"What do you think they'd pay to get him back?"

The other two men looked surprised. "Ransom him, you mean? Might as well. They're basically stealing the shims out of our pockets. As long as they don't know who we are, we can make it work."

"You're the leftover idiots from the contractors guild," Nym said. "Your whole ransom idea is stupid. I know who you are. I've seen your faces. Even if I hadn't, it's not like they don't know you guys hate them. You're the first people the constabulary will check."

"Er . . . kid's got a point, Tenny."

"Don't say my name, moron!"

"God give me patience," Nym muttered. He waited a beat. "No? No patience at all? Fine. I'll do it my way then."

"What are you mumbling about?" the man holding Nym asked.

Nym was not the same boy he'd been half a year ago when Senman tried to throw him off a cliff. He wasn't even the same boy he'd been a few months ago when those brothel recruiters had cornered him in an alley. He had options now. He could set the men on fire, or electrocute them, or just pick them up and drop them from fifty feet straight up. He could slice their skin open telekinetically, attack their minds and leave them dazed and drooling, or summon water to coat them, then freeze it solid. If he wanted to get creative, there were a few other options too.

In the interest of not being overtly obvious, Nym shaped little ridges in the road that cupped around the heel of each man's foot, then gave them a telekinetic shove. The two men opposite him tripped over immediately, while the one holding him staggered and clenched down on Nym's shoulder to keep his balance. Nym cast a quick, small slicing spell to slash across the hand squeezing him, and the man let go.

Nym walked away while the three men hurried to get back on their feet. By the time they chased after him, he had already disappeared into the crowd and sat on a nearby roof, watching them.

"Idiots," he said again.

"Who were they?" someone said.

Nym looked up to see a man leaning on the sill of a second-story window in the house next to the one he was sitting on. He seemed friendly enough, so Nym answered. "Just some guys who thought because they were bigger than me that they could do whatever they wanted. I'll let someone know, and it'll look bad on their whole guild. Maybe they'll get kicked out. Ha. That'd be funny."

"You going to tell them how you used magic too?" the man asked.

"Nah. No license. That'd just get me in trouble."

"You know you can use magic to defend yourself even if you don't have a license, right?"

"Really?" Nym asked. "No, I didn't know that. Still, no point in making things complicated. They tried to kidnap me, I got away. Wait, how'd you know I used magic?"

"You're sitting on my neighbor's roof, for one thing. For another, three adults against one kid usually ends in the three guys winning unless there's magic involved."

"Those are both good points. You're pretty smart."

"That's what they pay me for. My name is Constable Berndart. How'd you like to take a walk with me?"

Nym's face fell, and he started rapidly considering the merits of blasting Berndart with a daze spell and running off. The constable started laughing and said, "You're not in trouble, kid. I saw the whole thing. Come on, I'll take you to the station house to file a report, and we'll send a few guys around to pick them up. It won't take an hour of your time, and it'll get them off the street. Next time they might pick a kid who can't defend himself."

The constable's words made sense, but Nym was still wary about walking into a building full of people who might try to arrest him. "Can't you just make the report yourself? You saw everything."

"I can corroborate your story. But you're the one they tried to abduct, and they're already gone. Your descriptions will help us identify them and make sure we get the right people."

Nym considered his options. He could simply fly away and never look back. That would, once again, put him against the law, and he really didn't want to be dealing with that for the fourth time. He could play along and hope everything happened just like Berndart said it would. That would be the easiest thing to do, so long as there wasn't a wanted poster of him at the station that he would inconveniently stand next to for easy comparison.

"I'll meet you on the street," he said, hopping off the roof and floating down to the ground.

A minute later, the front door opened and Berndart walked out, his constable's hat on his head and his jacket in his hands. He led Nym a few streets over and about six blocks closer to the center of the city before they stopped at a wide, squat brick building. It was two stories too, but took up an entire block by itself, and something about the architecture just reminded him of a big, fat toad.

"What're you doing here, Berndart?" the constable at the desk asked when they walked in. "I thought you were off for the next two days."

"I was, but then some idiots decided to try kidnapping this boy right in front of my house."

They explained what had happened as best they could, with Nym reluctantly giving up the tale of his escape and his association with the earth mages that had led to him being targeted in the first place. When he was done, the constable on duty had him describe the three men, prompting Nym with a series of rapid-fire questions.

"The first one, anything to distinguish him? Scars? Missing any fingers? Notches in his ear, missing teeth? And the one who grabbed you, was it his left or right hand you cut? I see. I see."

The constable noted it all down and then called out another five men from a back room. "Go on down to the contractors guildhall and see if you can't find three men matching this description," he instructed. "They tried to abduct this kid off the street, and Constable Berndart here witnessed it happen."

"You got it, chief." The men saluted sharply and went off to make the arrests.

"See? Easy to do," Berndart said. "Now we can wait here together if you'd like, or if you want to tell me where you live, we can have someone come around to collect you once we've brought them in so you can identify them and make sure we got the right guys."

"Can I just come back in a few hours?" Nym asked.

"You could. Will you come back on your own?"

Nym's insides squirmed. He wasn't really planning to, didn't want to. But he wanted to stay on the good side of the law for once, so he nodded. "Yeah. I just want to go tell my friends what happened so they can watch out for anyone else trying to mess with them."

"Right, your friends the earth mages who are helping put up new buildings. What did you say they called their group again, the Earth Benders?"

"Earth Shapers," Nym corrected. It seemed like a boring name to him, but they'd collectively decided on it a few years ago, and that was what their business was officially called.

"Right, them. Actually, I'd kind of like to meet them myself. Do you mind if I go with you?"

"You do?" Nym asked, surprised. "Why?"

"Well they're involved in this whole mess too, aren't they? This only happened because they're poaching the contractors guild's business. I'm not saying they're in the wrong here, just that we need to get this whole thing settled before it escalates any further."

Nym squinted at the constable. "Isn't it your day off?"

Constable Berndart just rolled his eyes. "Come on, Ermy. Let's go talk to your friends and see if we can find some way to get this straightened out without it coming to blows in the streets."

CHAPTER 70

By the time they caught up with the earth-mage crew, they'd already finished the job and had gone to the Quarterhouse for dinner. When Nym and Berndart got there, they asked the host to fetch Bildar for them so as not to disturb everyone and make an unnecessary scene. The bearded earth mage came back a minute later, eyebrows raised when he saw Nym with a constable.

"What's going on? Are you in trouble?" he asked Nym.

"No, no, he's not in trouble," Berndart said. "I'm Constable Berndart. Your friend was almost kidnapped off the street by some members of the contractors guild who connected him to your group."

"*Almost* is a strong word," Nym protested. "I was not in any danger."

Bildar started swearing in some language Nym didn't recognize. "This goes too far," he said, "I understand their anger at the loss of business to us. The attack they made on us was not justified, but we are adults who can defend ourselves. To attack a boy just because he spent time in our company is wrong."

"I agree. I'd like to see this whole thing settled before it escalates further. Would you be willing to meet with the contractors guildmaster and try to find a peaceful solution here?"

Bildar bristled at the request. "Why should we have to do anything? They are the ones who are in the wrong. Should not the city be arresting the offending members and levying fines against the guild itself for allowing such behavior?"

"That's over my pay grade," the constable told him. He kept his voice measured and calm, trying to diffuse the riled-up mage. "Obviously we will be arresting the men directly involved in this incident, but that does not get at the heart of the matter. There is a feud between your group and the contractors guild, and as you are outside of the guild and poaching their business, they do have some legal standing to demand that you cease your operations."

Bildar opened his mouth, but before he could speak, Berndart cut him off.

"I am not saying they are right to do what they're doing in the eyes of the law, or that they'll get away with it. What I am saying is that it would be better for everyone if you agreed to meet with the guildmaster to find a way to settle this matter without it evolving into something that requires the constabulary to get involved."

Nym could practically see the march of different emotions crossing Bildar's face, outrage and indignation, followed by annoyance, begrudging acknowledgment, and finally concern. The earth mages were going to have to do more than just ignore the competition and hope that the city cracked down on them.

"I'm sorry we interrupted your meal," Nym said. "The constable saw the guys from the contractors guild make their move and got involved, and now he's just kind of dragging me around to help them with their stuff. We have to go back to the station so I can confirm the ones who get arrested are the right people."

"Which station?" Bildar asked.

"Station twelve," Berndart supplied.

"Give me five minutes to explain to my crew. I'll meet you there."

"That's not necessary right now," the constable told him. "I came along to make sure you were aware of what happened and keep an eye on Ermy, just in case anyone a bit smarter than those ruffians got it in their heads to try something."

"I understand. Regardless, I will meet you at the station shortly."

"Very well. We'll see you there."

"Why does everyone think they need to keep an eye on me?" Nym groused as he followed the constable back out to the street.

"I don't know. Do you get in trouble a lot?"

"No!"

"Is that really the truth?" the constable gave him a hard glare but broke down into a grin. "There are worse things in the world than having people care about you though. Okay, let's get the positive identification over with and get you back to your family. Or did you need to see someone from home first?"

"Don't have a family or a home," Nym said.

"Oh. I see."

"It's not a big deal. Don't get all weepy on me."

Berndart rolled his eyes. "I see a dozen kids like you every day. I'm just happy that for once you're not the one getting arrested. Try to keep it that way, huh? It looks like you've got some people who care about you. There's no need to get into trouble stealing."

"Did I do something to give you the impression that I'm a thief?" Nym asked.

"No, of course not. My apologies. That was wrong of me to assume."

Nym couldn't tell if the constable was mocking him or not. "Let's get this over with. I've got other stuff to take care of."

The constable nodded sagely. "Yes, of course. You've got a busy evening ahead of you, expensive fancy dinners, studying the secrets of the arcane worlds, not breaking into houses through unlocked second-story windows."

"I would never do that!" Nym said. It was even true. He had no intention of ever doing that again. Between the bookshop and the Feldstal manor, he'd had enough of being a sneak thief to last him his entire life. It was too easy with his magic, and he was bad at it to an embarrassing degree.

"You just make sure you get a license before you do any magic in the city. It might not be excused for self-defense next time."

"If only it were so easy," Nym muttered to himself.

"You got plenty of years left to get there. And no one is going to care if you decide to become a magister and live out in the middle of nowhere barely able to cast a second-circle spell."

Berndart was more than willing to banter with Nym the whole way back, though he suspected it was the constable trying to keep him distracted and in a good mood. It was probably part of his job to influence people he was responsible for and keep them amicable. Nym might have been more annoyed about it, except he expected to never see the man again after the whole thing was over and so far, it had been a relatively painless experience.

The walk through the station was easy enough, with Nym picking out the three men who'd tried to kidnap him from a group of six. It was over and done with before Bildar even got there. His sister walked into the station with him, and they immediately split up. Bildar went deeper in to set up his meeting with the contractors guildmaster, and Ophelia came over to Nym and Berndart.

"Hey, Ermy, you ready to get out of here?"

"Uh . . . Yes?"

"Great, Bildar will be back later. We decided you should probably stay with us until this whole thing gets resolved."

"No thanks," Nym said. "I've already got a room rented out for the rest of the week."

Ophelia frowned but nodded. "Fine. But consider relocating when the week ends?"

"Sure, I'll think about it," he promised. If Analia didn't show up before then, he didn't much care. The Lucky Barrel was fine, but he wasn't particularly attached to it. "How much does a room run at the Boot and Strap?"

"Two shields a week if you pay by the week," she said.

That wasn't terrible, but it was a bit more expensive than the Lucky Barrel. Nym supposed he could probably afford a single week there. At that point, he would be moving on from the city either way. Though things had gone well with his initial interactions with the constabulary, he didn't want to push his luck. He was still unsure about his position with the mage guild, but he was cautiously hopeful that he'd be able to use the teleportation platform without issues.

Ophelia must have read something on his face because she added, "I'm sure we can find some work for you to do for the crew even without a license to help cover the costs."

"Oh yeah? Like what?"

"You could inscribe runes for me. As long as I'm the one who's empowering them, you wouldn't need a license," she said. "I'll have to talk to Bildar. We're not really sure what the future is going to hold for us if this whole thing with the contractors guild doesn't go our way. We're thinking about heading west. I guess that undead outbreak rumor was real, and the army is digging in for a long campaign while they get to the bottom of it. They're going to need some forti-fications, so we should be able to find work there if we have to leave Thrakus."

Nym wondered about that. When he'd left Zoskan, it was just some loose seal that was spawning a lot of frost wraiths. Supposedly it would be patched up before it could become more of a problem. This wasn't the first time he'd heard about an undead problem to the west, but there was a lot of land west of Thrakus. It was probably just a coincidence and completely unrelated.

Then again, maybe it wasn't. If something had gone horribly wrong, he worried for Ciana. Palmara wasn't that far away from Zoskan and could be in trouble too. Perhaps in the near future, he would need to visit his adoptive sister. They could go see if his stalker shark was still patrolling the cove, waiting for him to come back.

It would have to be done delicately, with Nym staying well away from the village, but Ciana's shack was far enough away from Palmara that as long as he didn't go strolling through the village, he was confident he could fly past them with no one the wiser. He'd bring some money and food with him, maybe a new set of clothes. She'd like that.

He shook himself from his daydreams. He didn't even know if the Earth Shapers were going west to the battlefront, or if he'd be going with them if they did, or if the undead problems were in any way related to the incident he'd been involved with months ago. Then again, even if none of that was true, the only thing keeping him in Thrakus was waiting for Analia to arrive. If she never showed up, he could go in any direction he wanted, and Palmara was as good as anywhere else, so long as he was careful to stay away from anyone who'd recognize him.

"Ermy? What are you thinking?" Ophelia asked.

"Just considering what it would mean to go west again."

"Oh? You're not from Thrakus?"

"Not originally, no. I've wandered all over for as long as I can remember," he said. It wasn't really even a lie. He'd only spent a month or two in any single place since waking up on that beach. Abilanth had been the longest stretch at around three months.

"By yourself? That's awful. I hate traveling alone."

Nym shrugged. It was almost required in his case, since he did all his traveling by flying at this point. He could probably support one other person for short trips, but not over cross-country distances. He was hoping traveling with Analia would be easier than that since she could fly too.

Ophelia walked with him back to the Lucky Barrel, despite Nym's protests that he was fine. She refused to argue with him, just kept walking while ignoring him. Once they were there, she stayed to have a drink, told Nym she'd come pick him up tomorrow, and then left.

He rolled his eyes but smiled. It was touching how much they cared about him, despite only having known him for a few days. The Earth Shapers were good people who were entirely too worried about his safety. He hoped he got the chance to introduce Analia to them before everyone went their separate ways.

She needed to hurry up and get to Thrakus. He went to bed slightly annoyed that she hadn't showed up yet, even though she had some time left.

CHAPTER 71

True to her word, Ophelia was waiting for him in the common room the next morning. She was demolishing her breakfast, on her third plate at least judging by the amount of flatware scattered across the table when Nym sat down across from her, still rubbing at his eyes.

"How are you this perky?" he asked.

"I've always been a morning person," she said. Then she grinned wickedly and added, "And Bildar is really, really, really not. It drives him crazy, so I make an effort to be extra cheerful when I wake him up."

"You're evil."

"I know. It's fantastic."

Nym got his own food, and while they were eating, Ophelia asked, "What do you normally do with your mornings?"

"Go out of the city and practice my magic. It's one of the reasons I took a room here. It's close to the edge of town." He left unsaid his other new hobby of going by the Silk Box and scrying to look for Analia. He liked the crew, but he wasn't going to reveal her existence until after she'd already arrived and they'd had a chance to discuss future plans. Nym had learned his lesson already about giving information to adults who might decide they knew better than him how to run his life.

"What are you working on?" Ophelia asked, curious.

"Trying to modify an ice-golem spell to work with dirt and stone."

She let out a low whistle. "That's a tall order. I don't even know how to make a golem. Would you mind if I looked at the spell schematics?"

"I can draw them out for you if you want," Nym said. He doubted they'd be anywhere near as good as anything he'd seen in the spell books he'd learned from, but he was confident he could make something passable enough that it would make sense if he was there to explain it.

"No, no, not the modifications you're trying to make. The original schematic you're basing it off of."

Nym blinked. He didn't have anything like that since he'd learned the spell directly from the wolf-thing matriarch. "I don't have them," he confessed. "I learned it up north."

"How are you supposed to modify them if you don't have the original spell then?"

"Just kind of doing it in my head and playing around with different pieces to see what works."

"Playing around with . . . what? Okay, you're full of it. There is no way you have a spell to create a golem memorized."

Nym concentrated for a few seconds and raised a four-inch-tall ice golem out of his soup. It was more brown and yellow than frosty white and blue, and it only lasted a few seconds due to the haste with which he'd constructed it, but it waved a hand at Ophelia before collapsing back into soup. He shrugged and scooped up a spoonful. "If you say so," he said.

Ophelia's eye twitched.

Even the soup golem was a stretch of the spell. It only worked because the base was liquid, and because he'd spent so much time trying to figure out how to incorporate that stupid heating stone into the golem. Noodles and vegetables weren't quite the same thing, but a foreign object was still a foreign object, and his modifications to add it worked on a small, temporary scale.

"I would very much appreciate if you could draw out the schematic for the construct for me to review," she said slowly, through gritted teeth.

Nym ate another spoonful of soup and considered it. "Sure," he said after an appropriately theatrical pause. "It's the least I can do."

"This kid," she muttered.

Nym laughed quietly. That reaction never got old.

The pair stood in a field a mile or so outside the city. Nym demonstrated some of his elemental earth skills, and Ophelia gave pointers. He asked her to demonstrate a few spells that she was working on, just so that he could "see what the end result was supposed to look like," but also because it helped to get an uninterrupted, up-close, real-time viewing of the spell being cast.

Nym mostly ignored her advice, as it involved a lot of stuff like feeling the power of the earth beneath his feet and channeling its stability through his limbs. All that sounded suitably mystical, but he had no idea what it meant, and she refused to elaborate. The live demonstrations were much more useful, in his opinion.

Nym did sketch out the construct pattern for the ice golem in the dirt, along with his own modifications next to it. He pointed out the parts he was having trouble getting locked together, and explained how when making an ice golem, the biggest problem was that the arcana would start to freeze into place, and individual pieces would also freeze to one another before they were properly set.

"But with the earth-golem variation, that's not the problem I'm having. Instead, individual pieces start to sag. It's like the arcana is too heavy to support itself. It's actually a problem I've been having with everything I try, but most things are quick enough that I can get the spell off before it becomes an overwhelming issue," he finished.

"It sounds like you need to work on your intent filtering some more, like I've been telling you. You're not feeling the power of the earth and channeling it right," she said. "Yes, the arcana should be solid and heavy, but it should also be strong enough to hold its shape."

"I tried that, but then it became so rigid that I couldn't get it to form the construct."

"Well you're a smart boy. You'll get there," she told him.

"What happened with the meeting with the guildmaster?" he said, changing the subject.

"It's happening right now, way earlier than Bildar wants to be awake too."

"Any idea how it's going?" he asked, messing with the intent filtering. It would be so much easier if he could copy that from other people too. "How do mages fight if they have to keep changing their intent with every spell?"

"Nope. We'll find out soon enough, I suppose. Most mages stick to a single element if they get forced into a fight, or if they're doing something more complicated, they'll prepare in advance. That's why we're all earth mages. It's what we're good at. If a monster or a belligerent guildsman with a grudge comes at me, I'm going to use earth magic to defend myself."

Nym considered that. It wasn't really what he'd ever done. He'd switched intent filters rapidly during dangerous situations before, but his range of spells was extremely limited compared to someone like Ophelia. He wondered how much more effective he'd be if he could learn a full set of air-magic spells and blast them out one after another without having to pull in new flavors of arcana.

He could work on adding to his repertoire on his own, but it would be easier to find a spell book to study from. In the meantime, he'd just have to split his concentration between his evasive flying abilities and the more complicated lightning and fire attacks he already knew. As long as he didn't have to face down another hive queen in the near future, that would be good enough.

As the sun rose higher, Nym asked, "Do you need to get heading back? It's almost noon."

Ophelia sighed and stood up. The dirt on her flew away, repelled by her magic. "I suppose so. I don't want to be late. You'll come with me?"

"I have an errand to run, but I can meet you at the jobsite."

"Oh really? A secret errand? What is it?"

"It's secret," he said dryly.

"Is it about a girl? Ermy, your face is getting red. It is about a girl, isn't it?!"

"Not like you're thinking," he choked out. "Goodbye, Ophelia. I'll see you later."

Then he lifted himself in the air and flew off, leaving her behind.

"Hey," she yelled out. "If you're going to do that, at least take me with you!"

Nym just flew faster.

Another day of scrying revealed nothing. Nym just sighed and started to walk away. He made it back onto the main street and practically bumped into a person he hadn't realized was there. "Sorry," he muttered, looking up. He froze. "Analia?"

One look at her shirt was enough to figure it out. Of course he couldn't find her by scrying the Silk Box. Scrying had never worked on her. He could have sat there all day, and he never would have seen her with his magic alone.

"Nym! There you are. What took you so long? I've been here for over a week now."

"I've been looking for you since I got here about a week ago!" he said.

"I don't know how you could have missed me. I swear I spend hours sitting out in the open watching for you every day," she said. "Never mind, we found each other now."

She pulled him into a hug, which surprised him and he only tentatively returned. "Sitting out in the open where?" he asked.

"In the Silk Box, of course. That's where we agreed to meet."

"I didn't take a room here," he said, shaking his head. "It's way too expensive. I've just been coming by once or twice a day and scrying the place to see if you're here. And I just realized ten seconds ago why that plan didn't work."

"It's not that expensive. Only three shields a day."

"That's . . . that's twice what I paid for an entire week."

Analia's nose crinkled up, and she said, "What, are you staying in a stable?"

"No! It's a regular inn for normal people who aren't rich!"

She was just like he remembered her, dressed in expensive clothes with no concept of the value of money, but friendly and indifferent to their respective stations. Today she was wearing a long, frilly blouse with a matching skirt and a wide-brimmed hat. The clothes were all vibrant, and the runes stitched into them practically sparkled in the sunlight. A bright smile was plastered onto her face.

"How was your trip down here?"

"Cold and miserable. I got eaten by a giant worm," he said. "And yours?"

"Snuck out of the house and bought a teleport a week ago. It's been weird not having any servants, but the Silk Box's staff has been an adequate replacement. What do you mean you got eaten?"

"Big, giant worm was making the blizzard that hit the area. I had to kill it to clear the weather up so I could leave. It was . . . close." He shuddered at the memory.

"Wait, that was you who killed the tecula hive queen? There's been a ton of speculation about that back home. Some people think it was put there by the Korshics and that they lost control of it and had to kill it themselves."

"It was very much alive when I ran into it," he told her. "But anyway, it was an eventful trip that I never want to repeat. We're both here now though, so we need to figure out where we're going next."

"Come on, let's get lunch. I want to hear all about how you killed the tecula colony. I'll tell you some of the more outlandish theories that have been floating around."

"Er, I'm actually supposed to meet some people soon," he said. "Let me tell you about them though. I didn't want to let them know about you until we had a chance to talk and decide what we're going to do. They might be leaving town soon, and if they do, I thought maybe we'd go with them."

"Oh? Well, you can be a few minutes late. Come on, there's a charming little café just down the street. We can have a quick, light lunch while you tell me all about them."

Ignoring his protests, Analia seized Nym's arm and dragged him along with her.

CHAPTER 72

They briefly got caught up while they ate, with Nym giving her the abridged version of how he'd killed the hive queen and Analia giving him a dubious look. "How did you manage to hold three separate spell effects at the same time? Most mages can't even hold two," she asked.

"I . . . don't know? I just do. It's not easy or anything. I don't think I could do four, if for no other reason than I can't get a wide enough conduit to sustain that much magic at once."

"This is your stupid telekinesis spell all over again."

Analia pouted briefly before being distracted by a little cake the waiter brought to the table. Nym had a bite at her request, but it was so sickly sweet that he could barely swallow it. Analia didn't seem to have that trouble, and tore it apart in short order. "I've always wanted to do that," she said, smiling. "It takes forever to eat anything when decorum insists you always put the smallest sliver of your meal in your mouth for each bite."

"Yes . . . right." Nym couldn't say that he related. When he took small bites, it was usually because that was all the food there was. He did not miss those days at all. "So I should find out today if the mages I've been spending time with will be staying in Thrakus. One of them told me if they can't stay, they're going to go west to build fortifications for the army since some undead problem there is getting way out of hand. I'm sure we could go with them."

"That's where my father is," Analia said. "Though the army is big, and I doubt we'd run into him. There's always the chance though, and I'm not sure I'm ready to talk to him."

"Oh. The other option was leaving the country, but I think we got away clean enough that no one's looking for us at least."

"Eeeehhh . . . I might not have snuck out as easily as I made it seem."

Nym wanted to be surprised. Really, he did. But he knew there was more to her story than she'd told him, and he very much doubted it had been as easy as she'd claimed. With a sigh, he asked, "What happened?"

"Well you know, after our first attempt ended in me needing a healer to patch me up, my brother got really, really involved in every minute of my life. If he couldn't be there personally to watch me, he had Malk and Dansin both staring at me. It was a fight just to be allowed to use the facilities without one or both of them trying to escort me into the room."

"Who's Dansin?" Nym asked, trying to remember if he'd met anybody by that name but coming up blank.

"My father's shadowguard. He's been shadowing Bardin since Dad left a few months ago."

"I don't know what a shadowguard is."

"Oh, right. It's a noble thing. They're bodyguards you never see. Thus the name. They guard from the shadows. If you see a shadowguard, it's because something has gone very, very, very wrong. When Dad had to leave on assignment, he tasked his shadowguard with watching over Bardin until he got back. And then Bardin told him to start keeping an eye on me.

"Of course I didn't realize this right away because Dansin is a shadowguard. So the first time I try to sneak out, I'm about to float my trunk through a window only to see him sitting on it and oh so politely asking me to return to my room. Apparently, my brother gave him orders to reveal himself and interfere if I tried to leave the house on my own."

"You were basically a prisoner in your own home," Nym pointed out. "So how did you get away?"

"Ah . . . that. Well, I'd like to say that I am incredibly skilled in the stealth arts, but the truth is that I wasn't a 'prisoner in my own home.' I just wasn't allowed to go anywhere without an escort. So I went shopping, took a big purse with me, and then paid off the worker to let me slip out the back while I was trying on a new outfit. I just walked out in clothes my guards had never seen and headed over to the mage guildhall, then paid for a teleport to Thrakus."

Nym started laughing. After all the planning and scenarios they'd come up with, after failing to actually get away, she'd done it just by walking off in the middle of the day while her bodyguard waited in the next room for her to change her outfit.

"Hey, it worked!" she said.

"I know. I'm sorry. It's just . . . we put a lot of effort into our plans, and you could have done that at any time."

"I will stab you with this fork if you don't stop laughing at me," she threatened, waving around the fork, which still had flecks of cake on the tines.

"I'm not laughing at you, I promise. It's just kind of funny how easy it was when we went and made it so complicated."

There was a brief flash of arcana around Analia, followed by a black square of something launching itself through the air to bounce off Nym's face. He snatched it up before it could hit the table and took a bite out of it, only to make a face before he reluctantly swallowed it. "What . . . what is this?"

"It's chocolate, you godless heathen! Don't you dare try to tell me it's not good!"

"It's . . . very bitter." Nym set the rest of it back on the plate.

"You have no taste."

"I've eaten charred rat that tasted better," he told her, only somewhat untruthfully.

"That's gross. You have not."

Nym just stared at her. She stared back. "No, you're lying," she insisted.

"Only about it tasting better than your chocolate. And it's close."

Staring him in the eye, Analia picked up the piece of chocolate and put it in her mouth. She chewed and swallowed, still staring him down. Then she reached down to grab another piece and repeated herself. Nym rolled his eyes. "Whatever. You can have all the chocolate."

They finished their meal and parted ways, with Nym promising to come back to the Silk Box that evening to meet her after he found out what his new friends' plans for the future were. Analia wasn't entirely set against going west, but she wanted time to think about it first. Considering how complicated her feelings toward her father were after their discovery of his experiments, Nym couldn't hold it against her.

He caught up with the Earth Shapers just as they were exiting the Boot and Strap. "Hey, sorry I'm late, I was with a friend," he said as he ran up to them.

"A girl friend," Monick said.

"Ooooooooohhh," Nomick added.

Nym ignored them, and instead asked Bildar, "How did the meeting go?"

"Not good. Even though we're just making foundations, apparently we are still infringing on the contractors guild's rights, according to the city council. We would need to be licensed with the guild and have approval for jobs, else they have the right to censure us and take action to stop us. Basically, they can keep harassing us as much as they want, and at most they'll get a slap on the wrist if they do something illegal, probably because the guild paid off the people who are supposed to be in charge of enforcing these laws."

That was not how Nym had expected that meeting to go. The guilds had a lot more control over the local government than he'd expected, based on what Bildar was saying. It seemed to Nym that the contractors guild was clearly in the wrong, attacking the earth mages unprovoked and attempting to abduct Nym so they could ransom him back. The fact that the city council had sided with the guild despite all that made Nym a lot less eager to stay in the city.

That was too bad because he was starting to like Thrakus, other than the smell. And he'd gotten used to that. It was open and airy, which he always appreciated, and considerably warmer than Abilanth. There were rich districts and poor districts, but they weren't segregated by walls with posted guards whose only job was to keep the have-nots out of sight of the wealthy.

Thrakus was a trading city with a ton of traffic going through it all year-round, for all sorts of reasons. He supposed it only made sense that in a city so heavily focused on money, that those with bags full of crests would have the ability to influence the laws and politics in their favor. It wasn't fair, but that was life.

"If you can't do more foundations now, where are we going?" Nym asked.

"Oh, we can," Bildar said. "As many as we want. It's just that no one is going to stop the contractors guild from trying to punish us any way they see fit."

"That constable yesterday did not make it seem like this would be what happened."

"I'm sure he didn't. He'll do what he's told by the people who pay his wages, so from now on, any . . . disagreements . . . between us and the contractors would best be handled without the constabulary getting involved. No punishments are going to stick to them, and we'll be fined or jailed as much as they can get away with."

"They were really that blatant about it?" Nym asked. "Why didn't they just run you out of town on the spot then?"

"Too much effort on their part, I guess. Easier to let the guild shoulder the cost of getting rid of us, since it doesn't cost them anything to not arrest guild members, plus they probably figure they can squeeze us for more money at the same time, on top of whatever bribes the contractors guild paid them to rule in their favor."

"This kind of crap is why we don't do town jobs," Ophelia muttered darkly.

The mood was a lot less festive as they walked to the construction site. There was already a crowd gathered, and Nym recognized more than a few faces in it. The three men who'd been arrested the previous day were out and smirking at him, but before they could do anything, Constable Berndart walked up to them in full uniform and put a hand on one of their shoulders. He drew them away from the crowd and started talking to them, but it was too noisy for Nym to make out what was said.

One of them started arguing with him, his tone and posture belligerent. Nym could only assume the man, his head freshly swelled from getting out of trouble consequence free, was telling the constable to get lost. Whatever it was he said, Berndart didn't care for it. He reached out and grabbed the man, then pulled him forward and drove his knee into the man's gut. The man collapsed, and the constable squatted down to say something else to him. Then he patted the man's head, stood up, and walked away.

The man's companions helped him up, and all three cast hateful glares at the constable's retreating form, but none of them looked quite so smug anymore. "Ha," Nomick said softly next to Nym. "Looks like the good constable isn't happy about the decision either. Weren't those the three that took a swing at you yesterday?"

"Yes. I wonder what he said to them."

"That there were an awful lot of bad things that could happen to a man in a cell, even in the span of an hour or two, and it would be best for him to avoid the kind of trouble that would get him put there in the first place."

"What?" Nym shot Nomick a surprised look. "How do you know that?"

"I'm not *just* an earth mage, young man. I can do other things besides move dirt."

"You know sensory-enhancement spells?" he asked, suddenly interested.

"First and second circle," Nomick bragged.

"And he definitely learned all of them to aid with peeping on the girls when we were teenagers," Monick added.

"You'll never prove it!"

Nym wished he'd been paying more attention. He hadn't even noticed Nomick casting the spell. Oh well, he'd just have to get the mischievous earth mage to do it again so he could copy it.

CHAPTER 73

C ome eat with us tonight," Ophelia said.

"I . . . really can't afford to," Nym replied, not looking up from where he was inscribing the runes on the blocks. He'd learned that they weren't quite as simple as he'd initially thought, and that the runes were only meant to hold everything together temporarily. Interlocking lips were grown among the blocks after they were stacked up in such a way that they could not be removed without lifting everything on top of them up first. The runes would hold everything together for a week until the framework of the building was put on top of the foundation and driven through holes opened in the wall, at which point the weight of the structure would serve to hold the foundation it rested on in place.

"This doesn't seem like it should work," he said, studying the design.

"It is admittedly not as solid as some other methods, but it's designed to allow it to be repaired when it's impacted by something especially powerful, like a siege weapon or artillery spell. It might blow a few blocks out at the point of impact, but they can be replaced with minimal effort."

"And . . . that's necessary for foundation work in the residential district of a city that's part of a country that is not at war with anyone else?"

Ophelia shrugged. "Yeah, it's probably overkill. But hey, they're getting a hell of a deal."

"Why not just raise solid walls?" Nym asked.

"Harder to transmute that much at once. But don't change the topic. Come eat with us. We're going to discuss our future plans, and you should be involved with that."

"Me? You already said you couldn't take on an apprentice for months, and now you might have to leave."

"That was before we found out the city wasn't going to do anything to stop the guild from harassing us as much as they wanted. Now we're rethinking spending the summer months here, like I said. If our situation changes, we might be able to work something out."

Nym knew what the bill looked like for a meal at the Quarterhouse. It wasn't that he didn't have the money to cover it so much as he could eat for a week on what that single meal would cost, and his money was not unlimited. For the moment, he was set, but he wasn't really earning any income in Thrakus, and he might need every single wedge of that money once he and Analia finalized their own travel plans.

"Stop worrying about the money. You know we're going to cover it for you. You do enough work on our jobs to at least be worth a meal. We're probably getting the better end of the deal."

That wasn't really true. He wouldn't say he'd done a lot of work for them, certainly nothing Ophelia couldn't have done herself, and they probably hadn't saved much time since she'd been slowed down by both teaching him and going over his work. The Earth Shapers had been far kinder to a stranger than he'd deserved.

"I have to go meet my friend after we're done. I will try to get to the Quarterhouse when I can."

"Why don't you just bring your girlfriend too?"

"She's not . . . You know what, I'm not doing this. I will ask her, since one of the things we're talking about is leaving Thrakus and trying to figure out where to go."

"What? Just the two of you?" Ophelia asked. "That's kind of dangerous, don't you think?"

"Not really, no. She's also a mage."

"Still. Well, see if you can get her to come. I would love to meet your . . . ahem . . . friend. Who is a girl."

Nym rolled his eyes. "I'll see what I can do."

The doorman at the Silk Box was tall, handsome, well muscled, and plenty friendly with the inn's paying customers. For Nym, however, it was a different story.

"You renting a room?" he asked.

"No," Nym said. "I'm just here to—"

"Got shields on you?"

"What? Why would I—"

"That's a no. Look kid, if you're not a guest and you got no money, you're not welcome here. This is an expensive, exclusive inn, and our guests value their privacy. You're not getting in."

"I just wanted to see a friend who's staying here."

"I'm sure you do. Get your sticky fingers away from the door before I have to break them."

Nym was trying to edge past the doorman but pulled back. "Look, you don't want me in there, fine. I'm too poor, and it would offend their rich sensibilities. Can you at least send a message up to my friend to have her meet me somewhere else?"

"Nope."

"Why not?" Nym demanded.

"Not my job."

Briefly, for just a moment, Nym considered setting the doorman on fire. The temptation was there, and it was awfully strong. Nym pulled himself back and, through gritted teeth, asked, "How do I go about sending a message to my friend who is inside this building?"

"No idea. Not my problem."

Arcana poured into him, and Nym slammed a fully powered daze spell on the doorman. The man went slack-jawed and immediately slumped to the side. "You can barely notice a difference," Nym said, watching him. Then he stepped past the man and walked into the Silk Box.

The interior was every bit as posh as he'd expected from his scrying. Instead of a big, open room with a bunch of wooden furniture, it consisted of a series of booths lining the walls that were closed off for privacy's sake. The back wall was given over half to the bar and half to doors or stairs leading to other parts of the inn.

"Pardon me, are you a guest at the Silk Box?" a man asked, approaching Nym before he'd even gotten five steps past the door.

"I am not, no. And I am not looking to rent a room. I have a friend here I would like to send an invitation to meet me too, and then I will be on my way."

"Hmm . . . Very well. And the name of your friend?"

"Analia Feldstal."

"I see. I cannot confirm or deny a guest of that name, in order to protect our patrons' privacy. Assuming we do have such a person here, where and when would you like her to meet you?"

Nym could only think of one place he was sure they both knew the location of. "At the café down the street from here, as soon as possible."

The man bowed his head. "Very well. If you have no further need of our services, allow me to show you the door."

The man who'd stopped him inside the door gave him the boot, then paused to scowl at the doorman, who was still recovering from Nym's daze spell. Nym did not stick around to watch the rest of that, just in case the doorman realized what had happened and came after him. Instead, he went to the café and loitered nearby. He had no intention of going in if he didn't have to, though he was sure Analia would insist on it once she joined him.

He didn't have to wait long for Analia to show up. She bypassed him and immediately walked into the café, leaving Nym to follow with a wordless sigh. Sometimes he hated being right. The pair claimed the same table as their first visit, and before she could order food, Nym said, "My friends have invited us to eat with them at the Quarterhouse."

"Oh really? That's nice of them," she said. "They know about me?"

"No. They just know that I have a friend. Things didn't go well for them with that guild that's going after them, so they're going to decide if they're leaving tonight, and where to go. They . . . they asked me to go with them. I said we'd have to decide together."

Analia ordered drinks for both of them, ignoring Nym's protests, and sat back to think for a bit. "You said before they were considering going west to help the army."

"Yes," Nym said. "And you weren't sure you wanted to go. I thought we'd have more time, but it doesn't look like it."

"What do you want to do?" Analia asked.

"If it was just me and nobody else? I thought I might go west, but maybe not to the battlefront. There's someone I used to know out that way that I want to make sure is still alright. I don't know what I'd do after that."

"Maybe recover your missing memories?" she said.

"Sure. That'd be great. Any ideas on how to do it?"

"I . . . No."

"It would be great to know who I am, but I've got no idea how to accomplish that. I've just kind of gotten used to it. Right now I'm interested in the same thing I've always been interested in: learning new magic. One of them offered to take me on as an apprentice, but I'm not sure I want to focus that heavily on earth magic. I'm also not sure I want to be bound to an apprenticeship contract. We never discussed terms though, so maybe it's not as bad as I'm afraid it'll be."

Nym rambled on for a while, and Analia sipped from the porcelain cup sitting in front of her. When he was done, she told him, "I don't know what I want to do either. I've got so much to figure out. That's okay though. Let's go meet your friends and see what their plans are before we make any decisions."

"Just like that, huh?" Nym asked. "Why did you want to go with me, Analia?"

"I was afraid to be alone. I thought we'd have a better shot if we worked together. Also we can still teach each other magic. I want to learn that ice-golem spell you picked up, and meet your new wolf friends someday. You're still working on your runes, right?"

"I am," he admitted. "Ophelia taught me a few they use, but it's barely the first page in the book."

"We've got plenty of time," she said. "And if we're going to teach ourselves, we'll need a lot more money than we have."

"Ha! That's the truth. Books are expensive. It's kind of weird to see you worry about money though."

Her face flushed, and she mumbled something. Nym leaned over the table and said, "What was that?"

"I said . . . things are so expensive that I'm going to run out of money in the next week."

"Well, the cure to that is to stop spending it so fast, you know?"

"I have to eat though! I need a place to stay," she protested.

"Sure. I paid one shield five for a week at the Lucky Barrel. How much did you say the Silk Box is charging you?"

"Three shields even. A night."

Nym winced. "Well, I'm sure the beds are very comfortable."

"Oh shut up."

They sat in silence for a bit. Nym sipped the brown liquid from the cup in front of him and found it was nice. "What's this called?" he asked.

"Tea."

"I like it. Better than chocolate."

"Ugh. Uncultured peasant."

Nym laughed. He took another sip, thought for a second, and said, "Do you regret leaving?"

"Not yet. Do you regret not taking my brother's contract?"

"Never."

"It's really not that horrible of a deal. It's not like we send our retainers to the mines to do hard labor with the convicted criminals. But I understand. Freedom."

"Freedom," he echoed.

"Enough of this," she said. "Let's go meet your friends, enjoy a good meal, and see what new adventures are waiting for us."

That sounded hopelessly optimistic to Nym, but he appreciated the sentiment. Together, they got up to leave. Nym managed to not wince when Analia dropped a shield on the table. That was a ridiculous price for two small cups of tea, no matter how good it was. He was going to have to wean her off her natural inclination to buy the most expensive things she could find.

"Oh, I should probably mention, they don't know my real name," he said, leading her out the café.

"Is that so? What exactly do they know? Just so I don't spoil your cover."

"Let me try to remember . . ."

CHAPTER 74

The Quarterhouse was as full as always, but there were already two empty chairs between Bildar and Ophelia waiting for them when they got there. The host waved them past, pointing out the table the earth mages were seated around. Nym and Analia joined them, with him making introductions.

"Hi everyone, this is my friend Analia. This is Bildar, Ophelia, and the twins are Nomick and Monick."

"You got us backward," one of the twins said.

"Oh, sorry. Then this is Monick, and that's Nomick."

"Nah, he's messing with you. You had it right the first time."

"So these are the two blockheads who think they're funny. Their individual names aren't important."

One of the twins mimed gasping and clutching at his chest. "Such hostility! So cold and ruthless! I'm dying over here. Monick, save me!"

"If you die, I'm merging our names and becoming Monomick."

"Treacherous . . . dog," Nomick let out another fake gasp.

"Ignore those two," Ophelia said. "It's nice to meet you, Analia."

They'd agreed before arriving to use Analia's first name only and not reveal her connection to a noble house. It wasn't that Nym thought anything bad would come of it, but she had technically run away, and the search for her was probably more focused than anything Nym had to worry about. The less her full name was said aloud, the better.

After the introductions, Nym and Analia ordered some food, and the group talked while they ate. Bildar told them again about the meeting with the contractors guildmaster and the city council for Analia's benefit, and then laid out their plan.

"We're going to head out the west gate tomorrow morning. I've already got a wagon purchased for it and a pair of oxen for pulling it. It's not that big, but it'll hold enough supplies for three weeks of travel. Our first stop is going to be a town about four days west of here called Valcort. We'll stay the night and see if there's any work. The town's small enough that there shouldn't be any guild presence, but it might also be small enough that there's nothing for us to do or not enough money to pay for our services."

"What about going to the battlefront to make fortifications for the army?"

"We'll get there, don't you worry. But it's about five hundred miles, and to be perfectly honest, we're not exactly sure where they're stationed. A lot of what's out this way is just rumors."

"Their main base is in Ebalsan," Analia said.

The whole table turned in their seats to look at her. She just shrugged. "It's not news. This has been going on for months now."

"Right, well, that could be. We'll know more for sure when we get there. We've got two or three other towns to pass through, depending on supplies, which depends on how much the weather slows us down. With winter dying down, the roads are going to be getting muddy."

"You're earth mages though," Nym pointed out.

Bildar laughed and shook his head. "Sure, and if I need to firm up forty or fifty feet, that's no problem. Doing a few hundred miles is a different story. We'll get there quicker than someone who can't use magic, for sure, just not as quick as we would if we waited two months for the roads to firm up."

They took a break from planning to eat. The food was so good that even Analia had nothing bad to say about it, and with Nym's newfound appreciation of how expensive upper-class amenities were, he couldn't really say too much about the price either, not that he was the one paying. The Earth Shapers really did treat him far better than he had any right to ask.

Once they were done eating though, it was back to business. The route had been laid out; all four of the earth mages at the table were set on it. Supplies had been purchased, and a departure time scheduled. Bildar had argued for a slightly later time, but Ophelia bullied him into starting early, much to the twins' amusement. All the details for their trip were set, except one.

"Are you coming with us, Ermy? Your friend is welcome as well, providing you don't mind doing a bit of foraging to help offset the food cost."

"That's . . . I'm not sure. Analia, it's up to you," Nym said.

"Let me think about it tonight, and we'll meet you at Sunset Lane's end tomorrow morning," she said, naming the street that merged into the major westbound road they'd be traveling.

Everyone trooped out, this time without all the alcohol that had marked Nym's first dinner with them. It was a somber affair, with them saying their goodbyes in the street and then going their separate ways. Nym and Analia went back to the Silk Box together, talking quietly as they walked.

"I know you don't want to go to the battlefront, but there are a lot of stops between here and there," he said. "We could split off at any time between now and the at least six weeks it'll take to make it all the way to their destination."

"No, you're right," Analia said. "I think we should probably go with them. You like them, and trust them, and they trust you. But if we're doing this, we need to tell them the truth. It wouldn't be fair to get them caught up in our troubles if my family's retainers catch up to us and attack them one night while we're camping on the side of the road."

"That . . . Yes, we should do that," Nym said. "I guess I should tell them the truth about me too."

"Nym, nobody is looking for you," Analia said.

"What?"

"Not after the first day or two. I mean, if you walked back into Abilanth and announced to the guard who you are, they might put you in a room until someone came by to ask you some questions, but my family knows it was my decision to go with you, and the guard is more interested in Valgo than they are in you. I told them what you did to rescue me, and even if anyone tried to do anything to you, my family would come down on them."

"I bet Malk would probably still try to stab me."

"Oh come on. He wanted to do that from the first night he met you. It's not anything new."

Looking back on it, it was almost disturbing how casually accepting he'd been of the man's dislike, if only because he was assured that Malk was on a leash and wouldn't do anything without being ordered to. That had obviously not been true. He could still remember the toe of the bodyguard's boot digging into his chest.

"If I never see him again, it'll still be too soon," he said.

"Well, he was rather insufferable for the last few weeks. He basically stopped doing anything I told him and only followed my brother's orders. It was like being a prisoner the way he escorted me around."

Nym thought she had a rather distorted idea of what being a prisoner actually meant, but he kept that opinion to himself. "So we're doing this then?" he asked.

"I think so."

"What are you going to do tonight?"

"Well, the room is already paid for, so I guess I'll stay here. And you?"

"Same, at the Lucky Barrel."

"Meet me here in the morning with your stuff and we'll go to the edge of the city together?" Analia asked.

"How much luggage do you have?" Nym asked, squinting at her. "Is it so much that you need help carrying it?"

"No! . . . Yes."

"Of course it is. At least we don't have to fit it through a window this time. I'll meet you outside the inn? Last time the doorman didn't want to let me through."

"I'll tell them to let you in," she said, "But yes, I'll try to meet you out here and avoid the hassle."

"Sounds good."

She went into the Silk Box while the doorman stared daggers at Nym. It was the same man he'd dazed earlier to get through. "Uh . . . hi," Nym said.

The man gave him a rude hand gesture.

Laughing quietly, Nym shook his head and walked away.

Nym was up before dawn, quietly stuffing his few possessions into his pack and leaving his room key with the overnight attendant at the bar. Then he trudged across the city, rubbing sleep from his eyes and watching as the shadows slowly shrank with the coming dawn. At least the foot traffic was virtually nonexistent, though it was a strange experience walking through a city that almost seemed abandoned.

Analia was sitting on a trunk just outside the Silk Box, looking almost as tired as Nym felt. There was a glow of arcana around her, and he noticed the trunk floating an inch or so off the ground on the air cushions he'd taught her how to make. "You've been practicing that, huh?" he asked as he walked up.

"It's too useful not to use. I can fly with it, but only for short distances. It's still easier to use my old wind spell if I have to fly for more than a few minutes."

"Hmm. You've just got to build your stamina up. I used to only be able to fly for a few minutes at a time too, and barely faster than I could run. Six months later, I'm doing cross-country flights."

"Sounds cold," Analia told him.

"I bought warmer flying clothes, but then when I got stuck in a blizzard, I figured out how to modify a kinetic-barrier spell I got from your library into a thermal barrier. It won't help you warm back up, but as long as you keep it solid, you won't ever get cold."

"I think I'm a ways from that still. I don't know how you can just keep two spells running at the same time forever."

They talked while they walked, with Nym giving in and taking over the flight spell on the trunk after a few minutes when it became obvious that Analia was running out of stamina. Her aura winked out, and she let out a grateful sigh. "Thanks," she said.

"How did you ever get all of this to the Silk Box in the first place?" he asked.

"I bought it a few things at a time, and for the heavy stuff, I paid porters to deliver it for me."

"Ah, right. Money. That's how you did it. How could I forget?"

"Oh shut up." She gave him a good-natured shrug, and Nym retaliated by bumping her with her own trunk.

Neither of them realized that the people around them were not random city folk until they were fully surrounded. Twelve men and five women, about a third of which Nym recognized as guildsmen, formed a wide circle around them.

"Scuse me, kiddos. We're going to need you to come with us," one who was bolder or stupider than the rest said.

"Didn't you guys already try this a few days ago?" Nym asked. Without waiting for an answer, he turned to Analia and asked, "Did you ever get your license?"

"Nope, you?"

"Nope, but a constable told me they make an exception for self-defense."

"That's good to know."

"Hey, I'm talking to y—"

"Shut up," they both told man at the same time.

"Screw it. Pile on 'em. It don't matter none if they're in good shape, long as they're still breathin' at the end."

"We were leaving anyway," Nym said. "I guess we could cut loose."

"Try not to kill anyone this time," Analia said.

"Don't take all the fun out of it."

Then the guildsmen were on them, lunging in to grab at limbs to restrain the kids. Several of them had knives, clubs, or hammers, all typical craftsmen tools refurbished to weapons of war. It didn't help them much though, since Nym simply lifted himself, Analia, and her trunk up into the air.

"Do you want to handle offense, since I'm not allowed to use anything big?" he asked her.

She rolled her eyes. "I'm sure you have something that isn't instantly lethal to a dozen people, but fine. Watch."

She built a simple construct of air and water that materialized into a cluster of hailstones, then sent them flying at high speeds to pelt the guildsmen. Before they could recover, a strong wind ripped down the street, throwing up dust and dirt and blinding them. Nym hardened the air into a dome around them to prevent the spell from splashing them.

"Thanks," Analia said. "I didn't account for all the loose dirt on the road. I was just trying to knock them down."

One of the guildsmen took a running leap and flew into the air, far higher than a human could jump unaided. Nym saw a faint aura around him, almost completely clear, and figured the man was using some sort of first-circle enhancement spell. It didn't much help him though, when Nym hit him with a daze spell and then caught him in air cushions to prevent him from landing on his head when he fell down.

"See, I have restraint too," he told Analia.

A hammer came spinning through the air and struck him in the arm. "Ow!" he yelled, turning in place to glare at the woman who'd thrown it. A dozen telekinetic hands slapped her at once, bruising her face and arms and knocking her into the dirt. The attack seemed to inspire the rest of the guildsmen though, and all sorts of weapons were chucked their way.

Nym quickly threw up a kinetic barrier to protect them, and the weapons bounced off to fly back down toward the crowd at higher speeds than they'd been thrown. A few of the guildsmen took bad hits from their own thrown weapons and went down.

"Okay, I'm annoyed now and also not in the mood to deal with this," Nym said, rubbing his arm. "Should we just leave?"

Analia agreed, and the two flew off to the shouts and jeers of the guildsmen who were still on their feet. None of them were stupid enough to chase after the two mages.

CHAPTER 75

The Earth Shapers showed up about an hour after Nym and Analia got there. The two waited outside of the city a ways, with Analia guarding Nym while he scried up and down Sunset Lane watching for them. They waited, both of them sitting on the floating trunk, until the earth mages pulled up next to them.

"Coming along then?" Bildar asked, eyeing the trunk.

"For now, if you'll have us. We're not sure if we'll go all the way to Ebalsan though."

"That's fine. We're not sure we'll go that far either. I think we can fit this trunk in the wagon. Might be a bit tight. We'll have to unpack some stuff first."

"I'll take care of it," Nym said. The trunk floated over to the end of the wagon, which had a canvas roof stretched over its contents, and he peered inside. Objects started floating out, and the trunk slid all the way to the back, then the rest of the wagon repacked itself.

"Well he's handy," Ophelia said. "Why can't you do that, brother dearest?"

"Because I'm an earth mage, not an air mage. Though maybe I'm in the wrong line of work. But we'll see how he does when we're bogged down in the mud!" Bildar flexed an arm as he spoke. "That's when you'll see earth magic shine!"

"Who are you even talking to? Do you think any of us are impressed?" Ophelia asked.

"Aw shut it. You're just jealous I scored higher than you on the Helingar-Bistal Test."

"Oh please, like a twelve is anything to write home about. That's barely above average."

"But it's better than a nine, isn't it?" Bildar said.

It took Nym a bit to realize they were speaking about the soul-well-measuring test. "You took that, didn't you? I feel like we talked about it," he asked Analia.

"I did, yes. It caused a bit of a scene, and they made me redo it three times."

"Oh really? Why's that?" Ophelia asked.

Analia grimaced. "Twenty-six."

"God have mercy," Bildar swore quietly. "I've never heard of anyone getting above a fifteen."

"There are a couple of famous archmages who managed low twenties," Ophelia said thoughtfully. "Can't remember any of their names right now. Maybe one or two beat that, but you're going to go down in the history books when you grow up, girl."

"And what about you, Ermy? What'd you get? A five?" Nomick asked.

"I've never taken the test," he said. "And . . . speaking of, we decided that if we're going to be traveling with you guys, you need to know the whole truth. It wouldn't be right if you woke up one day and our problems caught up to us. You should know what you're getting involved in."

Analia stepped up next to him. "My full name is Analia Feldstal, of noble House Feldstal. I ran away from home about a week ago and took a teleport out of Abilanth. I have no doubt my older brother has quite a few people looking for me. They could catch up to me at any time and try to abduct me to return me home. My father is currently assisting the army in repelling the undead invasion, which is the reason I'm hesitant about going all the way to Ebalsan."

Before anyone else could cut in, Nym added, "My name isn't Ermy. It's Nym. I murdered a man who was trying to kill me and fled from home before I could be arrested for it. In Abilanth, a crime lord planted evidence to use against me and blackmailed me into trying to burgle the Feldstal estate. That's how I met Analia. I tried to help her escape, and in the process, we were both captured by the crime lord. I . . . I killed a lot of people escaping that, and burned down a building, and robbed the crime lord's vault to get enough money to survive while I fled."

"You robbed the vault?" Analia asked, surprised. "When did that happen?"

"After I took you to the healers. It was kind of by accident. He grabbed me with some sort of spell and dragged me into his hideout so he could kill me. I saw all the traps when I was scrying to find my way out of his hideout. When I went back to the healer to pay your bill, he told me your family had already picked you up and passed along your message."

"Wait, if you're rich now, why were you staying at the Lucky Barrel?"

"I'm not rich. I gave most of the money away before I left. I kept a few crests for traveling expenses and in case I needed an emergency teleport somewhere."

"Okay, hold up a second. Give us a minute to discuss this," Bildar said.

He pulled the other earth mages into a huddle, complete with an aura of arcana around Nomick. He watched the construct and committed the shape of it to memory. No sounds came from the group, though they were clearly talking to one another. A spell like that could be very useful. Absently, he wove arcana together to see if he'd gotten it right. Everything around him became muted, but he didn't think that was the intended effect.

If they didn't end up kicked out, he'd ask Nomick about it later. He'd probably messed something up, or it just didn't work quite as well with arcana that had no intent fused into it. It didn't matter. The whole project was just a distraction while he waited to see if his new friends still wanted the real Nym around.

He felt Analia squeeze his hand, and he looked down, surprised. "It's okay. I wouldn't blame them if they didn't want the potential danger we bring. We'll travel on our own if we have to."

"Easy for you to say. I'm going to be the one carrying that trunk."

"I am a noble. I cannot be expected to haul my own luggage around," she said pompously. "In fact, I should have a carriage to make this trip more bearable."

"You must have more money stashed away than I thought if that's your plan," he said dryly.

"Well no. I'm just saying that I *should* have a carriage, as befits my station."

"Your station as a runaway?"

"Give me my hand back. I'm never going to comfort you again."

She swatted him playfully, and Nym let out a rueful laugh. No matter how the next few minutes went, he wasn't alone. They fell silent and waited for the group to finish, which didn't take that long. Bildar walked over to them and said, "I understand why you would keep your history secret from strangers you just met, and I appreciate how hard it must have been to tell us the truth. And Analia, you must have a lot of faith in Ermy, er, Nym, to trust us on his word alone. That having been said . . ."

He paused and looked at the other earth mages behind him. Then, with a deep breath, he continued, "We've decided that you'll be assigned meal-clean-up duty, as no one here is very good at elemental water magic."

The tension drained out of Nym, and he left out a breath he hadn't realized he was holding. "You said it that way on purpose," he accused Bildar. The bearded mage grinned and didn't deny it.

"We want to hear some more details, but from your own admission, you acted in self-defense. I know how hard that is to come to terms with, and I can see that it weighs on you. We'll talk more as we go, and both of you are officially welcome to join us."

"Yeah, yeah," one of the twins said. "Enough of the speech. Let's get going. The sooner we're gone, the sooner I never have to see anyone from that contractors guild again."

"Oh, right, I forgot. Speaking of them, a bunch of them tried to ambush us again," Nym said.

"Tried?"

"They weren't very good at it."

"Alright, alright. We can hear this story while we travel. Let's get on the road, people," Bildar said, ushering them forward. The oxen started plodding along again, slowly until they got up to speed, and six mages walked away from Thrakus with the rising sun at their backs.

When they stopped for the night, Ophelia and Bildar approached Nym. "You said you've never done the Helingar-Bistal Test?"

"Nope. It never came up. I couldn't get the money together to go to the Academy."

"Not surprising. It's expensive. Our parents practically beggared themselves sending both of us. I think it was a good investment though. We've sent them a lot of crests back over the years. Anyway, turns out Ophelia knows how to do it, and I know enough to assist. So unless your rating is insanely high like Analia's, the two of us should be enough."

"Will it take long?" Nym asked.

"Just a few minutes."

Nym noticed Analia watching from over by the wagon, but she didn't say anything. "Okay, what do I need to do?"

"I'll cast the spell. All you have to do is fill your soul well up as full as you can. Then you close the conduit and push against the spell. Bildar and I will push back and take the measurements. Then we compare it against your age, and we're done."

"Oh, I don't actually know how old I am."

"Eh, not the end of the world. You'll have a range then, something like nine or ten, instead of knowing the exact number."

Nym started filling his soul well while Ophelia cast the spell. Auras sprang up around both, similar shades of soft green, almost identical. Once the spell was complete, some kind of magical orb formed around Nym, and Ophelia said, "Now push it all out. Don't draw any more in, just everything you've got in one go."

Releasing arcana without shaping it was a lot like exhaling underwater. It made him instantly want to draw in more to replace what he'd spent. The arcana rushed out of him all at once, and the orb around him blew out in three different spots. Ophelia yelped and practically fell over Bildar. "Ow!" she yelled. "What the hell was that?"

"Sorry," Nym said, trying not to panic. "I didn't mean it. Maybe I let it out too fast?"

Once everyone was back on their feet, Ophelia went over the spell again. "No, it worked, just . . . not really. I was starting to get the reading when you broke through the test bubble. Congratulations, you're stronger than the both of us put together, and not even half our age."

"That's kind of insane," Monick said.

"Very insane," Nomick added. "Do you want us to help?"

"Just one," Ophelia said. "It's easier to do the calculations with less people."

Nym refilled his soul well while she cast the spell again. This time, auras popped around all three of them, and a new orb appeared around Nym. "Ready?" he said.

"Ready! Give it all you've got."

Arcana poured out of him again and pressed against the orb. It strained for a second before deforming and splitting down the side. All three earth mages flinched and recoiled from him at the same time, but nobody fell this time.

"God's hairy balls, woman! Are you sure you're casting this spell right?" Monick demanded, clutching at his head.

"Of course I am!"

"Then why does he keep breaking the orb! There is no way Nym has got a bigger soul well than three adult mages."

"I don't know! Nomick, get over here and help!"

With some trepidation, they repeated the test a third time. Nym was almost afraid to let his arcana out, but at Analia's gentle nod, he mustered up his nerve and exhaled. Arcana pushed up against the orb, but finally, it held. There was some wobbling and stretching, but in the end, the arcana was contained. Ophelia let the spell dissipate and sighed.

"Wow. Okay, give me a few minutes to work this out. You two are both tens, right? And Nym, best guess on your age?"

"I don't know, somewhere between ten and thirteen?"

"I'll do the calculations for either end."

Ophelia spent the next half an hour sitting on the wagon scribbling numbers on a piece of paper while the rest set up the camp. Nym caught them giving him odd looks when they thought he wasn't looking, and he very much regretted agreeing to doing the test. It hadn't mattered to him before what the number was, but it was making things weird.

"I give up! I am obviously doing this wrong. These results make no sense. Bildar, we're going to measure you so I can run the calculations again and figure out where I'm making a mistake," Ophelia announced.

"It's fine, we don't have to figure this out," Nym said.

"The hell we don't!"

So they ran their test, and Ophelia went back to work. And finally, an hour later, she put the pen down with a sigh and started massaging her forehead. After a few minutes of that, she returned to the group and cleared her throat.

"I have triple-checked this. I ran the calculations again using Bildar's numbers so I know what the right answer is and that I did this right. Nym, as far as I can determine, if we assume you are thirteen years old so as to get the lowest result possible, your score on the Helingar-Bistal Test is a whopping seventy-four."

There was a round of stunned silence from the group, and then Bildar slapped him on the back. "Congratulations, kid. Looks like you're a demigod."

About the Author

EmergencyComplaints grew up reading fantasy and tried his hand at writing his first novel on an old MS-DOS text editor program when he was seven years old. That story didn't pan out; maximum character limits were a thing back then. Undeterred, he kept writing on other platforms, reading full-time, devouring JRPGs, and playing D&D, and he is now the author of the God Machine and Ascendant series. Check out his most recent work on Royal Road.

www.ingramcontent.com/pod-product-compliance
Lightning Source LLC
Chambersburg PA
CBHW030924120726
47906CB00002B/475

* 9 7 8 1 0 3 9 4 4 5 2 7 7 *